# So, I Met This ~~gorgeous man~~ ~~total fraudster~~ ~~absolute d##khead~~ Guy…

### Also by Alexandra Potter

*What's New, Pussycat?*
*Going La La*
*Calling Romeo*
*Do You Come Here Often?*
*Be Careful What You Wish For*
*Me and Mr Darcy*
*Who's That Girl?*
*You're The One That I Don't Want*
*Don't You Forget About Me*
*The Love Detective*
*Love From Paris*
*Confessions of a Forty-Something F##k Up*
*One Good Thing*
*More Confessions of a Forty-Something F##k Up*

# So, I Met This ~~gorgeous man~~ ~~total fraudster~~ ~~absolute~~ ~~d##khead~~ Guy...

**ALEXANDRA POTTER**

MACMILLAN

First published 2026 by Macmillan
an imprint of Pan Macmillan
The Smithson, 6 Briset Street, London EC1M 5NR
*EU representative*: Macmillan Publishers Ireland Limited,
1st Floor, The Liffey Trust Centre, 117–126 Sheriff Street Upper,
Dublin 1 D01 YC43
Associated companies throughout the world

ISBN 978-1-5290-9886-0 HB
ISBN 978-1-5290-9887-7 TPB

Copyright © Alexandra Potter 2026

The right of Alexandra Potter to be identified as the
author of this work has been asserted in accordance
with the Copyright, Designs and Patents Act 1988.

All rights reserved. No part of this publication may be reproduced,
stored in a retrieval system, or transmitted, in any form, or by any means
(including, without limitation, electronic, mechanical, photocopying, recording
or otherwise) without the prior written permission of the publisher.

Pan Macmillan does not have any control over, or any responsibility for,
any author or third-party websites (including, without limitation, URLs,
emails and QR codes) referred to in or on this book.

1 3 5 7 9 8 6 4 2

A CIP catalogue record for this book is available from the British Library.

Typeset in Sabon LT Pro by Palimpsest Book Production Limited, Falkirk, Stirlingshire
Printed and bound in the UK using 100% Renewable Electricity by CPI Group (UK) Ltd

This book is sold subject to the condition that it shall not, by way of
trade or otherwise, be lent, hired out, or otherwise circulated without
the publisher's prior consent in any form of binding or cover other than
that in which it is published and without a similar condition including this
condition being imposed on the subsequent purchaser. The publisher does not
authorize the use or reproduction of any part of this book in any manner
for the purpose of training artificial intelligence technologies or systems.
The publisher expressly reserves this book from the Text and Data Mining
exception in accordance with Article 4(3) of the European Union
Digital Single Market Directive 2019/790.

Visit **www.panmacmillan.com** to read more about all our books
and to buy them.

*For Trisha Jackson,
the best editor an author could ever hope for*

Dear Reader,

I'm often asked how I get ideas for my novels, and this one came to me when I was out walking the dog. It was a particularly damp and soggy day, and as I tramped across the park, lost in a world of my own imagination, I suddenly had this image in my mind of an old caravan in the corner of a muddy field, stuck out in the middle of nowhere. I could clearly see the woman who lived there. Her name was Maggie. What had happened to her? I wondered. What turn had her life taken for her to end up there? And as the scene played out in my head, I saw another, much younger woman, determinedly approaching the caravan. It was pouring with rain and she was getting filthy and wet through. Why was she there? What relationship did these two women have?

This scene was the inspiration for my new book, and while I knew I wanted it to be a fun, escapist read about the power of friendship and finding yourself – a story filled with adventure and joy and humour – there was a serious message, too.

More and more I'd been reading about the growing rise in romance fraud, where unsuspecting victims are scammed out of large amounts of money by someone with whom they've formed a romantic relationship. Often, these fraudsters target dating apps and social media, creating fake personas and spending weeks, if not months, building trust with their victims in virtual relationships in order to manipulate them into sending them money.

But it's not just happening online, it's happening in real life, too. And while it can happen to anyone, regardless of their gender, it's older women who tend to be the most targeted. Every day there seems to be another news story about a woman who has met and fallen in love with a man who she believed to be her soulmate, only to discover he's a romance fraudster. Women who might have recently gone through a divorce, be grieving the death of a loved one, struggling with mid-life or just feeling lonely and emotionally fragile are vulnerable to being exploited and manipulated by these cruel scammers.

Worse still, romance fraud isn't just about money. In fact, the psychological damage is often far worse than the financial. Because by masquerading as your soulmate, these fraudsters aren't just stealing your life savings, they're stealing your heart, your trust and your sense of self. It's a particularly cruel crime that leaves victims feeling emotionally and mentally scarred because it plays into everything we hold dear.

Love.

By falling in love you allow yourself to be vulnerable, to trust, to hope, to imagine a future together. Your partner is supposed to make you feel safe and protect you, so this fraud is the ultimate betrayal. I'd hear stories of people talking about how discovering the deceit had shattered their confidence and left them with extreme feelings of shame and guilt. Many spoke of being too embarrassed to go to the police since they blamed themselves. Isolated and depressed, and unable to trust anyone, including themselves, some even consider suicide.

Many, if not most of us, will know what it feels like to have our heart broken. But how does it feel to discover that everything you believed in is a lie? That the man you thought was your soulmate has stolen your life savings and effectively your life?

Which brings me back to Maggie. Maggie is every woman. She's all of us. A woman who worked hard to build herself a life that she loved. The only thing missing was someone special to share it with. What happened to her could happen to anyone.

And while this novel is a tribute to anyone who has ever been a victim of romance fraud, it's also for anyone who has ever suffered a blow so devastating they thought their life was over. Because Maggie is here to show you that it's not. Far from it.

But I'm getting ahead of myself – let's rewind back to the beginning. Back to how every story starts.

'So, I met this guy . . .'

# Prologue

*Off the Mediterranean Coast, late at night*

'Quick! He's getting away!'

Two women in evening gowns give chase. Rushing across the pool deck of the giant cruise ship, they dive past the live band and down the stairs. Darting and dodging through the uniformed crew and jiving guests that have gathered for the Dancing Under the Stars extravaganza.

'Sorry, excuse me, sorry,' apologizes the older woman.

'Get outta the way!' yells the younger.

Rainbow-coloured cocktails go flying; paper umbrellas rain down like confetti through the warm, floodlit skies as passengers are knocked fully clothed into the swimming pool with loud shrieks and splashes.

'What the . . . ?'

'Oh my God, I am SO sorry! Please, send me the dry-cleaning bill.'

But there's no time to stay and apologize. The cruise ship is nineteen decks high and the length of three Premier League football pitches. *And he's getting away.* Clutching on to the hems of their dresses, they race in hot pursuit. Adrenaline pumping. Chests heaving. Hearts hammering. There might be a generation gap between these two women but you'd never know it from the way the fifty-year-old is out-sprinting the twenty-six-year-old.

'Be careful, don't trip—'

*Too late. Spoke too soon.*

'Argh!' As the older woman races ahead her heel catches on the sequinned hem and she goes flying.

'Shit, you OK?'

'I can't run in these heels!'

'*Durrr!* Don't you know the high heel is a patriarchal tool to slow women down? Why do you think I'm wearing my trainers?'

'Oh, shut up and give me a hand.'

OK, forget the bit about the generation gap.

A whistle blows behind them. They both snap back and turn to see the cruise ship's own security team suddenly appear. They're uniformed and armed with batons and stun guns.

'Stop! Security!'

One of them shouts a command and waves a stun gun. *Hang on, is that a real gun?* Screams rise up from the crowds but the fleeing assailant has no intention of being arrested and now the security team join the chase as he leaps tables and overturns chairs, roughly shoving guests and crew out of his path as he makes his getaway.

'STOP HIM!' both women yell urgently.

'He's a thief!'

'A liar.'

Tossing her heels aside, the older woman clambers to her bare feet.

'The biggest mistake of my life!'

Way up ahead, on the dance floor, Dolores Lopez from Miami, recently divorced and celebrating her new-found freedom with a two-week cruise around the Mediterranean with her two best girlfriends from high school, is on her third round of strawberry daiquiris and enjoying some kick-ass moves, when the live music abruptly stops and she suddenly finds herself in the middle of all this commotion.

And now directly in the path of a dark-haired man sprinting towards her. Hearing the woman's cry, she's unexpectedly – and very annoyingly – reminded of her ex-husband. And she *really* doesn't want to be reminded of her ex-husband.

Which is the reason she decides to stick out her rhinestone stiletto.

'It was for all the years I had to wear flats 'cos he was a short-ass,' she tells local police the next the morning, showing them her six-inch stiletto as evidence when they come on board to take statements. 'And that was for all the years I had to do his goddamn laundry,' she adds, explaining why she tipped the rest of her daiquiri all over the assailant's white dress shirt as he stumbled and fell.

What Dolores doesn't tell the police is that for the split second he lay at her feet, he flashed her a cute smile. Or that, taken aback by his reaction, instead of whacking him over the head with her empty cocktail glass she stared, momentarily frozen. Then, unable to help herself, smiled back.

But it doesn't go unnoticed by the two women, even from a distance.

'Wait! *Is he flirting with her?*'

'Does a bear shit in the woods?'

'I don't know. Does it? You don't get many bears on the Pennines.'

And then before you know it, he's up and off again, disappearing through the crowds.

'Stop! Security! Surrender immediately!'

The team of security race past them. Crikey, where did they spring from?

'Don't worry. He can't get away. We're at sea.'

'He always gets away with it.'

'Not this time.'

'That's what you think.'

Breathless, the two women rush to catch up. As they near the helm of the ship they watch as he races up the staircase and leaps onto the glass railing. A loud gasp goes up from the crowd and a sound from a loudspeaker.

'Move away from the edge!'

There's nowhere further to go. Nowhere to run. Finally caught, he turns and looks back at the armed security team, scanning the crowds of passengers, until his eyes fall on the two women. They both stare at him as his gaze flicks from one to the other. A few seconds. A million emotions. Anger. Regret. Triumph. Loss. Heartbreak. Empowerment. Justice.

They reach for each other's hand, squeezing tightly as armed security move forward to arrest him. This is it. The End. It's over.

'Gotcha,' they mouth, fixing him with their gaze.

But instead of guilt and remorse, he stares back, unrepentant.

And then, with his figure silhouetted against the inky blackness, he turns to look at the wide ocean far below.

And he jumps.

*TWO WEEKS EARLIER*
A Field in the Middle of Bum-fuck Nowhere

# First Impressions

*Is this it?*

With a juddering halt, an ancient Volkswagen with one hubcap missing and a gaffer-taped bumper pulled up to the five-bar gate at the entrance of the field. It was pouring down. The windscreen wipers creaked back and forth leaving behind a blurry spot right in the middle, causing the driver to hunch down in their seat in order to see out.

Inside the car, Flick checked the directions on her phone again, but the map wouldn't load. No signal. Leaning forward across the steering wheel, she used the sleeve of her jacket to rub the fogged-up windscreen. The demisters had conked out too. Giving up, she rolled the window a crack to let in some air.

'Bloody rain,' she cursed, as a deluge of water followed, soaking her jacket. Hastily she rolled it back up again. It was the middle of July. What had happened to summer?

But Flick already knew the answer. Climate change. She didn't need to watch another award-winning David Attenborough wildlife documentary to know that everything bad that was happening in the world was the result of climate change. The planet was in crisis. Global warming was wreaking havoc with extreme weather, food scarcity, habitat loss and rising sea levels. It should be headline news, on the front of every newspaper every single day.

Except it wasn't.

She glanced across at the passenger seat and the latest edition of *The Local Echo*. Today their leading story was about a headbutting flock of sheep causing mayhem on the moors.

**WARNING TO HIKERS – EWE BE CAREFUL!**

It was terrible. Even more terrible was she'd written it.

**By Felicity Lomax. Community Reporter.**

Seeing her name in print gave rise to the usual feelings of pride and frustration. It was also a timely reminder. *This is why you're here, remember?*

Taking a swig of the cold dregs of her takeout coffee, she pressed her nose determinedly against the windscreen and peered out across the field ahead. Big, fat drops streamed down the glass, blurring her view, but then she saw it. In the corner. On the far right-hand side, between the trees and the stone wall.

A caravan.

And no, not a cute, vintage, candy-coloured-bunting-strung-across-Instagram-friendly caravan. But a knackered, mouldy-old-memories-of-wet-camping-trips-to-Wales-with-her-mum-and-Auntie-Pam caravan.

OK, so this definitely must be it.

Straightening up, Flick turned off the engine. The car fell silent; just the sound of the rain drumming on the roof. Brushing off the crumbs from her unfinished croissant, she checked her reflection in the rear-view mirror, making sure her liquid black eyeliner was perfect, complete with the signature flicks at the corner of her eyes. In her only good suit, a new pair of smart white vegan trainers that she could ill afford, and a hardcore blow-dry to get her fringe just as she liked it, she was aiming for savvy, confident and professional. An investigative journalist with a killer nose for a story and really good hair.

A twenty-something reporter from a crappy local paper stared back. Nerves jangled in the pit of her stomach. And she had really bad hair.

Shit.

Attempting – and failing – to flatten down the frizz that threatened to erupt from her head like one of those magic kitchen sponges that *pinged* the moment they encountered water, she grabbed her bag and umbrella, then reached for the door handle. It really was coming down now. Flick paused. She wasn't known for looking on the bright side – as a journalist she was a confirmed realist – but in a brief, uncharacteristic moment of optimism, she glanced at the leaden skies, hoping to see a break in the clouds.

But nope. Nothing but endless grey. She braced herself. There was nothing else for it.

Flinging open the door, she climbed out of the car.

And stepped right into a quagmire.

*What the . . . ?*

After several weeks of relentless rain, the farm track, previously a pretty wildflower lane, had been churned into thick, claggy mud and filthy puddles of water. Into which Flick's lovely new white vegan trainer promptly submerged itself.

*Fuck.*

As she yanked it back out, dripping wet and filthy, there followed a series of increasingly desperate manoeuvres that involved trying to lever herself out of the car and onto a central island of grass without ruining *both* trainers, whilst trying to put up her umbrella in the driving rain.

At which point Flick felt herself having one of those

out-of-body experiences where you suddenly look at your life and think, *How did I get here?*

Five years ago she'd graduated from university with high hopes and big dreams of being a journalist. Of adrenaline-charged newsrooms, breaking news stories and urgent deadlines. It all seemed so glamorous and exciting *and important.* Dashing around cities with a Dictaphone and a cigarette, doing exclusive interviews with famous people, investigating sources, digging deep to find answers.

Actually, no one uses a Dictaphone any more, and smoking gives you cancer, but you get the picture.

Nowhere in this vision of her exciting journalistic future did she see herself standing in a field in the middle of nowhere in the pouring rain, with feet caked in mud, getting piss-wet through.

For a brief moment Flick considered getting straight back in the car. Abandoning the whole thing. But there was so much riding on this interview. It wasn't just about her chance at proving herself, of getting a promotion and a pay rise, of making the leap from a local newspaper to a national one. If she turned around now, there'd be no hope of ever—

She stopped herself. She wasn't even going to go there.

Checking she had her phone and earbuds, she looped her bag over her shoulder, unhooked the gate and, making sure to close it behind her (memories of the headbutting sheep causing mayhem were still fresh in her mind), set off across the field.

She'd been over the moon when she finally got the job as a junior reporter at *The Local Echo.* But after nearly three years of covering local news stories about missing cats, Boy Scout jumble sales and wayward sheep, she was ready, *more than ready,* for an opportunity to prove she could be a proper journalist. For a story that would give her the break she desperately wanted.

Other reporters had been at the paper for years. Be patient, your time will come, they told her. But when? She'd be sitting around waiting for her big break for ever at this rate. She'd end up like Tupperware Tony, who'd been doing the Letters page for twenty-five years. Every day he brought in a packed lunch and announced to the rest of office what sandwich his partner had made. 'Ooh, what have we here? Tuna and sweetcorn, a true classic!' 'Cheese and pickle, hurrah, my favourite!' 'Roast beef and pesto, how about that for controversial?' Twenty-five years, and the most exciting thing to happen to Tony was his sandwich fillings.

No, big breaks don't just come. They don't just happen. You had to *make* them happen.

Which is why, last week, when Flick overheard a couple of people in the pub gossiping about some local scandal, her ears pricked up. From the snippets of conversation, it sounded terrible. *And completely fascinating.* She knew immediately it would make a great story; this was a hot topic of national concern right now and she kept hearing about it on the news or reading articles on the subject online. This was her chance to finally do some proper investigative reporting. To get her big break and make her name.

But it all hung on getting an exclusive interview with the inhabitant of the caravan.

Flick glanced at it now from underneath her umbrella as she tramped across the muddy field. Nerves jangled in the pit of her stomach, but she refused to acknowledge them. Off in the distance, she spotted a cow. She'd just covered a story about a rambler who was trampled by cows. The poor woman suffered broken ribs and was lucky to be alive. Not so much her poor spaniel. She quickened her pace. Rory, her boyfriend, would probably say it was her fault if she got trampled. He warned her about being too ambitious and going after her own stories.

'That's the problem with you, Flick, you're always getting ideas above your station.'

Of course, he only said things like that because he cared about her. He didn't want her to get hurt or be disappointed, especially so soon after losing her mum. He couldn't understand why she wasn't satisfied with being a reporter at *The Local Echo*. OK, so the money wasn't great but it was a steady job and they paid into a pension.

'I just don't want you getting your hopes up, that's all, babe. All these pipe dreams about having your own column in one of those fancy, big newspapers in London. Those are proper journalists, people who went to private school; they're not like us. Your articles are great, but it's not like you're a *real* writer. You need to stick to what you know.'

Constructive criticism, that's what he called it.

She kept trudging, head down, battling the rain, until eventually she reached the far corner of the field. Up close, the caravan was worse than she'd first thought. Chewing-gum white, net curtains, condensation on the windows: it had seen better days. Flick knew the feeling. Taking a tissue from her bag, she attempted to scrape the clods of mud from her now-filthy trainers, then smooth down her fringe. She hesitated. As a local reporter she'd stood on enough doorsteps in order to get an interview, but this was different.

Abruptly, a twist of anxiety threatened to derail her, but she quickly pulled it together. It was important to appear confident and assured. Taking a deep breath, she knocked on the door. No one answered.

'Hello?'

Actually, maybe this was a really bad idea.

She waited a moment, cleared her throat, then reached forward to knock again.

At which point the door was flung open to reveal a

barefoot, middle-aged woman wearing a pair of old sweatpants and a crumpled T-shirt. She peered myopically at Flick from behind a messy curtain of hair.

Immediately Flick was struck by two things: the woman was extremely tall, even with bare feet; and she looked surprised to see her.

'Hi. We spoke on the phone. I'm Felicity Lomax, from *The Local Echo*.' Flick spoke quickly and held out her hand. 'But everyone calls me Flick.'

'Oh, you're early!'

The woman looked like she'd just got out of bed. Pulling a scrunchie from her wrist, she scraped back her curls, which were the same colour as Flick's unfinished croissant, revealing grey at her temples and a face full of freckles.

'I am?'

And now it was Flick who was surprised. She prided herself on her timekeeping. She checked her watch, thus confirming to herself that she was bang on time.

'Didn't we say twelve on Friday?'

*Remember: confident and assured.*

'Yes, but today's Thursday. I was expecting you tomorrow.'

'Tomorrow?'

There was a pause as the cold realization trickled down the back of Flick's neck like the rain dripping off the broken spoke of her umbrella. And all at once she realized she'd made a mistake. Mortified, she reached for her phone in her pocket to check the date, but she already knew before she glanced at the screen. Somehow, with everything that had been going on since her mum died, she'd lost track of the days and got the dates muddled up. The funeral was six months ago, but she'd still not got back on track.

Unexpectedly her eyes prickled. Forget looking confident and assured; she looked like a total moron. She sniffed sharply, quickly pulling herself together. 'I'm so sorry, my mistake. I can come back another time if it's more convenient . . .'

Standing at the doorway of the caravan, Margaret Fletcher looked at the sodden young reporter with her muddy trainers and broken umbrella, its spokes sticking out at right angles, and considered this.

It really wasn't a good time. The place was a mess. Plus, she was so tired she couldn't face talking to anyone right now. In fact, all she really wanted to do was climb back into bed and pull the covers over her head. But then she felt like that most days now.

She opened her mouth to make some excuse, hand already on the door to close it behind her, thoughts returning to getting back into bed, disappearing underneath the duvet, making it all go away . . .

Then she noticed the reddening of her eyes.

Later, when Margaret Fletcher looked back, she would realize that this was the moment something clicked. The moment she recognized something in Flick. A vulnerability? A familiarity? A strange feeling of being untethered? She didn't know what it was, but she saw it reflected back at her and changed her mind.

'You're getting soaked, come inside.' Opening the door wide to let her enter, she forced a broad smile. 'And, please, call me Maggie.'

# Off the Record

'I'm afraid I don't have any sugar.'

Ten minutes later and the kettle was on, puffing out steam and condensing on the window. Well, what else do you do in times like this but put the kettle on?

*Should be the story of my life*, thought Maggie, who had lost count of the number of times she'd put the kettle on these past six months for want of something else to do. She attempted a quick tidy round; the place was a bit of a tip – worse, she'd just done a load of handwashing and the clothes airer was filled with damp bras and knickers that had seen better days.

'Oh, that's fine. My boyfriend says I'm sweet enough.'

On its way to being manoeuvred into a corner, the airer collapsed in on itself. They both looked at each other. Flick gave a nervous laugh, then shook her head.

'Actually, that's bollocks.'

Caught off-guard, Maggie smiled self-consciously.

The kettle clicked off.

'I'll do this later.' Abandoning the airer, she hastily turned her attention back to making the tea in the small galley that was her kitchen. Squashing teabags into the tiny plastic sink and stooping down to retrieve the small carton of milk from the miniature fridge, she tried not to think about her old kitchen, with its granite-topped island, acres of counter space and all the latest appliances.

At a memory of sitting at the kitchen island, sharing a bottle of wine and romantic meal for two, she felt a sudden yearning and caught herself sharply. No point thinking about that. It was gone, along with everything else in her old life. She firmly grabbed the two mugs.

'Here you go.'

'Thanks.'

As she passed Flick her tea, Maggie took in the young reporter who was now sitting at the small banquette in the corner of her caravan. It was the first time she'd had someone in her space and she felt acutely embarrassed by her situation. She noticed the mould around the windowpane and averted her eyes. What was she thinking, inviting her inside?

'I don't get many visitors.' Cradling her own mug in her hands, she sat down opposite, squashing her long legs underneath the Formica table. 'Don't have the entertaining space,' she added, forcing a laugh in a lame attempt at humour.

Flick smiled politely. 'I like caravans. They always remind me of holidays to Wales with my mum.'

'Nice.'

'Yes.'

Flick didn't mention the bit about the mouldy beds and never-ending rain. Best not.

The pleasantries over, the two women turned their attention to their tea. Flick took a large gulp – ugh, God, it was that awful Earl Grey stuff that tasted like perfume – and tried not to gag.

'So, anyway, after we spoke on the phone I printed off some pictures,' said Maggie.

After waiting what she hoped was enough time to not appear like she was trying to get this over and done with as quickly as possible, Maggie put down her mug and reached for the photos she'd set aside. At least she'd got that organized. Laying them on the table, she started showing them to Flick.

'So, this is George when he was a kitten. I called him after my best friend George, and also Dad's a big Beatles fan. I mean *was*,' she quickly corrected herself. 'George Harrison was his favourite. Said he was the most underrated Beatle. I mean, everyone goes on about Lennon and McCartney, but when it comes to song-writing ability you don't get better than "While My Guitar Gently Weeps", wouldn't you agree?'

Flick made an agreeing sound. She had no idea what Maggie was going on about. She made a mental note to check Spotify later.

'George isn't used to the countryside. He's been a city cat his whole life. My flat had a small roof terrace and he liked to sit on it and sun himself.' Maggie pulled out a photo of George doing exactly that and smiled, her thumb affectionately rubbing over his picture. 'We only moved up here a few months ago, after . . . well, after everything.'

For a brief moment her mind flicked back again, before she forced it briskly on.

'He's been missing over a week now. The farmer says there are foxes, but I think he might have just run away. I wouldn't blame him.' She smiled weakly. 'Anyway, you can take them if you want. I have copies on my phone.'

Shuffling the photos into a neat pile, she passed them across the table.

Flick smiled awkwardly. 'Actually, that's not why I'm here.'

'It's not?' Maggie frowned, confused. 'But when you called, you said you'd seen the posters I've put up around town about my lost cat.'

'Yes, I did. That's how I got your number.'

'I assumed you were going to write a piece for *The Local Echo*.' Maggie realized she was beginning to sound accusatory, but she didn't care. Her beloved cat was missing. She'd invited this reporter into her home to help find him. Reaching across to a stack of old newspapers, she found the one she was looking for and thrust it at Flick. 'Like this one. Look.'

Sure enough, there was an article Flick had written about a lost cat, entitled 'He's The Cat's Whiskers'. Flick cringed at the headline. That had been her editor's idea.

'And you said you had some information,' continued Maggie, refusing to give up.

'Yes, I do. But it's not about your missing cat.'

'It's not?'

Watching Maggie's face crumple with disappointment, Flick felt a stab of guilt. This woman was obviously upset about her pet. She should have explained more on the phone. Been more honest. Not come here under false pretences.

But she also knew if she had, Maggie would never have agreed to talk to her.

'So what is it about?'

Flick snapped back to see Maggie studying her suspiciously.

'It's in connection with a Mr Theo C. Stratin.'

At the mention of his name Maggie felt her breath catch in the back of her throat. Even now, over six months later, it was still so raw.

'Is this a missing persons thing?'

Flick quickly side-stepped with the deftness of a politician. 'I wondered what you could tell me about him?'

Maggie laced her fingers tightly around her mug. 'Not much really. We were in a relationship, we broke up.' She kept her voice even. 'The rest, as they say, is history.'

'I understand he scammed you out of your life savings.'

*Boom*. Maggie reeled.

'Who told you that?'

'It's a small town. People talk.'

Maggie's internal shutters came slamming down.

'I'm sorry, but I think you should leave. There's obviously been a misunderstanding.'

The caravan felt suddenly claustrophobic. Hastily, Maggie got up from the table and in her hurry she banged herself on the corner of the banquette and spilled her tea. Cursing under her breath, she rubbed her thigh furiously. She could feel the bruises beginning to form already.

*Well, that went well.* Watching her, Flick felt a stab of dismay as she put down her mug and reached for her bag. Mutely, she rose from her seat. Then paused. It was now or never.

'You're not the only one.'

'Excuse me?'

'You're not the only woman he's romance scammed. He's done it before and he'll do it again.'

'If you don't mind.'

Clambering over the collapsed airer, Maggie's foot caught in a bra strap, causing her to trip and bend down to unloop it. It was one of those T-shirt bras. Flesh-coloured with huge cups like giant jelly moulds. God, the indignity of it all. Standing upright, she glared at Flick, daring her to say anything.

'All right, look, I know I should've been honest about why I wanted to talk to you, but I thought if I told you, you wouldn't want to speak to me.'

Finally, Maggie lost her patience.

'You're damn right I wouldn't! Why would I? So you can write about me in your paper? Let the whole word know what a fool I was?'

'Well, to be fair, I don't think the whole world reads *The*

*Local Echo*. Our circulation is only about four and a half thousand an edition.'

Flick broke off as she caught Maggie's expression.

'And you're not a fool, you're a victim,' she added quietly, but firmly.

It took the wind from Maggie's sails.

'I've been doing my research into romance fraud, and more and more women – and men – are coming forward and the statistics are frightening. Men like Theo Stratin deliberately target vulnerable women. Apparently the most affected age group is usually over the age of forty-five; in fact, it's most often between the ages of fifty and seventy.'

'Great. Even worse. An *old* fool.'

'I didn't mean it like that.'

There was a lull as both women fell silent. Outside the rain was still lashing. Maggie watched the water seeping in at the windows.

'How old are you, Felicity?'

'Twenty-six.'

'How old do you think I am?'

Flick knew exactly how old Maggie was. She'd looked up her birth certificate, along with a few other things, as part of her background checks and initial investigations into the story.

'Late thirties?' she fibbed.

'I'm nearly fifty, almost twice your age, and any journalist worth their salt would've already looked up my birth records, so they'd know that. So either you're a crap journalist or that's a pathetic attempt at flattery.'

Flick felt her face go beetroot.

'I'm a good journalist and that's a crap attempt at flattery.'

Despite the insult, Maggie smiled at her admission.

'OK, so now we're being honest with each other, can I tell you something off the record?'

Flick nodded.

'He didn't just steal my life savings, he stole everything from me: my trust, my heart, my home, my livelihood, my self-esteem . . . all of it.'

As Maggie laid her vulnerability bare on the table between them, she was reminded yet again of the heavy weight of her guilt.

'Yet it's me who's ashamed. When I finally stopped crying long enough to go to the police, I felt like such an idiot—'

'But why? That's crazy!' interrupted Flick. She was indignant, but Maggie shook her head firmly.

'I was the one who'd willingly given him the money to invest in his new business venture. My father had recently passed away and left me a little bit of inheritance – not much, but it was something and it was just sitting in the bank making no interest, so I thought: why not? And when he suggested I sold my flat so we could pool our resources and buy a bigger place together, it was my idea to remortgage instead and also take out a business loan. I thought I was being so clever.'

Her voice threatened to break but she forced it to remain even.

'It was for our future. That's what he always said. It was an investment in our future. We were engaged, you see.'

As Maggie's mind flicked back, she felt a swell of hurt.

'Only, there was no international business venture. No new house. No joint account. No investments. It was all bogus. A con. A scam. What did you call it? A romance fraud.'

Followed swiftly by the usual feelings of anger, at both him and herself.

'After that, everything just fell apart; I lost my flat, my business . . . The police called him in for questioning, but he'd long disappeared, and my money with him. I tried calling the bank but they refused to reimburse me as I'd authorized all the payments . . . something about "contributory negligence". They'd even contacted me and read a fraud-warning script when I'd first sent funds internationally, but I'd confirmed it was to my fiancé's business and they were all genuine—' She broke off and laughed bitterly. 'Which is how I ended up here. I know it's not much, but this caravan was the only thing I could afford. If it wasn't for knowing the local farmer, and him letting me rent this field cheaply to put it in, I'd be homeless.'

The water leaking in through the windows had formed a pool and was now dripping onto the banquette sofas. Reaching for a roll of paper towels, Maggie started mopping it up.

'And you know the worst thing of all? The bastard even stole my dad's watch.'

A brief flash of anger. She couldn't bring herself to say his name. Tearing off a sheet, she folded it up and shoved it furiously in the cracks.

'It wasn't worth anything, Dad wasn't into material possessions, but it had huge sentimental value . . . It'd stopped working, so it sat in a drawer for ages, along with a few other bits of jewellery. I kept meaning to get it fixed, but just never got round to it. When I mentioned it to him, he offered to get it fixed for me; he was kind like that.' She laughs, bitterly. 'When he disappeared, the watch disappeared with him.'

Maggie broke off finally and the caravan fell quiet.

Flick had been listening, not wanting to interrupt, but now she spoke.

'Well, he's not disappeared any more. I've found out where he is.'

But Maggie shook her head firmly.

'I don't want to know. I don't ever want to see him again. If you want to tell someone, tell the police.'

'But we could stop him from doing this to someone else. We could save another woman from losing everything.'

'How?'

'By doing an exposé and revealing the truth about him. Letting the public know all the shocking facts. Confronting him and making him answer to what he did. You aren't the first woman he did this to, and you won't be the last.'

But while Flick's voice was urgent, Maggie's was weary.

'I'm tired. I just want to put all this behind me.'

'What about your life savings?'

'I'm sure the money is long gone.' Maggie shrugged with resignation. 'The last time I spoke to the police they said it was still under investigation, but there was little chance of getting it back even if it went to court and they got a conviction. Which seems unlikely, considering they've yet to find him to question him.'

'Well, even if the police can't do anything, the newspaper can still publish an article.'

Maggie looked at Flick. At this young, eager reporter with her whole life ahead of her. Was she like that once? She couldn't remember. She felt a sudden, strange affection for both Flick and her old self. And a crushing sense of sadness.

'Look, you seem really nice; really, you do. And I'm sure you're a really good journalist. And if you want to write a story, then I can't stop you; go ahead – but I don't want to be any part of it. What happened really affected me and it's taken me a long time to recover from it . . . In fact, I don't think I'll ever fully recover from it.'

She heard her voice catch in her throat and blinked rapidly.

'The police gave me some pamphlets with the details of

support groups, links to websites, numbers I could call . . . I thought about it, but I don't want to go over what happened to me. I just want to move on. Put it behind me, try to forget about it. The last thing I need right now is you dragging it all up again.'

She straightened up, her decision made.

'So, if you don't mind, I'm going to say goodbye now and it's nice to meet you. I'm sure you can find your way out.'

She'd said her piece and now Maggie looked at Flick, waiting to be challenged. But while Flick was a keen journalist and had learned all about questioning and trying to get answers, about eliciting information and being persuasive, she also knew when to call it a day.

'OK, fair enough.'

Putting her bag on her shoulder, she squeezed past Maggie and the collapsed clothes airer and walked the few paces to the door of the caravan. As she did, she caught sight of a black-and-white photograph on the side, of a little girl and her father. Curled up on his knee, she was laughing; he had his arms around her, hugging her tightly. It struck something inside and she gestured to it.

'Is that you with your dad?'

'Yes.' Maggie allowed herself to smile.

Flick looked at it again, noting his wristwatch.

'What about your dad's watch?'

'Oh, he's probably sold it by now.'

'But you said it wasn't worth anything.'

Flick hesitated, knowing she should probably leave it alone, but also knowing she couldn't.

'You said yourself, he didn't steal that watch because of the financial value, he took it because it was there and he can't stop himself. I doubt he ever had any intention of getting it fixed. He didn't care about its sentimental value, that it meant so much to you. Because you're right: Theo Stratin is a bastard.'

Always remain dispassionate. One of the golden rules of journalism, and yet here she was breaking it and getting personal.

'Don't you want to confront him? To warn other vulnerable women and men? Don't you want to show him and the rest of the world he didn't break you?'

There was a moment's pause and then Maggie spoke.

'But he did, though, didn't he?'

Maggie's voice was so quiet Flick almost didn't hear it above the sound of the rain.

'Look at me. My life's a mess. I'm broke, unemployed, living in a caravan . . . Everyone talks about mental health these days; well, he shattered mine. I wasn't always like this, you know. God only knows what you must think of me, but I used to have my own art gallery. A lovely home. *A life*. He ruined everything. I had confidence, faith in my abilities; I felt sure of myself. Now I can't trust myself. I can't trust my own judgement. Do you know what that feels like? Like everything was a lie.'

Broken, Maggie shook her head.

'The sad thing is I loved him. But you want to know the scariest? Part of me still does.'

Standing at the doorway, Flick absorbed her words before replying.

'Can I tell you something, off the record?'

Maggie nodded.

'Without you there is no story.'

The truth. That's what people always tell you to say. Because it's the truth that sets you free. But telling the truth is scary. It takes courage and vulnerability and trust.

And you have to be ready.

There was a pause as the two women looked at each other.

'I can't. I'm sorry,' Maggie finally said.

'You don't have to be sorry for anything.' Hiding her disappointment, Flick smiled kindly. 'But if you change your mind, you know where to find me.'

And leaving behind a business card, she opened the door of the caravan and stepped back out into the rain.

# The Local Echo

'You want to go *where*?'

'It's just for the weekend.'

'Hang on, so let me get this straight. You want to go gallivanting off to the South of France for the weekend to try to get an interview with some love rat?'

'Well, I wouldn't be gallivanting; I'd be investigating.'

'And you want the paper to pay for it?'

'Yes, that's sort of the idea.'

'Flick Lomax, have you taken leave of your senses?'

It was later that afternoon and Flick was in her editor's office.

After her conversation with Maggie, Flick had driven back to *The Local Echo*. Their offices were in town, situated just off the high street, in a converted Victorian woollen mill that backed onto the canal. It was actually a really nice building; they had their own floor and the others were occupied by a travel agent's, a bed manufacturer's, an accountant's and a funeral director. Which, when you think about things, and Flick was always thinking about things, summed up the basic cornerstones of life. Nice holidays, a comfy bed, death and taxes.

Which was either comforting or depressing, Flick wasn't sure. She'd mentioned it to Tupperware Tony once, asked him his opinion, and he'd looked bewildered and said he'd never even thought about it before. Which confirmed what

Flick had always suspected: that most people didn't think like her.

Most people would have left Maggie's caravan feeling dejected. So that was it. There was going to be no story. No exclusive. No chance of a promotion or pay rise. No Big Break. And, importantly, no answers. All that effort and for nothing. Most people would've walked back across that muddy field, feeling sorry for themselves about their ruined trainers and wasted time and career frustrations and stopped at the petrol station on the drive back to the office and treated themselves to some chocolate or crisps in a calorie-laden attempt to cheer themselves up. Hell, maybe they would have even bought both.

But Flick wasn't most people. Instead she drove right past that petrol station, hunched down low in her seat, windscreen wipers creaking furiously, as she hatched a plan. With or without Maggie, she was still going to try to write the story. She was a journalist, remember? And journalists didn't just give up at the first hurdle. No, they did not. They were tenacious and determined and when they got a whiff of a good story they chased it with integrity, ingenuity and a killer instinct.

Well, at least that's what they did in all those Netflix documentaries she watched.

Only, there was just one tiny problem – well, it wasn't exactly a problem, more a minor detail. One of several she'd conveniently left out when she'd pitched the story to Maggie.

She hadn't told anyone at the newspaper about what she was up to.

Not Simon on Features, Tupperware Tony, or Melissa, one of the subeditors who was known for her amazing skills at standfirsts and keeping the various indoor plants alive. And certainly not Seymour, her editor, whose office sat apart from the main news desk and into which she'd only entered a handful of times, once being the day she went for her interview.

No, instead she'd been working on her own initiative. Well, wasn't that one of the fundamental skills of being a journalist?

OK, so admittedly initiative seemed a *little* overrated – so far it had resulted in one expensive pair of ruined trainers and a caravan door (figuratively) slammed in her face. But she wasn't giving up.

Which is why she'd plucked up her courage, knocked on her editor's door, and spent the last ten minutes pitching her idea to Seymour. Who had sat across from her behind his large mahogany desk, mouth agape, listening to her telling him that no, she hadn't spent the morning at the town hall interviewing pole-dancing pensioners. But had, in fact, been miles out in the countryside investigating a story about a woman who had lost everything in a romance fraud.

'And he's not a love rat. The term is romance fraudster,' she finished.

'And I think you'll find the term is not on your nelly,' replied her editor.

Seymour, her editor, was in his sixties, with eyebrows that took on a life of their own and a fondness for Fair Isle vests, single malt whiskey and *pastéis de nata* from the Portuguese bakery on the corner. At least Flick thought he was in his sixties. She wasn't sure. It was hard to tell how old anyone was once they were over thirty. He also liked to use sayings she'd never heard of.

Leaning back in his leather swivel chair, he laced his fingers across his stomach and raised one of those bushy eyebrows of his.

'Let me ask you, how do you already know he's in the South of France? And what's more, how do you plan to find and interview this *romance fraudster* –' Seymour made a point of enunciating the words – 'if the police haven't?'

'I know where to look.'

'And where's that?'

'Social media, of course,' replied Flick, as if it was obvious. Because it was. Isn't that how everyone looked up their old boyfriends or girlfriends? Late at night, when you were feeling particularly bad about your life, eating what was left of the reduced-fat hummus and scrolling mindlessly in the hope of being reassured that they'd aged a lot worse than you and were still single. Even better, single with a really bad haircut.

Flick felt a niggle of doubt. Or was that just her?

Anyway.

'People like to show off,' she continued. 'They can't resist boasting about their holidays or their lifestyles and romance fraudsters are no different. Even if they change their name or their username and use aliases, everyone leaves a footprint if you look hard enough.'

'And how's that?' Seymour frowned, making his eyebrows flap like seagulls.

'Well, hashtags are often a dead giveaway, sometimes they even leave their location on, especially if it's a fancy hotel or restaurant, which of course isn't an accident, they *want* you to know where they are. To show off and say, "Look at me, look at how great my life is!" even though mostly it's just to convince themselves, because they're largely complete fantasists. But even if they don't leave their location on, there's cross-referencing between followers and friends, examining reels, their likes, screenshotting and zooming in on photos or landmarks in their stories to spot things in the background . . . and that's before you've even looked at their activity on TikTok or Facebook groups or X that used to be Twitter or Threads . . . There are clues everywhere.'

Her editor looked lost.

'Well, in that case you should tell the police if he's wanted for questioning.'

'And they'll do what exactly? The police are understaffed and overstretched as it is. According to Home Office data, eighty-two per cent of burglaries go unsolved. They're hardly going to cross the Channel to catch a thief if they can't even catch one on their own doorstep.'

'They might if they think they'll catch a suntan,' quipped her editor.

Sitting across from him, Flick frowned. Was he trying to be funny? She wasn't sure.

'OK, I'll tell them.'

'Good.'

'But I still want to go. It would make a great story. You know it would.'

It was a compromise of sorts. Flick knew the police wouldn't do anything. But this way she could still try and get her interview.

'Would it, though? I mean, a middle-aged woman falls for a con man? It's hardly headline stuff.'

'And pole-dancing pensioners are?' snapped Flick.

Seymour didn't reply. Underneath his Fair Isle vest, he could feel his shirt buttons straining from the extra pounds he'd gained since Gaynor, his wife, had left him six months ago. Too many takeaways and beers on the sofa. They'd met when he was a young, skinny-hipped reporter working in Fleet Street and he'd travelled to Liverpool to interview a band that was about to become the next Beatles. For the life of him, he couldn't remember their name now, but he'd never forget the pretty redhead who asked for his ticket at Lime Street station. Six months later they were married with a baby on the way and he'd given up his crazy London life for a steady job on a regional paper. He never regretted it, though sometimes he missed who he used to be. He glanced at his wastepaper basket, noting the empty box from the bakery and made a mental note to cut back on their custard tarts. Starting tomorrow.

And he really missed his wife.

He reached in his drawer for a packet of Monster Munch.

'I think you're forgetting this is a local newspaper,' he said, after a moment. 'We don't have that kind of budget. This isn't *News of the World*.'

'Actually, I don't think that exists any more.'

'But that's not the point, is it?' Seymour sighed heavily. 'You're supposed to be a local reporter. Reporting on *local* news.'

Through a gap in the vertical blinds, Flick caught sight of Simon on Features staring into Seymour's office. He was her senior and seemed to take great pleasure in giving her all the worst stories. He'd been dying to know why she was going to speak to their editor, but she'd refused to tell him. Now, with hope fast disappearing, she could imagine the smirk on his face when he found out.

Simon was someone who kept his location on and liked to post photos of himself drinking cocktails in bars around town together with the hashtag #cheerstome which, Flick thought, said everything you needed to know about Simon.

'But it is local news,' protested Flick. 'The woman's living locally in a caravan. That's local connections.'

But Seymour wasn't listening. 'Look, I know you've got ambitions. I was once like you. But keep working hard and one day you'll get here. You'll get my spot. You'll be in this chair,' he continued, his mouth full.

Flick looked at her editor, feet up on his desk, eating pickled-onion Monster Munch in his messy office. This was not the peak of her ambition.

'And, all right, perhaps it is a good story. But if it's a good story you want, I'll send you over to Clifton Park Reservoir.'

'What's happening at Clifton Park Reservoir?'

'Electric scooters. They're getting stolen and dumped there. Black market. Gangs. It's got all the hallmarks of a big story.'

'But it's not a big story, is it?'

'Well, that depends upon you. You're our community reporter. You can interview people. Follow up leads. Look at their footprint on social media,' added Seymour pointedly.

Flick felt her spirits sinking.

'If you write up a big piece, we can even think about the front page. How about that?' he enthused, flashing Flick a bright smile. He didn't want her feeling discouraged. She was a good reporter. Hardworking, enthusiastic, never missed a deadline. Not once during that whole time her mother was sick or even after the funeral.

'Or at the very least you could be on page three. Though not in the traditional sense, of course,' he added with a jovial laugh.

'Is that a reference to the tradition of sexually objectifying women by publishing photos of topless models in British newspapers that was finally banned in 2015 after a three-year campaign?' replied Flick.

Seymour nearly choked on a pickled-onion monster's foot.

'Right. Yes. That one.' Clearing his throat, he nodded vigorously, his expression stern. 'And not a minute too soon either, in my opinion. Thank goodness times have changed.'

'Thank goodness,' agreed Flick.

'Anyway –' eager to move off this subject, Seymour quickly grasped on to another – 'enough about work. Any summer holiday plans? I understand you've still got some annual leave to take before the end of August.'

'Yes, two weeks.'

'You know, if you don't use it, you lose it.'

Flick noticed Seymour chuckle to himself, there was obviously a joke in there somewhere, but she didn't get it.

'I'd rather be at work to be honest.'

Seymour studied Flick. She reminded him a lot of his daughter, when she was that age. Ambitious. Opinionated. Fearless. Before the drugs knocked all the stuffing out of her and tore their family apart. He felt suddenly protective.

'Look, I know you're dedicated, but it's all a work–life balance. Why don't you take some time off? Go on holiday with that boyfriend of yours, whatsisname?'

'Rory.'

'You two must be quite serious by now.' He raised an eyebrow.

Flick responded by returning the kind of smile she knew was required of her whenever anyone asked this question.

'Anyway, I'm sure Simon and Tony can manage on the Features Desk. Summer's always a quiet time for news.' He smiled genially. 'Think about it.'

'I will.' Flick nodded. But she didn't need to think about it. She didn't want a holiday. She wanted to break this story.

Pep talk over, Seymour threw the empty crisp packet in the bin and swung his legs back underneath his desk. It was Flick's cue to leave and, standing up, she walked over to the door and reached for the handle.

'Who is she anyway?'

Flick turned to see Seymour looking at her thoughtfully.

'This poor woman who lost everything?'

'Her name's Maggie. She used to own a little art gallery in Bath. Apparently she was quite successful.'

'And now she's penniless and living in a caravan up on the Pennines?' asked Seymour. 'Why move up here?'

'To be honest, I don't think she had anywhere else to go.'

Shaking his head, Seymour let out a low whistle. 'You just never know, do you? One wrong decision and your life's over.'

# Nothing to Lose

'It's been declined.'

'Excuse me?'

'Your card. It's been declined.'

Louder this time. The other people in the queue at the local farm shop turned to stare. Standing at the checkout, Maggie felt her face flush with embarrassment.

It was Friday afternoon, and she'd cycled to the local farm shop to buy a few groceries. Stock up for the weekend. Treat herself to a bottle of wine. At least that was the idea.

'Sorry, my mistake, it must have expired, let me try another one.'

Now, with all eyes upon her, she rummaged around in her bag. God, why did she carry all this crap around? Finally she located her purse and hastily pulled out another credit card.

'Here, this should work.'

As she held out her card, the teenage cashier gave her a blank look.

'Just tap the machine.' She pointed to the contactless symbol as if Maggie was an idiot.

'Sorry, yes, of course,' said Maggie, feeling like one.

Obediently she tapped the machine. Beneath the flaps of her jacket, she crossed her fingers, willing for the familiar *Card payment authorized, remove card* message to pop up on the display.

*Payment declined.*

'Don't worry, I've got cash!' She forced an overly cheerful voice, whilst trying not to think about the appalling state of her finances, and swiftly dug out the emergency twenty she kept in her purse. That should cover it. Worst case scenario, she could always put back the bottle of wine. Actually, no, on second thoughts the wine was an essential item. She'd put back the organic vegetables and locally sourced cheeses.

She zoned back to see the cashier looking at her with barely concealed contempt. 'We don't take cash.'

'You don't?'

Behind her, Maggie could feel the growing impatience of waiting customers. Meanwhile, the cashier, now clearly bored by this stupid middle-aged woman who was holding everyone up, pointed at the sign taped to the Perspex divider.

'It says on the sign.'

'Sorry, yes, of course . . . Sorry.'

Hearing herself say the word sorry for about the millionth time, Maggie wondered if she could sorry herself into non-existence. Each apology like an eraser, rubbing herself out like a line drawing until she simply disappeared.

'Right, well, um, that's all I've got.'

Briefly the thought struck her that if she were in a movie, this would be the point a handsome stranger would sweep in and offer to pay for her groceries. It would be the perfect meet cute. Swiping his credit card, the handsome stranger would disappear out of the shop before they even had a chance to swap names, and the rest of the film would be spent with her trying to find him and an opportunity to pay it forward.

But she was not in a movie. She was in a farm shop in the middle of nowhere. And this was definitely not a meet cute.

She locked eyes with the cashier, who was industriously chewing gum while staring her down.

'Right, well, I'll just put these things back . . .'

'Just leave the basket.'

'No, honestly I don't mind—'

'Will you get a frigging move on!'

A voice roared behind Maggie, causing her to jump. Turning around, she saw a huge queue had now formed behind her. An angry mob wielding organic produce and cartons of free-range eggs.

'We haven't got all day, there are people waiting!' A furious cyclist clad in Lycra waved his cold-pressed green juice at her.

'Sorry. I'm really sorry.'

Abandoning the basket on the counter, Maggie quickly skulked out of the shop. She could hear muttering behind her and was reminded of the journalist's visit yesterday; her saying how it was a small town and people talked. Abruptly, she felt a flash of mutiny and paused in the doorway. To hell with it. In for a penny, in for a pound. Give them something more to gossip about.

Turning back around, she marched up to the cyclist who, not expecting to be confronted, visibly paled.

'I've got a better idea,' she hissed, her face inches away from his rattish one. 'Why don't you stick that green juice up your Lycra arse?'

At least that's what her old self would have done. But this new, broken version of Maggie simply took the abuse and didn't answer back. Instead, she scuttled, shamefaced, out of the shop, the whispering ringing in her ears.

Twenty minutes later, back at the caravan, the state of her finances sank in. She'd known it was bad, but not this bad.

Logging into various banking apps on her phone, she checked the balances in her current account and on her credit cards. Since losing both her business and her flat above the gallery, which she had to sell after she could no longer pay the mortgage, she'd spent the last six months living off what little she had left and doing what she called the Zero Per Cent Balance Transfer Dance.

Less fun than the jive but more difficult than the Charleston, this involved moving debt around on her credit cards. It took a lot of time, practice and effort – timing was everything – and she was now something of an expert. Maybe they should think about having it as a category on *Strictly*.

Joking. Well, kind of.

She'd also been making a little bit of money doing some dog-walking for a nearby boarding kennels. She'd replied to an online ad. It didn't pay much but the only skills required were owning a pair of wellies, a pair of hands and liking dogs and she ticked all the boxes.

Which was quite something, as her life appeared to be ticking *none* of the boxes and there weren't many jobs out there for a middle-aged woman who had gone bankrupt.

Correction. *Almost* gone bankrupt.

She'd done everything to narrowly avoid that. When the bank had called in the business loan after she defaulted on the payments and the interest on her new, much bigger mortgage had sky-rocketed, she'd had no choice but to sell the gallery and her flat above it to pay off her creditors. Running an art gallery meant she didn't own any stock – what paintings she had were returned to the artists, all of whom were local and lovely and desperately sad to see her go – while the rest of the fixtures and fittings were sold off.

Luckily, she'd found a buyer quickly, but it was still a bitter blow. Last she'd heard the new owner had applied to the council to change the licence and open a coffee shop. It was as crushing as it was depressing. Like the world needed any more oat milk flat whites.

With what little she had left, she'd looked at renting, but everything was so expensive. Her friend George had said she could stay on his sofa bed in London, while one of her neighbours had kindly offered their spare room, but she didn't want to be a burden. Plus, their teenage son would need it in a few weeks when he came home from university.

Instead, she'd bought an old caravan on eBay, borrowed an artist-friend's Land Rover, and on a grey day in the middle of February, almost a year to the day since she first met the man she thought was the love of her life, she towed it two hundred and fifty miles up the M5 to the northern Pennines. Oh, the irony. To where Ainsley, an old university friend of her brother's who was now a local farmer and with whom she'd kept in touch, had a spare field she could rent. It was supposed to be a temporary solution, just until she sorted herself out, got back on her feet.

Except, getting back on her feet seemed to be taking a lot longer than she thought.

Reaching for her phone, Maggie texted the owner of the boarding kennels.

> **Hi Emma, do you need me to do any dog walks next week?**

She pressed send, then quickly added:

> **Just organizing my diary. Thanks, Maggie** ☺

Well, she didn't want to look too desperate. Even though she was. She'd even added a smiley face.

A few seconds later, the ticks went blue and Maggie could see Emma was typing. Hopeful, she stared at the screen, waiting for the reply to appear. It was taking an awfully long time. And now Emma had stopped typing, as if she'd changed her mind.

Finally, after what felt like for ever, a message appeared.

> Hi Maggie. Afraid next week's a bit slow.
> Will text you if we need you. Thanks, Emma

There was no smiley face.

Maggie stared at her phone, spirits sinking, before forcing herself to rally. Still, at least she had her emergency twenty-pound note – though she wasn't sure how much good that was to her if she couldn't find anywhere to spend it in this new cashless society. Getting up, she flicked on the kettle and checked the cupboards. She had a few tins, some pasta, a pizza in the fridge. There was enough food to last the weekend, but then what?

Anxiety bubbled, her mind flicking back.

When she lived in Bath she used to volunteer at the local food bank. Before she started volunteering, she'd assumed the people who used them weren't people like her. That they were different somehow. It sounded snobbish. Ignorant. Embarrassing, frankly, to even admit that she once thought that way, because she'd quickly realized how wrong she was. Lone parents, struggling families, low-paid workers, professionals who'd lost their jobs, pensioners who couldn't make ends meet, single men and women who'd suffered some unforeseen circumstance to push them over the edge. People just like her who thought it would never happen to them either.

The kettle boiled and she made tea. Chamomile. To calm the nerves. She thought about the bottle of wine she'd had to leave behind at the farm shop and felt a pang. Sod the chamomile, she could kill for a glass of that right now.

There was no shame. She knew that. And she was lucky enough to live in a country that had offered a safety net, of sorts. Amongst the pamphlets the police had given her, one had been for the local benefits office. But she'd ignored it, along with the rest. Somehow she felt like there were others much worse off than her, others that needed their help more. While she could manage, she would. Plus, would they even pay benefits to someone living in a caravan and without a permanent address?

She looked back at her phone. Perhaps she could do the Zero Per Cent Transfer Dance again? Surely there was bit of credit still left on one of her cards if she did a bit of tricky manoeuvring.

Maggie was just thinking this when her phone suddenly sprang to life and started ringing.

It was a WhatsApp video-call from George, one of her closest friends. They'd met at art college and spent a year together before she'd dropped out and moved back home. Still, they'd kept in touch and by their late twenties found themselves sharing a flat in London. By this time George had discovered it was actually quite hard earning a living as an abstract artist and was working as cabin crew for a big airline, jetting around the world. While she was getting experience in various galleries around Soho and Hackney, before finally moving out of the capital and opening her own.

Which, by the way, sounded very posh. An art gallery conjured up images of swanky locations and wealthy customers, but hers was a local neighbourhood gallery. Sandwiched between an antique bookshop and Jeera's Tandoori House, it was a small, but beautiful, creative space filled with local art of different mediums, all reasonably priced. There were a few expensive paintings, but most of it was affordable. After all, art should be affordable, shouldn't it?

Why should only the rich get to hang nice pictures on their walls?

And over the years she'd built up quite a reputation, discovering new artists and working with them for months to curate a show, supporting local sculptors and ceramicists, hosting different exhibitions, events and workshops. She was well known in the community and her gallery was a little hub of creativity.

She'd always loved art at school and dreamed of a career as a painter; getting into art college had been a dream come true . . . But things happen, and it wasn't to be. Still, that didn't stop her passion. The government seemed to think everyone needed to do maths and sciences, but arts were what made the world go round. What made it all bearable, she always thought.

Maggie stared at the vibrating phone in her hand. George was the only friend who ever called for a chat. No one had time these days. Everyone texted. Or left messages on various WhatsApp groups. Most of her girlfriends were dealing with husbands and partners and kids and ageing parents and jobs and traffic and menopause and everything else mid-life threw at you.

Plus, much to her shame, she'd lost touch with most of her friends when she met Him. Their love affair had been such a whirlwind, so all-consuming, she'd neglected her friendships. Plus, He preferred it that way. He wanted her all to himself. They didn't need anyone else, He would always tell her. At the time she thought it was romantic. Just the two of them, in this great big love bubble. She still couldn't believe how naive she'd been.

Much easier over texts to pretend that she was doing fine, everything was OK and she was starting over in her new life like it was one Big New Exciting Adventure. The only person she didn't have to pretend with was George. But still. She wasn't in the mood.

Rejecting the call, she texted instead.

> **Sorry, I'm busy. Will call you later x**

*Ping.* He replied straightaway.

> Bullshit. Busy doing what? You're unemployed and living in a field in the middle of bum-fuck nowhere. Call me back.

His text made her smile. George always had that effect, whatever the circumstances. Loud, opinionated and self-deprecating, he was someone for whom the phrase 'larger than life' was coined. But he was also deeply sensitive, with dark moods and a fragility witnessed only by those very close to him. Maggie always thought that's what made him such a brilliant artist. An ability to see beneath the layers, to glimpse light through the shadow and be able to draw it out.

Putting down her tea, she propped her phone against her mug and obediently video-called him back. Within seconds his wide smile was filling the screen, bright sunshine and blue skies making him squint against a backdrop of glistening skyscrapers.

'Where are you?' She could never keep track of George. Every time he rang he was somewhere different.

He swung the camera around so she could see the skyline. It was instantly recognizable as Manhattan.

'New York. Got a night stop. Wish you were here. We could go to the Metropolitan Museum of Art and look at Rothkos; it would be like the old days.'

'I wish,' she sighed, smiling. 'Forgive me if I don't swing

my camera around. The inside of the caravan doesn't have quite the same view as the Empire State.'

'So, how's it going?'

'Fine.'

'Liar.'

'Are you just ringing to insult me?'

He laughed good-naturedly. 'How long have I known you, Maggie?'

'Too long.'

'Exactly. Long enough to know nothing is ever fine. We're either fabulous and fuck-worthy or depressed and knackered or in love or heartbroken or *something*, but we're never just fine.'

Maggie smiled fondly at her friend.

George was a knee-jerk of exaggeration and drama. A working-class boy from Liverpool, he drank too much, loved too hard and always liked to joke about it. She was quieter, more rational, the sensible stooge to his funny man in the double act that was their friendship of over thirty years.

At least she was until recently.

'OK, so I'm not fine. I just got shamed out of the local farm shop.'

'Ooh, what did you do? Don't tell me. You gave a carrot a blow job? You got down and dirty with an organic cheese? You did something filthy with a side of grass-fed beef?'

Maggie shook her head as he fired her with filthy puns. 'Is this how your mind really works?'

George gave a throaty laugh. 'Don't look so shocked. We used to share a flat, remember?'

'Don't remind me.' Maggie gave a pretend shudder. 'Anyway, it was a lot more boring, I'm afraid. My credit card was refused and I didn't have any cash to pay for my groceries. Actually, that's not true,' she corrected herself. 'I had the cash, but they don't accept cash these days.'

'Of course not. It's a cashless society.'

'You knew that?'

'Where have you been?'

'In a field in the middle of bum-fuck nowhere, apparently,' she replied, repeating his words back to him. George looked sheepish.

'Sorry, I didn't mean that.'

'Yes, you did, and it's fine—' She caught herself and they both smiled. 'So, tell me, how are you, apart from being fabulous and fuck-worthy?'

'Actually, I feel completely *un*fuck-worthy. Since I finished with Joaquim it's been a total desert.'

Scraping his fingers through his shock of dark hair, he peered moodily into the camera. With his bright blue eyes and lantern jaw, George was the definition of handsome and he knew it. Still, it was an admirable attempt at modesty.

'But the good news is I'm painting. I just got a commission.'

'Wow, that's great.'

'You should start painting again.'

Maggie pulled a face. 'Oh George, I haven't painted for years.'

'I know. Which is why I'm always nagging you. You were good.'

'But not good enough. That's why I sell art. Or at least used to.'

George waved the statement away like an annoying fly. 'Well, now you could sell your own artwork. Look at it as an opportunity.'

Maggie gave him 'the look' that said to shut up and unusually for George he got the message.

'So, any news about my namesake?' he asked, changing the subject.

'Nope.' Maggie shook her head. 'George is still missing. It's been over a week.'

'I thought a local reporter had some information?'

'So did I, but turns it out it was about something else—' She broke off.

To be honest, the last twenty-four hours had been spent trying not to think about it. She was still reeling from the news that the man who'd blown up her life had been found – and all the emotions that stirred up – so she'd tried to push it to the back of her mind. Compartmentalize. Isn't that what they called it?

'Someone else.'

'*Someone?*' George raised an eyebrow. 'You mean, The Total Bastard Whose Name We Cannot Mention?'

'There must be an acronym for that.

'There is. It spells WANKER.' George was still visibly furious. 'Where he is?'

'She didn't say. To tell the truth, I didn't let her finish,' admitted Maggie. 'She said she wanted to write some article about romance fraud . . . to interview me and confront him and expose everything he's done. She wanted my help.'

'Do it.'

'You told me to forget about him.'

'But this is your chance to nail that bastard. When Joaquim cheated on me, I wanted revenge. I couldn't let him get away with it.'

'But he did get away with it. I lost everything. What good's it going to do now?'

'Have you told the police? Maybe they'll arrest him now.'

'No, and I'm not going to. It's just going to stir everything up again. I've moved on.'

'But you haven't really moved on, have you?'

'What are you talking about? I've moved to the opposite end of the country.'

'That's called pulling a geographic.'

'What's the difference?'

'If you'd really moved on, we wouldn't still be talking about him, would we?'

There was a beat as his words sunk in. He was right. And she hated herself for it.

'I'm going to go now, George,' she said, wanting to get off the phone. 'Have fun at the Met. Take a picture of Courbet's *Woman with a Parrot* for me.'

'Think about it.'

'Bye. Love you.'

'Love you more.'

The screen of Maggie's phone returned to her screensaver. A different George. Ginger and furry, he stared out her reminding her again of everything that was missing, everything that was lost. A sharp pain stabbed in her chest. She felt both annoyed by the phone call and anxious. It had stirred everything up again. Just thinking about Him gave her a knot in her stomach. A panic. A fear. She'd survived the tsunami of emotions that had once almost drowned her, but she was scared.

What if the tsunami came back? What if she didn't survive this time?

She got up from the banquette. After talking to George, the caravan felt quiet and claustrophobic. She turned on the TV for a distraction. Some daytime quiz show appeared, bright and loud, its chirpy presenter chatting to the contestants. She glanced absently at the screen, watching until it went to the ad break. And now it was all those awful commercials for funerals and stairlifts and starving animals, cynically scheduled to tug at the heartstrings of the retired. As if watching daytime TV wasn't depressing enough.

Quickly reaching for the TV remote, she turned it off. She felt restless. For so many years she'd had a purpose, a direction, a sense of control over her own life. But now she felt cast adrift. Like she had no control. And yet, if the truth be told, she was conflicted. Part of her wanted to hide away in this caravan for ever, to let life wash over her and not put up a fight. To admit defeat and just give up.

On the side she noticed the business card left behind by the journalist. She picked it up, tracing her thumb over the embossed lettering. She thought about her own business cards. All gone now. Her phone beeped, distracting her. It was a text from George.

> So I've been thinking. . . You know what's brilliant about losing everything?

> **Trust me, there's nothing brilliant.**

> That's not true. It's actually empowering.

> **How so?**

> Because now you've got abso-fucking-lutely nothing left to lose.

# Last Call

*'Thank you for calling 101. We are connecting you to Greater Manchester Police. If you require an alternative force, press hash.'*

Early Saturday morning and Flick was standing at a condiment bar in a cafe, looking for brown sugar for her oat milk flat white while listening to the automated voice in her AirPods. Ah, there it was. Grabbing a packet, she located a stirrer. Actually, on second thoughts. She grabbed several and pressed hash.

After following several prompts and giving the name of her local station, a real person came on the line.

'Hello, this is Police Constable Kahn. Can I take your name?'

'Hi, yes, it's Felicity Lomax – hang on, is that you, Tariq? It's me, Flick, from *The Local Echo*.'

'Oh, hi, Flick, you're at work early, and a weekend too! What can I do for you?'

The official voice gave way to a friendly one as he recognized her. Having spoken lots of times about various local crimes reported in the newspaper, Flick and Tariq were on first name terms.

'Actually, it's the other way around. I've got some information about a Mr Theo C. Stratin who is wanted for questioning in connection with a romance fraud.'

'I see. And what would that information be?'

'I've got reason to believe he's in Europe.'

'Right, well, in that case I'm afraid that's out of our jurisdiction. I'll enter it into our database along with your number and someone in the relevant department will be in touch. Anything else I can help you with?'

'No, I think that's it.' At the other end of the line, Flick felt a strange mixture of resignation and liberation. 'Oh, just one more thing. Any closer to catching the thieves who stole Mrs Robinson's new electric car? I interviewed her a few weeks ago and she was really upset.'

'Not yet, I'm afraid, but we're still working on it. Fighting crime never stops. Speaking of, I've got another call waiting so I can't chat, sorry Flick. Enjoy your weekend.'

'Thanks, you too.'

Flick hung up with the satisfaction of having ticked a box. While she didn't hold out hope of the police doing anything much – if they couldn't catch the local teenagers responsible for stealing Mrs Robinson's Citroen C3 from her driveway, despite having the whole thing captured on footage from her doorbell camera, then catching a romance fraudster on the run in Europe seemed unlikely – at least she'd done what she promised.

Because after talking to her editor, Flick had decided Seymour was right – and not just about telling the police. She did need a holiday. So she'd found a cheap, last-minute flight to Nice and booked into a little Airbnb for the night. Call it a *working* holiday.

Sipping her coffee, Flick wheeled her carry-on out of the cafe and across the departures lounge to a row of plastic chairs where she found a free seat and sat down. From here she could keep an eye on when her flight was boarding.

The only problem had been what to tell Rory, her boyfriend.

\*

'You're going away for the weekend?'

They'd met at The King's Head after work last night. Being a Friday night, it was busy, so she'd been helping out her stepdad Colin behind the bar. Her mum and stepdad had taken over as landlords when she was small, and ever since they'd lived above the pub. Memories of being allowed downstairs when she was a little girl, the familiar sights and smells of beer and perfume, her mum cleaning the counters, Colin changing the barrels. She loved the pub with its regulars.

After her mum got sick she'd finished her degree and put her plans on hold. While her university friends found jobs in the cities, starting their new, exciting careers and lives, she'd moved back into her old bedroom and her old life, working behind the bar until eventually she'd got a job at the local paper. Now, with her mum gone, they had full-time staff but she still liked to help out when she could. It made her feel closer to her mum somehow.

'It's just for one night. I'll be back Sunday evening.'

With the after-work rush hour over and a lull before the Friday-night regulars appeared, Flick was sitting at a table in the corner with a vodka tonic while Rory sipped his pint and fired her with questions. He was not best pleased with this new turn of events.

'I can't believe you didn't mention it. I thought we were going to the Odeon tomorrow to see that new Marvel movie.'

'Sorry, I totally forgot. What with everything that's been going on, it totally slipped my mind.'

'And what is it again?'

'Oh, some boring journalists' conference.'

She'd thought about telling him the truth. She really had. But then she'd remembered how Rory was always telling her not to get ideas above her station and thought better of it.

'Where is it, again?'

'I'm driving to Manchester first thing.'

'If it's only Manchester, I don't see why I can't come. I can stay in the hotel while you're at the conference. Make use of the spa facilities,' he grinned.

'What spa facilities? I'm not staying at The Hilton,' she quipped and he frowned.

'Well, where are you staying?'

'Oh, I don't know, probably some budget hotel chain.' She brushed it off evasively. 'It is *The Local Echo*, remember.'

Sipping his pint, Rory looked put out. 'Who else is going from the paper?'

Flick bristled as he showed his possessive streak. 'No one, just me. Most of the staff are married and have family commitments, so I got the opportunity.'

'Well, we know how to change that, don't we?' Putting his arm around her, he pulled her close and kissed her.

Flick kissed him back, ignoring the tightening in her chest. She was just anxious about lying, that was all.

'I'll just have to go out with the lads then. Have fun without you,' he said, finally seeming satisfied.

'I'll be back before you know it,' she smiled.

Draining his pint glass, he stood up. 'Same again?'

He didn't wait for her answer.

She wasn't really lying. She was *technically* in Manchester. OK, so she wasn't at a conference, she was at the airport, but still. The interpretation of the truth was very fluid these days. Everyone talked about speaking their truth, but wasn't that just their opinion? Flick found it all rather confusing. Shouldn't the real truth be the same for everyone? And wasn't her job as a journalist to find it?

She glanced up at the electronic screen. Her flight was

boarding. Last call. She couldn't wait any longer. Standing up, she began walking to her gate.

Maggie was late. The bus had taken for ever. She always used to take a taxi, but those days were long gone now. Which meant she'd had to change twice, standing around waiting ages for the next one to turn up.

Maggie noticed that a lot. All the waiting around. The loss of control. Everyone always thinks having money means being able to afford nice things, but it was less about buying stuff and more about having time and convenience and ease and agency. You jumped in taxis, bought takeout coffees, ordered Deliveroo and dropped clothes at the dry cleaner's. Convenient. Quick. Easy.

No having to try and run in flip-flops with your heart bursting out of your chest as you dashed through sliding doors into the airport and through security as you tried to make your flight before it leaves without you.

And then she saw her.

'Flick Lomax!'

As Maggie rushed down the long concourse towards the gate, she waved with her free arm at the reporter ahead of her.

'Wait!'

At least she thought it was the reporter. She looked different out of her suit and she had her hair in a ponytail. But as Flick turned, Maggie noticed she was still wearing the same trainers, only now they were free of mud. They'd cleaned up well.

'Maggie?'

'Sorry, the bus took for ever,' Maggie gasped, catching up with her. God, she was out of shape.

'I've been waiting for you in departures. I didn't think you were coming.'

Flick was staring at her with disbelief as she bent double, hands on her waist, trying to catch her breath.

'Of course I'm coming. You bought me a ticket.'

Yesterday, after speaking to George, Maggie had phoned Flick, who'd seemed surprised but pleased to hear from her. When Flick had told her she was still determined to get her exclusive and was flying to France in the morning, where she had reason to believe her ex was, Maggie had made the impulsive decision to go with her.

'I thought you might have had second thoughts.'

'Second, third, fourth and fifth.'

Straightening up, Maggie looked at Flick. A reluctant traveller, she was seriously out of her comfort zone, but she felt like she didn't have a choice. Without her there was no story; she had to warn other women. And when Flick had said the newspaper would buy her a ticket and the trip was all expenses paid, she couldn't refuse.

Especially since she'd woken up a couple of weeks ago to find an enforcement notice from the council slapped on the door of the caravan. Due to lack of planning permission, she was deemed to be living illegally and had twenty-eight days from the date of the notice to move the caravan otherwise they were taking her to court. So basically, in two weeks she was going to be homeless.

Like George said, at this point, what had she got to lose?

'I've got lots of questions.'

'Me too,' replied Flick. 'But they're going to have to wait.'

'*This is the final boarding call for flight 2103 to Nice. Will any remaining passengers please report to the gate immediately, as it's about to close.*'

For a split second the two women exchanged glances as they listened to the announcement, before grabbing their cases and dashing to their gate . . . to find it completely empty but for one member of the cabin crew who urgently greeted them, scanning their boarding cards and rushing them onto the plane.

It was only when they were finally in their seats, their seatbelts on, and the plane was taxiing down the runway that Maggie turned to Flick. 'So, He's in Nice?'

She still couldn't say his name.

'Actually, no.' Flick shook her head. 'In fact, he's not in France at all. My geography's terrible. I didn't realize it was a different country.'

'Huh?' Maggie looked at her, bewildered, as the engines began roaring and there was a sudden thrust as the plane took off.

'Didn't I tell you? We're going to Monte Carlo.'

# Monte Carlo

# To Catch a Thief

Monte Carlo. The Millionaire's – no, *Billionaire's* – Playground.

Just the name conjures up visions of glitz and glamour, with its world-famous casinos, celebrity super-yachts and the speed and excitement of the annual Formula One Grand Prix. Nestling on the glittering shores of the Riviera, this legendary district of Monaco, a tiny principality and home to the world's wealthiest, is characterized by wealth, luxury and extravagance.

Imagine arriving in style: the breathtaking views of the Mediterranean as you're whisked from Nice Airport during your exhilarating seven-minute helicopter ride. Or whizzing along the stunning coastline in a fancy sports car; the wind in your hair, exhilaration in your veins. Part of the endless stream of bright red Ferraris, canary-yellow Lamborghinis and blacked-out Range Rovers, sweeping up to the entrance of the opulent, five-star hotels.

Or, wait – what about the local bus?

*Cue the sound of a needle being dragged off a record player.*

Sitting with your luggage on your knees for what feels like for ever as you wind along the coastline, trying to stave off motion-sickness and cramp in your legs . . .

Squashed up against the window, Maggie rested her cheek on the glass, gazing out at the scenery but not seeing any of it, lost in thought.

'I suppose it makes sense,' she said, suddenly out loud. 'Where else would you go to catch a thief?'

'Huh?' Dozing off next to her, Flick opened her eyes and pulled out an AirPod. 'What did you say?'

'*To Catch a Thief*. You know, the famous thriller directed by Alfred Hitchcock and filmed in Monte Carlo.'

'Oh, right,' Flick nodded. 'Never heard of it.'

'Never heard of it?' Maggie frowned over the top of her carry-on suitcase. The wheels were beginning to dig into her thighs. The bus was packed so they'd had to put their luggage on their laps. 'It's a classic with Cary Grant and Grace Kelly. Actually, what's even more interesting is Grace Kelly went on to marry Prince Rainier III of Monaco and become Princess Grace of Monaco.'

'Who's Grace Kelly?'

Maggie shifted her body to turn to her younger travelling companion. 'You don't know?' she asked, incredulous. 'She was a beautiful Hollywood actress in the fifties, who gave up acting to marry a prince and become a princess. It was a real-life fairytale.' An image of Grace in her iconic wedding dress flashed across her mind.

'What's she doing now?'

At which point Maggie's face fell. 'She was tragically killed in a car accident.'

'Doesn't sound much of a fairytale to me,' shrugged Flick, closing her eyes again.

Which brought Maggie up short. Hang on a minute . . . She had the sudden, disorientating feeling of seeing something from a totally different angle, together with the thought that, actually, Flick might be right.

'Anyway, it should be called *To Catch a Con Man*,' continued Flick. Opening one black-liquid-linered eye, she squinted at Maggie and gave a wry smile. 'It's a much catchier title.'

They'd landed at Nice Airport over an hour ago and, after a bit of confusion, using Maggie's distant memory of GCSE French and Flick's iPhone they'd finally managed to switch onto the right bus to take them to Monaco and, from there, Monte Carlo, its most famous district. The journey was only supposed to take about an hour – not that much longer than a cab and at a fraction of the cost – but they'd been on it for what felt like for ever, stopping in various villages as they made their way along the coastal roads.

Resting her elbow on the armrest, her hot cheek against the glass, Maggie gazed absently out of the window, while Flick dozed next to her. Maggie envied her youthful ability to be able to fall asleep anywhere, at any time. She'd slept on the plane too, falling asleep as soon as they'd taken off. Maggie felt too anxious about everything. Was that a product of age? The constant seeing of life through a lens of worst-case scenario. Or was that because of Him?

With knots in her stomach, she'd ordered a gin and tonic from the in-flight drinks cart. It wasn't even lunchtime, but she'd needed something to take the edge off, to try to calm her nerves. Instead it had made her feel lightheaded and nauseous and she'd thrown up in the toilets. So much for taking the edge off.

Nice felt a world away from Northern England. The bright sunshine, blue skies and searing heat had hit as soon as they exited the aircraft and walked across the tarmac. Thankfully, the arrivals hall was air-conditioned and so was the bus. She'd forgotten how hot it could be abroad. Or maybe that was just the hormones talking. Bloody perimenopause. Her internal temperature was constantly being turned up and down, as if a couple had taken up residence inside her body and were arguing over the central heating thermostat.

Now, watching the blur of palm trees and glittering sea she felt the adrenaline slowly starting to ebb away. Felt the tension in her shoulders begin to ease and her body relax. And for a brief moment she felt an unfamiliar feeling of being disencumbered. Of feeling curiously lighter.

Before remembering why she was there and her stomach twisted itself up again.

Maybe she'd been too impulsive. Yesterday, after her conversation with George, she'd called Flick. She wanted to help; maybe by telling her story it would protect another woman. Maybe it would aid in his arrest. Maybe it would even help get back some of her money, or at least her dad's watch. Whatever the motive, she agreed to being interviewed. Just no horrible photos in the newspaper, please. You know the ones. Where perfectly normal-looking women were forced into fuddy-duddy wrap dresses and nude court shoes and made to look middle-aged and miserable so people could post mean comments online.

Though to be honest, these days Maggie felt middle-aged and miserable without any help from keyboard trolls.

It was then that Flick had proceeded to tell her the whereabouts of her ex. She'd been both surprised and not surprised, if that made sense. Of course he'd left the country. Of course he was in Europe, on the French Riviera, living it up while she was in a mouldy caravan in the corner of a muddy field in northern England, trying to make ends meet dog-walking and living off her credit cards.

And yet, while she felt angry and outraged at the unfairness of it all, there'd also been a sense of relief. That he was far away, somewhere else, out of the picture. Part of her hoped she'd never see him again. A big part of her. And yet, something inside of her – a flicker of her old self before everything fell apart – had reappeared in that caravan, like the Ghost of Christmas Past.

And before she quite knew what was happening, she was offering to go with the reporter. Packing an overnight bag. Catching the bus to the airport. It felt good to be finally doing something. Since losing everything, she'd gone from a woman who lived her life, to a woman who just reacted to events. She had things happen to her, instead of making things happen. Leaving to go somewhere, armed with her passport, felt like flexing an old muscle. She didn't know what to expect. She didn't know what she was doing. But doing something felt better than doing nothing.

Having *agency*. Isn't that what they called it now?

The bus rounded another corner, revealing another flash of the Mediterranean, and she took a deep breath, trying to steady her nerves. The doubts were creeping back in again. She felt exposed and uncertain. Back in the caravan, life felt constrictive and suffocating, but it also felt safe. Nothing bad could happen as everything bad had already happened. She was at rock bottom; there was nowhere further to fall. Forget Great Expectations, she had no expectations.

Still, it was only for twenty-four hours. Just one night and she'd be back home in the caravan. Though, with the enforcement notice fresh in her mind and tucked in her handbag, who knows how long she'd have a home.

Finally, after pausing at various bus stops in lots of different villages – *Villefranche-sur-Mer, Èze, Cap d'Ail*; Maggie read all the names in her best French accent – and passing lots of swanky hotels, the bus came to a halt.

'OK, I think this is us,' said Flick, eyes snapping open as

if she had an in-built timer and motioning for Maggie to get up.

'Great.' Maggie gratefully lifted her suitcase off her knees.

God knows why it felt so heavy, she hadn't brought much. To be honest, she didn't have a clue what to bring. After all, she was only there for one night. Plus, most of her stuff was in storage. The caravan had so little space, she'd packed all her nice clothes away, along with the rest of her belongings. Boxed them up. Wrapped them in masking tape. Stacked them up on top of each other in a tiny little unit in a vast yellow building on an industrial site somewhere off the ring road. She often wished there was somewhere like that you could put feelings. Pack them all away with the rest of your furniture. Turn off the light. Forget about them.

So she'd just thrown in a summer dress and some sandals, a pair of jeans, a T-shirt. She was hopeless at packing at the best of times. She was always a sucker for those articles that appeared every summer in magazines and newspapers, telling you how to pack 'a capsule wardrobe' with a few rolled-up items. However, she couldn't ever remember reading, 'What To Pack To Confront The Man Whose Name You Refuse To Mention Because He Stole Your Entire Life'. No one ever seemed to write those articles. So she'd just had to wing it.

They clambered off the bus with their wheelie suitcases.

'Where are we staying?' She looked over at Flick who was glued to her phone. The whole time they'd been passing all that lovely scenery, her travelling companion had been either asleep or nose-to-screen, continuously scrolling. Missing everything.

'Is this the hotel?'

Maggie gestured across at the hotel opposite. It looked nice. Quite swanky, actually. With flags flying outside and a uniformed doorman. She felt a beat of something that, dare she even think it, was suspiciously like excitement. After months of living in the caravan, just the thought of a nice bed, hot shower and lovely ensuite bathroom for one night made all of this worth it.

She couldn't remember the last time she stayed in a nice hotel. Well, actually, she could. It had been with Him. Last year. For her birthday. He'd taken her away for the weekend – to one of those trendy boutique hotels in the country, with velvet sofas and quirky picture walls and a Michelin restaurant offering small sharing plates and overpriced cocktails – then accidentally forgotten his credit card. Of course. At the memory, Maggie felt a painful stab.

'Actually, no.'

Maggie snapped back. 'No?'

Flick finally looked up from her phone, squinted in the sunshine, and shook her head. 'All the hotels were full, what with it being peak season, but I managed to find an Airbnb.'

'Oh, OK.'

Which was fine. Totally fine. But she must have looked disappointed as Flick continued.

'Ideally I would have had more time to sort out accommodation, but this trip was spur-of-the-moment,' she explained, reaching into her backpack and pulling out a pair of large tortoiseshell sunglasses, which she pushed up her nose until they almost covered her whole face.

'Being a journalist, it's almost impossible to plan as you never know where the story is going to take you. It's unpredictable and you've got to be able to move quickly at short notice. To be flexible and spontaneous as you never know where you're going to end up. News is of the moment. Hence the term, breaking news.'

Flick said this so seriously, and with such a sense of knowing it all, that Maggie had to almost stifle a smile. She'd googled Flick after she'd paid her a visit and left her business card, mostly just to double check she was who she said she was. Having gone through what she'd just gone through, Maggie found it almost impossible to trust anyone.

Fortunately Flick checked out. She was indeed a community reporter for *The Local Echo*. In fact, she'd now read quite a few of her articles, not just the one about the cat's whiskers. However, as enjoyable as they were, she wouldn't have classified them exactly as 'breaking news'. Unless, of course, Boy Scout brownie-eating competitions were making the headlines these days.

'Before you called I was actually booked into a hostel in Nice, so it's lucky I was able to find something here in Monaco.'

'Oh, I would have been fine with a hostel,' protested Maggie, looking at Flick and wondering why she wasn't sweating. She could feel it trickling down her cleavage, yet her companion looked as cool as a cucumber. But then Maggie had that typical British freckly skin, a throwback from her Scottish ancestors; it came with the red hair, which had faded to a pale yellow as she'd grown older. One sign of sunshine and her nose went pink. And not in a cute way.

'You shouldn't have worried about me. I could have slept in a bunk for a night. I remember my interrailing days roughing it around Europe with a backpack,' she smiled, with a rush of nostalgia.

She was lying, of course. Nostalgia or not, the last thing she felt like doing was sharing a dormitory with a load of strangers. But she didn't want this twenty-something thinking she was an old fart.

Flick suddenly looked a bit awkward. 'Actually, I did try to book an extra bunk but there's an age limit. You have to be under forty . . .' She trailed off.

'Oh, I see.'

Right, well, that told her. She was officially an old fart.

'Anyway, the Airbnb is in a much better location,' continued Flick, pinching the screen of her phone and peering at it in concentration. 'In fact, it should be around here . . .'

Punching the address into the app on her phone, she pressed start and after a few moments of waving it around like a divining rod to see which way the arrow was facing, she set off with Maggie behind her. Together they followed the directions, which led them along steep, winding streets. Zig-zagging further and further away from the swanky hotels and seafront restaurants, they climbed up the hill, huffing and puffing.

Well, actually, Maggie noticed only she was huffing and puffing. Flick seemed to be taking it all in her stride. But then she was wearing trainers, observed Maggie, who resolved to change out of her flip-flips as soon as she got to the Airbnb. They had no arch support. Podiatrists always tell you that. It was obviously the reason why she was so out of breath, and nothing at all to do with the fact she'd lost her gym membership along with everything else.

And, no, walking a few springer spaniels a couple of times a week for the local kennels and living on frozen pizza did not replace Body Pump three times a week.

'This must be it!'

Finally Flick stopped climbing endless stairs and came to a standstill outside an incongruous-looking building. Puffing up the stairs behind her, lugging her wheelie case, Maggie felt a wave of relief. All she could think about was taking a cold shower and being horizontal.

'Perfect,' she panted.

*Note to self. When flying to the Mediterranean in the height of summer, do not dress for a northern climate in jeans and a thick sweatshirt with nothing underneath but your T-shirt bra which is now glued to your under-boob sweat.*

'Is there a code to get inside?'

'Yes, it's keyless entry, hang on,' replied Flick and then, after punching in a few numbers, the door released with a buzz, and they entered.

OK, so she wasn't expecting five-star but as Flick opened the door and surveyed the dingy room before her, her heart sank to the bottom of her vegan trainers. Oh God, this was beyond awful. This had to be one of the grottiest Airbnbs she had ever stayed in, and there had been some grotty Airbnbs in her time. Thanks mostly to Rory, who was not exactly known for pushing the boat out when it came to accommodation, his favourite phrase being 'It's just a bed for the night.'

As the two women squeezed inside, their backs to the wall, she was momentarily lost for words.

Which, for anyone who knew Flick, was almost unheard of.

'Oh well, it's just a bed for the night,' she said cheerfully.

But as she said it out loud, she couldn't bear to look at her travelling companion. When Maggie had offered to come with her on this ~~madcap scheme~~ first chance at investigative journalism, she was delighted by her support, but nervous as hell. She was flying by the seat of her pants, but she couldn't let Maggie know that. She wanted to look like a professional journalist – someone proficient and capable, who had a handle on every situation. Someone with experience, whom Maggie could trust.

And yet there they both were, standing in a room with a bare lightbulb hanging from the ceiling. The kind of room that wouldn't look out of a place in a TV crime series about drug smuggling and kidnapping. As for the size – bijou would be one word; broom cupboard would be another. And all with a view of someone's dirty washing and a brick wall covered in graffiti.

'Is that a penis?' Maggie gestured towards it now.

'Um, maybe a rocket ship?' said Flick, hopefully.

*You know those nightmares? Where you're running down the high street naked and everyone is looking at you? Well, this is worse*, thought Flick. *Much, much, worse*. She glanced across at Maggie, who gave her a reassuring grimace.

'It's not so bad.'

'It's awful,' groaned Flick. 'It didn't look like this on the website.'

'What? You mean, there were no photos of giant graffitied penises?' joked Maggie and Flick felt herself relax ever so slightly.

'I'll take the sofa; you can have the bed, obviously.'

'I don't think there is a sofa.'

'Huh?'

Flick looked around the broom cupboard. Maggie was right. There was no sofa. Just two small stools, a table and some misshapen wire hangers. The wardrobe door was missing.

'I'm happy to share the bed, if you are,' suggested Maggie. 'Unless of course you want to call your editor and see if he can find you something else? Surely it's the newspaper's responsibility if they've sent you here to try and get an exclusive?'

And that was another thing.

Flick hadn't yet told Maggie that she'd *gone rogue* and was here under her own steam, which included paying for it all herself, including both their airline tickets. That when she'd pitched the story to her editor, he'd almost laughed her out of his office.

She'd get round to that later.

'Well, it is only for one night.'

'Exactly.'

They both sat down on the edge of the bed, then winced. 'Bit soft and lumpy.'

'The story of my thighs,' quipped Maggie.

Flick smiled. She couldn't help it. And she suddenly felt a blast of gratitude towards this woman she hardly knew. A woman who'd had the shittiest thing happen to her, and who was trying to make her feel better. Who'd trusted her enough to fly out here and face her fears.

She also felt a huge weight of responsibility. She was the one that got her out here.

Maggie's voice cut into her thoughts.

'So, what's the plan of action?'

'Well, first, I thought we'd get showered and changed.'

But even as she was saying it, it crossed Flick's mind that there might not even *be* a shower and frankly she was almost too scared to look as otherwise it was going to have to be *a flannel wash*, as her nana used to call it, and God only knows how she would explain that to Maggie. 'Then let's go out and get something to eat for lunch and I can talk you through it.'

There. Hopefully that sounded professional. Plus, it gave her a bit more time to think.

Because, in truth, she'd been so preoccupied with making arrangements to fly out here, while making excuses to Rory, her stepdad and her editor, that she hadn't thought much further ahead. But now she was here she had to think and she had to think fast.

Still, this was part of the job description. As a journalist she'd been taught to use her initiative. To think on her feet. To multitask, be flexible and formulate, and to be prepared to travel at short notice to get the story.

In other words, Flick's plan of action was currently called Winging It.

# Winging It

'I remember coming here when I was nineteen with my friend George. It feels like a lifetime ago.'

Less than twenty minutes later, Maggie was feeling so much better. Having showered and changed into a sundress and sandals, she was sitting at a bustling cafe up near the royal palace, in the comfortable shade of a candy-cane-striped sun awning. She almost felt like a different person.

'Though we could never have afforded to sit down at a cafe,' she continued, looking across at Flick. 'We were backpacking and had no money. I remember watching someone drink their coffee and leave half a croissant on their plate and George swiping it.'

As the waiter handed them their lunch menus and Flick glanced at the prices, she felt like stealing food from people's plates too. *How much for a salad?* Picking up her phone, she began googling the currency exchange rate. Thank God they were only here for one night.

'You know, until we sat down, I'd completely forgotten all about that.'

In the middle of reminiscing, Maggie's face clouded. For a brief moment, she'd been nineteen and carefree, excited for the future, with no idea of what lay ahead – and now suddenly she was about to be fifty. Blink and thirty years had passed.

'Sometimes I wish I could reach back through time and warn myself about the future.'

'You can't do that; it mucks everything up.'

'Sorry?'

Maggie looked across at Flick. She'd presumed Flick wasn't listening. Half the time she seemed to be in a world of her own, or on her phone. She felt like part of one of those couples you see, sitting across from each other at restaurants, glued to their phones, not speaking.

'It's always in those time-travel movies you see on TV. You change one thing in the past and it affects all the stuff into the future,' said Flick.

'They call that the butterfly effect,' nodded Maggie.

As she spoke a brightly coloured butterfly landed on the condiments on their table. They watched it briefly flapping its wings before it flew away again.

'Maybe you're right. Maybe it's a sign.'

'I don't believe in signs. After Mum died, every time my Auntie Pam saw a white feather, she'd say it was her.' Flick rolled her eyes. 'People fool themselves to make themselves feel better.'

Maggie looked at Flick. In her crop top and denim shorts, she appeared the embodiment of young and carefree, but she was anything but.

'I'm sorry. About your mum.'

'Thanks. It's OK.' Flick attempted to shrug it off. 'It's been over six months now.'

'Six months isn't very long, especially when it's a parent. I lost my dad two years ago. It still feels like yesterday.'

They both looked at each other across the table, for the first time realizing they shared a common bond.

'It wasn't long after that I met Him.'

'Perfect timing.'

Flick was being sarcastic, but Maggie missed the sarcasm and sighed.

'It certainly felt that way at the time. I was so sad and then there was this man who made me smile again.'

'From everything I've read, romance fraudsters target women when they're vulnerable.'

'Can someone really be that cold-hearted and manipulative?'

Sitting across from her, Flick felt a flash of pity. Could someone really be so naive?

It wasn't really a question. Maggie already knew the answer, but even now, a big part of her still couldn't believe it.

'Well, that's what we're here to find out,' replied Flick as a waiter appeared at their table to take their order.

They both looked at the menus. Maggie wasn't very hungry and ordered a small salad. Flick was starving but felt nauseous at the prices and ordered a small salad too. To drink they ordered tap water. The waiter looked pissed off. Cheap tourists. *Pah*.

Dumping down a breadbasket, he scooped up the menus with a flick of his wrist and quickly headed over to check on the table of six drinking champagne and eating lobster.

Flick dived on the bread and immediately begin buttering.

Maggie watched her enviously. She didn't have an appetite. Her stomach was still off. For a few moments she could fool herself they were on holiday but there was a more serious reason why they were there, and it was making her deeply anxious.

'Tracking him down and exposing him is one thing, but why on earth do you think he would agree to talk to a journalist?'

'Because you've agreed.'

Reminded, Maggie's chest tightened. Was it too late to change her mind when she was in Monte Carlo at a fancy restaurant having lunch with the journalist all expenses paid? She sipped her water and wished she'd ordered wine.

'And from my experience, everyone wants to tell their side of the story; their truth, even if it's a pack of lies . . . criminals especially always seem eager to give you their version of events.'

Maggie nodded while wondering if she should voice her doubts.

'He didn't want to answer the questions the police wanted to ask him.'

'That's different. No one wants to talk to the police,' replied Flick, pulling a face. 'Not even the innocent. Though to be honest, once you get to know the person behind the uniform they're just like us.'

Flick thought about Police Constable Khan down at her local station. They were on first name terms. She'd got to know Tariq over several years and had become quite friendly. He was actually quite attractive, now she came to think about it. She quickly shoved the thought out of her mind. She had a serious boyfriend, remember? One who'd texted her this morning and she'd promised to call later.

'And, anyway, this way you get to ask the questions you wanted the police to ask.'

'What if he says no comment?'

'Did you ever know him to say no comment?'

Maggie gave a rueful smile. 'No, he had an answer for everything.'

'I had a feeling that might be the case.'

Flick finished off the bread roll and started on another.

'What I still don't understand is how you first heard about him?'

'Easy. I googled you.' Flick shrugged. 'When I heard the gossip in the pub, I looked you up. It's the journalist in me, I'm afraid. That's how it all started. I saw a photo of you at an exhibition you held at the gallery. He was standing next to you.'

'Oh, yes . . .' Maggie trailed off, remembering. 'That would've been when we hosted an exhibition for a successful local artist. It got quite a lot of press.'

'The caption mentioned you and your fiancé and gave me his name. And the rest, as they say, is social media.'

Maggie's face fell as she thought back. 'I haven't looked at his social media since . . . well, since after he disappeared. I did at first . . . Drove myself crazy with the constant scrolling, hoping to find out where he was and what had happened to him, until finally I deleted the apps from my phone.'

'I've done that before,' nodded Flick. 'I think everyone does it with their exes, don't they?'

'Really?'

'Trust me, you don't need to have dated a romance fraudster to want to know what your ex is up to,' said Flick, wryly.

Maggie smiled, despite herself.

'Thing is, I came to realize I didn't want to see what he was doing. I just wanted to erase him. To delete him. Like you do when you remove all the website data from your laptop.'

'Clear your history.'

'Exactly. Only, it's not so easy in real life.'

'I just put everyone on mute,' confessed Flick.

'Does that work?'

'Kinda. Though to be honest, you end up putting so many people on mute, you'd be better off deleting the app from your phone, but of course no one can as we're all addicted.' She took the final piece of bread from the basket. 'You're lucky. You didn't have social media when you grew up.'

'We had phones stuck on walls in kitchens and had to conduct every conversation under the watchful eyes and ears of our parents,' countered Maggie.

Flick grimaced.

'And with a father who kept yelling, "What are you talking about? You were just with them the whole day at school!"'

'Actually, maybe social media is better.'

They both laughed.

'Well, to be honest, you probably wouldn't have found him as he's got several accounts with different names,' said Flick, her face falling serious.

'How do you know?'

'I did a deep dive into his social media. He seems to have multiple aliases and accounts if you cross-reference.'

Opening various apps on her phone, she waved her screen towards Maggie to show her, but Maggie immediately shrank back.

'No . . . thanks . . . I don't want to see it.' She gave a little shudder. 'I don't think I'm ready for that just yet.'

*If ever*, she wanted to add.

Maggie still felt like she was on the edge of a big dark hole whenever his name was mentioned, one she could so easily slip into, and she hated herself for it. It was a strange, breathless, disoriented feeling. She felt so weak. So pathetic. She'd come here to face her fears and yet just thinking about it left her feeling panicky and unbalanced.

She sipped some water and stared out across the view of the Mediterranean, forcing herself to regain her balance. Refusing to fall again into that hole.

'I've got a photo of me taken here when I'm nineteen,' she said, changing the subject. 'I can still see it now. I'm wearing cut-off denim shorts, not unlike yours, a bikini top and red Converse. I had to borrow a long dress to go into the chapel. George started crying over Grace Kelly's grave.'

'Started crying? Why?'

'George is like that. He cries at everything.' She smiled,

fondly. 'He once cried over my haircut. I chopped all my hair off and dyed it purple. When I got home to the flat, he took one look at me and started bawling like a baby.'

'I can't imagine you ever having purple hair.'

'I wasn't always this age, you know. In fact, I wasn't much younger than you are now.'

Their conversation was interrupted by Flick's phone beeping up a message. Maggie watched her glance at her screen and bite her lip.

'Is everything OK?'

'Oh, yes, it's nothing. It's my boyfriend, Rory.'

'I see.' Maggie nodded. Though she didn't really. Still, she didn't want to interfere. She looked at Flick; she was still squinting at her screen, her face troubled.

'Is it serious?'

'We've been together since we were at school; we've talked about moving in together, getting engaged—' She broke off when she saw Maggie's expression and realized she'd misunderstood. 'Oh, I thought you meant the relationship.' Her face coloured. 'No, it's nothing, he's just checking in, you know.'

Maggie sensed something was up.

'And you don't want to?'

'I'm not sure.'

'Well, no need to rush; you've got plenty of time.'

Flick knew Maggie was right. There was no need to rush. And yet, was she unsure or was she stalling? Surely she should know by now? She was constantly seeing photos of friends showing off engagement rings on their socials, grinning proudly into the camera with a new Shellac manicure and a diamond solitaire. Always liking the posts and adding the required comment of *Congratulations!* plus several love hearts and a party popper emoji.

Privately, she would wonder if there was an emoji for the sense of claustrophobia she always felt when she saw those posts. The feeling of being trapped. Of her future being all mapped out. Engaged. Married. Kids. Rest-of-your-life stuff. It was terrifying. And yet no one else looked terrified; they looked over the moon. Which was even scarier.

She looked back at the text on her phone.

How's the conference? Miss me already?

She deliberated, she didn't want to lie any further, but she'd dug herself into a hole. And in more ways than one.

**Boring** ♥

She typed back and added a love heart emoji. Rory loved emojis. Sometimes she thought Rory might love emojis more than her. After a moment's deliberation she added a few more love hearts in various rainbow colours just for good measure.

'OK, so what's the plan? Do you know where He is right now?'

Maggie's voice broke into Flick's thoughts, and she snapped back.

'He's here in Monte Carlo. He posted a photo of himself standing next to a Ferrari and overlooking the port with the hashtag #montecarlovibes.' Flick pulled a face.

'Who's he with?'

Immediately Maggie hated herself. She felt a wave of embarrassment for even asking such a thing. 'Not that I care, of course.'

'Of course.'

The two women looked at each other in mutual understanding.

'It's a selfie,' replied Flick, looking again at the photo. 'Are you sure you don't want to see this? It might help prepare you for when you see him in real life.'

Maggie paused. Tempted, but afraid of what it might unleash. 'OK,' she agreed finally, reaching for the handset.

There was a pause as she peered at the screen. Angling it away from the bright sunshine, she stared at the once-familiar figure, at this suntanned person in a blue shirt and chinos, trying to recognize the person she would reach for in the middle of the night, who would tell her he loved her, who brought her tea and toast in the morning. It was like looking at a stranger. She pinched the screen to zoom in.

Sitting across from her, Flick observed Maggie.

'How does that make you feel?'

'Weird.'

'That's it?' Flick was indignant. 'It should make you feel angry. He's here living it up in Monte Carlo with your money and you're living in a caravan in a field in the middle of the bloody Pennines. I'd be furious.'

Maggie felt the youthful outrage waft across the table. She felt so weary in comparison. 'True,' she nodded. 'But it takes so much effort to stay angry. It slips away when you're not looking and you're just left with all these unanswered questions.'

'Exactly, and we're here to ask them.'

Maggie knew Flick must think her pathetic, but she was too resigned to care.

'So what shall we do? Go to where this photo was taken?'

'Well, he won't be there now. The selfie was posted yesterday.'

'In that case, how do we even know he's still here? In Monte Carlo?'

'We don't.'

Maggie looked at her, surprised.

'Just call it a hunch.'

Flick couldn't let her confidence slip. There was a lot riding on this weekend. She couldn't let Maggie catch a whiff of doubt. Couldn't allow herself to admit to any either.

'Well, your editor obviously believed in your hunch, so I've every confidence in you.'

As Maggie gave a supportive smile, Flick felt a twist of guilt. She hated lying to Maggie – after everything Maggie had been through, she needed people to be honest with her. Flick resolved to tell her later. After it was all over.

'Can I ask you a question now?' she said instead.

'Of course.' Maggie steeled herself.

'What do you think he's done with all the money he stole from you?'

'I've no idea. Spent it most likely. Isn't that what thieves do?'

'On what? Designer clothes? Fast cars? Drugs?'

Maggie snorted, suddenly amused. 'He used to make a fuss about taking a paracetamol when he had the Man Flu, so I don't think it's drugs. And he didn't drive a particularly fancy car or seem interested in them . . .' She broke off and looked back at the photo of him posing next to a Ferrari. Did she ever know him at all? 'But he did like to wear nice suits. I remember thinking how smart he looked when I first met him.'

'So how can you be sure he's spent it all? When I first came to your caravan, you said the money would be long gone. But what if he's got it all squirrelled away in a savings account somewhere?'

Maggie raised her eyebrows in mock derision.

'What, you think he's opened a savings account at the Post Office?'

Flick coloured. 'I meant a digital currency account, something untraceable.'

'Oh, I don't know, maybe. Does it matter? I doubt I'll ever see a penny of it.' Maggie shrugged; she'd wasted so many hours, days, weeks, months, her mind on a loop, going over and over it. 'The police thought he might have a hidden stash somewhere or a gambling habit, apparently that's quite common.'

'Well, that's easy then!' Flick looked triumphant.

'Huh?'

'Where would you find a gambler in Monte Carlo?'

And there it was. Staring them both straight in the face. They both spoke at the same time.

'*The casino.*'

# Sorry Not Sorry

There was just one small problem:

'The Casino de Monte-Carlo has a strict dress code.'

Twenty minutes later and they were in Place du Casino, with its fountain and palm trees, standing outside one of the most famous buildings in the world. With its iconic golden facade and sweeping main entrance, it was surrounded by expensive sportscars and crowds of starstruck tourists.

And two women on the hunt for a romance fraudster.

'To enter this legendary venue, visitors are required to wear smart attire in the evening,' continued Flick, who was googling and reading aloud from her iPhone. 'Details can be found on the official website.'

'Patrons wearing shorts, jeans with holes, running shoes, flip-flops and sandals will not be admitted,' finished Maggie, who'd picked up a leaflet from tourist information on the way.

They both paused from reading and turned to each other, taking in each other's outfits. Collectively they were wearing every banned item on the list. Minus the holey jeans, thought Maggie, but she had a pair of those in her suitcase.

'Fuck.'

'Gordon Bennett.'

Both cursing at the same time, Flick turned to Maggie. 'Who's Gordon Bennett?'

Maggie shrugged. 'I have no idea. It's just an expression.'

Flick stared at her. What was it with the older generation and their use of bizarre sayings?

'Sorry. It's what my dad used to say. Sometimes when I get nervous it just pops out.' Maggie fanned herself with the leaflet. It must be a hundred degrees. She could feel her chest going all blotchy, like it did when she got all hot and bothered.

At the mention of Maggie's dad, Flick felt a stab of sympathy. Her mum was never far from her mind either. 'You don't need to apologize,' she said more kindly.

'Sorry, I know, it's just—' Maggie caught herself apologizing again, shaking her head with an awkward laugh. 'Honestly, I don't know what's wrong with me. I can't stop saying sorry these days.'

'It's not your fault. We live in a patriarchal society. Women are taught to over-apologize, for taking up space, or having an opinion, or being ambitious. Basically everything men do without thinking. You know men hardly ever feel guilty?'

'They don't?' Maggie looked at Flick in astonishment.

'No, I've asked Rory. He looked at me like I was bananas. "*Guilty? For what?*" And yet women are constantly made to feel guilty for everything.'

'And now I'm feeling guilty about feeling guilty,' admitted Maggie, which made Flick laugh.

'See. A total waste of our time. Talking of which –' she glanced at her watch – 'we need to get a move on if we're going to find something to wear for tonight.'

'You mean, we have to go clothes shopping?'

Maggie's heart sank. There was a time, when she was younger, when she loved nothing more than shopping for clothes. But now it filled her with dread.

'Yes,' Flick nodded. 'It says men have to wear a blazer and smart shoes, but it doesn't say what women have to wear.

But I think we'll be OK in a dress and heels. You know, something suitably glitzy.'

'The patriarchal society at work again?' Maggie raised an eyebrow and Flick made a face.

'Unless you brought a dress and heels?'

Maggie gave Flick a look that needed no words.

'OK, well, neither did I. In that case, we don't have anything to wear.'

Maggie's face clouded. 'I'm sorry, but I can't afford to buy any new clothes. Especially not here, it seems to be all expensive designer shops.'

'No need to apologize! And I'm sure we can find something cheaper.'

'Can you expense it on the newspaper? Will they cover the costs?' Maggie realized she was already feeling guilty. Flick was right.

'Um . . . yes, I'm sure that's fine.'

'OK, then let's go find some sequins.'

And now it was Flick's turn to look horrified.

Thankfully, nestled amongst the designer shops with their designer price tags were several high-street chains selling outfits that wouldn't break the bank of Monte Carlo. However, finding something suitably dressy was more of a challenge.

'Isn't it a bit shiny?'

'It's satin; it's supposed to be shiny.'

'I can't wear a minidress; it's too revealing.'

'So why are you giving it to me?'

Flick and Maggie were having a stand-off in the middle of the store.

'Because you're twenty-six. You can wear anything at twenty-six.'

'You can wear anything at forty-nine if you want to.'

Actually, Flick liked the minidress. It would look good with her trainers. Then she remembered the strict dress code. Shit.

'*Technically*,' agreed Maggie. 'But just because you can wear it, doesn't mean you should.'

'What exactly does that *mean*?'

Maggie paused from pulling clothes off racks. 'Actually, I've got no idea. I read it somewhere.'

'OK, I'm getting this one.' Switching the satin dress for a full-length version, Flick decided she was going to try and hide her trainers underneath.

'What about this for me?' suggested Maggie, holding up a long, navy-blue linen shirt dress. 'It's even on the sales rack.'

Flick wrinkled her nose. 'It's a bit boring.'

'It's not boring, it's classic.'

Unconvinced, Flick turned back to the sale racks. 'Ooh, look, sequins!'

'I was only joking about the sequins.'

But Flick was already pulling out an emerald-green halter neck dress, holding it up in front of Maggie and enthusing, 'Look at the colour! It's perfect with your hair!'

'It's not me.'

'Exactly!'

Maggie looked at her doubtfully. 'What does that mean?'

'It means you get to be someone else for the evening. Someone who wears bling and goes to a casino and hasn't lost everything to some pathetic fraudster, including their confidence and self-worth. By wearing this you're showing him that all he got was your money and your dad's watch. That you're made of stronger stuff and he didn't break you. That you're someone who says fuck you and not sorry—'

Flick broke off, her chest heaving, and looked at Maggie,

waiting for her to say something. It hadn't meant to turn into a speech and she wondered if she'd gone too far when, without a word, Maggie grabbed the dress and marched over to the cash register.

'Wait? You're not going to try it on?' she called after in astonishment.

'Nope.' Shaking her head, Maggie looked back and smiled. 'You had me at fuck you.'

# Place Your Bets

There's something rather thrilling about only spending one night in a foreign country. It feels spontaneous, impulsive, decadent almost.

Especially when that one night happens to be in Monte Carlo.

As dusk fell the legendary district began to work its magic. The day-trippers and the shorts-and-T-shirts tourists disappeared, glittering lights illuminated the crescent-shaped harbour and an impossibly glamorous crowd began to appear. Everything was bigger, bolder, brighter. The warm evening air felt charged with excitement and, to the people having their photos taken on the steps of the casino or sipping cocktails on the terraces of Café de Paris, it felt like you were at the centre of the universe.

But Monte Carlo divides people: into those that love the thrill of it all, and those that see it as a symbol of everything that is wrong with the world.

Flick was most definitely of the second camp.

'Honestly, this is why the world is in such a mess,' she grumbled, as they made their way from their Airbnb towards the casino later that evening. 'Too much bling and excess. Too many rich people. Too many cars—'

Her voice was drowned out by the loud roar of a bright green Lamborghini as it revved its engine – a deliberate move by the driver so that everyone would turn and stare.

'And we wonder why the environment is in chaos and the planet is in freefall,' she huffed, waving her arms around to no one in particular. 'Do they even *know* what a carbon footprint is?'

Maggie walked beside her mutely, trying to make agreeable noises, while secretly being very much in the first camp. She was entranced by Monte Carlo. As they made their way around Port de Fontvieille, lined with luxury yachts and super-sleek sailing boats, the marina felt almost like a fairyland of polished decks, white sails and exotic boat names.

'I mean, look at that!' said Flick, pointing at the giant cruise ship moored in the outer harbour of Port Hercule, the deepwater port that stood in the shadow of the Rock of Monaco.

'Wow, yes,' nodded Maggie. Rising out of the water with too many decks to count, the *Galaxy Goddess* was like a huge floating hotel. 'That's incredible.'

'Incredible?' snorted Flick. 'It's an environmental catastrophe. Did you know that going on a cruise is actually worse than flying?'

'Says the woman who flew to Monte Carlo for the night,' retorted Maggie. 'How's your carbon footprint?'

Which shut Flick up. 'OK, point taken. I'm being a hypocrite.'

'You said it.' Maggie grinned, because at least she could admit it.

They'd got ready in their rather shabby Airbnb. Taking quick showers before the hot water ran out. Trying to do their hair when the plugs and mirrors were on opposite walls, so you had to be a contortionist. Now, dressed up in their outfits, Maggie felt a bit like Cinderella going to the ball. It would be exciting if she didn't have to keep remembering why they were here – then it became terrifying and she felt sick with nerves.

But for now, she was enjoying staring at all the bling and the excess and the ridiculously loud and expensive cars. It was hard to compute that only a few hours ago she was in her wellies, in a muddy field, and now here she was, walking along the harbour front, in a sequinned halter dress. *And with blisters.*

'I'm going to have to take these off,' she winced – her heel was rubbed red raw.

They'd both bought new footwear. Maggie had gone for a nice pair of heels – a rather foolish choice, she realized now, for two reasons: firstly she was old enough to have bought, never worn and given away enough high heels to know that unless you spend an absolute fortune on a pair, they were always excruciatingly uncomfortable and impossible to walk in, and these were less than thirty euros; and, secondly, when on earth did she last wear a pair of heels? She couldn't remember.

Whereas Flick had been a lot more sensible and gone for a pair of flat sandals after deciding that trying to hide her trainers under her dress probably wasn't the wisest idea.

'I told you to buy some of these flats,' she was saying now, in that rather annoying way she had of I told you so.

'I know, but I thought if I was going to see Him, I wanted to look my best.'

Flick looked at her like she'd gone a bit mad.

'Heels make me look slimmer,' she explained.

'We're going to confront him. You're not trying to date him.'

Maggie felt her cheeks flush underneath her bronzer. Like she'd been caught. She doubled down.

'It might be hard for you to imagine this, as you're in a relationship. But imagine you were going to see your ex – how would you want to look?'

'Strong. Confident. Like he was something I scraped off my shoe,' replied Flick.

'Well, that too,' nodded Maggie. 'But I also want to look slimmer.'

She caught Flick gaping at her with horror.

'What? Why are you looking at me like that? Most women do, otherwise there wouldn't be a multi-billion-pound industry in control pants.'

'You're not wearing . . . ?' Flick broke off.

'Kill me now and nail me to your feminist Gen Z cross,' snapped Maggie, who was growing sick of being lectured to. 'Yes, I am wearing tummy-control pants. And, yes, I brought them with me.' She glared at Flick, challenging her to say something. 'Though they're bloody uncomfortable in this heat,' she added, fidgeting underneath her sequins.

'Well, you look great anyway,' said Flick, suitably reprimanded. She might have spent all her time projecting confidence about this evening but she was as nervous as Maggie. Even if for very different reasons.

'So do you,' said Maggie, returning the compliment.

They turned to look at each other, taking themselves in, then both smiled at their transformations. Not bad, considering.

'OK, come on.' Flick threw back her shoulders. 'Let's do this.'

On arriving at the casino, they discovered that, like the rest of Monte Carlo, it had transformed at night. Lit up against the night sky, it was flanked by a fleet of expensive cars and a flashy set of people were swirling around the bottom of the steps at the main entrance.

Joining them, Maggie scanned the crowds, a fluttering in her stomach at the possibility of seeing him again.

Was it nerves? Fear? *Desire?*

As the thought popped into her head, she almost tripped on the hem of her dress as she climbed the stairs and had to grab hold of Flick's elbow.

'Wait, are you OK?' Flick glanced at her, concerned.

'Yes, yes, fine . . . absolutely fine,' she garbled. Fine being the universal language for absolutely not fine, not in the slightest.

*Get a grip*, she told herself firmly. Smoothing down her dress, Maggie tried slowing down her breathing.

At the entrance they were greeted by uniformed doormen and, after showing their passports and paying their admission, which Flick put on her credit card while trying not to think of the costs she was racking up, they were suddenly inside the famous casino.

And it was breathtaking.

A large atrium, flanked with marble pillars and ornate chandeliers, which spilled from the ceilings like crystal waterfalls, greeted them as they entered. It was grandeur on a level that neither Flick nor Maggie had ever seen before. Luxurious rooms with swagged red velvet curtains, huge floor-to-ceiling paintings and stained-glass windows gave way to rows of slot machines and gaming tables, their familiar green baize and polished mahogany appearing like islands, around which sat dozens of players with throngs of excited bystanders jostling behind the roped-off sections.

'Wow, this place is really incredible,' murmured Maggie, gazing up at the frescoed ceilings with awe. 'Look at these paintings.'

'Look at the bar with all the crystals,' gasped Flick, who seemed to have left her soap box at the door and was momentarily stunned by the opulence. It was a world away from the bar she often pulled pints behind at home. 'It's so busy, there's so many people.'

'It's probably full of rich playboys,' whispered Maggie, gesturing towards the gaming tables, where the minimum bet was more money than she had in the bank.

'Well, we only need to find one playboy,' Flick reminded her, snapping back to the matter at hand.

They moved through the different gaming rooms, scanning the crowds, while trying to be discreet. Maggie was focused on remaining calm, but she was a bag of nerves. Adrenaline and anticipation, mixed with fear of the unknown and the casino's highly charged atmosphere, made for a complicated cocktail of emotions. Meanwhile, Flick was quickly swooped upon when she pulled out her phone – they were strictly prohibited in the casino – so she couldn't check for updates on His social media.

Instead, they concentrated on scouting the different salons, including the bar where they traded in the two drinks vouchers, which had been included in the price of the admission, for one expensive cocktail. The minutes ticked by. Ten. Twenty. Half an hour. An hour.

*He isn't coming.*

Doubts swirled in their minds. *We've got it wrong. What were we thinking? It was such a long shot.* But when they caught each other's eye they'd stop chewing their lips and fiddling with their hair and instead swap reassuring smiles and *I hadn't noticed the time* shrugs of unconcern. Despite their differences, they had something in common: both were terrible actors and they saw right through each other.

'Maybe we should get another drink,' suggested Maggie.

'At these prices?' Flick blanched.

'Isn't the newspaper paying?'

Flick imagined Seymour getting a bill for two cocktails at a casino in Monte Carlo. The thought both terrified and amused her. It was a struggle to get him to pay parking, despite the local car park only charging two pounds a day. Can't you park at Tesco's? he would always grumble.

'Um, yes, of course,' she nodded, forcing a smile.

*He isn't coming.*

And then suddenly, there he was.

Maggie sensed him before she saw him. Like you can sense the change in atmosphere just before there's a thunderstorm. The room felt electrically charged. A sudden whiff of his familiar scent. A flash of him amongst the throngs of people. Was he alone or with other people? She couldn't tell. It was so busy. Emerging briefly through the crowd, he strode through the salon as if he owned it, oozing confidence. It was the first time she'd seen him since he walked out of her flat and her life and now here he was, in a casino in Monte Carlo.

The room blurred. The noise muted. Everything seemed to shift on its axis.

'*That's Him.*'

She said it under her breath, without barely moving her mouth. Flick saw the look on Maggie's face, realized immediately and quickly turned. Until that moment she'd only ever seen a photograph, but there he was in the flesh. She recognized him instantly.

The two women stared, frozen, for a split second, before Flick sprang forward.

'Excuse me!'

As Flick suddenly moved towards him, Maggie snapped to and tried to follow, but before they knew what was happening, he was being swept through mirrored panels, which made up a secret doorway, and had disappeared.

'*Excusez-moi*,' stammered Maggie. Two burly men in suits

turned to her, blocking their way. Both said something in French that neither she nor Flick understood.

That was the problem trying to converse in a different language. Speaking it was one thing, understanding it was quite another.

'I'm afraid I don't understand—' Maggie began apologizing, but Flick interrupted impatiently.

'We need to speak to the man who just entered that room.'

One of the doormen shook his head. 'This is for members and VIP players only,' replied the other, his face expressionless.

'It's important,' urged Flick.

'Please,' added Maggie. She smiled sweetly, teenage memories of trying to charm nightclub bouncers resurfacing, but the two men remained, sentry-like, in front of the concealed doorway.

Flick scowled furiously. 'I can't believe it. That's ridiculous. They can't just bar us from entering.'

'They just did,' said Maggie, as she led a furious Flick away before she caused a scene and they were thrown out.

'But there must be a way in.'

'There is if you're a high roller.'

Flick gave her a blank look.

'A person who spends a lot of money gambling,' explained Maggie.

'You mean a lot of other people's money, in his case,' snorted Flick furiously. 'And your money, more to the point.'

Maggie didn't reply. She was still reeling from seeing him. Still partly in shock. It hadn't quite sunk in. He was here. *He was actually here.*

'Well, at least your hunch was right,' she said, after a moment. 'At least that's something.'

'We're not giving up,' said Flick adamantly. 'We know

exactly where he is. If he's gone in there, he's going to have to come out.'

'So we just wait?'

Flick nodded. 'And when he finally does, we've got him.'

# All Bets Are Off

By midnight, they were still waiting outside and he still hadn't appeared. They'd made their very expensive drink last until the ice cubes had long since melted, Maggie's feet were killing her and Flick was checking her watch for the millionth time.

'Stake-outs always look fun in the movies.' Maggie winced, wondering if anyone would notice if she took off her shoes.

'We can't have missed him, we've had our eyes glued.'

'He could be in there until the early hours, if not longer. What if he's on a winning streak?'

No, it would be terrible. Barefoot in the casino was not a good look.

'I don't know, but I definitely feel like we're on a losing streak just standing around waiting out here,' grumbled Flick.

Maggie sighed. Her earlier nervousness at seeing him had turned into a frustrated weariness. There's only so long adrenaline can last, and exhaustion had now taken over. She just wanted to get it over with. The face-to-face meeting. The confrontation. Whatever.

Finally, she snapped. 'This is ridiculous! I'm not waiting any longer. He's caused enough trouble as it is. He's in there having a fun time with my money and we're out here like a couple of lemons? He's put me through enough. There's patience and there's wanting to get these bloody high heels off.' Stirred into action, she slammed the watery dregs of the drink down on a table. 'I'm going to go and talk to them!'

There is a moment in every woman's life when she reaches a point. When a mixture of tiredness, desperation, hormones, having seen it all and years spent pleasing everyone – together with the enormous amount of shit she's had to put up with – causes the dam to break. It's a powerful moment. It's also often fleeting, which is a shame because if women could hold on to it, they would truly rule the world.

Regardless, this was one of those moments for Maggie.

'Talk to whom?' Flick was taken aback.

'Our friendly bouncers.'

Flick watched as she marched over to the doorway and spoke to the doormen. They appeared to be having a conversation. There was some gesticulating. Another member of staff appeared. Then Maggie's face paled.

She came rushing back, limping. 'He's gone! He left hours ago!'

'What?' Flick was aghast. 'But how?'

'There's another exit, apparently.'

'Why didn't I think of that?' Flick clamped her hand to her forehead, stricken.

'So I said not to worry, and I'd catch up with him at his hotel.'

'Did you get the name of the hotel?'

'That's just it! He's not staying at a hotel. I just spoke to the manager who organized a taxi for him to the port. He told me he'd left hours ago as his cruise ship, the *Galaxy Goddess*, was departing at 10 p.m.'

*Cruise ship?*

They stared at each other, both remembering their walk to the casino, past the harbour where the giant cruise ship was docked. No. Surely not. It couldn't be. But as they rushed to the outside terrace, with its view across the port to the rock of Monte Carlo and the jetty, they saw that where earlier was nineteen decks of floating hotel, now there was just an empty space. The cruise ship had departed. It was gone.

And with it, so was he.

# Love Is a Losing Game

Behind the magnificent mahogany and crystal bar in the Salle Europe lounge – one of the casino's finest rooms – Jean-Paul, the bartender, busied himself polishing the rim of a champagne coupe. Said to be modelled on the breasts of Marie Antoinette, each glass was made of the finest cut crystal, and every one had to be spotless.

Jean-Paul took this job very seriously.

Using a soft, white, lint-free cloth, he lightly polished the base and stem (never allow your bare hands to touch the glass!). Then taking a second cloth, he placed the shallow bowl inside his palm, carefully cleaning the inside and outside (not too much pressure or you can break the delicate crystal!). Before lifting each one up to the chandelier for closer inspection (it has to sparkle!). Only when he was satisfied, did he move on to the next.

Usually, he was totally focused on the task, but that evening he was distracted by two women on the opposite side of the bar. Dressed in satin and sequins, they were seated together on the velvet bar stools. Heads bent close, one fair, one dark, they appeared deep in conversation. Every so often there'd be a flurry of gesticulation – forehead slapping, clutching of chests – loud groans, deep sighs and a fair amount of cursing. Followed by slumped shoulders and another order of drinks.

Were they a mother and daughter having an argument? A couple breaking up? Or just friends drowning their sorrows?

And if so, over what? Usually, when women were angry or upset there was a man involved, but as far Jean-Paul could tell, they were alone. It was all very confusing.

As a bartender of over thirty years, Jean-Paul had learned more from working behind a bar than you can learn from any university. He'd listened to people pour out their hearts. He'd watched couples start and end relationships in front of him. Been privy to surprise proposals and clandestine affairs. Hookers, politicians, celebrities, royalty, presidents; the casino welcomed all walks of life. It was not his job to judge; it was his job to serve drinks to them all. Even James Bond, *shaken not stirred*. He'd seen and heard more than you could ever imagine, witnessed the highs and the lows, met the winners and the losers, been tipped by the rich and the poor. He might not have fancy letters after his name or a framed certificate on his wall, but he had more insight into people than any psychiatrist.

And yet, he couldn't suss these two out.

He continued polishing the glass.

One thing he was certain of: they were on their third round of cocktails and getting very drunk.

'I can't believe he got away.'

'I can't believe there was another exit.'

'Why didn't I think of that?'

'Why didn't I?'

After discovering they'd been given the slip, Flick and Maggie were back inside the casino, sitting at the bar, drowning their sorrows.

'We came all this way for nothing.'

'We were so close.'

'We had one chance.'

'And we fucked up.'

'A rookie error.'

'And now he's gone and we've lost him.'

'What are we going to do now?'

'Go home. Get on with our lives. What else can we do?'

Back and forth they went, their laments louder and their sighs deeper with each round.

'We can't chase him around Europe as he sails around the Mediterranean on his luxury cruise—'

'That I've paid for!' finished Maggie, feeling a flash of anger. She drained the rest of her martini. 'I didn't even know he liked cruises!'

'To be fair, you didn't know a lot of things,' Flick responded.

'But why a cruise?'

'Maybe it's the all-you-can-eat buffet?' quipped Flick, but Maggie didn't laugh. 'Or maybe it's the perfect place to find his next target. All those lonely, rich, solo travellers looking for love on the high seas. You know, I once read an article about a wealthy widow who lived on a cruise ship for seven years—' She broke off as she saw Maggie's expression. She looked upset. 'I dunno, does it matter? We've lost him.'

'Hi, would you gorgeous ladies mind if we joined you for a drink?'

Probably not the best time to be chatted up. Maggie and Flick were oblivious to two men approaching them, until one of them spoke to Flick.

'Yes. We would,' snapped Flick.

In the middle of sliding onto bar stools next to them, the two men paused, their charming smiles wavering.

'Oh . . . OK.'

'Sorry, we're just having a private conversation.'

Maggie smiled apologetically as they reverse-slid off the bar stools while Flick scowled.

'Will you stop saying sorry!' she hissed as the men beat a hasty retreat.

'Sorry.' Maggie hiccupped and covered her mouth. 'I didn't want to be rude.'

'We're not being rude. And, anyway, we can buy our own drinks.'

'At these prices I'm not sure we can.' Maggie screwed up her face and blinked, trying to bring Flick into focus as the two men slunk away. 'Thank God your editor's paying.'

'Fat chance,' muttered Flick, under her breath.

*Correction*: it was meant to be under her breath, but alcohol turns up the volume and Maggie heard her.

'Oh no! Do you think the newspaper will refuse to reimburse you if they don't get a story?'

'The newspaper's not paying,' admitted Flick.

'Can they do that?' Maggie looked stricken.

'Well, yes, they can, actually . . .'

'But that's terrible!'

'Well, it's not really . . .'

Flick hesitated, wondering how she could put this, how she could fudge it, or spin it, or be selective with the facts. But she'd drunk three very strong cocktails on an empty stomach. The only thing spinning was her head.

'My editor doesn't know I'm here,' she confessed at last. 'No one does.'

Well, she was always planning to tell Maggie. She'd just been waiting for the right time, only it never seemed to arrive.

Maggie frowned and shook her head as if she had water in her ears. What Flick was saying was taking a while to compute. Her hair had come loose from its top knot and hung in long, pale auburn waves around her face. In her drunken state she liked to think it made her look like a pre-Raphaelite painting, but she had a feeling it just made her look a little unhinged.

'I don't understand,' she said finally.

Avoiding Maggie's gaze, Flick fiddled with the rings on her fingers. One of them was her mum's and she twisted it around like a talisman. She wasn't sure this was the right time, but considering everything had gone tits up, what did it matter now?

'My editor doesn't know I'm here. The newspaper didn't send me.'

Maggie looked blank so Flick soldiered on.

'When I pitched the idea to my editor, he was interested, but not enough to fly me out to Monte Carlo. So I thought I'd use my initiative and pay for my own flight and accommodation.'

There. That sounded a lot more professional than *not on your nelly*.

'I was planning to come by myself. See what I could find out. And then you called.'

Silence. When Flick looked up, Maggie was still staring at her intently.

'And you paid for my flight? And my lunch? And this dress?'

Maggie's mind was whirring backwards, thinking of all the things they'd been spending money on, mentally adding up the whole trip. Arithmetic had never been her strong point, but it must be well over a thousand pounds, probably more.

'But why?'

There was a pause.

'Because it's a good story.' Flick raised her eyes to meet Maggie's. 'An important story and I wanted to be the one to tell it. Men like Theo Stratin ruin women's lives and think they can just get away with it. I wanted to expose him. To confront him and try to get some answers.'

'For me?'

'For you and all the victims of romance fraud. So many feel stupid or ashamed. They don't speak out. I've read about some victims wanting to take their own lives, and it's happening more and more . . . If by exposing him and telling your story we can warn others, if we save one person from what he did to you and—'

Flick stopped herself, swallowing down whatever it was she going to say.

'And I did it for me too,' she admitted, after a moment. 'I'm a journalist. I can't write about jumble sales and missing cats any more. No offence, I know you're still upset about your cat George, but I can't . . .'

Maggie sat very still on her plush bar stool absorbing this information. The alcohol had made things spongy. She wasn't as sharp as she should be. But still, one thing was very clear.

'You lied to me.'

Flick blanched.

'After everything that's happened to me . . . that's the one thing I can't bear. Someone lying to me.'

'I'm sorry.'

'And now you're saying sorry and you've told me to stop saying sorry.'

'For stupid stuff, yeah, but not this. I *am* sorry and I should apologize, but I just knew you wouldn't come if I told you the truth.'

The two women looked at each other.

'And you're probably right. I wouldn't have done,' admitted Maggie. 'But don't you understand? I can't have people lying to me. Not after what happened. I don't trust anyone any more. I don't even trust *myself* any more. You can do anything, but you can't lie to me, Flick. You've got to be honest with me—'

She broke off, her emotions racing as Flick's admission sank in.

'Is there anything else you've got to tell me?'

Flick paused. Now was the time to come completely clean.

'I don't know how we're going to pay this bar bill,' she confessed.

And it was at that moment the awful mess of the situation, the whole disastrous evening with all its stress and anxiety and ridiculous sequins and satin, suddenly became hysterically funny. Who was it that said tragedy and comedy are two sides of the same coin? They didn't know, but unexpectedly they both burst out laughing.

On the other side of the bar, Jean-Paul the bartender paused from polishing a champagne coupe.

See. He couldn't work them out. Couldn't work them out at all.

# Against All Odds

Flick wasn't remotely religious. She was a journalist. She believed in facts. In truths that could be researched and fact-checked. In remaining objective. In a commitment to reporting only accurate stories, without skewing or embellishing the facts. Which is why she'd fidgeted her way through her Catholic primary school assemblies as a child, sitting cross-legged as she listened to the stories from the Bible about faith and miracles. But where was the proof? she would ask, shooting her hand up, much to the impatience of her head-mistress. Where were the facts?

But now, some twenty years later, even she hoped for a miracle as she handed over her credit card.

Thankfully Mastercard performed one and her payment was accepted. She didn't look at the bar bill. Just closed her eyes and said a little prayer. Her headmistress would be delighted.

'OK, time to call it a night,' yawned Flick, as they both slid off their bar stools and began making their way past the roulette tables.

'Really?'

Flick glanced at Maggie, surprised by her reaction. She'd assumed Maggie would be more than ready to leave the casino and go to bed.

'It's been a long day, and we've got an early flight tomorrow. I'm beat.'

'Yes, I know, me too.' Maggie paused on the swirly carpet. 'Except . . . we've got one night in Monte Carlo. We're in the world's most famous casino. Are we really going to go back home without having a flutter?'

Flick frowned. 'With what? We're both broke. After that bar bill, I don't think it's just you who's lost their life savings,' she wisecracked and kept walking.

'C'mon, just one game of cards.'

'You're drunk.'

'Yes, I am.' She smiled tipsily. 'And so are you.'

Maybe it *was* the three strong cocktails. Maybe it was being in Monte Carlo, away from real life. Maybe it was seeing Him again. But while she'd been reluctant to come here, now Maggie was reluctant to leave. As soon as she walked through that exit, the spell would be broken, and she'd be back to reality.

'When am I ever going to get this chance again? You know, I used to be pretty good at cards. Dad taught me how to play blackjack. We used to play all the time when I'd visit him on his canalboat. I might not have got his watch back but I'd like to play a game of cards, just for him.'

Flick faltered. It was the mention of Maggie's dad that did it. She knew what it was like to lose a parent. The things you remembered. The things you did to make them feel close again. The lengths you'd go to. Plus, let's be honest, she was more than a little bit drunk herself. Those cocktails had gone straight to her head.

'OK, why not?' Why not humour her? At this point, it wouldn't do any harm; plus, she still felt guilty not telling her the whole truth about the trip. 'There's just one problem – we don't have any cash.'

'Aha, well, that's where you're wrong. As luck would have it . . .' Maggie opened her wallet and pulled out her emergency twenty-pound note. 'Ta-dah,' she said, brandishing it.

She knew it would come in useful at some point. All that talk about it being a cashless society. There would always be one place happy to take your cash: *a casino*.

OK, so perhaps happy wasn't quite the right word.

A few minutes later, the cashier peered rather sniffily at Maggie's paltry twenty-pound note. He was used to players with big amounts. The person in front of her had just exchanged enough for piles of chips. She handed over her money. She got one chip back.

'That's it?'

'*Oui*,' he replied, his face deadpan.

'OK, then.' She smiled brightly, undeterred. One chip was better than no chips. When the chips are down and all that.

Together she and Flick walked over to one of the blackjack tables.

'How much are you going to bet?' asked Flick.

'There's a minimum to play, so I'll bet the lot.'

Flick nodded and felt rather pleased. She was tired and totally ready for their soft and lumpy bed. This should be over in no time. One game and Maggie would lose her money and they'd be going back to the Airbnb.

As Maggie took her place at the table amongst the rest of the players, she put down her chip and the dealer dealt her two cards. Stick or twist? She twisted and won.

'Wow!'

As Flick watched the croupier hand Maggie her winnings, Maggie felt an unexpected shot of adrenaline. It was the first bit of luck in she couldn't remember how long. The first time she'd won money, not lost it. She felt a buzz of excitement.

'Let's go again.'

'Hello, can I have the old Maggie back?' joked Flick as Maggie placed another bet and won. And then another. And another.

But what Flick didn't know is this *was* the old Maggie. The Maggie who was adventurous and confident and fun. The Maggie she used to be before she fell in love with a fraudster who stole her life. She was back.

Time flew by and before she knew it, Maggie had won two hundred and fifty euros, which included her original bet. Time to quit while she was ahead.

'Wow, you're really good!' congratulated Flick. She was wide awake now. Watching Maggie gambling was invigorating. She knew nothing about playing cards, but Maggie obviously did. Choosing to stick or twist with the seriousness and certainty of someone who'd played a million games of blackjack, even if it was with her dad at the kitchen table and not a fancy casino in Monte Carlo.

'I had a good teacher,' grinned Maggie, gathering up her chips and leaving the table. The croupier nodded in respect. As did a few other players, men that weren't used to be being beaten by a woman, especially not one as unassuming as Maggie. 'And by the way, it's yours.'

'What?' Flick looked confused.

'To pay you back for my flight and the dress and lunch and everything. It's not nearly enough, but at least it's something.'

'No, don't be silly. It was my stupid idea.'

'It wasn't stupid. It was the first time I've had fun in a long time. Please, take it.'

Flick hesitated. She should be sensible. Cash in the chips. Use the money to pay off some of her credit card. And yet, even though she'd never admit it, Maggie wasn't the only one caught up in the spell of Monte Carlo. Tomorrow she'd be back home to face the music, but it wasn't tomorrow just yet.

'How about we gamble it all?'

'Huh?'

Impulsively she pointed to a table with a roulette wheel. 'What have we got to lose?'

Maggie had heard that somewhere before. She thought of her friend George. 'Two hundred and fifty euros?' she replied and together they both started grinning.

It was so out of character for both of them. Flick had spent her whole life being sensible, while Maggie no longer trusted herself to take any risks, but they were both drunk and in the most famous casino in the world.

'*Faites vos jeux!*'

'What does that mean?' hissed Flick as they took their place at the roulette table.

'Place your bets,' whispered Maggie. 'You must place them yourself on the green baize.'

All around them people were placing their chips on the table.

'Do you want red or black?'

'Can you bet on a single number?'

'Yes, but then the odds are really against us,' warned Maggie.

'What's new?' replied Flick and they both met each other's gaze.

'OK, what's your lucky number?'

'Nineteen. It was my mum's birthday.'

With a flick of his wrist the croupier spun the roulette wheel as Maggie slid all their chips onto number nineteen on the table. It wasn't much, but it was everything they had.

'If we win thousands, what are we going to spend it on?'

Flick's nerves jangled. Too late to change their minds now.

'Paying off our credit cards?' suggested Maggie, her chest tightening.

'*Rien ne va plus.*'

So this was it. No more bets. The moment when everyone held their breath, their eyes riveted on the roulette wheel, waiting for the ball to come to rest.

'That's boring. How about we use the money to catch a thief?'

And then suddenly the croupier was announcing the number and it was flashing up on the screen and people were whooping and clapping.

'*Dix-neuf.*'

Nineteen. They'd won. Oh my God. They'd won!

# The Hangover

No, not the movie with Bradley Cooper, a tiger and a baby. But the beast that was pinning Maggie to the bed and making her feel like death. Actually, maybe she was dead. Death by cocktail. Blearily she opened her eyes . . .

'Great! You're finally awake!'

*WTF?*

Chirpily sitting on the sofa, all bright-eyed and bushy-tailed, was Flick. Looking like she'd only ever drunk sparkling water.

'Ugggghhh,' was all Maggie managed to say, spittle oozing onto the pillow.

She desperately wanted the room to stop spinning. Nausea gripped her by the throat, while there was throbbing coming from deep inside her brain. Actually, maybe death would be better than this.

'You're up,' she managed to croak, pointing a finger towards a fully dressed Flick. She noticed she had the shakes.

'I've been up for hours, since the crack of dawn. I've been out asking questions, doing some investigating.'

Maggie looked at her askance. Well, she would've done if she'd actually been able to focus properly. Because this, my friends, was the difference between being in your late forties and your mid-twenties, she thought to herself. It wasn't about wrinkles or life experience. It was about being able to get completely shit-faced and wake up five hours later *with absolutely no hangover.*

'OK, so I've made a plan of action.'

Flick was sitting up on the sofa, sipping a takeout coffee, notebook in hand, madly scribbling.

'A plan of action?'

Groggily, she dragged a pillow and hoisted herself up against the headboard. It was a superhuman effort. Compounded by the fact she was still trying to focus.

'I need coffee,' she croaked, her voice hoarse, like a whisper.

And it wasn't just her throat that was all scratchy, her whole body was too.

Out of the corner of her eye she spied a flash of sequins. Hang on, was she still wearing her dress? Ugh. She must have slept in it.

'Did I black out? I have no memory of me getting home.'

'You don't remember singing in the street? Something about being as hungry as a wolf.'

'I sang "Hungry Like the Wolf"?' Maggie was mortified. 'In the middle of Monte Carlo?'

'Drew quite a crowd.'

'Oh my God.' She clutched her head, then thought better of it as it thudded in her hands. This was even worse than she feared.

'I must have been drugged. Someone must have spiked my drink. You read about it all the time in the papers.'

'Nah.' Flick laughed and shook her head. 'You were just drunk.'

'Oh God . . .' Maggie had to swallow hard to stop the bile rising in her throat.

'You let your hair down. You needed it.'

'What I need is a coffee.'

'Here.' Flick passed her one over. She'd got two from the takeout place. 'Might not be very hot still, but caffeine is caffeine.'

Maggie took a sip and grimaced. It wasn't coffee. It was some horrible-flavoured syrup thing.

'So, like I was saying, we need a plan of action. I've been out already and found out about the cruise ship, and I've managed to get online and pull up the itinerary of all the destinations.'

'Hang on. Rewind. *Itinerary?*'

'Last night. I thought we agreed. We're going to go after him.'

Somewhere in the dark recesses of Maggie's alcohol-sodden mind, she had a vague memory of Flick saying something along those lines if they won at roulette.

'That was just the alcohol and the adrenaline talking, wasn't it? We didn't really mean it—' she began to protest, then broke off as Flick's face fell in dismay. She changed tack. 'And anyway, how can we? We're going home today. Our flight leaves in a few hours.'

'But that's just it. We don't have to. I've emailed my editor, Seymour, and told him I'm going to take the two weeks' paid holiday he's been nagging me to take for ages. And it's not like you've got a job to go back to,' she pointed out.

Maggie's face clouded.

'I didn't mean . . . what I meant is . . . I was just saying.'

Like a car that's stuck in the mud and turning its wheels, only to make them go deeper, Flick's attempts at explanation were only making things worse.

'It's OK. No offence taken. You're right. I don't have job. I lost the gallery, along with everything else.'

'Well, then, what's stopping us?'

'What about your boyfriend Rory? What have you told him?'

Flick faltered momentarily at the mention of Rory. Reminded of his texts which she'd been responding to with vague replies and emojis, she felt a moment of doubt. 'I'm sure he'll understand when I explain,' she replied unconvincingly.

'Or what about the small fact that the man we came here to catch is now on a luxury cruise ship in the middle of the Mediterranean?' continued Maggie.

Actually, this coffee wasn't so bad.

'Ah, but that's just it. I know where it's headed. Apparently the first stop is Rome.'

'And?'

'With the money we can rent a car, drive to Rome.'

'*Drive to Rome?*'

Maggie couldn't work out if Flick was joking or being serious.

'And what happens if we don't find him in Rome?'

'Then we go to the next destination, the next port, until we do.'

Flick leaned back and folded her arms. She looked very pleased with herself.

Maggie observed her. 'Is writing about local charity fundraisers and headbutting sheep so bad?' she said after a moment.

'Huh?'

'So bad that you want to chase around Europe after The Man Whose Name I Cannot Mention.'

'We need an acronym for that.'

'That's what George says. Not my cat, my best friend,' explained Maggie, sensing the confusion. 'Though he just calls him The Wanker.'

'Come on, Maggie,' Flick sighed. 'We were so bummed when he gave us the slip and got away, but now with our winnings we can go after him.'

'How much did we win again?'

Reaching into her suitcase, where she'd hidden it in her underwear, Flick produced a wad of bank notes.

'Eight thousand, seven hundred and fifty euros, plus the original two fifty wager, so nine thousand total.'

As Flick said it out loud, they had to take a moment to let it sink in.

'That's so much money.'

'I know.'

They both stared at the bundles of cash, neatly bound in their paper wrappers.

'With my half I could pay off some of my credit cards, maybe even get together a rental deposit for a flat . . .' Maggie was thinking out loud as possibilities began opening up before her.

'Or together we could afford to rent a car and pay for hotels and go after the bastard who stole your entire life savings,' finished Flick.

'But that's just crazy.'

'Is it, though?' Flick frowned. 'Women are always being called crazy, or emotional, or irrational, or hysterical – "the psycho ex", "the crazy ex-wife" – but we never are. We're just reacting to bad situations. We're taking control and standing up for ourselves and refusing to take it lying down. It's not us that are crazy, it's the situation. Notice men are never called crazy,' she added, raising an eyebrow.

A memory of seeing Him last night flashed through Maggie's mind. The rest of the evening was a blur, but not that. That was clear, like she was watching it in high definition. Seeing him again. The way he moved confidently, the way he looked across the salon as if he owned it. The way his eyes glossed over her without even seeing her.

But then he never did see her, did he?

'Don't give up now, Maggie.'

Instead, he told her she was crazy.

When her gut instinct had told her something was up, he'd said she was being crazy and she'd believed him. She'd doubted herself and trusted him. And look where that had got her.

She thought about the enforcement notice in her handbag. The wreckage that was her life waiting for her back in the UK. Why had she really come here? What was her real motive? Was it truly to help protect other women? To seek justice? Find closure? Was she hoping to recoup some of her money or get her dad's watch back? Or was it to try and get revenge? To make him pay for what he did to her? Seeing him last night had brought hot flashes of fury; he was going on a luxury cruise while she was about to become homeless.

*Or is it something else?* a voice whispered deep inside of her. *Are you here to see if you still love him? If there is any chance he still loves you? If he ever loved you?*

Oh, Maggie.

'I know when you agreed to come, it was for just one night . . .' Flick's voice broke into her thoughts. 'So I know I'm asking a lot.'

Maggie shifted her gaze to Flick. Every scared, reluctant, bruised and battered cell in her body was telling her to get on a plane and go home. But she didn't have a home. Not for much longer anyway. And after so many months of feeling numb, feeling scared was better than feeling nothing.

She smiled. 'How's your Italian?'

# Rome

*Day Two*

*Twelve more days to go*

# The Road Trip

'So, have we got everything?'

Putting on her seatbelt, Flick adjusted the rear-view mirror. Having finished up the car rental paperwork, she was now sitting in the driver's seat of a bright red Fiat 500. Despite her outward confidence, she felt abruptly nervous. She'd never hired a car abroad, let alone driven on the right-hand side of the road, but she wasn't about to admit that to Maggie.

'Yes.' Finishing putting the suitcases in the boot, Maggie and her hangover slid next to her in the passenger seat in dark sunglasses. 'Apart from our minds, but we lost those hours ago.'

Choosing to ignore her, Flick turned the ignition, put the car into first and pulled out of the car park. And straight into oncoming traffic.

Put it this way, there were screams.

'They're on the wrong side of the road!!!'

'No, you're on the wrong side of the road!!!'

As the two women yelled and shrieked at each other, Flick quickly swerved into a layby, narrowly missing a silver Ferrari. The Fiat stalled. The Ferrari blasted its horn. Both drivers looked at each other. Flick had gone as white as a sheet and was shaking.

'How about I drive?' suggested Maggie. 'And you can navigate.'

'I'm sure I'll be fine with a bit of practice,' Flick feebly protested.

'Or dead,' replied Maggie, opening the car door and getting out. Because if her hangover wasn't going to kill her, Flick's driving was.

Without further discussion they swapped seats.

'So how long's the drive?' Checking her mirrors, Maggie safely pulled out onto Avenue Princesse Grace.

'Seven hours, forty minutes,' replied Flick, peering at the directions on her phone. For the first time in her life, she actually felt relieved *not* to be in the driving seat.

'Ouch, that's a long journey.'

'How about we listen to some music to help pass the time?'

Flick turned on the radio and the next few minutes were spent scrolling through stations. Cue terrible pop music with a curious amount of synthesizers and news channels in French which, despite Maggie's GCSE and Flick's translation app, neither could fully understand. Every so often spirits would be raised as a classic Rolling Stones record or a catchy Dua Lipa hit blasted over the airwaves and the volume would be turned up together with the mood in the car. Only for the song to be drowned out by static a few seconds later as the signal became weak and then disappeared.

There was a metaphor for life in there somewhere.

Finally Flick gave up and turned it off.

'I've got Spotify.'

'OK, great.' Focused on navigating a roundabout, Maggie followed the directions onto the autoroute. 'What shall we listen to?'

Flick fiddled with her phone, scrolling through various playlists. 'What are you in the mood for?'

'Something that won't make my headache worse.' Maggie rubbed her temples.

## SO, I MET THIS GUY . . .

Despite the trifecta of caffeine, croissants and paracetamol – the usual guaranteed cure – her headache was proving to be like one of those guests at the end of a party who refuses to leave and takes up residence in your kitchen.

'How about this band? They're pretty chill.'

Music flooded the car. At least, Maggie assumed it was supposed to be music.

'God, they're terrible,' she said, wincing, after a few minutes. 'How about we listen to some eighties instead?'

'*Eighties?*'

'What's wrong with the eighties?'

'Big hair. Leg warmers. Acid-wash jeans . . . seriously, I've seen Mum's old photos.'

'Ah, the good old days.' Maggie smiled fondly, then caught Flick's expression. 'Just kidding. The fashion was awful, but the music was amazing. God, I used to have such a crush on Simon Le Bon.'

'Is that the guy from *Britain's Got Talent*?'

There was a beat. Surely she hadn't heard that right?

'No, it is not!' she cried, in disbelief. 'That's Simon Cowell!'

*Uh-oh.* Flick tried to hide beneath her sun visor.

'Are you telling me you don't know who Simon Le Bon and Duran Duran are?'

Flick pretended to have something in her eye as Maggie drew herself up indignantly behind the steering wheel and went on about how if she hadn't heard 'Hungry Like the Wolf', and no, her singing it drunkenly in the street didn't count, she hadn't lived.

'Seeing as we can't agree on music, what about listening to a podcast?' Flick suggested, a few moments and one imaginary eyelash later.

'OK.' Maggie shrugged, still slightly in a huff.

'How about some true crime?'

'I don't need to listen to true crime, I've been living in a true crime.'

*Fair point*, thought Flick, as Maggie threw her a sobering look.

'I know,' suggested Maggie, 'what about a celebrity podcast instead? There are some new ones I've been reading about.'

'You mean, the ones where rich and famous people we can't relate to interview other rich and famous people we can't relate to?' remarked Flick.

Maggie laughed then. 'I take it you're not a fan of celebrities?'

Flick shook her head. 'No, it's not that. It's just the people I find the most fascinating aren't even remotely famous. They're ordinary people who are just quietly going about their lives, but they have all really interesting stories to tell, they just haven't got a voice . . .'

Breaking off, she stared out of the window as the French countryside sped by in a blur. 'That's why I wanted to become a journalist. To give a voice to those that haven't got one. Because everyone's got a story to tell, you just have to listen.'

She shook her head, invigorated now.

'I mean, don't get me wrong, I enjoy watching chat shows but mostly famous people are just there to promote their new film or album or book. Same when you read their interviews. I'm not really interested in hearing another Hollywood actor's life story; I'm interested in people like us. You know, normal people.'

'Not sure I call what we're doing normal,' retorted Maggie, putting her foot down and overtaking a truck.

'Exactly!' Flick turned back to look at Maggie, her face energized. 'But that's why it's so interesting. It's like your story. One day you were just like everyone else, living your everyday life and the next it's all stolen from you—'

'And you're on some mad caper across Europe to try and get it back,' finished Maggie with a grimace. 'That doesn't make me sound normal; it makes me sound like I'm nuts.'

'No, it does not,' rubbished Flick. 'Women will relate to you. If it can happen to you, it can happen to them, too.'

But Maggie didn't look convinced.

'They'll find it shocking and unbelievable but mostly inspiring.'

'I'm hardly an inspiration, more like a complete idiot for making such a massive mistake.'

'I think you're inspiring.'

Maggie glanced across to see Flick looking at her and felt oddly touched.

'I just never want anyone else to go through what I went through.'

'And that's exactly why I wanted to interview you, so you can explain why and how it happened, so you can warn other women.'

'Oh, it's a long story.'

'Well, we've got seven hours and forty minutes and six hundred and seventy-nine kilometres,' said Flick, pointing at the sign ahead that said Roma. 'It's either that or Eye Spy.'

'What? You want to interview me now?'

'I'm not going to record it. Just tell it to me, in your words.'

She heaved a sigh. 'God, I wouldn't know where to start.'

'Oh, that's easy.' Flick smiled. 'In journalism, they call it the inciting incident.'

Maggie glanced at Flick with interest.

'It's something, however big or small, that happens in your life which sets in motion a sequence of events.'

Tightening her grip on the steering wheel, Maggie focused back on the road ahead.

'In other words, how it all began.'

# Maggie

So, I met this guy.

Well, isn't that how every love story starts?

It was a Tuesday afternoon in February last year and I was at the gallery. I remember the date as it was Pancake Day and I was thinking about my dad. He'd died the summer before. Pancakes were his favourite and every year I'd catch the train up to see him, armed with a bag of flour and a dozen eggs. Dad would fire up the frying pan, I'd make the batter, and we'd both take turns in trying to flip them. I was hopeless. There'd be more on the floor than in the pan. Not that Dad cared. Greedy bugger would smother them in golden syrup and gobble up the lot.

So, I'm feeling a bit tearful, sitting in the back with a cup of Earl Grey that's gone cold and half a packet of stem-ginger cookies, lost in thought and wondering who I'm going to make pancakes for now, when the doorbell chimes.

I pop my head out.

'Hello?'

'Hi. Is it OK to browse?'

And abruptly all thoughts of pancakes vanish and There He Is. A tall, dark, handsome stranger. Standing in the middle of my little gallery. Literally.

'Yes . . . yes, of course.'

I quickly brush biscuit crumbs from my cardigan. They're all caught in the pink mohair. Tiny guilty ginger crumbles.

'I've just moved to the area and I'm looking for some art for my new apartment.'

'Well, you've come to the right place then,' I joke.

It's a bit feeble, but it makes him smile and I notice he's got a really nice smile. The kind that reaches the corner of his eyes and makes them go all crinkly. And somewhere, deep inside this grief-stricken soul of mine, I feel a flicker of something.

'If you like landscapes, we're currently exhibiting some wonderful paintings by a local artist,' I continue, pointing to the walls where various large brooding oils are displayed.

'Hmm . . . yes . . . I like their use of colour.'

'Isn't it extraordinary?'

He nods and continues walking slowly around the gallery. Pausing in front of each painting. I watch him studying each one. Meanwhile I take the opportunity to study him. His dark hair is swept back off his temples, his face is tanned and he's wearing a woollen overcoat. Deep blue, with the collar turned up, it's beautifully cut and looks expensive.

I feel abruptly self-conscious in my jeans-and-cardie combo and faded old suede boots.

'And if you're looking for something a little cheaper, we have signed limited edition prints too,' I add, though somewhat redundantly. This does not look like a man that needs to worry about money.

'I'm afraid I don't know much about art.'

'Oh, you don't need to. I always think it's whatever you feel a connection with.'

'Is that so?'

He turns to me with a cheeky smile and raises an eyebrow. Wait. Is he flirting with me? I feel myself go all hot underneath my armpits and deeply regret my mohair cardie. No. Don't be silly. Of course he's not. No one's flirted with me for years. Since my last relationship finished in my mid-forties, I've been single and invisible.

I take off my cardie and hang it over the back of my chair.

'Sorry. It's a little hot in here. I think I turned the thermostat too high,' I say, thanking God I wore a bra under my T-shirt.

'I'm still getting used to the British winter,' he says, motioning to the fact he's wearing a scarf. And not the bright, stripy, Tom-Baker-as-*Dr-Who* kind of scarf that I wore to work today wrapped around my ancient sheepskin coat that I found in a flea market years ago, but the luxury, butter-soft cashmere kind that's pale grey and knotted perfectly at his throat.

'Oh, you've been away?' So that explains the tan.

'For the last twenty years, yes. I live in LA. Or I *did*,' he quickly corrects himself. 'I just sold my house and moved back to the UK.'

It's the casual way he says LA. I feel my interest piqued. Not that it wasn't already.

'Bit different from sunny California,' I say, gesturing to the leaden skies outside the gallery windows.

'Just a little,' he nods. 'So, you know Los Angeles?'

'Only from the movies. And *The Real Housewives*,' I admit, then, seeing his confused expression, add in explanation, 'It's a reality TV show set in Beverly Hills.'

'Oh, yes, I haven't seen it,' he confesses. 'I work in film.'

'*Film?*'

It comes out a bit high-pitched. Well, it's not every day I get handsome men who work in film walking into my little art gallery on the outskirts of Bath. It's all very glamorous. Usually, it's tourists browsing for a souvenir or a local landlord decorating yet another holiday let. Yesterday it was one of my neighbours, looking for something for their new downstairs loo. They went for a lithograph print of a vase of flowers.

'It's not as glamourous as it sounds. I scout filming locations.'

'No, working in Hollywood doesn't sound very glamorous at all,' I reply, and he laughs.

'Well, put like that . . .' He breaks off and looks at me and I get that funny feeling again.

'So, what brings you back to the UK?'

'Mum had a fall.'

'Oh, I'm sorry, is she OK?'

'Yeah, yeah . . . she's fine now but she's not getting any younger. I wanted to be nearer, what with her being a widow now. I'm an only child and we're very close . . . Plus, I've been thinking about moving back for a while, ever since the divorce—' He breaks off. 'Sorry, I didn't mean to pour out my whole life story.'

'No, honestly, it's fine.' I smile reassuringly. 'I understand.'

Underneath the smart coat and suntan, I see a vulnerability and feel an unexpected connection. He looks about my age, maybe a few years older. We're in that time of life when the roles have reversed and it's us that worry about our parents. Doesn't matter whether you're in a designer coat or not.

'I lost my dad last summer, so I know how important it is to spend time with our parents while we can.'

'Oh, I'm sorry. I hope I didn't upset you.'

'No, not at all.' I shake my head. 'In fact, it's nice to talk about it to someone who understands.'

'You must miss him.'

'Yes.'

And it's hearing myself admit it out loud, to a complete stranger, that catches me by surprise. It's been a tough six months. Losing a parent is hard for anyone, but Dad's death had crushed me. My parents divorced years ago and while Mum had remarried and moved to Spain, we were never close. I'd always been Daddy's girl.

All through my childhood and teenage years he was my constant protector and champion. Even as an adult I knew nothing bad could ever happen to me as long as Dad was alive. Boyfriends came and went – there was even a short-lived marriage in my twenties, a six-week disaster which ended when I ran home shamefaced and crying that I'd made a terrible mistake and Dad just hugged me and told me everything would be all right. He was the only man who had ever loved me unconditionally and his loss was profound.

Grief overwhelmed me. I cried constantly. I never thought I'd feel joy again. Friends were kind and supportive, but they had families and busy lives and after a while the sympathy cards and the texts stopped and people just assume you're getting on with it. It's your father. Losing a parent is normal. It happens to us all. Perhaps it was being single and not having a partner's shoulder to cry on, but it hit me incredibly hard.

Feeling my eyes welling up, I go to quickly brush the tears away when I notice him reach into his pocket and he holds out a packet of tissues.

'Trust me, I don't usually walk around carrying these but this freezing cold weather has been playing havoc with my sinuses.' Then he grins and pulls a face. 'Too much information?'

'Too much information,' I sniff, smiling as I take them from him.

The bell chimes as the door opens. A few tourists enter, take a cursory glance around the gallery, ask about the price of a sculpture, then leave. Several moments pass.

I look over towards my handsome stranger. He's still here. Waiting for something.

*Someone?*

'So, anything in particular that catches your eye?'

'Yes.' He turns to me. 'But I don't know if it's available.'

And as we hold each other's gaze we both know he's not talking about the artwork any more.

'I'm Theo, by the way.'

'I'm Maggie.'

And I realize that flicker of something I first felt as he walked into the gallery was a flicker of me coming back to life.

There's a beat.

'Do you like pancakes?'

And just like that, we're not strangers any more.

# But First, Pizza

According to the famous saying, all roads lead to Rome.

Well, no, apparently not, thought Maggie, as they finally arrived later that evening after circling the city, taking one wrong turn after another, as the city sweltered and the traffic fumes choked and the air conditioning on the Fiat decided to conk out. Not when Flick was in charge of the directions.

Still, any frustrations and weariness were soon swept away by the sheer engulfment (was *engulfment* even a word?) of finding herself in Italy's capital city. After climbing three flights up the narrow staircase of a little backstreet *pensione* – the only accommodation they could find available online at such short notice – the bickering and the bad moods seemed to instantly evaporate as they opened the full-length windows, folded back the heavy wooden shutters and stepped out onto their tiny balcony.

And there it was, stretching out before them, a sea of Roman terracotta rooftops, studded with church domes and lit by a blazing crimson sky, streaked with golden pinks, caramelized tangerine and clouds that hung like deep purple bruises.

'What's that?' asked Flick, pointing into the distance at the large dome that dominated the skyline.

'St Peter's Basilica.'

'Wow.'

There were so many adjectives at her disposal, so many

ways to convey things and Flick fiercely prided herself on her vocabulary and use of language. On her clever metaphors and carefully inserted similes. She was a writer; her job was to communicate. But now, gazing at the panorama before her, she was rendered speechless but for one simple, clichéd exclamation.

'Just. Wow.'

There. She'd said it again.

Standing beside her, Maggie glanced at Flick, at her eyes lit up, reflecting the sunset. And that kind of magic that comes from travel and finding yourself somewhere beautiful. She felt it too and for a few moments they both stood together, side by side, looking out across the rooftops, breathing it all in and forgetting the reason they were there.

The evening air was sweltering. The city buzzed beneath them. The sounds of ancient church bells, revving Vespa engines and suitcases being wheeled across the cobbles, mingling with laughter and glasses clinking and delicious aromas from the restaurants below. All sounds and smells of life. It was all here.

'So, what's the plan?' asked Maggie, reluctantly breaking the spell and turning back to the matter in hand.

'Well, according to the itinerary the cruise ship doesn't dock until first thing tomorrow morning.'

'Where is it now?'

Flick pulled out her phone and pinched at a document on her screen.

'Elba, wherever that is.'

'It's an island. Where Napoleon was exiled to.'

'Cool.'

Maggie noted Flick didn't even pretend to be interested in what she thought was actually an interesting bit of information, but was now focused on taking a photo of the view.

'Do you want me to take one of you in it?' she offered.

'Oh. No. Thanks. I hate myself in photos.'

'Why? You look lovely.'

Flick pulled a face and went back to taking a photo and Maggie thought about how she used to be the same when she was her age, always thinking she looked awful, hating to be photographed because she thought her thighs were too big or her face too spotty and she wasn't wearing a full face of make-up. And now, whenever she looked back at old photos of herself, all she saw was someone young and beautiful and she wished she could reach back in time and give herself confidence. To take herself by the shoulders and tell her that one day in the future she would kill to look like that again.

And now here she was, wishing she could explain all that to Flick and realizing that no, she couldn't, you just had to learn it yourself.

'Well, in that case, I guess we've got the evening off,' she said instead.

'It's like being on holiday.' Flick grinned.

'A Roman holiday.'

'Is that another film reference? 'Cos I know that one.' Flick looked triumphant. 'Audrey Hepburn and Gregory Peck.'

'So you don't just watch *Love Island*?'

Maggie was teasing, but Flick looked offended.

'Not everyone in their twenties watches that mindless rubbish.'

'Who says it's mindless rubbish?'

'I do. It's just women parading around in bikinis.'

'And men parading around in tiny shorts. My friend George loves it. He's always sending me screen grabs to cheer me up.'

Flick threw her a withering look.

'Maybe you should watch it,' suggested Maggie. 'Before you form an opinion.'

Flick bristled. Forming opinions about things was something she prided herself upon. First impressions. Gut instinct. It was how she made sense of the world. Protected herself from all the confusing, complicated stuff, of which there'd been plenty in the last few years.

'*Roman Holiday* was one of my mum's favourite films,' she said, changing the subject. 'She loved Audrey Hepburn—' She broke off, her expression thoughtful as she looked back out across the city, taking it all in. 'She said she always wanted to bring me to Rome. To show it to me. She said the first time you see Rome it has to be with someone who loves you.' She felt her eyes well up. 'But she never got the chance.'

'Maybe she's with you here now.'

'Oh, I don't believe that stuff.' Flick gave a brisk sniff and shook her head firmly. 'I'm not going to see a white feather or a rainbow and think it's a sign from Mum.' She glanced across at Maggie. 'Do you? With your dad?'

'No, not really,' she confessed. 'But I like the idea.'

'And why does it always have to be a feather or a rainbow, anyway?' she tutted derisively. 'If Mum was going to give me a sign, it would be something that cheered me up.'

'Like what?'

'I dunno.' Flick leaned against the balcony, peering down into the street. 'Pizza?'

And the mood was suddenly lifted and they both turned to each other and laughed.

'Actually, pizza would make me really happy right now,' agreed Maggie. 'I'm starving.'

'Me too.'

'Right. Come on then, let's quickly shower and change and

then I'll take you to this great pizzeria I know. The last time I was in Rome I had *the best* pizza.'

'Much better than a feather.'

'Much better.'

Grabbing her toiletries from her suitcase, Flick went to use the shower in the ensuite while Maggie hung a crumpled dress on a hanger and hoped the creases would fall out. As Flick walked to the bathroom, Maggie turned to her.

'I know I'm not your mum, but I want you to know you're in Rome with someone who cares about you. And for what it's worth, I'm glad I get to show you the city.'

There was a pause and for a moment Maggie feared she'd overstepped the mark. Oh dear. Was that insensitive? Had she said the wrong thing?

But as anyone who has lost anyone knows, the only wrong thing to say is nothing at all and Flick's pause wasn't because Maggie had been insensitive. It was because, of all the sympathy shown to her by family and friends, this simple act of thoughtfulness by a woman she'd only just met floored her. It was one of the kindest things anyone had ever said.

'Me too.' She smiled and opened the door.

It was a July evening in Rome and after the sweltering lethargy of the brutal midday sun, the city had revived itself from its *riposo* and come alive in the dusky shadows. Narrow cobbled streets were crowded with freshly showered tourists eating gelato and shopping for souvenirs, while piazzas thronged with restaurants, street musicians, faded stucco and fountains and the orange glow of a thousand Aperol spritz. A glorious jumble of life past and present.

After fifteen minutes of weaving their way through the backstreets, Maggie suddenly turned to Flick.

'Wait, I have to blindfold you.'

'I thought we were just going out for pizza?'
'We are, but I need to cover your eyes.'
'Why?'
'Don't ask why. It's a surprise.'
'I hate surprises.'
'You'll like this one. Trust me.'

Flick was unconvinced. Once, on a school coach trip to Windsor Castle, she'd learned about coats of arms with Latin inscriptions and decided her motto would be 'Trust No One'. Only, she didn't know what that was in Latin because she went to a local comprehensive and they didn't study Latin. Plus, her ancestors were all coalminers; they had outside loos, not family crests.

Still, it was probably just a royal family thing. Something from medieval times, along with the suits of armour and swords. Or so she thought until she'd gone to university some years later and been teased about her accent by posh boys wearing gold pinky rings with family crests, and realized it was actually a real thing.

*Magnus stultus.*

'OK, OK.' Surrendering with a sigh, she allowed Maggie to put her hands over her eyes and lead her faltering across the cobbles.

'Mind the kerb . . . Careful, there's a scooter to your right . . . Nuns incoming!'

Maggie barked out instructions, while Flick, feeling incredibly vulnerable, clung on to her arm and allowed herself to be steered down the street.

'Ow,' she yelled, as she bumped shoulders with a passing tourist. 'This better be worth the surprise.'

'It is, trust me.'

She was led a bit further, trying not to trip on the cobbles.

'OK, now you can open your eyes.'

As Maggie removed her hand, Flick blinked in the evening sunlight.

'*Ta-dah!*'

Flick gave a sharp intake of breath. She was standing next to the most magnificent fountain, surrounded by candy-coloured buildings – which, she learned from googling later, were examples of baroque architecture – in the middle of a large square filled with restaurants and terraces and tourists.

As anyone who knew Flick would tell you, she wasn't often lost for words, but as she tried to take it all in, she was overwhelmed.

'Where am I?' she managed finally.

'Piazza Navona.'

'Is this even real?' she marvelled. 'It's like a film set or something.'

She twirled around slowly, allowing her gaze to fall upon restaurants and cafes packed with diners enjoying pasta and people-watching, while street performers entertained and traders threw brightly coloured balls in the air and people took selfies to send to family and friends around the globe. Thousands of livingmybestlife hashtags winging their way out of an ancient Roman square and into the metaverse.

'And look! The restaurant is still here!'

Maggie was jubilant. It was several years since she'd been to Piazza Navona. She couldn't remember when, exactly. It had been with George; he'd got her a cheap midweek flight, and they'd spent a whirlwind twenty-four hours soaking up the sights and as much art as they could consume. It was all a bit of a blur, thanks mostly to George's love of red wine – he kept ordering bottles of Montepulciano – but she did remember the pizza. Did that make her a philistine? Forgetting the baroque masterpieces but still savouring the memory of the salty anchovies of her pizza di Napoli.

'Can we get a table? It looks totally full,' asked Flick dubiously, following her now as she set off across the cobbles to the row of red-and-white-checked tablecloths.

'Let's ask, you never know. *Scusi?*'

Maggie tried to catch the eye of the waiter, but he was flitting between tables in his salmon-pink waistcoat, and for a few moments she stood at the sidelines, ignored and invisible.

'Excuse me?'

As luck would have it, she was with a twenty-six-year-old and as Flick spoke and stepped forward, the waiter's eye was caught and he came over, fluttering and preening like a flamingo, two menus flapping like wings, instantly finding them the best seats in the house: a table overlooking the piazza. Whilst also trying to flirt with Flick, who either chose to ignore him or didn't notice.

Probably the latter, thought Maggie, as they ordered the ubiquitous Aperol spritz and olives. Who notices male attention when you're that age? It's just the norm. Meanwhile, sitting across from Flick, she felt like an elderly spinster on the grand tour of Europe with her young charge.

'The waiter was cute,' she prompted.

'Was he?' Flick peered at her phone.

Maggie gave up and turned to the menu. 'What do you fancy?'

'Not the waiter.'

She glanced up with a mischievous grin and Maggie laughed.

'So you *did* notice?'

'I couldn't help it.' Flick pulled a face and reached for her menu.

'Trust me, you'll miss that attention when you get to my age.'

'You get attention.'

'What are you talking about?'

'That man over there.' Behind her menu, she made a gesture with her eyes. 'He's been staring at you ever since you sat down.'

'Who?'

'Don't look.'

So of course Maggie did exactly that and turned to look. To see a man a few tables away sitting by himself with a glass of wine and a book, which he appeared to now be reading. Until he suddenly glanced up, in that way people do when they can feel someone looking at them, and caught them both staring at him.

'Oh shit, he wasn't staring; *we* were staring.'

Maggie turned away quickly, embarrassed.

'He looked at you,' said Flick.

'He was probably looking at you.'

'Don't be ridiculous. He's old enough to be my dad.'

'*And?*'

They were interrupted as the flirtatious waiter returned with their drinks and took their pizza orders. 'I can't believe he's reading a book.'

'Some people do actually read books, you know,' said Maggie. 'Not everyone wants to be glued to a phone,' she added, as Flick's lit up and started vibrating on the table.

A few seconds passed.

'Aren't you going to answer that?' asked Maggie.

'It's Rory. He wants to speak to me.'

'And you don't want to?'

'He's furious I lied about the work conference. He wants me to get on the first flight home.'

'Well, that's to be expected.'

'I tried to explain. I told him about you and Theo Stratin and the whole romance fraud, but he says I'm being ridiculous. That I've made him a laughing stock amongst all our friends. Which frankly is him being ridiculous as I said it's got nothing to do with him,' she added with annoyance.

'That's probably the problem.'

Flick looked blank.

'Look, I don't know Rory, but in my experience men like it to be about them.'

'But it's not.'

'Exactly.'

Flick sighed and rubbed her forehead. 'So, what am I supposed to do?'

'You're asking advice from me?' Maggie gave a wry smile. 'I'm hardly the person to be giving out advice about romantic relationships.'

'I've said I'm sorry. I've apologized.'

'Well, then, that's all you can do.' Maggie shrugged. 'Try not to worry. These things have a habit of working themselves out.'

Flick nodded and stabbed her ice cubes. Several texts popped up on her phone. She read them and chewed her lip, looking troubled.

'What if they don't?'

'You'll be fine.'

'I love Rory, you know.'

'I'm sure you do.'

They both sipped their drinks, but Maggie could feel the tension.

'How did you meet?' she asked, trying to dissipate it.

Flick shrugged. 'I've known him for ever. We were friends a long time before we ever got together. He was in the year above me at school. He's always been *there*, you know? Solid. Like part of the landscape . . .' Flick chewed her straw thoughtfully. At least it was paper not plastic, so there were some things to be happy about. 'I went away to uni and we lost touch for a few years, but when I came home and moved back above the pub, we started up where we left off. He'd come into the pub with his friends, but I think half the time he hung around 'cos he wanted to talk to me—' She broke off. 'God, does that make me sound like I've got a big head or something?'

'No, of course not.'

'And when Mum got sick, he was so good, really kind. My stepdad Colin loves him. Everyone loves him.'

'Including you,' added Maggie.

'Yeah, including me.' She nodded, and finished up her drink, sucking it up loudly through the straw as the pizzas arrived, hot and steaming with melted cheese and cracked pepper from the biggest pepper grinder Flick had ever seen.

And between delicious mouthfuls, they talked about their plans for tomorrow, before tiredness caught up with them both and, stifling yawns, they headed back to the hotel to get an early night. Where the conversation about Rory was forgotten, along with the waiter and the stranger with his book.

Well. Not quite.

At 2 a.m. Maggie woke, unable to sleep, and gazed up at the shaft of moonlight on the ceiling. Worried and anxious about the day ahead, about what was going to unfold, she let her mind return to the restaurant. As they left, she'd glanced back at the exact moment the stranger had looked up from his book and they'd both caught each other's eye and smiled. It was nothing, just a casual, friendly smile. But for the briefest of moments, after the longest time, a tiny bit of her felt seen again.

# Meet and Greet

'Wow, it's a bit busy.'

'Busy? It's absolute *chaos*!'

Early the next morning Maggie and Flick found themselves seventy kilometres northwest of Rome in the modern port town of Civitavecchia, standing on the edge of the docks, mouths slightly agape as they surveyed the scene before them. It's not what they expected. But then nothing could have prepared them for this kind of scale.

As one of the busiest cruise ports in Europe, and the biggest near Rome, it was a major international hub, servicing millions of passengers a year. And frankly, looking at the sheer size and number of the colossal white cruise ships and crowds of passengers disembarking like an endless stream of ants – that is, of course, if ants wore shorts and T-shirts – into the waiting coaches, minibuses and private cars to be whisked away for daytrips to Rome, it would appear that all those millions were arriving today.

'It's impossible,' sighed Maggie.

'He's got to be here somewhere,' reasoned Flick.

'We're never going to find him. It's like looking for a needle in a haystack.' Maggie shook her head hopelessly. 'We should have got here earlier.'

It was hard enough to locate the ship, let alone find one person, and having geared themselves up for The Big Confrontation, they were both feeling a massive disappointment.

'Don't be such a defeatist,' snapped Flick.

'I'm being a realist,' argued Maggie, but of course, she was the only one who would admit to it.

They'd got up at the crack of dawn. According to the map on their phone, the port was one hour and twenty minutes' drive away. However, after yesterday's stressful journey into the city, Maggie didn't want to repeat the experience of driving in Rome. She'd never played video games, but yesterday she'd felt like she was in the middle of one. Dodging cars, navigating one-way lanes, being attacked by scooters and cyclists that came at her from all sides, honking and yelling, while always being on the lookout for humans who liked to appear from nowhere and throw themselves in front of you, with dogs and children and prams in tow.

What fun! *Not*.

Her cortisol levels had gone through the roof, her nerves had been shot and, despite getting them both to their destination, alive and without any incident, she hadn't gone up any levels or scored any points. She'd just been bloody stressed and exhausted.

So instead they'd decided to take the train that morning. Apparently it took less than an hour and there were two trains an hour. They'd be there, waiting, as the cruise ship sailed into the docks and the passengers disembarked. See. Easy.

Except, when it comes to travelling in a foreign city, especially Italy, the words *apparently* and *easy* should always be used loosely. Because by the time Maggie and Flick had managed to find the correct train station, navigated the confusing ticket machine that was only in Italian – *Scusi, non capisco* – realized they'd read the timetable wrong, resisted arguing about whose fault that was, located the correct platform and got on the right train, they were already running late.

Add to this their discovery on arrival at Civitavecchia that it was a further twenty-minute walk to the port, and the queue for the cabs was a mile long, running late turned into them being *too late*.

'The cruise ship docked over an hour ago, most of the passengers will have disembarked and already gone off on their daytrips,' continued Maggie, digging a wad of tissues from her bag and dabbing her face.

It was still early but temperatures were already in the high twenties and the sun was blazing. Plus, they'd had to run from the station and while Flick had set off with ease, all ponytail swinging, she'd trailed behind, clutching her chest and cursing silently.

*Well, sorry, but no one told me we were going for a sprint, otherwise I'd have worn a bloody sports bra*, she'd cursed silently, because of course, it was Flick who'd read the timetable wrongly.

'He's probably on a coach, halfway to Rome at this point.'

Flick ignored her and carried on defiantly scanning the crowds, while Maggie fell silent and sat down in the shade, mopping up trickles of perspiration. These days she felt like her body was falling apart. Why did no one ever warn you that being in your late forties was like living in an old house that required constant maintenance to just stay habitable? With cracks appearing on a daily basis, a thermostat on the blink and a roof that was forever springing leaks.

Scooping into her sundress, she wiped up the drips between her boobs. Lovely.

And yet, despite her crushing disappointment, there was a relief that she wouldn't have to see Him looking like this, all red-faced and sweating. She'd got up early that morning, all anxious and apprehensive, to wash and style her hair, put on some make-up and shave her legs. Well, if you're going to see your ex, you want to look your best. Even if you don't have feelings for him any more; it was a pride thing.

At least that's what she told herself.

'Fuck.'

She snapped back to hear Flick curse and watch as she slumped next to her. She looked gutted.

'I think you're right. We've missed him,' she admitted.

It was one of those moments when there was no satisfaction to be gained from being proved right.

'We've totally messed up again.'

'No, we haven't.' Maggie realized that she'd been so consumed with how she would feel if she saw Him, that she'd lost sight of Flick's feelings.

'Yes, we have, we should have planned it better, got here earlier—'

'It's fine, don't worry. We'll find him,' she lied, in an attempt to reassure Flick.

'But how? He could be anywhere.'

'Rome isn't that big; it's actually quite compact.' Seeing Flick's disappointment, Maggie swung into encouragement mode. 'If he's gone on one of the sightseeing tours, it's likely he'll be visiting all the major touristy spots, like the Trevi Fountain or the Sistine Chapel or the Colosseum. We'll just have to do our own sightseeing. See if we can bump into him.'

*Bump into him.* Maggie couldn't quite believe she was saying this so casually, as if bumping into The Man Who Broke Her Heart was as inconsequential as bumping into an acquaintance.

'And if we don't?'

'We get to see some of the most incredible things in the world.'

Flick still looked defeated.

'I didn't think it would be this hard,' she finally admitted.
'Remember, we've got two weeks.'

Maggie seemed to have found herself in the strange position of the roles reversing, and she was now the one convincing Flick.

'I know, but . . .'

'But nothing.' Jumping to her feet, Maggie attempted to cheer her up. 'We can't feel sad, we're in Rome!'

'We're actually seventy kilometres north of Rome,' corrected Flick, heaving a sigh at what a wasted journey it had been, trekking all the way out there for nothing. She was annoyed with herself and the whole situation and for a moment her northern grit left her and all she wanted to do was sit and sulk.

But Maggie wouldn't let her. 'Come on,' she said, grabbing her hand.

'Where are we going?'

'I'm going to show you something that changed my life.'

# The Space In Between

The two fingertips are almost, but not quite, touching. With their muscular arms outstretched towards each other, there is still a small gap between Adam, lying completely naked on a grassy hill, and God, floating above him in the heavens, his pink cape billowing out behind him, surrounded by cherubs, as he reaches out to touch him.

'Why aren't their fingers touching?'

'I think it's more powerful that way, don't you?'

With their necks cricked right back, Flick and Maggie were standing in the middle of the Sistine Chapel, staring up at the frescoed ceiling and Michelangelo's *The Creation of Adam*.

'There's so many theories, about it being the moment humanity is created, before the spark of life jumps from God's fingertip to Adam's.'

'It reminds me of that moment in *E.T.*'

'*E.T?*'

'When he touches Elliott's finger.'

Maggie turned to look at Flick, and she blushed and pulled a face.

'Oh bollocks, did I just say something really stupid?'

And now she felt like a complete idiot. She knew Maggie had owned a gallery and was all knowledgeable when it came to art and lots of other middle-class things.

But if Maggie thought her a philistine, she didn't show it.

'No, not at all,' she said, shaking her head. 'Maybe Spielberg was inspired by Michelangelo?'

They both smiled, then turned back to staring at the ceiling, along with the rest of the tourists who were being herded through the chapel with slack-jawed awe.

'Why's God always got to be an old white man with a beard?' observed Flick. 'Why can't God be a woman? Or a person of colour? Or my age?'

'I think in the old days that was supposed to be the traditional image of wisdom.'

'What's changed? The world is still run by old white men. Pale, male and stale. Look at politics.'

'Do we have to?' Maggie groaned. 'I'd rather look at these beautiful frescos.'

But Flick was feeling irked now. That was the problem with all these old religious paintings. These famous masterpieces that were always painted by men hundreds of years before she was born, and which she was always being told were important – but why exactly? She could never see herself or her generation reflected in them, could never relate to their view of the world. OK, so these old guys might be good at art – hell, she could barely draw a stick figure so she was seriously impressed by their skill – but so what?

'They might be beautiful, but they don't mean anything to me.'

That caught Maggie's attention.

'I mean, this painting might have changed your life, but it's not going to change mine. For starters, I'm not religious.'

'It doesn't matter, you don't have to be. That's the wonderful thing about art. It's never just about the subject, but about how it makes *you* feel. It allows you to see things within yourself. Everyone sees something different. Everyone gets something different.'

'Like what?'

'Like in this painting there's a tension. It's this big, dramatic moment, and yet it's so breathtaking in its simplicity.'

Titling her head on one side, Flick squinted up at the ceiling. 'I don't see it.'

'Look at that gap, between the fingers. To me that symbolizes that space in between where life truly happens. Like that moment just before a storm breaks, before the lightning crackles and lights up the sky. When the atmosphere changes and you hold your breath and wait for it to begin.' Maggie gazed up at the ceiling.

'It's the split second before you walk onto a stage, or leap into the unknown, or make any big life decision. When you first meet someone and there's an electricity, an anticipation, a spark between you both. Before you kiss someone for the first time. That's when you feel most alive.'

Flick nodded and tried to think about Rory, but nothing came.

'All those things come flooding back when I look at this painting. It makes sense of all those emotions and feelings, in a way that I can't explain properly—' Maggie broke off, flushed. She suddenly felt rather embarrassed. 'Sorry, I went on a bit there, but does that make sense?'

Flick looked at her, curiously.

'If you love art so much, why did you drop out of art college?'

There was a pause and Maggie uttered four words.

'Because my brother died.'

How can four words describe the magnitude of such an event?

It wasn't the answer Flick was expecting and she turned to Maggie. 'Sorry, I had no idea.'

'It's OK. It's a long time ago now. Motorbike accident.'

Short phrases. Keep it simple. Even now, all those years

later, the feelings threatened to come flooding back. The knock on the door. The policeman. Her mother dropping to her knees, howling.

'My parents needed me.'

Her brother's bedroom, kept exactly the same as the moment he left to go back to university that term, never to return. The duvet cover freshly washed each week. The faded posters. The silence. The blame. Her parents' marriage never recovered. Had any of them? Funny, sweet, clever, reckless Charlie. He was twenty-one, just a year between them. Her big brother. Motorbike mad. Skinny-hipped, biker jacket, patchouli oil. Even now she couldn't smell that scent without thinking of him ruffling her hair and feeling the weight of his fingers on her scalp.

'So, have I changed your mind?' Forcing herself back to the present, Maggie turned to Flick. 'Does it mean anything now?'

Flick nodded. 'Yeah. Maybe.'

'OK, I'll take maybe.' Maggie smiled.

'And I admit, it's a very good painting.'

'I'm sure Michelangelo will be pleased to hear that.'

Flick grinned and went to pull out her iPhone from her bag to take a photo but was stopped by a security guard who spoke a torrent of Italian and waved his arms.

'No photos,' translated Maggie.

Flick quickly put away her phone.

'You'll just have to remember it. Like we used to do when we'd travel before smart phones and we'd run out of film for our cameras.' Catching Flick's horrified expression, Maggie laughed. 'Take a photo with your eyes instead.'

'Like how?'

'Like this.' Maggie stared up the ceiling without blinking. 'Imagine you're going to have to describe it later to someone, notice the colours, the use of light and perspective, then really focus on the details, look for the surprising ones, hidden away, like little jewels for you to uncover.' She paused, her eyes searching them out.

Flick watched her. Transfixed. She'd never looked at art like this before. No one had ever explained or talked about it in this way. On school trips, she would race around art galleries, bored. She remembered once when she'd gone to Paris and seen the *Mona Lisa*. She just remembered how *small* it was. How disappointing. Couldn't see what the fuss was all about.

But this. This was different.

'Think about how it makes you feel, how it inspires you or takes you out of yourself into something bigger; think of all the people who have stood where we're standing now and looked up, all their dreams and aspirations projecting onto the ceiling above.'

*All those people who won't ever get to stand here and see this*, thought Maggie, an image of her brother swimming before her eyes. And suddenly she was right back in that space in between. Between throwing her arms around his neck in a casual goodbye and the sound of his voice – '*Bye, Mags, see you in you the summer*' – and the knock on the door.

They were so close and yet so different. The joke in the family was that she got all the looks while he got all the brains, but that wasn't true. He got both. While she failed every A-level except art, Charlie excelled at school. He was studying medicine to be a doctor, just like their dad and grandfather before them. He would tease her that he was taking one for the team, so she could pursue her life as an artist. In the three decades since he died she'd been seeing art for him, looking at it with her eyes and wishing he could see it too.

'OK, I've got it.'

Flick's voice caused Maggie to zone back in.

'It's saved to the memory bank. Better than a photo.' She grinned. 'No carbon footprint from data storage using up all that energy in some building out in the desert somewhere.'

'Er, right, yes.'

Before coming on this trip, Maggie had thought doing your bit for the environment meant recycling and reusable carrier bags, but sometimes being with Flick felt like being on holiday with Greta Thunberg. It was both educational and terrifying. That said, Greta would have never got on a plane, so there you go.

'I don't think he's here. At least I can't see him.'

'Sorry, what?'

'Our romance fraudster. Theo C. Stratin. Or whatever he's calling himself now.'

Maggie snapped back to reality. It took a second to realize who she was talking about. For a moment there she'd been somewhere completely different. She'd forgotten all about Him.

But now she was sharply reminded.

'No . . . no, me neither.' She shook her head. She knew she should be disappointed, but it was hard to conjure up dismay when she was looking at something so beautiful. Art did that to her. That was its power. After Charlie first died, she used to visit art galleries and sit on the benches for hours and just stare at the paintings, as if somehow their beauty would cancel out the pain.

'We could try going to the Colosseum. Or the Pantheon . . . is that how you pronounce it?'

Flick was chattering away and had pulled out her phone and was reading from it again, despite the security guard circling.

'Yes . . . yes, we should . . .'

Maggie heard herself mumbling. She didn't want to think about Him. Not here. Not ever. She felt annoyed by his intrusion.

'You know, I'm reading this list of all the things to see in Rome. There's loads, he could be anywhere.'

And then immediately foolish. *Why do you think you're here, Maggie?* a voice in her head piped up, sharp and critical. *You're not on holiday, you silly idiot.* And now guilt and shame were piping up as well. *How could you fall for all his lies? Of course he never loved you. How could you be such a fool?*

'Oh look! He's posted a photo!'

'Sorry, what?' Dazed, Maggie zoned back. Her euphoria from looking at Michelangelo's ceiling had now disappeared and been replaced by self-loathing.

'Aha, I knew he wouldn't be able to resist. Look!'

Flick was waving her phone in her face and she had to step back slightly. Not just because she needed her glasses and couldn't focus, but because seeing him again, so sharply, was like a strike to her chest. She hated herself for letting him have that power over her. She felt so pathetic.

'That's the Colosseum,' she managed.

She felt almost woozy. Her heart was hammering and she had to steady herself against the railing.

'What's he doing? Trying to be the Gladiator?' scoffed Flick.

Maggie rolled her eyes, affecting the expression she knew was required of her, while trying to mentally pull herself back together.

'*Scusi!*'

And now the security guard had spotted the phone and was making his way over.

'Come on, let's get out of here,' said Maggie, grabbing Flick's elbow, 'before we get thrown out.'

# Birdy

Birdy Carmichael had been married six times. Or was it seven? She couldn't remember. She was in her seventies now and her memory wasn't as sharp as it used to be, not that she'd ever admit it. Or look it. Thanks to a facelift from one of the best cosmetic surgeons on the Upper West Side. Plus, to be honest, there were some husbands she'd rather forget.

So she used the rhyme, like Henry VIII.

What was it, now? Oh yes.

*Divorced, Beheaded, Died. Divorced, Beheaded, Survived.*

No, only six. She counted them off on her diamond-clad fingers. And none were beheaded, though she wouldn't mind. Still, instead of cutting off their heads, she'd taken them to the cleaner's. Well, that's what they'd said, according to their lawyers, though the language had a been a bit more . . . well, one could say fruity, another could say, 'You Fucking Cunt!'

That had been husband number four. But then he would say that, as she'd caught him in bed with his secretary, which was so much of a cliché, she couldn't be bothered getting annoyed about it. She'd simply changed the locks on their Park Avenue apartment, transferred all their stocks and mutual funds from their joint account and into her name (like she didn't keep a note of all the passwords? What was she? Some dumb-ass wife?) and called her lawyer.

Much better than cutting off anyone's head. Less messy.

Much better to cut off their balls instead.

So now here she was: single, on vacation and ready for romance. Sitting outside a glorious cafe in Rome, surrounded by designer shopping bags and enjoying her second negroni, she was watching the world go by. Europe in the summer was so much more fun than being back on the East Coast. Everyone she knew decamped from Manhattan to the Hamptons with their families; all beige-knit crews, white-washed houses and casual elegance. All those women trying to be Diane Keaton in *Something's Gotta Give*, only with fat, balding banker husbands who were nothing like Jack Nicholson.

Now, *he* was *something*.

Talk about dull. Not Jack, of course, he was a blast, but the Hamptons. Everyone was bored out of their fucking minds, but no one would say it. Casual elegance might look stylish in a magazine shoot, but in real life it was mind-numbing. Who cared about the size of their new kitchen island? Or their guest lists? Or that they were featured in *Architectural Digest* with their driftwood furniture and ocean neutrals?

As for walking barefoot on the beach collecting pebbles, it was totally overrated. The sand got fucking everywhere and she had flat arches.

Plus, frankly, the only rocks she was interested in were the ones on her fingers.

Birdy adjusted her oversized sunglasses and bestowed her gaze upon the piazza, which was teeming with tourists from all walks of life, locals going about their daily business, delivery vans, scooters, workmen. So much better being here amongst all the chaos of life. There's a reason people listened to ocean waves to send them to sleep. Being in the Hamptons was like being in a coma.

She stirred the ice in her drink; it made that magical clinking sound against the glass, which just had to be one of the most wonderful sounds ever. She once dated a guy who said one of the best sounds was morning birdsong. He used to rise at the crack of dawn to stand in one of those wooden huts with his binoculars. Total opposites. She liked to get up late and her favourite sound was champagne corks popping. Or live music in a late-night, underground jazz club in Paris. Or the cabin crew instructing her to 'Turn left, ma'am' as she boarded an aeroplane.

No, they were not a match made in heaven. Which was where he was now, God bless his soul. He ended up being husband number three, but they were only married a few months before he died. Apparently the sight of a Kirtland's warbler, one of the rarest songbirds in North America, got him so excited it caused a massive heart attack. And they say cigarettes and alcohol kill you. Birdwatching could be deadly.

Think about that when you're hanging your fat balls in the garden.

Birdy removed her straw and took a sip of her negroni. Always remember: sip, not suck. At least when it came to drinks. Straws should be illegal. Everyone went on about the environmental damage they caused, but did you have any idea the damage they do to your lips? All that puckering up made your mouth look like a cat's ass. It would cost you thousands in filler to repair the damage to your cupid's bow and you needed someone skilled with a needle. Mouths were tricky. Manhattan was filled with women with bloated, overfilled trout pouts pretending they looked different because they'd just got a new lipstick.

Yeah right. It was like when celebrities shared their beauty secrets and it was always 'Drink lots water and get eight hours' sleep', and never the number of their surgeon.

No, always sip. Much better, much sexier too.

*Woah, who was that?*

In the middle of sipping her drink, she clocked a young Italian priest walking past. He threw her a smile and she tipped her sunglasses onto her nose, raised an eyebrow and smiled back. See, that's why she loved Europe. Growing up in the US, she'd spent her entire teenage years desperate to be twenty-five – then the next fifty being told she had to remain looking twenty-five to be attractive.

It was such bullshit. European men appreciated women of all ages. They found them sexy and sophisticated and desirable. You could be mature *and* sexy. Even to men of the cloth.

She thought about her girlfriends back home with their brood of grandchildren, enjoying sticky-fingered kisses and finger painting while their husbands played golf and eyed up the twenty-something nanny. No thanks. Give her a hot priest any day.

'Sorry, excuse me, I mean, *scusi*, are these seats taken?'

Hearing a British accent, she turned to see a frazzled-looking woman hovering beside her table. Her face was flushed with the heat and she was wearing a shapeless linen sundress, one of those that completely hide your figure for the sake of being comfortable. Why did women do that? Since when was looking good about being comfortable?

And she must only be in her forties too, thought Birdy, her gaze sweeping over her and noticing those ugly sandals that all these women wore these days, like something out of Woodstock. No, you needed height. A wedge, preferably, with these cobbles. Hers were from Gucci and added four inches.

Birdy adjusted her own silk wrap dress that clung in all the right places and crossed her legs.

'Sure, honey, take them, they're all yours.' She smiled graciously, and as the woman moved to sit down she spotted the younger woman standing behind her. That must be her daughter, though they looked nothing alike.

'Oh, thank you *so much*!'

The frazzled forty-something collapsed in a chair with a loud sigh – and that was another thing, making all those weird noises when you got up or sat down really aged you – while the younger one slipped silently onto the seat beside her. Now, she was adorable. All flicky black eyeliner, short bangs and charming outfit. Cute as a button. Something about her reminded her of Audrey Hepburn in *Roman Holiday*. And the boys liked her, she noted, watching the waiters' eyes swerving over like boomerangs.

Birdy reapplied her lipstick, showed a bit more cleavage and recrossed her legs.

'It's so kind of you to let us share your table, it's just so busy everywhere, all the cafes and restaurants are full and we couldn't find anywhere to sit . . . and we're exhausted!'

The older woman was talking and fanning herself with both hands and now, up close, Birdy noticed she was actually quite attractive. But those freckles! Had she never heard of SPF and lasers? Pretty face, though; lovely eyes and good hair, a natural strawberry blonde by the looks of things, though she needed to do something with those roots.

Or maybe she was one of those women she'd been reading about recently, all those magazine articles about women who were embracing going grey. Embracing! They gave themselves all kinds of names like Silver Warriors or Gunmetal Gals, which were supposed to sound liberating but all she could think was *Over my dead body*.

Birdy stirred her ice cubes and resisted the urge to give the older woman some advice. She could really do something with herself. Nothing a bit of red lipstick and a good colourist and blow-dry wouldn't solve.

'We've been sightseeing all day!'

'Maggie's been giving me the grand tour!'

Maggie, not Mom. So that wasn't her daughter, thought Birdy, as the younger woman spoke.

'We must have walked miles.'

'In this heat?' Birdy raised an eyebrow. Well, as best she could. She'd had Botox just before the trip. 'Is that wise?'

'We had a lot of places to visit.'

'The Colosseum, the Pantheon, the Trevi Fountain . . .' The younger woman was ticking them off on her fingers.

'And did you find what you were looking for?'

It was meant to be tongue in cheek, a gentle tease, so she was surprised when she saw the look that passed between the two women. As if she'd touched a nerve. She couldn't place it; they seemed nervous, guilty – but what on earth could these two have to hide? The older one especially. She looked so *unassuming*.

'Um . . . not really.'

'We saw lots, but there's so much to see, you can't do it in one day.'

Birdy waved a dismissive hand. 'Oh, I don't bother with all that, you can see all the sights you want to see sitting right here. Once you've seen one fusty old church, you've seen them all.'

She smiled broadly and while the older woman looked unsure, the younger girl let out a hoot of laughter.

'Forgive me. I'm forgetting my manners. My Southern mama would kill me.' She extended a hand in greeting. 'I'm Birdy with a "y".'

There were a couple of blank expressions.

'As opposed to "ie",' she added, in explanation. 'No one wants "die" at the end of their name, cuts a little close to the bone at my age, don't you think?'

## SO, I MET THIS GUY . . .

'Hi, I'm Flick . . . with a "k",' added Flick, smiling.

'I can see you and me are going to get on just fine.' She gave a wink.

'Maggie – nothing so exotic, I'm afraid.'

'I disagree; doesn't it have Greek origins meaning pearl?' Birdy smiled. 'And next to diamonds, pearls are my weakness. Something I share with the great, late Elizabeth Taylor. La Peregrina, now *that* was some pearl.'

'Oh, I didn't know. I'd always thought Margaret was quite boring, not that anyone ever called me Margaret. I've always been Maggie, or Mags . . .'

But Birdy was gesturing to the waiter and not listening.

'What are you having?'

'Just sparkling water and maybe a bite to eat—'

'Another negroni, and two more for the ladies.'

'Oh, no, we couldn't possibly—'

'Relax. You're in Italy. Embrace *la dolce vita*.'

'I'm afraid I don't speak Italian,' confessed Flick with a shrug.

'It means the sweet life,' translated Maggie, helpfully.

'It means exactly what we're doing right now, sugar,' smiled Birdy, her eyes twinkling. 'To pause and appreciate the sweet moments. To not stress. To chat to strangers.'

The waiter brought menus and a breadbasket. Birdy watched with astonishment as both women dived upon it. Carbs hadn't passed her lips since 1972.

'You have amazing jewellery.'

She turned back to see the young girl looking at her rings, fascinated.

'Why, thank you. They're not real.'

'They're not?'

'Oh no.' Birdy laughed. 'In this town? I'd be a fool! What with all the pickpockets. No, the real diamonds are in the safe at home in New York. Trust me, no one can tell the difference.'

'Wow.'

The waiter came and took their food orders.

'Would you care to join us for something to eat?' asked Maggie.

'Thank you, but I prefer a liquid lunch.' She raised her almost empty glass as proof. 'Though it's a little too late for that,' she said, noticing the time on her wristwatch, a gift from an old *amour*, who'd collected expensive watches and taught her to be quite the expert when it came to timepieces. She'd wanted a Patek Philippe, so had been somewhat disappointed to open the box and discover it was your basic Cartier. *Cheap fucker*.

'Ah, and there's my car, right on time.' She smiled as a sleek black Mercedes pulled up. 'Apologies, but I must go.'

Reaching into her Chanel handbag, she drew out a wad of euros and placed them on the table before standing up.

'Well, my darlings, wonderful to meet you. Enjoy the rest of your trip.'

And waving farewell, she sashayed across the cobbles to where her driver was holding open the door, waiting to take her bags, and slid onto the cool, air-conditioned leather upholstery, where she kicked off her wedges. They didn't call them killer heels for nothing. Her feet were fucking killing her. Well, no one ever said looking this good didn't come at a price.

But then, didn't everything?

# The Amalfi Coast

*Day Four*

*Ten more days to go*

# The Next Morning

'OK, so where are we headed? Where's our next stop?'

'Positano, on the Amalfi Coast.'

'And how long's the drive?'

'Four hours without traffic. *According to my phone*,' added Flick, looking slightly sheepish and wanting to quickly shift any blame ahead of today's drive. On their last car journey, her navigational skills had left much to be desired, resulting in it taking far longer than first thought. And Maggie nearly killing her.

But if she was expecting a sarcastic reply, she was surprised when Maggie turned the ignition and announced, 'Driving the Amalfi Coast's always been on my bucket list.'

'You have a bucket list?'

'Yes, don't you?'

'No, I don't believe in them. It's always things like jumping out of planes or swimming with dolphins. Can't we leave the poor dolphins alone? I'm sure they don't want to swim with us idiots.'

'Well, aren't you a ray of sunshine this morning?'

Flick caught herself at Maggie's quip, but doubled down.

'It just all feels like too much pressure. What happens when you tick them all off? Do you die? And what happens if you don't? Do you spend your life in regret?'

'I think you might be overthinking it.'

Pulling out into traffic, Maggie followed signs for the

autoroute while Flick fell silent at the reminder that most people didn't think like her and fidgeted with her phone. She'd woken up to a flurry of drunken texts from Rory and was feeling stressed. He'd been out last night, celebrating the birthday of one of his work colleagues, and while his messages had been sweet and loving at the beginning of the evening, saying how much he missed her, complete with love heart emojis, his mood had gradually darkened as the evening wore on and more alcohol was consumed.

'Well, anyway, it's supposed to be one of the most beautiful drives in the world,' continued Maggie, as they headed out of the city. 'And the most romantic.'

Flick felt suddenly bad and threw her a look of sympathy. 'Sorry.'

'What for?'

'Being with me instead of some guy.'

'Don't be silly.'

'I'm guessing this isn't exactly how you imagined it was going to be.'

'The story of my life,' shrugged Maggie and the two women exchanged glances.

'We'll just have to make our own romance,' teased Flick.

'Why do men have the word bromance but there isn't a word for female friendship?'

'Womance?'

Maggie laughed. 'I bet Birdy would know a good word.'

'Oh, yes, wasn't she great?'

'And so generous to pick up our bill. I couldn't believe it when the waiter told us she'd paid ours as well after she'd left.'

'I think she must have been really rich. Not sure I believed the stories of the diamonds, they looked real to me. And did you see all those designer shopping bags? She must have spent a fortune!'

'Do you think she was on holiday on her own?'

'I don't know, but I do know I like negronis now. I'm going to have another one when we get to Positano,' grinned Flick.

'OK, but we've got a long drive first.'

'Great. It's a good chance to carry on with your story.'

'I can't remember, where did I leave off?'

'When he walked into your art gallery and you first met him.'

'Oh yes . . .' Maggie nodded, her mind flicking back as the road stretched ahead. 'That was the day that changed everything.'

# Maggie

Love-bombing, isn't that what they call it?

When someone sweeps you off your feet and showers you with gifts and affection and all their attention?

Or is it just plain old-fashioned falling in love?

Those whirlwind first weeks when two people meet and you can't get enough of each other. Every minute spent texting, talking, being together. Discovering you share the same sense of humour, dreams and desires. When the world both shrinks and expands with possibility and it's like catching a wave.

The sudden feeling of being alive. Really alive.

Exhilarating. Intoxicating. Can't-catch-your-breath alive.

It all happened so quickly. So unexpectedly. I wasn't looking for love; I was grieving. But then Theo literally walked into my gallery and my life and everything changed. I'd been in such a dark place and now I was bathed in sunlight.

Three months later, he suggested we move in together.

'It makes sense.'

'What, do you mean financially?'

'No, not financially,' he frowns. 'Do you really think I'm so unromantic?'

'Of course not, silly.' I laugh, and ruffle his hair as he pouts in his striped butcher's pinny. 'You're the King of Romance.'

'Which makes you my Queen,' he replies with mock-theatrics, picking up a tea towel off my kitchen countertop and performing an over-exaggerated royal bow as I stop stirring the pan to hoot with laughter.

It's a Saturday evening and we're cooking dinner together in my flat, the radio tuned to his favourite Classic FM. This is how I spend my weekends now. Him in my pinny, me with a glass of wine, moving in synchronicity around my kitchen island, chopping vegetables, peeling garlic, stealing kisses as my le Creuset pans provide an orchestra of aromas. Even they look happy now, their bright orange faces cheerfully bubbling and steaming and sizzling. Gone are the days of a bag of Kettle Chips and hummus for one on the sofa with just my ginger tomcat George for company. Now it's a scene of cosy domestic bliss. The kind you want to hate unless you're the one luxuriating in it.

We're so comfortable with each other. Like we've known each other for ever. I can't remember a time before he was here – in my flat, in my kitchen, in my bed. Even my cat loves him. I watch as George rubs himself against Theo's legs, purring.

'I want us to move in together because when you know you want to spend the rest of your life with someone, why wait?' Taking the bottle of red wine, he tops up our glasses. 'It's like the line from *When Harry Met Sally*.'

The breath catches at the back of my throat. Not only is that one of my favourite films, but did he just say he wants to spend the rest of his life with me? I take a large gulp of wine, feeling suddenly overwhelmed.

'I love you.'

He strokes the side of my face, lifts my chin towards his and kisses me.

'I love you, too.'

We've been telling each other we love each other for the last few weeks now. He said it first, but I was quick to follow. It feels so natural. As if it was meant to be. Which sounds crazy, as I don't believe in fate. And yet there's something about Theo that might make me change my mind.

'It's just . . .'

'Just what?'

Still, there's a little part of me that can't let go and embrace what's unfolding between us. The part of me that's experienced heartbreak and heartache: the flings that went nowhere, the relationships that failed, a starter marriage in my twenties that lasted six weeks and should never have happened. The part of me that's loved deeply only to discover those feelings weren't returned; that's been disappointed and rejected and stood staring into the mirror wondering *why not me?* The part of me that's spent my whole life looking for exactly this connection and yet, now I've found it, is holding back, protecting myself, not quite believing I'm worthy of this love.

Who frankly is shit scared and looking for reasons why it can't be true.

'If we move in together, I want it to be for the right reasons.'

'Meaning?'

'I don't want it to be a way to save money.'

As soon as I speak, I regret it – he looks so offended.

'Is this because I borrowed a thousand pounds to pay the storage company?' he accuses. 'I paid you straight back, didn't I?'

'Yes, of course, I didn't mean—'

'Maggie, please. I've just been having a little cash flow problem because it's taking so long to get the funds from the sale of my house in LA. The whole US system is so different to over here. Have you any idea how many emails I've been firing off to the realtor? I've been giving him hell!'

Slamming down his wine glass, he shakes his head. He looks so upset and furious, and I feel horribly guilty. I should never have said anything.

'I know, you said it's been difficult . . .'

I try stroking his arm, but he moves away, his jaw set. Awkwardly, I return to the stove to attend the orchestra of pans.

'It's hard enough not being able to access the funds yet – but having to ask the woman you love if you can borrow money? It's embarrassing frankly.'

'I'm sorry, I didn't mean to embarrass you.'

But still he's refusing to look at me and is staring down at his feet, the muscle in the side of his jaw twitching. The atmosphere has changed and I kick myself. We were having such a nice time, cooking pasta, making up our own recipe, in our little bubble, and now it's all spoiled.

For a moment I fear he might go, that the evening is ruined and then –

'Look at you, taking care of me. I want to take care of you.' Coming up behind me, he puts his arms around my waist. 'I want to be the one looking after you.'

I feel my body relax and relief floods through me. Just as quickly as his mood blew up, it's gone again, like clouds moving quickly across the sun. And now I'm back in the sunlight, bathed in his rays of sunshine and adoration.

'Are you for real?' I tease.

'Pinch me.' He laughs as I pinch him. 'See.'

I laugh and fall back into his arms.

'And we spend all our time together; it doesn't make sense me renting my own flat.'

'I still can't believe you haven't invited me over there.'

'Because it's still filled with boxes and the rest is still in storage. I never got round to unpacking. I meant to, but then I went to look for something to put on the walls and got a little distracted.'

I smile, flattered.

'Am I distracting?' I flirt.

He raises an eyebrow. 'Very.'

'Plus, I've been away a lot with work these last couple of months, scouting locations for this new movie.'

'I'm not sure I'd call flying all over the world visiting exotic locations for film shoots work,' I tease, and he laughs. 'I still can't believe someone gets paid to do that. Why did the career's teacher never tell me about that job?'

'Trust me, it's not as glamorous as it sounds. The jetlag is a killer. Not to mention, I hate leaving you.'

It's true. Every time he packs a bag and leaves for the airport he insists he doesn't want to go, that he misses me already and wishes he could stay.

'It was different before, when I was married. Things were so bad at home, I'd relish going away, being able to leave, but not now. Now it kills me to even tear myself away to grate the parmesan.'

He nuzzles his face against my neck and I laugh, feeling his hot breath, and kiss his cheek before he makes his way across the kitchen to my large double fridge.

At first, when he went away, I suggested we video-call, but he was on some tiny island in Indonesia and the time difference made it too difficult, plus often he was out scouting remote locations and the WiFi was non-existent, so instead we had to make do with texts.

Though later he confessed he preferred it that way. 'Seeing you will just make me miss you more. Make me realize how far away I am. Let's just text. Or leave voice messages. I like hearing your voice last thing at night or first thing in the morning when I wake up.' So now we leave each other voice messages and I listen to them when I'm in bed before I turn out the light or pull back the curtains. It's amazing how close you can feel to someone who's far away.

'And then of course I've been visiting Mum,' he says from across the kitchen.

I nod sympathetically. 'I'd like to meet her one day.'

'She'd love you. It's just . . .'

I turn to see his face clouding and I stop stirring and go over to give him a hug.

'What?'

His eyes water. 'I'd hate you to see her like this. She's just a shell of who she was. She'd hate anyone to see her like this.'

I nod sympathetically.

'I know, it was like that with Dad at the end in the hospice. Cancer really does a number on you.'

'Try dementia.'

I stroke his arm supportively. Just last week they'd got the diagnosis he was dreading. Theo's mum has dementia and is probably going to have to move into a residential care home. He's been finding it difficult. He's had so much emotional upheaval in recent years. There was me thinking I was in a vulnerable place when I met him, but he was too. Both of us were grieving the loss of our old lives; I'd lost Dad, but he'd gone through a divorce and moved across an ocean. Two lost and lonely souls, looking for love and hoping to start over. We were so lucky to find each other.

'Which is why we've got to grab happiness when we find it,' he says, grabbing me to prove his point. 'Live life like there's no tomorrow. We're not getting any younger.'

'Is this just your excuse to open another bottle of red,' I laugh, but he looks hurt.

'Don't make fun of me, Mags.'

'Oh love, I'm sorry. I wasn't . . . I didn't mean . . .'

Releasing me, he reaches into the fridge for the parmesan, then opens a cupboard and pulls out a grater. I watch him, allowing myself to feel a small, delicious moment of contentment. He knows where all my ingredients are. Where my spoons go and where I keep my cheese grater. There's something so basic about all of that, so comfortable, and I feel a rush of love. Back in my twenties I craved adventure and excitement, but now in my forties the domestic thrill of someone knowing where my kitchen utensils go is what I want.

'I was just joking, being light-hearted; cancer and dementia are pretty depressing.'

'But I'm being serious. There are no guarantees and life is short.'

My eyes meet his.

'Come on, let's get a place together, let's move in together.'

'Seriously?'

'I've never been more serious about anything.'

'But shouldn't we move a bit slower? I mean, it's all moving so fast.'

'What are we waiting for? We're both grown-ups. Neither of us has kids. We're footloose and fancy free!'

I pause. Trying to be sensible, but his enthusiasm is infectious and the possibility of what this might become is bubbling beneath the surface, threatening to overwhelm me. And this time it's in a good way.

'We could get something amazing together if we pool our money. You could sell this place, I've got the money for the house sale in LA once all the paperwork's done, we could buy a place in the country—'

'The country?'

'Get some animals . . . a couple of donkeys, some chickens . . .'

'Since when did you want chickens?'

He's getting all excited now, twirling me around the kitchen, and I'm laughing.

'Imagine it, just you and me against the whole world.'

But I don't need to be told, I am imagining it, though I can hardly believe it. Just a few short months ago I was at my lowest, feeling lonely and still grieving Dad. Life seemed hopeless, pointless, and now look. It's unbelievable how one person can turn it all around.

'But the flat's part of the gallery, I won't want to sell it.'

As I speak I see his mood dip, like when the wind suddenly goes out of a boat's sails, his face crushed.

'But I can remortgage,' I suggest quickly.

'No, it's OK. Forget I mentioned it.'

'No, no, but I want to.' I'm insistent now. 'I can remortgage and that way I can keep the gallery and rent out the flat. If we need more money, I can even take out a business loan.'

'You don't have to. Seriously. It's not about the money.'

'I want to be in this all the way. Fifty-fifty. You and me.' I'm powered up now, absolutely convinced. 'I want to do this. You're right. What am I so scared of?'

'Allowing someone to love you, allowing yourself to be loved,' he says.

And just like that, it floors me. For so long I've been protecting myself. Ever since my brother died, I've been building a wall around my heart. Looking after myself, never relying on anyone, determined that no one could ever hurt me, or let me down, or leave me. My eyes blink back tears. The grief. It was so overwhelming. I felt like I was drowning. I thought I'd never recover from the loss of Charlie, we were so close, but I did, and I've been doing everything myself, trying to remain in control. But then my dad died and I realized just how lonely I was. How exhausted I was of being alone. And now here's this man asking me to let down those barriers, to allow myself to be vulnerable, to let him in, to let myself be loved.

I start crying then, and he takes me in his arms. The pasta pan starts to bubble and boils over. Spilling water all over the stainless-steel hob. But he doesn't let me go. He's never going to let me go. Everything that I've been looking for my whole life and that I never thought I'd find is here with this man.

'I love you,' he whispers over and over. 'I love you.'

I don't know how long we stay like this but his eyes never leave mine, and when he asks, it feels inevitable.

'Marry me, Maggie.'

# Twists and Turns

You've got to hand it to the younger generation. They think they know everything. Which is both incredibly annoying and, of course, absolute nonsense. They haven't *done* anything to *know* anything. With age comes wisdom and all that. Except sometimes, thought Maggie with irritation, it turns out the most annoying thing is they're actually right.

'I can't believe this was on my bucket list! Romantic? It's a bloody nightmare!'

After being stuck for the last twenty minutes behind four coaches, not being able to move an inch forward or backwards, Maggie was flopped in the driver's seat, fanning herself with her sunhat and fast regretting their decision to drive the Amalfi Coast.

OK, so the scenery was stunning, with dramatic cliffs and colourful coastal towns, but *hello?* Who can look at the scenery when you're too busy white-knuckling the steering wheel as the road itself is frankly terrifying?

Filled with blind turns, giant buses and hundreds of motorcycles weaving in and out of traffic, she'd spent the last couple of hours narrowly missing hitting several vehicles that had veered over the centre line. Meanwhile with all the twists and turns it had been a nauseating ride for poor Flick, who had chosen that moment in her life to discover she suffered from motion sickness and had spent most of the journey chucking up in a plastic bag.

Ah, the romance.

'You were right. Bucket lists are ridiculous things. I'm throwing mine away!'

'You mean, you actually have one written down?'

Hanging outside the window, trying to get some air, Flick sounded incredulous.

Choosing to ignore her, Maggie swigged the last of the water from her bottle. The sun was beating down and she pulled back the sun visor and tried to angle it to shade her. It was hopeless. They'd had to turn off the engine as the petrol gauge was running dangerously low, and with it the air conditioning, which they'd managed to get working again. Even with the windows open it was about a hundred degrees. A hot blast of air blew in.

'And now I need to pee.'

That's the thing about road trips, you get *very* close, *very* quickly.

'*Again?*'

'I can't help it; my doctor says it's the perimenopause.'

From outside the car, Flick pulled a face. 'Is it contagious?'

'Ha ha, very funny.'

'Oh look, we're moving.'

Ahead the stuck coaches suddenly belched fumes of exhaust and forced themselves through the tiny gap, like corks popping from a bottle. Immediately there was an impatient honking from behind. Literally, not a second had passed and there was Mr Middle-aged Sportscar, blasting his horn. Turning the ignition, Maggie felt a sudden rage.

'Oh, go fuck yourself,' she cursed, giving him the finger in the rear-view whilst Flick stared at her in utter astonishment.

The horn promptly went silent.

'Woah, Maggie, I've never seen you get angry! You should do it more often, it suits you.'

'It's not me, it's the perimenopause,' she protested, embarrassed by her outburst. That was *so* unlike her.

'Well, in that case I hope it *is* contagious,' said Flick and they both turned to each other and started laughing.

They finally arrived in Positano much later than they'd intended, having totally underestimated the amount of traffic and lack of anywhere to park. And with only a couple of hours until the cruise ship was due to set sail.

'Hang on. Where's the ship?'

As they both climbed out of the sweltering Fiat, which they'd managed to wedge into a tiny spot at the side of the road, Maggie pointed to the small harbour where only a couple of small white sailboats were bobbing on the turquoise waters.

'I don't see it! Have we missed it?'

'No, it's too big to dock here. It says Amalfi/Positano on the itinerary, but I think they anchor off Amalfi and use tenders and local boats to bring the passengers to Positano—' Flick broke off, looking a little doubtful.

'You *think*?'

'Well, according to the internet forums.'

Maggie felt a beat of frustration. 'You mean, we've driven all this way and you're not even sure where the cruise ship is stopping?'

'I'm a reporter, not a cruise ship expert!' snapped Flick.

The two women bristled. The heat and tiredness were getting to them both.

'And, anyway, after this the next stop is Sicily and that was too far to drive in one day, so we had no choice but to break the journey.'

There was a beat as they stood side by side in the shade, looking out across the view of the glittering Mediterranean.

Spotless blue skies stretched out before them. Positano was a chic resort town perched on a cliff; ice-cream-coloured houses clung to the hillsides together with splashes of bright pink and purple bougainvillea. The scent of jasmine wafted towards them on the warm breeze, along with the soft sounds of lilting music.

It felt totally different to Rome, with its urban chaos, grand piazzas and colossal ancient buildings around every narrow, cobblestoned corner. Here everything felt as if it had slowed right down. As if Italy had just taken a long exhale, ordered itself an aperitif and was taking in the sea view.

'I suppose there are worse places to spend a night,' shrugged Maggie, giving a mock grimace.

'Oh, I don't know, it's pretty awful.' Flick wrinkled her nose, playing along. 'But I guess it'll have to do.'

See, that was the thing. On paper they really shouldn't get along. They were too different. And yet that's the problem with having the same sense of humour. It's impossible not to.

Which was lucky when it came to checking into their hotel.

Being peak season, everything had already been booked, apart from one slightly cheesy-looking hotel Flick had found online, and all it had left was a suite. Thankfully they had their winnings to pay for it – suites on the Amalfi Coast in summer are *not* cheap – but it was only when they were shown to their room and discovered towels shaped like swans and a bed strewn with rose petals that they realized they were in the honeymoon suite.

'What was that you were saying about making our own romance?' grinned Flick, brushing the petals off the eiderdown.

'Be careful what you wish for,' laughed Maggie, flopping down on the double bed.

'Hey, that's my side.'

'Is it? Sorry.'

'Don't be daft, I'm only joking.'

As they lay side by side, relieved to be horizontal, in an air-conditioned room, they both dug out their phones. Maggie's was turned off. She didn't want the council ringing her about being in breach of planning and the enforcement notice – she had enough on her plate right now – but she lived in hope of receiving a message about George the missing cat. Turning it back on, there were several voicemails from a number which she was pretty sure was from the local council, plus three WhatsApps from George the human.

*Ping.*

> Hey babe, how was Monte Carlo?

*Ping.*

> You haven't replied. Where are you? Did you find The Wanker?

*Ping.*

> Babe! The ticks aren't going blue. WHAT'S GOING ON??!!!

Maggie wasn't sure how to reply.

Meanwhile Flick was reading aloud the activities from the cruise ship, along with its itinerary. It was all a bit of a long shot. They'd missed him in Rome, despite hitting all the major tourist spots and Flick showing everyone a photo of him on her phone, as if they were looking for a missing person, which technically she supposed they were. The chances of finding him here were slim. Even with Flick's forensic approach to his social media.

'OK, so he hasn't posted any photos, but someone's tagged him in their stories.'

'Great!'

Maggie had no idea if this was great or not. In fact, to be honest, she found it all a bit bewildering. OK, so she'd stalked a few ex-boyfriends on Facebook, who hadn't? But this was on a whole other level and involved hours spent scrutinizing stories and reels, cross-referencing posts, following the breadcrumbs of hashtags to various other accounts and apps until you ended up in a world of TikTok videos with strangers challenging you to do all kinds of weird and crazy things with loud music that drove you bananas.

(*Confession*: she still didn't know exactly what a reel was and had never done a TikTok challenge, but was too embarrassed to admit this to Flick for fear of looking like an old person.)

Watching Flick now poring over her phone, fingers flying as she scrolled through different screens, Maggie was reminded of an article she'd once read about MI5 wanting to recruit more women to be intelligence officers as they were more intuitive. Forget journalism, Flick should have been a spy.

'The photo's taken from the deck of the ship. It's a group shot.' Flick pinched the screen with her fingers. 'Problem is, I can't see him in the photo, so that doesn't make sense.'

'Maybe he took it?' suggested Maggie, randomly.

'Oh, well done!' Flick looked at her, like she'd just cracked a code. 'Why didn't I think of that?'

'And the view in the background definitely looks like the Amalfi Coast,' Maggie continued, peering over Flick's shoulder. 'I recognize that lighthouse, we drove past it.' She felt quite pleased with herself. So what if she'd never done a TikTok challenge? She wasn't completely useless.

'I don't remember seeing any lighthouse.'

'That's because you were too busy throwing up in a sick bag.'

'Oh God, don't remind me.' Flick grimaced. She felt nauseous just thinking about it. 'Only problem is it was posted four hours ago.'

'By who?'

'Technically, it's by *whom*.'

'Are you going to give me a grammar lesson or are we going to try to find him?'

'It's an old couple. Judging by the wedding photos they posted last week I'd say they were on honeymoon.' Flick's face crumpled into a smile. 'Aw, sweet. Later-life love.'

Maggie looked at the photos. They looked like they were in their early fifties. Is this what later-life love looked like? Fifty used to seem so far away and now it was just around the corner. Literally, days away. How did that happen?

Flick's voice pulled her back from the edge of that particular rabbit-hole. 'At least he can't be trying to romance scam a couple of honeymooners.'

'But where is he?'

'I don't know. The rest of their stories are a lot of kissing selfies.' Flick pulled a face at the horror of old people fancying each other and quickly swiped past their page. 'But we're on the right track, we're going to bump into him at some point.'

'Are we, though?'

'It's bound to happen if we keep going to the same places. It's the law of averages. I mean, I'm forever bumping into my weird neighbour at my local supermarket. In fact, it can be a bit annoying.'

'The Amalfi Coast is a bit different to your local Tesco.'

'You know what I mean.'

Maggie still wasn't convinced, but she'd committed to the road trip. For reasons that were less about confronting her past and more about wanting to avoid her future. What did she have to go back to? A missing cat, torrential rain and an eviction? Her home was a mouldy caravan and, judging by the number of voicemails from the council, which she was putting off listening to, she wasn't even going to have that for much longer.

Unless by some miracle she managed to turn things around and get back her life savings, she was going to be homeless. And then what?

Maggie couldn't even face thinking about it and being here meant she didn't have to. Being here felt like running away. She turned to look out of the open window, to gaze at the glittering Mediterranean on the horizon, to breathe in the warm lemon-scented breeze and lie on clean sheets in dappled sunlight. To feel a million miles away from a wet muddy field and the mess of her life.

Frankly, running away felt pretty good right now and, feeling sleepy after the long drive, she let her eyes close, feeling herself drift, until Flick's voice suddenly jolted her awake.

'Oh my God! *He's here!*'

# The Fraudster

The boats were at the shoreline, waiting for the crowds of passengers to embark. Being the height of summer, there were multiple cruises in town, and it was exceptionally busy. Tour guides, their brightly coloured umbrellas held aloft, were herding queues of people on board, where they would be ferried to Amalfi, before being tendered back to the giant cruise liners anchored offshore.

Only, he didn't queue. Never had. Never would.

In life there were two kinds of people: those who got in line, obediently waited their turn, allowed others to tell them what to do and when they could do it. And those who pushed to the front and broke all the rules. Who didn't wait for permission. Who stuck two fingers up at authority, whether it was some bouncer at an Essex nightclub, a British copper in a uniform or an Italian tour guide with a bright umbrella.

He was the second kind. You weren't ever going to see him standing obediently in line like some loser. Sod that. He didn't wait around for someone to give him permission to have what he wanted. He used his wits and he took it. And right now, that was getting on one of those boats and getting a ride back to the cruise ship.

'*Scusi* . . . *scusi* . . .' Waving his hand, he attempted to move past hordes of people waiting in line and motioned to the tour guide ahead. As she spotted him, he flashed her a grateful – and his most charming – smile.

'Please. Wait in line,' she instructed, gesturing for him to go to the back as several people tutted and muttered at him for pushing in.

A queue-jumper. Was there anything worse?

His smile froze, but only ever so slightly.

'I'm afraid it's something of a medical emergency.'

He lowered his voice so people didn't overhear. Something so private, he didn't want everyone knowing, but he mustn't have lowered it enough – several passengers in the queue turned round to look at him, their initial expressions of annoyance filled with concern at the mention of a medical emergency.

Oh dear. What a pity. That was never his intention at all.

The crowds parted, allowing him through, and he strode to the front, tipping his Panama and flashing apologetic smiles to the other passengers. Several women smiled back, charmed by this dark, handsome stranger.

He had a gift. A seductiveness. He'd felt it from a young age. Some could play the piano, others were good at sport, but his talent was his ability to make people feel special, to get what he wanted, to manipulate. 'A charmer,' that's what the teachers used to write on his school reports. Not that anyone ever read them, his mum was always too wasted, high on drink and drugs with some random bloke who used to beat him black and blue. That's when he had to toughen up and get wise.

'What's wrong? Is everything OK?'

The tour guide greeted him impatiently. He knew what she was thinking. He looked perfectly healthy, like there was nothing wrong with him. And she'd be correct of course, there was nothing wrong with him, he was as a fit as a fiddle, but when did the truth ever need to get in the way?

She looked circumspect as he began explaining.

'I'm a diabetic and I totally forgot to bring my insulin with me. I desperately need to get back to the ship.'

His granddad had Type 1 diabetes, so he knew all about it. The need for careful monitoring of blood sugar and injections. Not that it stopped him living a long and healthy life before retiring to Florida and playing golf all day, until his eighty-third birthday when he'd passed away in the golf cart on the way to the eighteenth hole. Not a bad way to go. Much better than being in one of those horribly expensive nursing homes with dementia, like so many old people you hear about. Thank fuck his pathetic excuse for a mother had died early from alcohol poisoning and he'd never had to deal with that. Good riddance. He didn't even bother going to the funeral.

Guilty? No, he didn't feel guilty. Guilt was a wasted emotion.

'And your name is?'

'Stratin. Theo C. Stratin.'

The tour guide glanced at her clipboard. She was one of those no-nonsense official types. A tough nut to crack.

Tough, but not impossible.

Taking off his Ray-Bans, he let his gaze rest upon her face until, sensing his eyes upon her, she looked up from her clipboard. Their eyes met.

'Did anyone ever tell you you've got really pretty eyes?'

*Bingo.*

Instantly her demeanour changed, and he watched her blush beneath her thick panstick make-up. It wasn't just about giving the compliment, it was the way you gave it.

'Please, sir, if you'd like to come this way.'

And quickly escorting him to the front of the queue, she unhooked the rope and waved him onto the boat.

'Have a pleasant journey. I hope you feel better soon.'

'Oh, I will . . . just as soon as I get that shot . . .' He mimed giving himself an injection, then glanced at her name tag. '*Grazie, Veronica.*'

'*Prego.*'

Briefly, he wondered about asking for her number, then quickly discounted it. She was just a tour guide. He was here to catch much bigger fish. This cruise was costing him a fucking fortune and that was after the weekend spent in Monte Carlo. Fifteen euros for a beer! And don't get him started on the price of the hotel. Shoving his sunglasses back up his nose, he looked around for a place to sit. The boat was pretty full inside already, but there were a couple of empty seats on top on the open deck. He climbed the stairs, holding down his hat as the breeze threatened to remove it, took one of the few empty seats and gazed back at the shore, waiting for the last few remaining passengers to board.

And that's when he felt it. A strange feeling like he was being watched. He turned around, glancing back up from the shoreline to the line of cafes and restaurants, bathed in the golden evening light, his gaze sweeping over the tourists enjoying an evening cocktail. He adjusted his sunglasses. He had a sixth sense for these things. You do when you're on the run.

'Excuse me, honey, but is this seat taken?'

He heard the drawl of an American accent and turned to see an attractive older woman, gesturing at the seat beside him. Wide-brimmed sunhat, red lipstick, lots of cleavage. What must she be. Sixties? Seventies, maybe?

'Please, be my guest.' He smiled politely, distracted.

As she squeezed in beside him, she held out her hand in introduction. 'Hi, I'm Birdy, pleased to meet you.'

Which is when he noticed the huge diamonds on her fingers and everything changed.

## SO, I MET THIS GUY . . .

Including his name.

'Hi.' His eyes flicked to her Louis Vuitton handbag covered in its famous logo. 'I'm Louis,' he smiled, taking inspiration from the brand of her handbag and holding her hand in his just a fraction longer than necessary. 'And trust me, the pleasure's all mine.'

The engines started and as she laughed at his flirtation he felt that familiar rush of pleasure, the kind he always thought hunters must feel when they spot their prey, an exhilaration mixed with a quiet, calculating resolve.

'Hold on to your hat,' he yelled, above the roar of the engines and, as the boat pulled away from the shore, he turned for one final look back at Positano.

And that's when he saw her. Amongst the crowds of tourists left behind, a face he never thought he'd see again.

*Maggie.*

# Missed Connections

Was that him? The man in the Panama? Maggie squinted, the sun in her eyes. But she couldn't see properly – his face was hidden and she was too far away – and now he'd disappeared. No, she must have been mistaken, she decided, taking a sip of her wine.

Back on dry land, the cafes were gearing up to their busiest period of the day: the Golden Hour. That magical time when the sun began its slow descent into the sea, bathing everything in a warm, Mediterranean glow, including the tourists who were fast trying to locate an empty seat at one of the many pavement cafes. To sit, drink in hand, and watch Positano's pastel-coloured buildings silhouetted against what was going to be another incredible sunset.

One of whom was Maggie, who was feeling very pleased with herself. By sheer fluke she'd bagged two of the best seats in the house. After leaving the hotel and walking around town, on the lookout for You Know Who, she and Flick had found themselves down by the harbour where the boats were ferrying passengers back to Amalfi and the various cruise ships anchored offshore. It was the perfect vantage point and, when she'd seen a couple asking for the bill at a nearby cafe, she'd pounced.

Are you leaving? Yes, they were on a cruise and had to get back to the ship. A cruise? Was it the same one as their friend? *Friend*, that made her choke, a bit, but what was Flick supposed to say? No, theirs was a different cruise. They were heading to Greece, but sorry, they mustn't be late. They'd heard stories of passengers being left behind. There were videos on YouTube. Have you seen them? One couple spent thousands chasing a cruise ship around the Med. Can you *imagine?* OK, well, bye, enjoy your drink.

'We should've told them we don't need to imagine,' said Maggie, tilting her face to the evening sunshine. 'But they'd think we were crazy.'

'Depends how you define crazy.' Flick shrugged, drinking a beer. 'I think working five days a week for forty years in the same job is crazy, but some people think it's perfectly normal. Same goes for living for ever in the same town you were born, or getting excited over what sandwich filling you're having for lunch.'

'*Sandwich filling?*' Maggie raised an eyebrow behind her sunglasses.

'A work colleague at the newspaper,' explained Flick, but it was pretty obvious to Maggie this wasn't about her work colleague; this was about Flick and how she saw her future.

'You only get one short life. Look at my mum.'

Maggie turned to her then, but Flick was gazing off into the distance, her eyes fixed on the horizon. 'Not taking a risk in life,' she continued, speaking almost to herself. 'That's what seems crazy.'

The waiter came and they ordered more drinks. And there they sat. Front row, with a great view of the harbour – it was the perfect lookout. But there were so many people, so many different tours and cruise companies, it was hard to distinguish anyone in the crowds. Once or twice, Maggie thought she might have spotted Him.

But to be honest, did she really want to?

Because, while she couldn't admit this to Flick, a big part

of her didn't want to find Him. She was beginning to like this new-found freedom of being on this road trip. Waking up in a different place every day. Moving forward. Never looking back. She didn't want it to stop. What would happen *if*, and *when*, they eventually found Him? When they reached their goal?

What then?

She tried to imagine it, but couldn't really. It went all fuzzy and messy, like those old-fashioned Etch A Sketch drawings. And then it would be over and she'd have to go back to face the music.

And, no, it wouldn't be the sound of some Italian crooner singing 'That's *Amore*'.

Basking in the warm evening sunlight, she gave a shudder. It was so lovely here, she didn't want to spoil it.

'Well, we're definitely getting closer.'

Maggie zoned back to see Flick had picked up her phone and was scrolling through various social media apps. She called it 'following his digital footprint'.

'Definitely.' Maggie nodded, encouragingly.

'He was here. We must have just missed him by minutes.'

'Next time.'

'Totally.'

'Absolutely.'

Maggie was wondering how many more synonyms they could come up with, when Flick let out a groan.

'Oh shit, he wants to FaceTime!'

'*FaceTime?*' Maggie shrank back with horror, pushing her chair away from the phone like it was a live hand grenade. How did he get Flick's number? 'I knew you shouldn't be digging around in his social media, this is what happens—'

'*Huh?*' Flick looked confused. 'I'm talking about Rory.'

Abruptly, Maggie felt foolish. She was being paranoid. 'Right, yes, of course. Well, that's nice.'

'No, it's not nice.' Feeling stressed, Flick took a slug of her beer and shoved her phone on the table. 'He's going to have a go at me.'

'Why?' Maggie frowned. 'I thought you two were fine now. You've been texting each other all day.'

The whole time she was driving today, Flick had been constantly on her phone. So much for looking at the stunning views of the Amalfi Coast. Her face had been buried in her screen.

'We were having a fight.'

'Still?'

Flick nodded. 'He still doesn't get it. Why I'm here. He thinks I'm with someone.'

'Well, you are.'

'Not *you*!' she tutted. 'You don't count.'

'Cheers.' Maggie raised her wine glass in mock salute, causing Flick to redden.

'I mean, another bloke. I told him we were on the Amalfi Coast and he googled it and said it was a top honeymoon destination and there was no way I was here for work. He doesn't believe me.'

'Maybe it's better if you talk to each other; have a proper conversation,' suggested Maggie. 'Texts are so easy to misinterpret.'

But Flick's face remained troubled.

'I don't think you know Rory. He's even got my stepdad Colin giving me grief now.'

'Why, what's he saying?'

'Asking me what's going on . . . telling me to come home . . .' Flick broke off to take another much-needed swig of her beer. 'I told him not to worry. That I'm here to break a story. To get an exclusive. I tried telling him all about romance fraud, how it's a really important issue right now, that this could be my big break.' She rubbed the top of her nose. 'He's always been really supportive, he knows how ambitious I am. I think he just worries about me, especially with Mum not being around to worry about me any more.'

There was a gap in the conversation. Maggie looked at Flick and felt suddenly maternal. She was too young to lose her mum. Too young to know that kind of grief. It changes you as a person. She should know.

'Are you close to your stepdad?' she asked, after a moment.

'Yeah . . . at least, we used to be.' Flick looked troubled. 'I always wanted a dad when I was little. I never knew my real dad. He disappeared when Mum got pregnant, so it was always just the two of us. I think I was about seven or eight when Mum met Colin. I remember him first coming to the house, being all goofy and playing in my Wendy house with me, pretending to have tea. . .' She smiled at the memory. 'I was so excited when they got married and I got to be a bridesmaid. I'd always wanted to be a bridesmaid.'

She paused, her mind flashing back to being eight years old in a confection of pink tulle.

'But then Mum got sick and things changed. We'd had our ups and downs before, when I was a teenager, but this was different. When we lost Mum, it was like something broke, like the glue that stuck us all together wasn't there any more . . . do you know what I mean?'

Maggie's mind slipped back to when they'd lost her brother, how everything had fallen apart in their family when he'd died, as if he was the glue and they'd come unstuck.

'Yeah, I know what you mean,' she began, before being interrupted by a jangling noise. It was Flick's phone.

'Oh crap, he's trying to FaceTime me.'

'If he doesn't believe you're telling the truth, why don't you FaceTime him here? Show him your sexy Italian Stallion is actually a very *un*sexy middle-aged woman,' suggested Maggie, smiling, but Flick frowned.

'You're not unsexy. You look great for your age.'

'*For your age?*' Maggie pulled a face.

'What? That's a compliment!'

'No, it's not, it's basically telling someone they don't look too bad for being old.'

'That's not true,' protested Flick, then frowned. '*Is it?*'

'I think you'd better answer that.' Maggie gestured to the phone which was still vibrating away on the table, Rory and Flick's faces beaming up from the screen, a symbol of happier times.

'That's a nice photo.'

'We were at the Isle of Wight music festival. That was taken before I saw the portaloos . . .'

As she grimaced, the call rang off and her phone fell silent. For like a second. Then started again.

'He's persistent, I'll give him that,' quipped Maggie, but Flick's sense of humour had deserted her.

'Maybe better if I take it in the room.' Snatching up her phone, she stood up. 'I don't want to have another row and spoil this lovely evening for everyone.' She gestured to the tourists sitting all around them, enjoying drinks. 'You OK here by yourself?'

'Don't worry, I'll be just fine. I'll finish my wine and watch the sunset.'

'Enjoy.' Grimacing, Flick quickly dashed off.

'Love to Rory.' Maggie raised her glass as she called after her.

Relationships, huh? Who'd have one?

# You Again

After Flick disappeared back to the hotel room, clutching her phone with a look of dread that Maggie was pretty sure shouldn't be the expression worn by a young woman about to speak to her boyfriend, Maggie remained alone at the cafe drinking her glass of wine. In a sea of couples, she felt a bit like Shirley Valentine.

God, she loved that film. It had been on TV one rainy afternoon a few weeks ago and for a couple of glorious hours she'd been transported from a damp, soggy caravan in northern England to a sun-filled Greek island. The first time she'd watched it, she'd been a teenager, and she remembered thinking Shirley was this frumpy, old, middle-aged woman, so it had come as quite a shock to discover Shirley was only forty-two.

Forty-two!

Talk about feeling ancient. She was older than Shirley Valentine!

As the sun began to sink into the sea, streaking a tangerine sky with purplish clouds, Maggie felt her mood dip. For years she'd had this dream of being on the Amalfi Coast, drinking wine and watching the sunset, and now here she was, sitting by herself, her life in tatters, staring down the barrel of fifty. The years had gone by so fast. What happened to that young, free-spirited Maggie, with all her hopes and possibilities and big dreams? Where did she go? Where did *they* go?

And now she was really feeling sorry for herself.

Finishing her wine, she decided against another glass. They had another early start and she'd regret it in the morning. Plus, while a couple of glasses of wine might feel empowering, in a strong, independent woman kind of way, spending the evening drinking on your own felt a bit sad and pathetic.

A flashback: *her kitchen. The two of them sharing a bottle of wine. His proposal.*

She stood up, forcing herself back to the present, and left a fifty-euro note. It was expensive here and they were burning through their winnings. Pretty, but a tourist trap. You paid for the view, but there was nothing to see here. The boats were all gone. The harbour had emptied out. Yet, instead of feeling disappointed, Maggie felt only relief. She could relax now. Being in a constant state of anticipation was exhausting. She wanted to pretend she was here on holiday. Explore the backstreets and lose herself in souvenir shops. Be a tourist, like everyone else.

Slipping her bag on her shoulder, Maggie set off walking. She was wearing her trainers, which were not the kind of cute fashion trainers Flick wore, but the ones she used for dog-walking. With scuffed fabric and faded laces, they'd seen better days. Which, thinking about it, was a good metaphor for herself. But, oh boy, were they comfy. She could walk for miles in these. Plus, one of the joys of getting older was caring more about comfort and less about how things looked.

Which was just as well, as no one was looking at her anyway. Something which the media seemed to want her to be upset about. She was constantly reading interviews with female celebrities her own age, dolled up to the nines, filtered beyond recognition, sticking up a proverbial finger to a society that wanted them to be invisible. *Fuck that! Look at me! Better than ever!* Which was wonderful and good for them and You go, girl.

And yet, while Maggie felt she should be outraged too, she was secretly finding she rather enjoyed this new invisibility. (And rather guiltily, as she was worried this didn't make her a good feminist.) After all, wasn't being invisible supposed to be a superpower? Didn't Harry Potter get a cloak? Finally freed from the male gaze, in fact, *any* gaze – including her own, as she had spent years peering in the mirror, wracked with insecurities – now she could look any which way she wanted and no one batted an eyelid.

Which was rather lucky, as the ugly trainer-and-sundress combo was quite something.

Positano was heaving with tourists and she soon found herself amongst them, strolling along the main street, admiring the shops filled with silks, handmade sandals and ceramics. She thought about how on past holidays abroad she'd loved shopping for souvenirs and gifts. Now she couldn't afford to buy anything. Not even a kitschy fridge magnet.

Though, to be honest, that was less about the price tag and more about the fact that she no longer had her large, freestanding stainless-steel fridge. It was sold along with her flat, and magnets wouldn't stick to the little plastic fridge she had in the caravan.

Still, she was lucky. Some people didn't even have that. But then neither would she, soon enough. She thought about the enforcement notice stuffed into her suitcase, the missed calls on her phone. She'd listened to the voice messages. One was from someone at the council, the other was from Ainsley, the farmer whose field she'd been renting. Someone from the local planning committee had been over, said he needed planning permission for the caravan, and threatened him with a fine and prosecution if he didn't move it by next weekend. He sounded both furious and apologetic.

'*Fucking bureaucracy, telling me what I can do on my own land. Sorry, Mags. If it was up to me, you could stay as long as you wanted.*'

He was an old friend of her brother's, doing her a favour. She didn't want to get him into trouble. Drag him into the mess she'd got herself into. She needed to sort it out, but not here. Not tonight.

Firmly shoving it to the back of her mind, she weaved her way through the legions of couples enjoying a romantic evening stroll, their arms entwined around waists and slung around tanned shoulders. Past the families with their small children out late, the sleeping babies in strollers, the men in freshly ironed shirts, the women in their new holiday wardrobe. The streets smelling of aftershave and perfume and fresh lemon soap, buzzing with the good mood that being on holiday brings.

Thrust amongst them, Maggie didn't feel lonely; on the contrary, she relished the feeling of being anonymous. Back in England she'd felt as if everyone was talking about her when she went to the local shops, gossiping about the foolish, middle-aged woman who'd fallen for a fraudster and lost everything, including her own mind. Like Flick had said, 'It's a small town, people talk.'

But here, no one knew her, no one was paying her any attention. She could be anyone. She was just a tourist. One of many wandering around, eating gelato, window-shopping, taking arty photos of Italian doorways to add to the dozens they'd already taken and which they'd probably never look at again once they get home.

*Me included*, thought Maggie, pausing to take a photo of a particularly lovely door with peeling paint and ancient patina and smiling to herself.

Because here, in this tiny corner of paradise on the Amalfi Coast, she felt as if she'd shaken off the heavy clothes of being the woman that had lost everything. For the first time, in a very long time, she felt the weight of shame and grief and self-loathing lift from her shoulders – and she was free of it all. Free of herself. That was one of the gifts of travelling. Being able to leave behind your ordinary life, with its well-worn pages, and venture into a whole new fresh one. One made up of blank pages ready to be filled, where you could be anyone you wanted to be.

After a while Maggie left behind the shops and galleries, curious to explore. The village was built on a cliff and, having read about the best view being much higher up, she set about climbing the endless stone steps. The ascent was steep and soon she found herself high above the sea, where she paused to catch her breath, and not just because she was puffed and out of shape. Dusk had fallen and all the lights had come on. It was so pretty, it almost felt magical. From here, the houses appeared to cascade down the cliff, their amber lights glowing in the evening dusk.

She gazed at the view. All the tourists that had come to watch the sunset had already left and, finding herself alone, she leaned against the railing, taking it all in.

At least she *thought* she was alone.

'It's beautiful, huh?'

Hearing a voice, she turned to see a man standing a few feet away in the shadows, leaning against the same railing. There was something faintly familiar about him.

'Yes, very,' she nodded, trying to place him.

Tall, with blond hair, he was dressed in a pale blue shirt and shorts, a small backpack slung over his shoulder. Was he famous? An actor, maybe? She'd once smiled and said hello to someone in Waitrose, thinking it was someone she knew, only to realize she recognized them because they were an actor in a famous long-running soap. Talk about Mortified in the Cereal Aisle.

'Hello again.'

And now he was smiling and saying hello to her like he knew her. And she *definitely* wasn't an actor in soap. Though recently life had felt as if it had taken on one of their outrageous plot lines.

'Sorry, have we met?'

'Sort of, not really,' he shrugged, still smiling.

Well, that cleared things up.

'The pizzeria in Rome . . .'

Of course. Suddenly it clicked. This was the man reading the book. The stranger she turned around and stared at. Who caught her eye when she left the restaurant and looked back. So he *was* looking at her. He *did* notice her. All these thoughts whooshed through her mind, but all she said was, 'Basilico's, Piazza Navona,' and smiled, like it was no big deal.

Because it wasn't, right?

'Yes, that was it.' He nodded. 'You have a good memory.'

'Not always,' she smiled ruefully, 'but I do when it comes to food.'

'How was the pizza?'

'Wonderful. Yours?'

'I went for the pasta carbonara.'

'No!'

He laughed at her outrage. 'Is that terrible?'

Embarrassed by her reaction, she laughed. 'I'm sure it was delicious, but they're famous for their pizzas. They do the best crusts. You missed out.'

'Next time.'

His eyes met hers. Darkness was falling, but even in the half-light she noticed how strikingly blue they were.

'I'm Sander.' Taking a few steps towards her, he held out his hand in introduction.

'Maggie.' Smiling, she shook it. It felt curiously formal. Sweet, though. And his handshake was warm and friendly. 'You have a cool name,' she added.

'Not really. I'm Dutch. It's quite common in the Netherlands.'

So that explained the blue eyes and blond hair. Memories of visiting Amsterdam when she was much younger and being amazed by how tall and blond and good-looking everyone was flicked through her mind. As someone who'd been a gangly teenager, shooting up to five foot eleven by the time she was fourteen, it had been wonderful not to be the tallest for once. To actually stand in a crowd and not be head and shoulders above everyone else. To feel like she fitted in. Well, apart from the blond, good-looking bit.

'So, you're on holiday?' she asked, snapping back.

'Sort of. My son is taking a gap year to travel before he starts his university degree, so I thought why should all the teenagers have the fun? Why not do that myself?'

'You're on the gap year together?'

'We're close but not that close.' He laughed. 'He's in Thailand and Indonesia, going to festivals and full moon parties. But I've been there and done that. I read *The Beach*.'

Maggie smiled at the reference. They must be the same age.

'Every backpacker read that novel.'

'It was our bible,' he nodded. 'Now I sit in restaurants and read books about history and order the wrong thing.'

He smiled then, a mischievous, teasing smile that would normally put someone at ease and make them laugh, but instead made Maggie immediately put up her defences and feel guarded. She'd had this kind of connection with someone before. Thought someone was nice and friendly and cute and funny. Laughed at their jokes and felt flattered by their interest.

*And they blew up her life.*

'And you?'

For a split second Maggie faltered as Sander threw back the question, not wanting to reveal her situation, to explain why she was there, before suddenly realizing she didn't have to. She could be anyone here. She didn't have to be Maggie, the woman who lost everything, the fool who fell for a man who told her he loved her, the penniless loser living in a caravan. She could rewrite her life. Escape from her reality, at least for a little while. After all, she was never going to see him again.

'I've taken the summer off to come to Europe and study art history.'

It just came out.

'A sabbatical?' Sander's eyes widened and he looked at her, his expression one of genuine interest.

'Yeah, sort of.'

*A sabbatical.* She liked that idea. She was taking a sabbatical from her life.

'And what do you do?'

'I'm an artist. Painter. Mixed media. Oils mostly.'

'Fascinating.'

*Fascinating.* For so long she had been anything but that. But now in this warm evening breeze on the Amalfi Coast she was chatting to a handsome Dutchman who found her fascinating. It felt intoxicating.

'I was in tech, but recently I needed a change so I sold my company. Now I have a bicycle shop and do guided tours.'

'Wow, that's so interesting.'

'No, really, it's not as interesting as what you're doing.'

She felt a stab of guilt. He was being so nice.

'Do you ride a bike?'

'Yes, back in England, not here.' Maggie gestured to the steep stone steps and he laughed.

'Well, if you ever find yourself in Lisbon, you must come rent a bike from me. I'm by the seafront. Look for the yellow sign with the windmill.' He smiled. 'I'm joking about the windmill.'

'Lisbon?'

'I moved to Portugal. I needed a change.' He didn't go into details and she knew there was something more he wasn't telling her, but she didn't ask. She didn't want to know. For a few moments she wanted to enjoy being in this make-believe bubble.

'Do you want me to take your picture? It's a good one.' Changing the subject, he pointed to the view behind her.

'Oh, no, I don't think so, I look a mess.'

She gestured to her outfit, but he ignored her and, putting down his backpack, took out his phone.

'No, seriously, I have a good eye. The sky is very pretty.'

Feeling self-conscious, she smoothed down her hair and leaned against the railing, trying not to think about her crumpled sundress and scruffy trainers. She felt slightly ridiculous as she smiled for the camera.

'What's your number? I'll WhatsApp it to you.'

'You could just AirDrop it.'

'I could, but then I wouldn't have your number.'

And now Sander was the one smiling and looking self-conscious.

'It's not just the sky. You look very pretty too.'

'Sorry, I don't give my number to strangers.'

Abruptly Maggie felt herself snap back, pulling her

crossbody bag to herself, like a barrier. She'd done that before, remember? Given her number to a stranger and blown up her life.

'Oh, sorry, I didn't mean—' Seeing her body language, he quickly held up his hands as if in surrender, his smile apologetic; a man who'd attempted to flirt and misread the signals. 'I hope I didn't make you uncomfortable.'

'No, it's fine.'

Oh God, he was just being nice and she'd gone and freaked out and now it was all so awkward. What happened to the make-believe bubble? To fun, fascinating Maggie on a sabbatical? *Real life, Maggie. That's what happened. Real life.*

'Well, nice to meet you.'

And now he was picking up his backpack and throwing it over his shoulder.

'Yeah, I've got an early start; we're driving to Sicily.'

'Sounds amazing, I'm heading to Greece for a little bit, then back to Lisbon.'

'Well, have fun.'

'You too.'

They both turned to walk away, and she turned back.

'I suppose you're not really a stranger.'

He turned.

'Seeing as I know your name and where you live and what you do for a living. And that you prefer pasta to pizza,' she smiled.

It wasn't real life that had brought her to her knees. It had been one man. And that wasn't the same man standing in front of her.

'0786 . . .'

It wasn't the same man putting her number in his phone.

And as she walked away, down the steps, back towards the hotel, a few minutes later, she heard her phone ping. And, smiling, she reached for her phone in her bag, expecting to see the photo he'd just sent her.

Except it wasn't a photo from Sander. It was a text from a number she didn't recognize.

> Hi Mags, it's me, Theo. It's been a long time. How are you, babe?

# Sicily

*Day Five*

*Nine more days to go*

# Maggie

Everyone loved him.

All my friends thought he was handsome and charming and that I was so lucky. When we announced our engagement, they couldn't have been happier for me.

'He's perfect, Maggie!'

'Congratulations!'

'Amazing news. We're so pleased for you both!'

'What a beautiful ring!'

We'd arranged to have dinner at our local Italian and invited just a few close friends. As Theo disappears to the loo, they crowd around me, hugging and kissing. Mike and Pat, my old neighbours; Jenny and Samir, two amazing local artists; and George, who made a special trip up from London to be here tonight.

'What about his friends?'

'Huh?'

As George clinks his champagne glass against mine in celebration, I laugh giddily, not understanding.

'What are you talking about?'

'Well, these are all your friends.'

'They're our friends now. *Mi casa, su casa.*'

Buzzing with happiness and alcohol, I can't take the grin off my face, but George frowns.

'I just think it's odd that he doesn't have any friends.'

'Odd, why? He's lived in LA for the last twenty-plus years.

All his friends are in America. He's starting again over here. And anyway, what does it matter?' I break off, irritation threatening to ruin my good mood. 'Don't tell me you're jealous,' I tease.

Actually, when I said everyone loved Theo, I should have said *almost* everyone. George doesn't, but then George can be very territorial when it comes to my boyfriends. He hasn't liked many of them and no one is ever good enough. He hated my ex-husband with a passion – thankfully it was brief – and barely tolerated my last relationship with a sculptor, who I was with for several years, before it fell apart because of his drinking. In many ways George is like the protective older brother I lost. In others, he's the bitchy best friend. Tonight he's being the possessive lover.

'He's got a fabulous arse, I'll give him that,' he admits, almost reluctantly.

I laugh. I know that's as close as I'm going to get to his blessing.

'Definitely fit.'

'Thank you.'

'Just feels a bit weird, that's all.'

'Not everyone has as many friends as you, George,' I point out. 'You're like the pied piper. Everywhere you go you attract people.'

'Classic insecurity,' he grins. 'Can't stand my own company. Tortured soul.'

He affects one of his brooding looks and I roll my eyes.

'I surround myself with people so I don't have to be alone with my own self-loathing.'

'Don't say that!'

'I'm only joking. Sort of.' He raises a perfect eyebrow. 'Total FOMO.'

'FOMO?'

'Fear Of Missing Out.' He breaks off. 'God, is that even a thing any more? Nothing ages you more than a dated acronym.'

He looks so stricken, I throw my arms around him. I love George, even if he is the most melodramatic man I've ever met.

'Well, he says he doesn't need any friends, he just wants to be with me. It's romantic.'

'You mean claustrophobic.'

'George, please be happy for me,' I plead.

Breaking apart, I grab him by the shoulders and stare at him with my most deadly serious stare. The one I used to use when we were both students and drunk on cider and George would try and persuade me that doing tequila shots at 2 a.m. whilst listening to the Counting Crows' 'Mr Jones' on a loop was a good idea. Which of course, it never was.

'I am, of course I am!'

Raising his glass, he drains it in one. A classic party trick. Back in the day, George would drink everyone under the table, but now he's *slightly* more measured. Saying that, everyone is a bit drunk and woozy, after all the wine we've had to drink and now the champagne.

'So, are you talking about me?'

Theo reappears from the bathroom as I'm refilling George's glass.

'Oh, didn't see you there!' I jump as he comes up behind me, sliding his arms around my waist. 'We just were talking about our happy news.'

'Wonderful, isn't it?' Not letting me go, he looks over my shoulder at George. 'Don't you agree?' It's almost as if he's challenging him to disagree.

'Amazing. I'm so happy for you both. Maggie deserves the best. You're a lucky man.'

'And don't I know it.'

Theo nuzzles his face into my neck and I laugh as his stubble tickles. I'm being silly. George is making me paranoid. Theo isn't challenging anyone. There's no weird vibe between them. It's totally fine.

'So, George, will you be the one giving Mags away?'

'Oh, I don't know about that, I don't think I could ever give Maggie away. You'd have to steal her from me.'

'Is that so?'

OK. Maybe I was wrong. There's definitely a vibe.

'Hey, I am here, you know.' Freeing myself from Theo's arms, I put myself between them. 'You're talking about me as if I'm not here!'

Laughing, I try making light of the matter.

'And what's all this giving away business? It's a bit old-fashioned. I'll walk myself down the aisle, Meghan Markle style.'

'Show what a strong, independent woman you are,' smiles Theo, approvingly.

'It all kind of went a bit tits up after the wedding, though, didn't it?' quips George.

Poor George. He's such a royalist. He was so excited when Prince Harry married Meghan and so upset when it wasn't the royal fairytale ending everyone hoped for and they moved to America. No one loved Princess Diana more than George, he couldn't get out of bed for days when she died, and he's been in quite a state about her two boys, the princes, falling out.

'Meaning?'

That said, it was probably a bad joke to make, under the circumstances, and I see Theo's face cloud. Sensing the tension between them, I feel a twist of anxiety. I so want him and George to love each other. They're the most important men in my life.

'Just joking, mate.'

*Mate*. George never calls anyone mate.

'We're mates, are we?' Theo looks at him so coolly, it makes my inside freeze.

'Let's get the bill, shall we?' I interrupt, trying to be all cheery and provide a distraction. 'It's getting late.'

'So have you two set a date yet?'

Another friend, Samir, a photographer who exhibits in my gallery, appears by my side tipsy and grinning.

'No, not yet. We're still looking for a house and work has been crazy,' replies Theo, motioning to the waiter to try to get his attention.

'Theo's been away such a lot, filming,' I add, glad of the change of subject.

'Ooh, sounds glamorous.'

'That's what I always say,' I laugh, 'but he assures me it's hard work being with all those famous actors in exotic locations.' I roll my eyes and I'm relieved to see Theo laugh, his good mood restored.

'It can be pretty demanding.'

'Aren't they all going to be replaced with AI?' pipes up Pat, my neighbour.

'Well, it's funny you say that.'

'Tell them about your new business idea,' I interrupt excitedly.

'Darling, please,' he quickly shushes me, but I'm a bit drunk and in proud fiancée mode.

'It's amazing! Everyone should invest in it!'

'Ooh, what's that, got any insider tips?'

My friends gather round, ready to be let into a secret, but Theo just laughs.

'You can be put away for that, you know. No, it's still early stages, but I'm working with a Hollywood source on some new AI technology. I think it's going to revolutionize movies.'

'Wow, sounds amazing.'

'You're going to get married *and* rich, Mags!'

'I hope so! We've sunk all our savings into it!'

'Not all, darling,' Theo swiftly corrects me. 'We have other investors. And we're not sinking anything, we're *investing* in the future. *Our* future.'

He breaks off as the waiter returns with the bill and Theo goes to get it. He's so generous like that, always buying me gifts and flowers and treating me to lovely restaurants. I watch him telling everyone not to be silly and to put their cards away, please, it's his treat, he's just pleased everyone could come to celebrate with us and I feel a swell of happiness. A disbelief that this is really happening to me. That love and happiness really does come for everyone in the end, you just have to be patient and wait – your turn will come.

'Oh damn, I can't believe it.'

I notice he's patting the back pocket of his jeans and now doing the same with his jacket, which he's slung over the back of the chair.

'What's wrong?'

'I've only gone and brought the wrong wallet.' Furious with himself, he flicks it open to reveal a bunch of dollar bills. 'This is my old one, the one I used in LA.'

I'd bought him a new one as a gift for his birthday a few weeks ago. A lovely leather one I'd had monogrammed with his initials.

'Oh, it's my fault,' I quickly reassure, squeezing his arm. 'Buying you a new one and getting you all mixed up. That always happens to me when I swap handbags. Don't worry, I'll get this.'

I quickly pull out my credit card and hand it to the waiter. Out of the corner of my eye I notice George giving me a look. I ignore him.

'Thanks, darling, I'll pay you back.'

'Don't be ridiculous, it's my engagement dinner too.'

'These feminists, they won't let you pay for anything these days.'

Theo slips his arm around my waist affectionately and there's laughter from my friends.

'Don't you have Apple Pay?'

I hear George's voice and notice he's not laughing.

'Nah, don't trust it.'

'Really? But it uses AI technology to enhance security.'

'So?'

'Well, I would have thought you of all people would be into that. What with your new business?'

There's a split-second pause.

'Oh right, yeah. . . well, it's a totally different use of AI technology,' explains Theo. 'To be honest, I leave that side of things to my tech guys; they're the experts.'

'I see. Wow, fascinating,' nods George.

'Yeah, it really is,' agrees Theo.

George catches my eye and I smile, pleased to see both men getting on so well and agreeing on something, finally. And as the waiter returns with the card reader and hands me my receipt, I feel a swell of happiness. Maybe they'll be besties after all.

We leave the restaurant and we gather outside on the pavement for a few minutes, saying our goodbyes. Everyone is in a good mood, all smiles and hugs, and we fill the warm May evening with the sounds of warm wishes and laughter.

'Are you sure you don't want my sofa bed?' I say to George, but he shakes his head.

'You two lovebirds don't want me snoring and farting on your sofa bed, now, do you?' he protests, bashing away the invite. 'Talk about a passion killer. No, one of the cabin crew has given me his Airbnb for the night, mates' rates.'

He grins broadly and Theo laughs and we all hug and say goodbye, waving each other off, as he jumps in a cab and everyone goes their separate ways.

We set off walking in the opposite direction. It's not far to my flat, only fifteen minutes, and buoyed up by such a lovely evening, I reach for Theo's hand. We always hold hands when we're walking down the street, that's one of the things I love about him. How he's so affectionate.

That's when I first sense that something is up. He has his hands in his pockets.

'So, that was a lovely evening,' I say as we set off down a side street. I go to link my arm through his instead. I'm imagining it. Being silly. I am a bit tipsy, after all.

Silence; then, 'Well, it was until you showed me up.'

It was like the sound of a chord in a minor key.

'Sorry? What?'

I look at him. It's late and dusk has fallen, but it's still light. The warm smile that's been on his face all evening has vanished and he looks pinched.

'You heard.'

It's like all the geniality and warmth of the evening has disappeared. Like it was an illusion. Even though it's a summer's night, it's as if there's a sudden chill in the air.

'I'm sorry, love, have I done something wrong?'

I frown, not quite understanding what I've done to cause his good humour and affection to be so suddenly withdrawn.

'If I said something to offend you somehow, I didn't mean to—'

'You and your mate George, making fun of me.'

'We weren't making fun of you,' I reply, astonished he could think such a thing. 'It was just George, messing about—'

'It was patronizing and belittling. You tried to make me look like a fool.'

'I did? No, don't be silly, I didn't—'

Everything is unravelling.

'Silly? I'm being silly?' He fumes, breaking apart. 'I think you've said enough.'

'No, please, Theo, don't spoil this evening.'

'Me, spoil this evening?' He turns on me now, his face furious. 'I think you need to look at your behaviour, Maggie, not mine; the only person spoiling anything is you, showing me up, showing yourself up, flirting with everyone—'

'*Flirting?*' My mind is whirling, trying to make sense of it all. The whole evening feels as if it's suddenly been tipped on its axis. 'What are you talking about? They're my friends—'

But he's not listening. 'Trying to emasculate me in front of everyone.'

'Is this about me paying the bill?'

As soon as the words leave my mouth, I know I shouldn't have brought it up.

'See! I knew it! I knew that's why you did it. Pretending in front of all your friends like it was no big deal! Trying to make me look like some cheapskate.'

'What? No! I don't think anything—'

'All your friends must think I'm a total loser. That I can't provide. That I'm not good enough for you.'

It's like a car crash. It's all happening so fast. I can't control it.

'Theo. Please. Stop. I don't know why you're saying all this.' I can feel myself on the verge of tears. 'You'd brought the wrong wallet, I was just trying to help, my friends don't think anything, they love you—'

He stops then on the pavement and twirls around to face me. When I see his face, I almost don't recognize him. Gone is the charming smile he just bestowed on George and my friends. The affection. The kindness. The consideration. Gone is the love. His eyes are dark and flashing and his jaw is set.

'I love you,' I plead.

I'm so desperate to return to the happy mood of the evening. For it to be how it was. How could it have all turned on itself like this? I wait, desperate for him to say it back to me.

But there's nothing. Just silence where the words should have been.

Instead he turns away from me, almost in disgust, and continues walking. Him slightly ahead, me behind. I follow, my mind and body reeling. Frantically trying to work out why I'm being punished, to remember what I've said or done that has upset him so much, to think how to make it right. But my mind is foggy from the wine and champagne, and I can't think straight.

'I'm sorry, Theo, please . . .'

I'm begging now. I feel terrible. Guilty. Wracked with remorse. I just want the Theo I know back, the affection, the love, the intimacy. It's our engagement party night. Our celebration. We're supposed to be the happiest we've ever been.

But he ignores me and keeps walking, our footsteps the only sound I hear until we reach the art gallery and the side door that leads to my flat. Digging his set of keys out of his pocket, he opens the door and lets us both in. I follow him meekly inside and upstairs, my head bowed, my whole self subdued.

The flat is in darkness and as I turn on a lamp, George the cat comes out to say hello and wind around our ankles. I scoop him up, burying my nose into his soft, warm fur. I've never felt more wretched.

'I'm going to bed.'

Without looking at me, Theo turns and goes into the

bathroom, brushes his teeth, then disappears into the bedroom. When I go in a few minutes later the bedroom is in darkness and he's turned away from me.

I climb in beside him, pulling the covers around me. I feel so alone. On my bedside table, a flash of light illuminates the blackness. It's my phone. It's on silent, but as I go to turn it off a text beeps up; it's from George, saying thanks for the lovely evening and a love heart. A tear silently trickles down my cheek as I look at the diamond on my finger.

I send a love heart back.

# It's the Journey, Not the Destination

'So what happened afterwards?' asked Flick, as Maggie finished telling her the story about the night of their engagement dinner. 'When you woke up the next day?'

As Maggie turned off the engine, the car fell silent.

'Nothing.'

'*Nothing?*' Sitting beside her, in the passenger seat, Flick was incredulous. 'Seriously?'

'Seriously.' Maggie nodded. 'When I woke up the next day, it was like nothing had happened.'

After over seven hours on the road, one ferry and five hundred and fifty kilometres later, a dusty red Fiat and its passengers had finally arrived at its destination: the beautiful hilltop town of Taormina. Spectacularly perched on a mountainside, high above the sea and with a view of Mount Etna, this was one of the famous stops on the Grand Tour, the journey made by nineteenth-century aristocracy, who came to learn about art and history and archaeology.

Fast-forward a couple of hundred years and following in their footsteps were Flick and Maggie. Minus the crinolines, parasols and footmen, they'd pulled into the large gravel forecourt outside their hotel, tired and weary from the long journey.

And they weren't here to educate themselves, they were here to catch a con man.

'But I don't understand . . .'

'At the time, neither did I, it was the weirdest thing.'

Maggie rested her hands on the steering wheel, her mind flicking back.

'I was bracing myself for an argument, to find him still in a bad mood, rehearsing what I might say to make it all better, but when I walked into the kitchen the radio was on, fresh coffee was brewing and he was at the stove, cooking me breakfast, all cheerful and happy—' She broke off, back in the moment. 'And when he saw me he gave me the biggest smile, like I was the best thing he'd ever seen.'

'He didn't mention the night before?'

'Nope.' Maggie shook her head. 'It was like it had never happened. And I didn't mention it, because I didn't want to bring it all up again.'

'How weird.'

'To be honest, I was just so relieved that the man I knew and loved was back. That everything was normal again.'

Parked in the shade of a row of large cypress trees, with the windows of the Fiat buzzed right down, a welcome breeze blew through the car. They both knew they needed to check into the hotel, go through the whole paperwork and passport process yet again. But for the moment they remained sitting in the car, not yet ready to drum up the energy needed.

'But it wasn't normal, was it?' Maggie spoke quietly.

For so long she'd deliberately locked these memories away and reliving them now was both painful and illuminating.

'I should've said something. Called him out on it. Had a conversation about what had angered him so much and made him so upset. Maybe if I had done, I wouldn't have got myself into such a mess.'

But Flick wasn't having any of it. 'That's ridiculous!' she retorted. 'It's not your fault. You didn't get yourself into the mess, it was him.'

'But I let him, didn't I? I was the one who allowed it.'

Resting her hands on the steering wheel, Maggie let herself be transported far away from the summer heat of Sicily, back to the kitchen of her old flat. Despite the summer heat, she felt herself go cold.

'"Eat up, babe, your eggs will go cold." That's what he said. And then he gave me a kiss.'

She turned to Flick, smiling, but it was the saddest smile Flick had ever seen.

'And you know what's the worst part?'

Flick shook her head.

'I kissed him back and told him he made the best omelette and I ate my breakfast like a good girl.' Maggie's eyes flashed with tears, but she refused to let them fall. 'And afterwards I convinced myself that I must have drunk more champagne than I thought the night before. That I'd remembered it all wrong. That I must have said something, or done something, but it didn't matter now, because everything was good between us again.'

She sniffed sharply. She was damned if she was going to cry another tear over Him.

'You mustn't blame yourself.'

'But that's just it. I do blame myself. I ignored that voice in my head that told me something was wrong . . . I told myself everything was fine, that we loved each other . . . and for a long time I didn't realize what was happening to me, until it was too late . . .'

As Maggie spoke, Flick felt a mixture of guilt and tremendous responsibility. She was the reason Maggie was having to relive all of this. If it wasn't for her turning up at her caravan, digging for information about a Theo C. Stratin and asking her to tell her story, she wouldn't be having to go through all of these painful memories. She wouldn't be here now, reliving all of this.

And for a moment, she allowed the doubts to take hold. Had she been right in pursuing him? Involving Maggie? Dragging her halfway across Europe on some madcap scheme? Because listening to Maggie talk, to hear about her experience in these unscripted interviews on the road, where she spoke about what had happened to her, it was clear to Flick that this wasn't about the money. It was about much more than that. But then she always knew that, didn't she?

'. . . because what I didn't know then, is this is how it all starts.'

'You mean the deception?' Flick felt herself snap back. 'Defrauding you out of your life savings?'

But Maggie shook her head. He'd stolen so much more from her than that.

'No. I'm talking about the coercive control. The emotional abuse. The breadcrumbing. The gaslighting.'

She turned to look at Flick. Only now was Flick really beginning to understand what had happened to Maggie.

'I didn't even know what those terms meant before He walked into my art gallery. I'd probably heard of them, read them in a magazine article, but I'd never experienced them, never thought that could happen to me. You don't, do you? You think you'd be wiser, stronger. I wasn't some naive young girl – I was in my forties; I owned my flat, ran my own business; I'd been married, had relationships . . . It was only afterwards, when I went to the police and they gave me some leaflets, links to support groups and websites . . .'

Looking down at her lap, Maggie began picking an invisible thread on her dress. Flick watched her, ignoring the impulse to tell her it wasn't her fault. That fraudsters were heartless. Master manipulators. Experts at lulling their victims into a false sense of security and trust, at convincing everyone that they were something they're not.

'I started reading up on it and recognized the patterns of behaviour, the description of the silences and bad moods, the mind tricks and constant threat of him taking away his love and affection. I started living on eggshells, feeling isolated . . .'

'But what about your friends? What about George, what did he say?'

Maggie looked embarrassed. 'I stopped seeing most of them,' she admitted, raising her eyes to Flick's. 'I'd make excuses, say I was busy. Pretend I'd forgotten to return their calls. I didn't want to risk a repeat of what had happened that evening, it just felt easier this way. Looking back, now I realize it was his way of isolating me from my friends. After a while, people assume you're busy and stop trying to meet up. They think you're newly engaged and planning a wedding, that you're in some kind of love bubble.'

'Gosh, Maggie, I'm sorry. What a mind fuck.'

'That's one way of putting it.'

She smiled then and Flick felt an urgent need to reassure Maggie that the experience was more common than she thought, that she was determined to write the exposé to broaden awareness and warn others so it wouldn't happen to them.

'You know, if it's any consolation, you're not alone. I've been doing my research and I've read about this happening to lots of people. Both men and women. The victim is desperate for affection from their abuser, it becomes a vicious cycle. That's how they get away with the lies and deceit for so long. They're unscrupulous.'

'Yeah, I know.' Maggie nodded. 'And all the time they tell you they love you. And you want it so much to be true, you believe them.'

## SO, I MET THIS GUY . . .

There was a pause and Flick reached out her hand, squeezing Maggie's in hers.

'He's not going to get away with this. We're going to find him and make him face up to what he's done. I promise.'

Maggie nodded, grateful for her kindness and confidence, and thought about her phone burning a hole in her pocket, about the text she received out of the blue from Him last night. She hadn't told Flick that he'd made contact. Neither had she replied. It had been such a shock to hear from him, she was still processing it. Deciding what to do. Though, of course, there shouldn't be any decision to make. She needed to tell the police. To tell Flick.

'Actually, there's something else—'

'*Buon pomeriggio, signore, e benvenute nel nostro hotel.*'

They were interrupted by loud Italian voices and, turning, saw two uniformed porters striding towards the car, ready to welcome them to the hotel with huge smiles and a silver tray on which balanced two tall glasses.

'Wow, hi.'

'Thank you so much.'

As they both quickly clambered out of the car, they found themselves being presented with chilled lemonade cocktails, as their luggage was swiftly removed from the boot.

'Sorry, what was it you were saying?'

Flick turned to Maggie, a drink in her hand, her head spinning. She felt like she'd just stepped into some five-star fairytale.

'Oh, nothing.' Maggie shrugged. 'I'll tell you later.'

And together they were whisked across the gravel courtyard to reception, in a whirl of scented blossoms, delicious cocktails and handsome Sicilian men in uniform.

Whatever it was, it could wait.

# Trouble in Taormina

'I think we should split up.'

'*Split up?*'

Twenty minutes later and they were both horizontal on two sun loungers by the pool. Having flopped their weary – and rather tipsy, thanks to the welcome cocktails, of which they'd had two – bodies in the shade of a yellow-and-white-striped parasol, while they waited for their room to be ready, Maggie was just drifting off to sleep . . . when she was abruptly woken by Flick breaking up with her.

'Uh . . . sorry . . . have I missed something?'

Groggy and discombobulated, she realized she'd been drooling on her fancy hotel towel. Oh God, how embarrassing. She forced herself to sit up.

To see Flick wide awake and staring at her.

'Rather than sticking together, like we have been doing, I think we should split up, that way we can we cover more bases, double our chances of finding him.'

'I thought we were having a day off today?'

'We are. I'm talking about tomorrow, when the cruise ship arrives.'

'Oh, right, yes. Good idea.'

After four days on the road, both Flick and Maggie had come to the realization that trying to chase a cruise ship around every port of call was not only exhausting, it was totally impractical. The distances were just too huge and trying to arrive before the ship had docked and the passengers had disembarked was proving impossible. It was like constantly being late to the party.

Not that it was much of a party. Staying in a different place every night might sound like fun, but it was beginning to take its toll, both physically and mentally.

This is what it must feel like being in the witness protection scheme, Flick had remarked only that morning as they'd packed their bags and left as the sun was rising. It was ironic, but they were beginning to feel like *they* were the ones on the run.

So they'd decided: they weren't going to try to follow the whole cruise, but choose a few strategic places on its itinerary. Starting with Taormina, where they were going to spend two nights. This way they could relax and recuperate, ready for when the ship arrived in Messina, close by, the next morning.

'I've managed to get hold of the list of tours and activities and there's a bunch.'

As Flick began scrolling on her phone and reading off the screen, Maggie tried to engage her still-half-asleep brain.

'You can climb up Mount Etna, which is still an active volcano; take a tour of the various Greek theatres, apparently there's loads around here; walk in the footsteps of *The Godfather* and visit the various filming locations; take a cooking class where you learn how to make your own lasagne and tiramisu—'

'Do you get to eat it?'

'Um . . . yes, it says here you get to have it for lunch.'

'Oh, I like the sound of that one.' Maggie's stomach rumbled. Since breakfast she'd only had a packet of crisps bought from a motorway service station when they refuelled and the few olives the waiter just brought them, as an accompaniment to their drinks. She felt weak with hunger. Unlike Flick, who was always full of energy. People talked about the generation gap between Gen X and Gen Z, but was from where she was sitting, it seemed to be more a gap in energy levels.

'I want to see Mount Etna.'

'You want us to hike up an active volcano?'

The thought of putting on her trainers made Maggie's heart sink. She was exhausted after today's drive.

'Don't worry. Not us. *Me*.' Flick laughed at her expression. 'We can do things separately. Obviously, the tours are just for the cruise passengers, but a lot of these activities are open to the public. Like the cooking school or Mount Etna.'

'Perfect.' She felt a wave of relief, then a thought struck. 'Hang on, but what if it erupts?'

'Well, it would certainly put me on the front page.' Flick looked unalarmed.

'I'm not sure those are the headlines you want. Haven't you heard of Pompeii?'

'BRITISH JOURNALIST BURIED ALIVE IN HOT LAVA.' Putting on her best movie trailer voice, Flick used her hands to spell out the words in the cloudless stretch of blue sky. 'Got quite a ring to it.'

'Flick, it's not funny.'

'You're right. Bad taste. I know.' She looked sheepish. 'But you know me, I'll go to any lengths for a story.'

Maggie lay back on the sun lounger. It was a small, boutique hotel and there were a few people around the pool. Mostly couples. Everyone looked relaxed. Respectable. Reading books, listening to podcasts, their AirPods firmly in situ. Absently, she watched a wife rubbing suntan cream into her husband's hairy back. This was the kind of place she'd envisioned for her honeymoon.

'Either way, I have a feeling we'll find him tomorrow.'

She snapped back. Now would be a good time to tell Flick

about His text from last night. She didn't like keeping secrets. She needed to be honest.

'So, about last night—'

But before she could finish, Flick let out a loud groan. 'Oh God, don't. I don't want to think about it.'

Maggie was momentarily confused.

'Note to self: never FaceTime your boyfriend to put his mind at rest that you're not having an affair, while *in* the honeymoon suite.'

'Oh no.' As it became clear what she was talking about, Maggie clamped her hand to her mouth. 'I didn't think.'

'Neither did I.' Pulling a face, Flick lifted her sunglasses and did her scary wide eyes.

Despite the thirty-something-degree heat, Maggie noticed she'd still applied her trademark flicky eyeliner and wondered how it didn't smudge in the heat. She'd given up with the mascara, even waterproof had melted down her cheeks, making her resemble a giant panda.

'I went back to our room to have it out with him and totally forgot.'

'But how could he tell?'

'Well, the swan-shaped towels might have been a bit of a giveaway but I think it was the plaque above the bed with the big love heart and "*Amore*" that might have swung it.'

Maggie let out a strangled groan. They both looked at each other. The situation was dire. Which, of course, made it all the more funny, and they both snorted with laughter.

A few guests around the pool looked over to see what the commotion was.

'Don't, we must be serious,' hissed Flick, wafting her hands in front of her face in an attempt to suppress the giggles. But it was impossible. Why is it that when you're not supposed to laugh, things are always a million times funnier?

'So what happened?' whispered Maggie, her face half buried in a towel.

'We had another massive row and I tried to explain and he got all upset, and then we made up. At least I think so.' She pauses. 'I dunno. I'm not very good at relationships,' she added, as an afterthought.

'Who is?' consoled Maggie, shooting her a look of solidarity as she wiped her eyes. 'I met a man last night and acted all weird. I mean, God only knows what he thought of me.'

'Wait a minute.' Flick threw out her hand. 'Back right up. *You met a man?*'

Realizing how it sounded, Maggie shook her head. 'No, not like that. I didn't meet him, *meet him*. I knew him before. We both do. Well, sort of.'

'How sort of?'

'It was the man at the restaurant in Rome. Where we had the pizza.'

'The handsome stranger who was staring at you!' Flick looked triumphant. 'No way!'

'Way.' For once Maggie felt quite hip.

'I knew he fancied you! What did he say?'

'Don't be silly, he didn't fancy me. He was just being friendly as we recognized each other. We'd both climbed up to the famous viewpoint. His name's Sander, he's Dutch.'

'And?'

'And nothing. We chatted for a little bit, then we said bye.'

'Did you get his number?'

Flick was suddenly seeing Maggie in a whole new light. While she'd been holed up in her hotel room, having another tedious argument with Rory, Maggie had been out on the Amalfi Coast, being chatted up by a handsome stranger. Unexpectedly she felt a twinge of envy.

'No, of course not.' Meanwhile Maggie was fast wishing

she hadn't mentioned it. She wondered why she had. 'Though I gave him mine,' she added, almost as an afterthought.

'You did?!'

Except it wasn't an afterthought. She wanted this younger woman's respect and approval. Flick had met her at her lowest. She'd seen her not as the woman she used to be, but as the woman she'd been reduced to. And watching Flick's eyes light up, Maggie felt a curious flicker of pleasure. There was something satisfying about seeing yourself cast in a different role. To prove something, to herself, to Flick, to both of them? She wasn't sure.

'Yes. He wanted to send me a photo.'

Flick raised her eyebrows, teasing.

'Not *that* kind of photo.' Maggie blushed. 'The photo he took of me on his phone.'

'You want to be careful; he'll be sending you a dick pic next.'

With her broad accent, Flick was never one to whisper and several guests around the pool turned round and stared. It was a discreet, adults-only hotel, the kind of place people talked in hushed voices and wore stylish outfits. Apart from Maggie and Flick, who'd only packed for one night away and were wearing the clothes they'd been travelling in which, after several long car journeys, were crumpled, stained and in desperate need of washing.

'Wow, you're a dark horse.'

'It was nothing. There was a nice view. That's all.'

'So, let's see the photo, then.'

Flick gestured for Maggie's phone and she felt herself freeze, reminded of the text from Theo. She didn't want Flick looking at her phone and seeing it.

'Well, actually, that's the thing. He never sent it.'

She was telling the truth about the photo, but not about

the text. Just thinking about it made her stomach clench with anxiety. Her phone lay beside her on the towel and she reached for it, squeezing her fingers tightly around it as if somehow she could keep the genie in the bottle.

'Huh. Strange. Maybe this Sander guy got your number wrong.'

'Yeah, maybe.'

Or maybe he'd had second thoughts and decided she was a weirdo. Maybe he'd deleted her photo and gone to chat to a nice, normal woman who didn't go around pretending to be something she wasn't, because she'd ruined her own life and lost all her confidence.

Their conversation was interrupted by one of the hotel staff who came to inform them that their room was ready and, gathering their things, they followed them through the gardens, with their lemon trees and mosaic paths, to a beautiful light-filled room, with twin beds and a small terrace. Not for the first time did Maggie feel grateful for their winnings. A hotel like this didn't come cheap, and they'd been lucky to find a room in town, due to a late cancellation.

Kicking off her trainers, Flick padded barefoot out onto the terrace. It felt a world away from the industrial northern town where she'd grown up and still lived. 'I never knew places like this existed.'

'There's a whole world out there.'

'Yeah.' Flick nodded, her face thoughtful. 'Have you been to Sicily before?'

'No. It's my first time too.'

'See. Told you we had to make our own romance.'

Maggie laughed at the joke.

'So what shall we do now? We've got the rest of the day off. I've been googling and there's so much to see and do.'

*Now.* Now was the time to show her the text, thought Maggie. After all, the two of them were in this together. Except, they weren't. Not really. She was the one who'd fallen in love with a fraudster. Who'd discovered everything she thought was true was a lie. Who'd beaten herself up for months with shame and guilt and self-loathing. She needed some answers for herself first. Ever since he'd disappeared she'd been having furious, tearful, anguished conversations with him in her head, and now was the chance to have one for real. She wanted to know how this had happened to her; she needed to know why.

And then she'd tell Flick.

'Let's do what everyone does when they're on holiday,' she suggested, her mind made up. 'Let's go to the beach.'

'Really?' Flick looked thrilled. For a moment there she assumed she was going to be dragged around Greek amphitheatres. Not that there was anything wrong with Greek amphitheatres, but she really wouldn't mind just lying on a beach and getting a bit of a tan. Which she knew was terribly bad for her, what with the ozone and skin cancer rates and importance of wearing SPF50 and sitting in the shade. But sometimes, once in a while, doing something terribly bad for you felt terribly good. 'OK, great, but there's just one problem.'

'What is it?'

'To get there we need to catch a gondola.' Reading her phone, Flick frowned. 'I thought they were only in Venice.'

'It's not that kind of gondola.' Maggie stifled a smile. 'It means a cable car.'

'It does?' Flick bristled. 'Why doesn't it just say that then?'

'But you're right about it being a problem. I'm terrified of heights.'

## *Later*

Hi Mags, it's me, Theo. How are you, babe? It's been a long time.

**Is this really you?**

Yes, it's really me.

**Why are you contacting me?**

I want to explain everything.

**Explain it to the police. You're wanted for questioning.**

I understand why you're angry and I don't blame you.

**You stole my life savings.**
**You lied about everything.**

Please don't say that.
I loved you. I wanted to marry you.

**Is that why you disappeared?**

I did it to protect you.
There are some bad men after me.

**I don't believe you.**

It's true. I had no choice.
I tried paying them off. That's why I needed the money.
They threatened to kill me.

Maggie felt herself reel, but quickly caught herself. It couldn't be true. It must be another one of his lies. She'd read about this online. About how fraudsters made up life-threatening stories of danger to extract money from their victims. Plus, she'd just seen him swanning around Monte Carlo and getting on a luxury cruise. He didn't look like a man in fear for his life.

**Why didn't you go to the police?**

You don't go to the police about men like this.

**I don't believe you. You're lying again.**

Mags, can I ask you something?

**What?**

Will you meet me?

Maggie's stomach lurched. She wasn't expecting that. She hesitated. And then.

**Where are you?**

I can't say. It's not safe. I'll text you a place later.

He was avoiding her questions. This was just another one of his make-believe stories. The man was a fantasist, remember? A serial liar. She thought she'd heard the last of him. What did he want? Why did he want to meet her? Surely this wasn't another attempt to try and con her out of money? Not that she had any left. Maybe he wanted to try and persuade her to drop the charges by making her believe his life really was in danger. Did he really think she was that gullible? After everything that happened? She should ignore him and show Flick the messages; together they could decide what to do.

And yet, while Maggie had doubts about a lot of things,

she knew that if Theo found out she was in Europe with a journalist who was intent on hunting him down, she risked never hearing from him again. He could disappear, and for good this time. And with him, the opportunity to look him in the eye; to rage, to vent. To ask: why? To demand: how? To say everything she wanted to say and get the closure she so desperately needed. It was just too big a risk.

She needed to let him think she believed him. That she'd fallen back under his spell. That because she loved him once, she could love him again.

**Just say yes.**

And what she couldn't admit to anyone, even herself, is that, despite everything, she needed to see if she still had feelings for him. For the man she thought he was.

Her thumbs moved over the keyboard as she typed one word and pressed send.

**Yes.**

# Al Dente

So it turns out the cable car wasn't that scary after all and after a lazy day spent at Isola Bella beach, recharging their batteries in the clear turquoise water, renting eye-wateringly expensive sunbeds and beach umbrellas and getting sand in all the wrong places, Flick and Maggie woke bright and early the next morning. Both had a big day ahead of them, though Flick's was slightly bigger – a whole three thousand metres bigger in fact, in the shape of the highest and most active volcano in Europe.

'Are you sure you'll be OK?' asked a slightly worried Maggie, as the minibus arrived at 8.30 a.m. to pick up Flick.

'Of course! We're going to get the cable car up and then hike around the perimeter of some extinct craters and lava flows, before going into a volcanic cave after lunch.'

'It sounds dangerous.'

'You know fear and excitement are actually the same emotion.'

'So I've heard. Please be careful. What if you slip?'

'Don't worry,' assured a jovial tour guide, as an eager Flick clambered inside. 'We have hiking shoes and hard helmets. Your daughter will be fine.'

As Flick tried to stifle a snort of laughter, Maggie rolled her eyes. The tour guide looked about fifteen. What was it with everyone looking like children these days? Every time she saw a doctor, they seemed to be getting younger. Or was it her that was getting older? And the policeman she gave a statement to couldn't have been more than twenty-something.

A memory of walking into a police station six months ago, to report the disappearance of her fiancé along with her life savings, flashed through her mind. She'd been at her lowest ebb.

'*Ciao, grazie.*'

Now she felt like an Italian mother waving her child off on a school trip. Smiling at Flick's excited expression, she called out as the minibus began to drive away.

'Enjoy the hike, but remember if you see him, don't do anything silly!'

'What? Like push him in the volcano?'

'I'm being serious!'

'Me too!' Flick laughed. 'Enjoy the cooking class! And don't forget, whatever happens, keep calm and pasta on!'

Maggie laughed then and stood in the morning sunshine, watching until the minibus disappeared, before stooping down to stroke one of the cats that hung around the hotel. Plump and ginger, he reminded her of George. There was still no news. He was still missing. She hoped someone had taken him in and was feeding him.

And yet, for the first time she felt a glimmer of hope seep in around the edges. She'd been lost for a while too but on this tiny corner of a tiny island, wearing a new brightly coloured beach dress she'd bought yesterday from a souvenir shop, and with the morning sun on her face and the kitten purring by her ankles, Maggie was starting to feel found.

There were lots of cooking classes to choose from in the area, but the most popular and highly rated was in an old stone farmhouse, deep in the Sicilian countryside and surrounded by olive trees. It was run by a grey-haired matriarch called Mamma Lucia.

'But you can call me The Godmother,' she announced, as she welcomed her mix of students through the large wrought-iron gates and led them through her impressive vegetable garden and into her large kitchen.

Trailing at the back, Maggie assumed she was joking. Only, she didn't look like she was joking. In fact, she looked rather scary, in her navy-blue apron, black-framed glasses and wooden clogs. Which clattered loudly on the flagstone floor as she barked instructions to them in Italian.

'Sorry, what is she saying?' whispered a fellow student nervously.

'She wants us to put on our aprons,' translated a young American from Boston who Maggie had overheard earlier saying he was travelling through Sicily to explore his heritage and the cooking class looked like 'a fun thing to do'.

'Be quiet! I'm talking!' bellowed The Godmother.

Everyone fell silent. There were many words to describe the cooking class so far, but currently the word fun didn't look like it was one of them.

'Cooking is serious business,' she continued, her sleeves rolled up, elbows covered in flour as she began demonstrating how to make today's menu – lasagne alla zucca, parmigiana di melanzane, tiramisu – starting with the fresh pasta for the lasagne.

Everyone nodded mutely. The way The Godmother was cracking those eggs with a sharp flick of her wrist – *smash* – down on the marble top, spilling the whites and piercing the soft yellow yolk so that it oozed into the moat of flour, made everyone flinch. There was something very metaphorical about those eggs. Well, this was mafia country.

Careful not to be caught not paying attention, Maggie

snuck a tentative look around the class. It was a mixed bunch of about fifteen students, of all ages and races. Apparently several had come on tours from different cruise ships. But there was no sign of Him. That said, she wasn't really surprised. Despite his love of cooking, a class wasn't really his thing. He was never one to follow recipes, preferring to make things up as they went along.

Maggie caught herself at her choice of words. Oh, the irony.

'*Signora*, your attention, please!'

She jumped as The Godmother noticed her being distracted and paused from pounding and kneading the dough, to shoot her a furious scowl.

'Sorry. Of course. Absolutely.'

Nodding vigorously, Maggie gave her full attention as she turned back to pummelling and beating it into shape. She needed to stop thinking about Theo or his texts, and focus. Like The Godmother said, cooking was serious business and at this rate she was going to get into trouble.

Which is why, when she heard the door creak open behind her and the scurry of footsteps, she didn't turn around at first.

'*Scusi, scusi*, sorry to intrude . . .'

It was only when she heard an unmistakable Southern drawl she dared glance over her shoulder. To see a woman in a leopard-print pantsuit and heels, tottering towards them. Despite the cool shade inside, she was still wearing her sunglasses and wide-brimmed sunhat, while in the crook of her arm she was carrying a designer tote bag that was so oversized it was almost bigger than she was.

*Birdy.*

Maggie recognized her immediately as the woman she and Flick had met in the restaurant in Rome. What on earth was she doing here? And, more importantly, was she going to survive the wrath of The Godmother, who looked up sharply at this sudden intrusion.

Maggie braced herself. As did the rest of the class.

'They sent me to another culinary school, but it was run by complete schmucks! Luckily my driver is local so he knew all about your world-class reputation and drove me here with his foot on the gas . . . I just hope I'm not too late to join your class.'

But if Maggie was thinking Mamma Lucia was going to scream at Birdy and shoo her out of her kitchen, she was very much mistaken. Instead, seemingly flattered by these compliments from this glamorous American woman who, quite possibly, was of a similar age, The Godmother's back visibly straightened, her chest inflated and, with a smile not unlike that of the *Mona Lisa*, she gestured for her to take an apron and join the rest of the students. Which Birdy dutifully did.

'*Grazie.*'

'*Prego.*'

The two women nodded respectfully to each other, like a couple of prize-winning boxers. In one corner there was the brassy American, in the other the terrifying Sicilian. It was as if both knew they'd met their match. It was quite remarkable actually.

Ten minutes later the demonstration was over and the students were asked to pick partners and move over to their work stations to begin their various tasks.

'We meet again.'

As Birdy appeared at her side, Maggie was now the one who felt flattered.

'You remember me?'

'I'm good with faces. I had six husbands.'

'Gosh.'

'Though I rarely remember all their names.' She laughed, removing her sunhat and sunglasses. 'But I remember yours. It's Maggie, right?'

'Yes.'

Taking a silk headscarf out of her bag, she proceeded to deftly wrap up her hair in an elaborate turban as Maggie watched her in fascination. Honestly, she couldn't look more fabulous. Meanwhile her own frizzy curls were pulled back into an elastic scrunchie.

'Where's your cute little friend?'

'Hiking a volcano.'

'Wowee. She's got some energy, that one. A real firecracker.'

'Yes, I know.' Maggie smiled fondly as she thought about Flick's earlier excitement. But this was coupled with a pang of anxiety. She hoped she wouldn't do anything stupid up there. It was an active volcano after all. 'So, what a coincidence, seeing you here!'

'Oh, I don't know about that. I don't believe in coincidences, do you?'

'*Allora!*'

The Godmother appeared beside them, rapping the countertop with a spatula.

'The pasta must be rolled thin before we make the lasagne!'

That said, if you were talking hot and dangerous with the risk of violent eruptions, look no further than this kitchen. And we're not just talking The Godmother. Huge frying pans of hot oil were bubbling and smoking on the giant stove, into which slices of aubergine were being dropped; butternut squash (and students' fingers) were being roasted until the flesh was tender; and there was a very dicey situation going on with the young man from Boston, an electric whisk and the bechamel.

'She's very serious,' muttered Maggie, as The Godmother moved on to the next nervous students.

'Food is a serious business.' Birdy rolled out the dough with surprising expertise. 'I've had countless men fall in love with me for my buttermilk fried chicken and mashed potatoes.'

'They sound delicious.'

'Well, I wouldn't know, honey. I never ate any.'

'Whyever not?'

'I was keeping my figure.' Birdy patted her tiny waist. 'But I can tell you something. They didn't marry me for what I could do in the kitchen. Do you know what I'm saying?'

As Birdy raised an eyebrow and let out a low chuckle, Maggie blushed.

'You ever been married?'

'Once. A long time ago.'

'You're just getting started.' She laughed as she rolled out the dough and passed a piece to Maggie to feed through the pasta maker to make into lasagne sheets.

'I don't think so.' Maggie shook her head. 'I was engaged recently, but . . .'

'It didn't work out?'

'That's kind of an understatement.'

'Don't tell me. He's gay.'

Maggie blinked. 'Excuse me?'

'Sorry, that's me projecting. Husband number five was a lavender marriage. I was the last to find out. We're the best of friends now, though; I love his new husband. Total hottie and a real hoot.'

It was as if she had no filter and Maggie listened with amazement. Something about being with Birdy made her own story seem less shocking somehow.

'He was a fraudster.'

The words just came out.

'Oh, aren't they all.' Birdy shook her head and carried on rolling.

'No, but he really was. Evidently there's a term for it. A romance fraudster.' Maggie felt a sudden urge to open up to this woman she hardly knew. 'He was a con man. A thief. He stole everything from me. My life savings. My home. My business. My self-worth.'

She looked up to see Birdy staring at her. For once, she appeared lost for words.

'He was even petty enough to take sentimental family stuff like the diamond earrings I got for my twenty-first birthday and my dad's watch, not that it was worth anything, but it was all I had left of him . . .'

Maggie bit down hard on her lip to contain her emotions.

'He left me with nothing.'

'Well, honey, that's not true.'

'It is, he was a total scam artist and I had no idea.'

'No, what I'm talking about is he didn't leave you with nothing.'

Maggie looked at her blankly.

'You're not a nothing, Maggie. You're a something.'

She said it with such conviction that for a split second, Maggie almost believed her.

'I don't feel like a something,' she whispered quietly, a single tear unexpectedly trickling down her cheek.

'Well, I'm here to tell you you are. Trust me. Birdy Carmichael knows a something when she sees it.' Reaching across, Birdy gently but firmly wiped away the tear with a polished red fingernail. 'I don't care what you say, but there's a spirit inside of you.'

The older American woman fixed her with a steely expression.

'He didn't steal everything from you. No, siree. You are resilient and resourceful, and what doesn't kill you makes you stronger. Men underestimate us, but you must never, *ever* underestimate yourself.'

Birdy's eyes flashed with defiance and, despite her situation, Maggie felt herself buoyed up. Her temerity felt contagious.

'*Cosa sta succedendo qui?*'

A loud voice caused them to twirl around to see The Godmother behind them, listening. Having been so focused on their conversation, neither had noticed the fresh pasta had fallen in misshapen ribbons all over the counter.

'I'm sorry, we were talking—'

'No talking!' she bellowed, snatching up the ribbons and kneading them back into a ball of dough. Handing Birdy the rolling pin, she instructed her to feed the dough through the pasta maker, before turning to Maggie.

'Think of yourself like pasta,' The Godmother instructed. 'You have to be *al dente*.'

Maggie stared blankly, not understanding.

'*Al dente* means to the tooth. It has to have a bite to it –' she mimed gnashing her teeth violently and Maggie took a step backwards – 'too soft and mushy isn't good. It needs resistance. *Capisce?* You need to be like pasta!'

Maggie nodded at the advice. She needed to be *al dente*. She needed to toughen up.

'I need a drink,' declared Birdy, when they'd finally finished making their lasagne and put it in the oven and The Godmother had moved away to terrify another couple of students. 'Where's the vino?'

'In the fridge, but I think we're supposed to be having that with lunch.'

'It's called a liquid lunch, remember?'

Swooping on the large refrigerator while The Godmother's back was turned, Birdy pulled out a bottle of red, and quickly uncorked it.

'Here, have a glass.'

Pouring out two large tumblers, she passed one to Maggie. She didn't refuse.

'Isn't it a bit early to be drinking?'

'It's five o'clock somewhere.' Clinking her glass against Maggie's, she took a large swig. 'So, where were we? Ah yes, your ex-fiancé. So come on, where's the fucker now?'

Maggie looked over at Birdy, leaning against the counter, observing her.

'That's just it, I don't really know,' she shrugged. 'My friend Flick, she's a journalist. She found out he was in Monte Carlo, so we flew out last weekend, only he gave us the slip. But we know he's on a cruise ship, so we rented a car and we've been driving across Europe, following its itinerary, trying to find him ever since.'

'And what are you going to do when you find him?' Birdy raised a smile. 'Kill him?'

Maggie laughed. She actually laughed.

'And that's why you're in Taormina?'

'I know it sounds crazy.'

'I like crazy.' Birdy grinned. 'Being normal is totally overrated.'

The two women looked at each other as they realized they had more in common than they first thought.

'It sounds like quite some adventure. So where next?'

'Spain. We leave tomorrow.'

'Whereabouts?'

'Palma in Mallorca.'

'Well, would you believe it, that's where I'm heading.'

Maggie stared at her in surprise. 'No way. When's your flight?'

'Oh, I'm not flying, honey.' Draining the rest of her glass, Birdy reached for the bottle and refilled her glass. 'I'm on a cruise.'

# Letting Go

'And it's the same cruise.'

'Shut up!'

In the garden of a small trattoria, tucked away down a cobbled side street, Flick paused from diving on the breadbasket and stared wide-eyed at Maggie across the white linen tablecloth. It was one of those romantic restaurants, strung with fairy-lights, that catered for couples who liked to sit close together around a fountain, on tiny tables that forever wobbled, however many times you folded up a napkin and shoved it under various metal legs.

Still, the hotel had made the reservation and they were lucky to get a table as, being the height of summer, everywhere was fully booked. They'd arranged to meet here, rather than back at the hotel, and while Flick might have reasonably assumed that a day spent hiking an active volcano at three thousand metres would be more interesting than a cooking class, it turned out Maggie was the one with the exciting news.

'So has she seen him?'

'You just told me to shut up.'

'It's an expression of disbelief,' gasped Flick, exasperated. Honestly, sometimes Maggie felt like her mother and not in a good way.

'Well, it's a stupid expression.'

'So, has she?'

'She couldn't recall meeting anyone of that name. But then, there's thousands of people on board.'

As soon as Birdy had said she was on a cruise, Maggie had felt her stomach drop. Turns out it was the very same *Galaxy Goddess* he'd embarked in Monte Carlo. Yet when she told Birdy she didn't seem surprised at all, saying, 'See. I told you I don't believe in coincidences.'

'Didn't you show her a photo of him?'

'I don't have any. I deleted them.'

'All of them?'

That's what the policeman had said too, when Maggie had finally reported him missing, along with her life savings. He'd seemed incredulous and doubtful that anyone would do such a thing. As if somehow this made her story less believable. Why would she purposefully destroy the evidence? Obviously it had never happened to him so how could he possibly understand the desire to erase it all? He was young and newly married, judging by his shiny wedding ring. No doubt his photos were in silver frames and displayed proudly on the mantelpiece.

'Maybe I was a fool to delete them all.' Maggie shrugged. 'Not that it was easy.'

'Oh, you mean letting go.' Flick shot her a sympathetic look.

'No, I mean from iCloud.' She laughed then, unexpectedly. 'Have you any idea how hard it is to delete things from your iCloud? I am *so* not computer savvy. It took me for ever.'

'Harder still to delete them from your heart, though, huh?'

Flick's words caught Maggie by surprise. Was it that obvious, *still*?

But before she could deny it, Flick was tearing open a bread roll and buttering it.

'God, I'm starving. It's been a long day.'

'Sorry, I hijacked the conversation.'

'Hijack? Don't be daft. You had important news.'

'Well, not really. They're on the same cruise, but so what? So are thousands of other people.'

'It's another lead, though. Did you get her number?'

'No, I didn't. Sorry, I'm not an investigative reporter.'

But she had His number, thought Maggie, guilt stabbing. They'd texted each other. Arranged to meet.

'No worries.' Flick shrugged. 'Somehow I don't think we've seen the last of Birdy.'

'I know.'

As soon as she'd got some answers, she'd tell Flick. They could confront him together and she could get her story. She didn't know how, but she'd figure it out somehow. She just had to keep the secret a little bit longer.

'So how was the volcano? I'm dying to hear,' asked Maggie, changing the subject.

Flick paused from tearing up her bread roll, trying to find the right words. Her whole life, she'd relied on words to articulate her feelings, but for once, language felt inadequate to describe how she'd felt today. Standing on the edge of a volcano in Sicily, with its dramatic lunar landscape, looking down at the Ionian Sea. Doing something so completely different to her normal everyday life, with a bunch of strangers whom she'd probably never see again, but for those few hours felt like the best of friends.

She'd heard all the clichés about travel broadening the mind and being transformative, but she'd never really got it before. Never felt it, until today, when their guide had led them up to the crater and she'd felt a delicious moment of insignificance. Of getting out of her own head. Of abandoning the desire to always be in control, because up here even she knew she couldn't control a volcano so what was the point? Just let it go.

She thought for some time, then took the easy way out.
'Bloody amazing.'
'That's so great.'
'What about the cooking class?'
'Well, it was certainly an experience.'
'But did you enjoy it?'
'Yeah, it was good. Especially the food.' Maggie smiled, remembering the huge lunch they'd had afterwards, out in the garden, where they'd all sat at a long trestle table and feasted on one delicious dish after another. How could she be hungry again? 'Though The Godmother was pretty scary.'
'Was she really called The Godmother?'
'Yes, really. And trust me, she was *terrifying*.'
'What, you mean like this?'
And shoving the bread roll into the side of her cheeks, Flick then proceeded to do a terrible impression of Marlon Brando, which made Maggie laugh and snort the water down her nose, just as the very sniffy-looking waiter in a white jacket and bow tie came to take their order and several whispering diners glanced over. Including a couple who were fellow guests at the same hotel.

These two English women again. What are they like? Where are their husbands? asked the husband whose wife had dutifully rubbed suntan cream into his back as they'd sat by the pool. And the wife looked at her husband who she no longer had anything in common with and wondered the same thing. She wished she could join them. They looked like they were having so much fun.

After a large carafe of wine, two huge plates of linguine con vongole, plus dessert and espresso, it was time to head back to their hotel.
'I ate too much,' groaned Flick, looping her arm through

Maggie's as they navigated the winding back streets. 'I need to lie down.'

'You shouldn't have had the cannoli.'

'Oh my God, those things were delicious.'

'I can't believe you've never had one before.'

'I was a cannoli virgin.'

The two women laughed as they walked through the backstreets back to their hotel. It was such a lovely evening. Taormina was so beautiful at night. The way it was illuminated. The streets had emptied out with tourists and it felt almost like their own secret. Soon they reached the entrance to their hotel: a discreet stone archway, covered in bougainvillea.

Flick stopped walking. 'OK, I'm off to bed, I'm exhausted.'

'I'll be up in a minute.'

'Where are you going? It's almost midnight.'

'I just want to stretch my legs a bit. Walk off some of that linguine.'

Unlinking arms, Flick went into the hotel and Maggie continued down the stone steps. She could hear faint music and followed it, turning a corner into a square, where a bunch of people were gathered outside the church. There appeared to be a woman, teaching the steps to a dance. The music was lilting folk music and as they joined arms, dancing in a circle, Maggie stood in the shadows watching, as they looped and twirled.

An old man dancing looked over to her and said something in Italian. Maggie smiled and gestured that she didn't understand, but he smiled and gestured back for her to join them.

'*No, grazie.*' She smiled, shaking her head. She didn't know the steps.

But he ignored her protestations. Another woman held out her hand. And before Maggie knew it, she was holding their hands and part of their circle, smiling and laughing and looking at her feet, as they taught her the steps. She couldn't remember the last time she'd danced. She must have been in her twenties, a teenager maybe; was it before her brother died? She'd always felt too self-conscious, that she wasn't a good dancer, but here in the moonlit square in Sicily, with a bunch of strangers, as the clock struck midnight, none of that mattered any more and she felt herself letting go.

Can you still meet?

**It depends where.**

Maggie thought about the itinerary Flick had meticulously planned and wondered where he was going to suggest. She felt suddenly doubtful about her plan.

I'll be in Palma, Mallorca, in two days.

She felt a strange rush of relief. So would they. To meet his cruise ship.

**Spain??**

Well, she had to act surprised.

Yes. Will you come?

**OK, I'll try.**

Great. I'll text you the address later.

**How can I trust you again, Theo?**
**After what's happened?**

I swear on my life. Just don't tell anyone, right?

**OK.**

Thanks, Mags. I'll make it up to you. I promise.

*Liar, liar, liar.* Maggie stared at the screen, then typed one letter:

**X**

# Mallorca

*Day Seven*

*Seven more days to go*

# Viva España!

The Spanish flamenco dancer wore a red frilly dress with gold spots and black netting, her shiny black hair piled high in an elaborate bun and fixed with a comb from which hung a lace mantilla, while in her tiny plastic hand, lifted high above her head, she held a fan.

As a little girl, Flick had loved that doll. It might have only been seven inches high, but it was her most prized possession and took pride of place on the mantelpiece of their pebble-dashed two-up, two-down. It had been a gift from Auntie Pam and Uncle Dave, who'd once swapped their traditional two weeks on the Isle of Wight for a package holiday to Spain and had returned home with sunburn, dodgy stomachs and a steely resolution to never leave for foreign shores again.

'I mean, can you believe it, they eat octopus!' had shuddered Uncle Dave, while digging into a plate of tripe and onions in the safety of his limed-oak kitchen.

'And all that sunshine can't be good for you,' observed Auntie Pam, applying calamine to her red and peeling shoulders while she waited for the rain to stop so she could hang out their holiday clothes on the line to dry.

But seven-year-old Flick hadn't listened. Instead she'd looked with wide-eyed wonder at her souvenir from Spain. She'd never been into dolls before, with their boring pinafores and blonde plaits, or worse still, the ones that looked like babies and which you were supposed to feed with a bottle and change its nappy. But this doll was different.

With her brightly coloured clothes she looked like an exotic bird and Flick was fascinated. She was so beautiful and so bold; with her arms thrown defiantly over her head and leg kicked out high, she felt less of a doll and more of a superhero. Whenever Flick had a bad day at school, she'd come home and take her down from the mantelpiece and together Flick and the Spanish flamenco dancer would run away from the bullies who picked on her in the playground for not having a dad, away from her mum who worked three jobs and was always tired and cranky, away from a two-up, two-down terrace in a northern industrial town and go on exciting adventures to Spain.

'I wonder what happened to that doll . . .'

'S'cuse me?'

Flick snapped back to the present to see Maggie staring at her from across the back seat of the cab. They'd just flown into Palma from Sicily and were travelling to their hotel.

'Oh, I was just daydreaming.'

'About a doll?'

'About being in Spain,' she corrected, embarrassed. 'I can't believe I'm here, finally.'

Buzzing down the window, she gestured to the palm trees and promenades and parasols whizzing by.

'I know.' Maggie nodded. 'We've been travelling for hours. It was that three-hour layover in Barcelona that did it.'

But that's not what Flick meant by finally. Finally wasn't about a few hours, finally was about all the years that had passed since she was that confused and upset seven-year-old who played with her Spanish flamenco dancer and dreamed of visiting Spain one day. And now here she was and she couldn't quite believe it.

But how can you explain stuff like that, in the back of a taxi on the way from the airport, to someone you only met a couple of weeks ago? Maggie was no longer a stranger; they'd grown close, yet when it came to sharing certain details of her past, she wouldn't know where to start.

So instead she just nodded in agreement and glanced at her watch.

'It's six thirty.'

'Perfect timing. We can dump our bags and go get a sundowner.'

'I'm not sure we can afford one. Did you see the price of the car rental?'

Maggie blanched. After deciding their next destination was going to be Palma, in Mallorca, they'd soon realized they were going to have to fly to the Spanish island. Which meant saying goodbye to their rental car. As luck would have it, the company had an office at Catania Airport, so they could drive there, leave the Fiat, and get straight on a flight. Perfect!

Except, have you ever tried to do a one-way rental? Worse still, picking up in one country and dropping off in another? Last-minute? No, neither had Flick and Maggie and they nearly fell on the floor when the salesman gave them their bill.

'It would have been cheaper to buy a Fiat 500,' Maggie was saying now.

'Good job we won at Monte Carlo.'

'You won at Monte Carlo?' The cab driver's ears pricked up. It was the first time he'd spoken during the journey, other than to ask them the name of their hotel.

'Yes, we did,' replied Flick. Only now, saying it out loud, did she realize how crazy it sounded. He probably thought they were millionaires.

'Wowee.' He let out a low whistle. 'What did you spend your winnings on?'

The two women looked at each other. How to answer that?

'A trip of a lifetime,' replied Maggie, catching his eye in the rear-view and giving a wry smile.

'Man, I need a holiday.' Shaking his head wistfully, his face split into a grin. 'So, c'mon, tell me, where've you been?'

'Well, we started in Monaco.' Flick began playing along. Well, it felt rude not to. 'Then drove to the French Riviera, Rome, the Amalfi Coast, Taormina.'

'Where's that?'

'Sicily.'

'You drove all the way to Sicily?'

Said like that it did sound a bit mad.

'And what's been the best bit so far?'

Flick and Maggie glanced at each other, their minds flicking back. Walking through the backstreets of Rome. Time standing still in the Sistine Chapel. Watching the sunset on the Amalfi Coast. Dancing in the square at midnight. The negronis. The pizza. The view from the crater of the volcano. That first cold shower when they'd been driving for hours.

It was different for both of them, and yet it was the same.

Until now they'd been so focused on finding him, and on all their private fears and frustrations, that they hadn't given it much thought. But suddenly there it all was, like a highlights reel thrown up by their iPhone.

'The gaps in between,' replied Flick.

The driver frowned. 'Huh, I don't get it?'

But the two women did. Because it wasn't about any of the highlights. And as Maggie looked at Flick across the back of the taxi, they both made the same gesture with their forefingers. Almost, but not quite touching. Because that's where life truly happens.

*

'OK, we're here.'

A few moments later, the taxi pulled up in front of a large, high-rise hotel. Surrounded by palm trees and with several flags flying above the entrance, it was a world away from their first Airbnb in Monte Carlo.

'Wow, this looks swanky,' said Maggie, as the taxi driver left with a large tip and an instruction to enjoy the rest of their trip. 'It must have cost a fortune.'

'No, it was on special. I booked it a few days ago on my app,' said Flick, as they stood on the pavement outside with their wheelie suitcases. 'I thought I'd try to be organized and not leave it to the last minute.'

'You've got an app for booking hotels?'

'Of course. There's an app for everything.'

'*Everything?*' Maggie raised an eyebrow.

'Pretty much.'

'OK, so what about doing the laundry, or shaving your legs, or unloading the dishwasher?'

Flick threw her a withering look. 'Of course not.'

'Well, there isn't an app for everything, then, is there?' Grabbing her suitcase, Maggie headed towards the entrance.

'Maggie, you sound like an old person.'

'I am an old person. I turn fifty on Monday.'

'What? It's your birthday?' Flick hurried to catch her up, but Maggie was already inside the revolving door. Waiting her turn, she quickly followed her into the lobby of the hotel. 'Why didn't you say?'

Maggie shrugged. 'I'm trying not to think about it.'

'We'll have to celebrate.'

'That's why I didn't mention it.'

'*Buenas noches.*'

As they both headed towards the large front desk, they

were greeted by Juan, who welcomed them to the hotel and took their passports.

'Actually, there probably is one for doing the laundry,' added Flick, as they were being checked in.

Maggie looked at her blankly.

'An app.' Digging out her phone, she started scrolling. 'Not sure about shaving your legs, though.'

'You have a message.'

Abruptly, Juan caught their attention.

'A message?' repeated Maggie, as they both turned to him in surprise. 'From who?'

Flick resisted the urge to correct her.

'He didn't give his name. It was from an English gentleman.'

The two women looked at each other, their minds racing.

'Who knows we're here?'

'No one.'

'Have you told anyone?'

'Like who? My missing cat?'

There was a heavy pause.

'You don't think . . . ?'

'What? That's Him?' Maggie's mind was falling over itself as she thought about their secret text exchanges. That's exactly what she *was* thinking. Had she said anything? Given anything away? 'No, of course not,' she quickly dismissed the idea.

They were interrupted by Juan clearing his throat for attention.

'He asked me to tell you he is waiting for you in the lounge bar.'

Flick and Maggie froze.

'Please. Allow me to send your luggage up to your room and one of our front desk will show you to the bar.'

Suddenly they were being escorted through the lobby and into the lounge.

'Maybe he's found out we're following him,' whispered Flick, her heart racing. Maybe they hadn't found him, *he'd found them*.

'And the hotel we're staying in?' Maggie didn't look convinced. It didn't make sense. How could that be? And yet, abruptly she felt sick with nerves. Was this it? Was this the moment?

Hearts thumping, minds racing, they were met by a waiter who led them past tables of hotel guests, over to a booth by the window where a man was sitting, his back turned away from them.

'*Señor?*'

There was split second before the waiter got his attention. Later, it would transpire he'd been wearing his AirPods and listening to a true-crime podcast; they were his favourite, and he was just at the part where the killer was about to get caught red-handed . . . But then, abruptly, he saw them out of the corner of his eye and jumped up from his seat, flinging his arms out wide and yelling.

'Surprise!'

And that's when Flick got the shock of her life.

'*Rory?*'

# It's Complicated

If there's one thing in the world Flick didn't like, it was surprises. Some people love them. Flick was not one of those people. Surprises made her deeply anxious. If the pressure to look pleased and happy and excited by this unexpected event wasn't stressful enough, it was the sudden loss of control over the situation.

And as far as surprises go, having your boyfriend fly to Mallorca and show up at your hotel was one hell of a big one.

'I can't believe it. What are you doing here?'

It was a few minutes later and Flick was sitting in a booth with Rory, still staring at him in disbelief. After brief introductions, Maggie had made her excuses and gone up to their room. 'I'll leave you two lovebirds to it,' she'd smiled, disappearing to take a shower. And now it was just the two of them.

'Well, that's not the welcome I was expecting,' he laughed.

'But how did you know where I was?'

'Call me Sherlock.' Winking, he tapped his nose.

'No, seriously.'

'We share the same hotel booking account, babe.'

*Of course.*

'And I had the weekend off, so I thought I'd fly out and surprise you.'

'Well, you certainly did that.' She forced a bright smile,

while trying to hide the complicated feelings inside her. There were many things she was feeling right now, but one of them definitely wasn't lovebirds.

'Good one, huh?'

'Brilliant.'

They were interrupted by a waiter who came to take their drinks order. Rory ordered another beer. He was in shorts and T-shirt, thrilled to be in Spain. He'd got there earlier and was red from sitting in the sun. Flick realized she felt irritated by his surprise appearance. Also, she felt like a completely different person since she last saw him. Was it only a week? She'd changed so much and seen so much. She'd even hiked a volcano.

'And a vodka tonic for the lady.'

'Actually, can I have a negroni?'

Rory frowned. 'What's got into you? You always have a vodka tonic.'

'I don't know, I just fancied a change.' Flick shrugged. 'Have you had one? They're delicious.'

'What's in them?'

'Um . . . gin and Campari, I think, and something else. I can't remember.'

Rory wrinkled his nose. 'I'll stick to beer.'

'You can try mine if you like, see if you like it.'

'No, thanks. I'm not into fancy cocktails.'

'It's not a fancy cocktail, everyone was drinking them in Italy.'

As soon as she mentioned Italy, Flick knew she shouldn't have. Rory's face clouded.

'Well, you won't be drinking those when you're back home.'

'Oh, I don't know, I'll have to get Colin to serve them at the pub,' she teased, but Rory didn't laugh.

'I missed you.'

'I've only been gone a week.'

'Didn't you miss me?'

'Of course.'

She was lying. She hadn't missed Rory at all.

'Come here, you.'

Draping his arm around her shoulder, he pulled her in close for a kiss. Flick tried to relax, but he was being all weird and insecure. Flying out here, surprising her like this. What had got into him? Rory hadn't been like this when he'd gone off with the lads to Germany last month to watch the UEFA Champions League. A whole week in Munich and she barely heard a peep from him, other than a couple of thumbs-up emojis whenever she'd texted to see how it was going. Or the time he'd gone camping in Scotland for Callum's stag weekend – which from her memory, was a very *long* weekend – and he'd gone off-grid. Which she suspected was another word for whisky-tasting.

'Nice place this.' Rory looked around at the hotel bar. 'Can't believe *The Local Echo* stretched to this! How does it work then, do you just put in your expenses at the end?'

'Um, yes.'

'Must be doing better than we thought, old Seymour.'

'Hmm.'

'Charges an arm and a leg for the classifieds. Remember when our kid got married?'

Our kid being Rory's brother. Flick nodded vaguely.

'So—'

'So—'

'What shall we do this weekend?'

'Well, to be honest, I'm supposed to be working.'

'Oh, c'mon, I've flown all this way to see you! Can't you take a day off? What's so important about this story anyway? What's the big secret?'

Flick felt herself clam up. She didn't want to tell Rory. He always trivialized her job on the paper. 'It's not like you're saving lives,' he'd retort, if ever she got stressed about work. And while she knew he was just saying that to make her feel better – 'I'm just trying to put things in perspective, babe' – she couldn't help wondering whose perspective exactly, because it only made her feel worse. In fact, just the fact he'd shown up, expecting her to drop everything to make time for him, was indicative of his attitude towards her career.

'Oh, it's nothing.'

'Can't be nothing. Not if it's top secret and they've got you out here,' he continued. 'I thought the local paper was supposed to be about local news, anyhow?'

Rory frowned and swigged his beer, his forehead creasing. It was the colour of beetroot. That was going to be painful tomorrow, thought Flick absently.

'Don't tell me, it's drugs.'

'What?' She snapped back.

'It's a drugs ring. All that weed they're selling down by the canal. It's coming from out here, isn't it? Is that why they've got you gallivanting across Europe? Chasing the source?'

Rory broke off, shaking his head; the effect of his second beer, his true-crime podcast and too much sun were beginning to fuel his imagination.

'Bloody hell, Flick, you be careful.'

'Don't be silly.'

'Haven't you seen *Narcos*?'

'Rory, please, it's not a drugs ring.' Flick felt a stab of guilt. She felt bad lying to Rory. 'And I think a Colombian cartel is slightly different to the teenagers from the local comp smoking spliffs by the canal,' she teased, trying to diffuse the situation. 'You've been listening to too many of those true-crime podcasts.'

But Rory looked put out. 'It's not funny, you know.'

'I'm sorry, you're right.' Flick felt suitably chastised. Rory had a habit of always making her feel like she'd said the wrong thing.

'Honestly, I don't know what's got into you, Flick. Ever since you lost your mum . . .'

At the mention of her mum, Flick felt herself brace.

'I'm worried about you.' Rory softened, leaning forward and rubbing her arm.

And now she was actually feeling a bit terrible. None of this was Rory's fault. She was being totally selfish. He didn't know her and Maggie had all these plans for tomorrow, and now they were ruined. He'd flown out to see her, because he missed her and was worried about her. So many of her friends at uni had been in shitty relationships with bad boyfriends who didn't seem to care, but she was lucky. Rory had always been there for her. Ever since she was sixteen. She should be grateful that he cared, that he wanted to see her.

*Control her.*

A little voice in her head. She brushed it aside swiftly.

'Why don't we get something to eat?' she said brightly, changing the subject. 'There's supposed to be some lovely restaurants down by the port.'

'What about your work colleague?'

For a moment she wondered who he was talking about, before realizing.

'Oh, I'm sure Maggie will be fine. She'll probably be pleased to get a night off from me.' She forced a laugh.

'I feel like I've seen her before.' Draining his beer, Rory looked thoughtful.

'You might have, she's living just outside town. That's how we met. We're working on a story together,' she added quickly, before he could ask where exactly she lived.

'Investigative journalism, eh?' Rory spoke slowly,

enunciating every syllable, then laughed as if this was the funniest thing ever. 'Sorry, I'm not taking the mick, I'm just teasing.' He leaned in and gave her a kiss. 'To be honest, I'm just relieved you're not with another bloke.'

'Rory,' she protested, irritated again.

'Well, when I saw that honeymoon suite, what did you expect me to think?'

Flick shook her head. Honestly, those bloody swan-shaped towels had a lot to answer for.

'Made me realize a few things.'

'Well, I'm not with another bloke, am I? I'm with you,' she said briskly, determined to get off this subject. 'So, what do you fancy doing?'

'You.'

'Are you drunk?'

'On two beers?' he protested, looking affronted, but his squiffyness betrayed the several more he'd drunk in the airport and on the plane.

'I might go take a shower, get changed.' It was all too much. Flick needed a few minutes by herself to decompress.

'I got us another room,' he winked. 'Bit pricey, but we've got a lot of catching up to do.'

'It's only been a week.'

'A week's a long time in the life of Rory Armstrong.'

Flick hated it when he spoke about himself in the third person. She stood up.

'I'll wait for you down here in the bar. I've already had a shower and got changed before you arrived. Wanted to look my best for you,' he winked, pulling the room key from out of his shorts and passing it to her.

'Thanks.' She gave him a quick peck on the lips.

'Don't be long, I want to hit the town, it's Friday night,' he said, as she began walking away. 'And, hey, babe?'

Flick turned. Rory was sitting in the booth, a drunken smile on his face.

'Good surprise, eh?'

She forced a smile. 'Yeah, good surprise.'

Are you here?

                                                            **Yes.**

Great.

                    **So where do you want to meet?**

Meet me at Bar Tio.
It's on the corner, by the port.

                                   **What time?**

How about 5 p.m.? Is that OK?

Maggie hesitated. Was she really going to go through with this?

                              **Yes, it's fine.**

Be good to see you, Mags.

                                 **You too, Theo.**

# A Change of Plan

On Saturday morning, Maggie found herself in the curious position of waking up in a hotel room completely alone.

It felt weird, to be without Flick. Over the past seven days and God knows how many European towns and cities, she'd got used to her being there – her stuff strewn all over, the wet towels on the bed, the sheer amount of time she took in the shower. Seriously, you'd think a human being would dissolve in there. Er, hello? Weren't they supposed to be *conserving* water?

Maggie had never known anyone be in the bathroom that long. Which seemed more than a tad hypocritical, considering Flick's stance on the environment, which she was forever banging on about. Honestly, you should've seen the fuss she made when she'd caught Maggie using a packet of facial cleansing wipes.

'But it says they're biodegradable,' she'd protested weakly.

'In about a million years,' retorted Flick, morally brandishing a flannel.

Of course Flick had an answer, because she had an answer to everything. Which is why she could be insufferable and infuriating. Thing is, she could be equally wonderful, with her funny observations, wry sense of humour and tendency to overthink. Maggie had never seen herself as a mother, having discovered quite early on that instead of the maternal urge everyone talked about, she just felt a deep panic whenever anyone thrust a newborn at her. But being with Flick had made her think it might be rather nice to have a grown-up daughter.

That said, it was pretty fabulous being able to get in the bathroom.

After showering and getting dressed, she went down for breakfast. As expected, there was no sign of Flick or Rory. No doubt, they were doing what most twenty-something couples do in hotel rooms. And it's not getting up early to make the continental buffet, thought Maggie, trying to decide between all the delicious-looking pastries, then thinking sod it and piling them all onto her plate.

Finding an empty table, she sat down and pulled out her phone. Rory's surprise arrival had thrown all their plans out of the window and, with Flick otherwise engaged, Maggie was now on her own for the day. Which meant the onus was on her to try and find Him; only of course, she didn't need to *find* Him. She didn't need to head down to the port where the cruise ships dock to scan the crowds for disembarking passengers, or spend all day in the searing heat scouring the island for possible sightings. Because she knew exactly where he was going to be: come 5 p.m. he was going to be waiting for her in a bar in town.

Her stomach flipped and she stared again at his texts. If she was hoping she'd feel pleased, triumphant even, at this major coup, she was mistaken. Anxiety churned. It was still hard to believe that it was actually happening. That in a few hours they'd be face to face for the first time since he disappeared over six months ago. Since he stole her life. Broke her heart. Detonated a bomb in her world. Left her in the wreckage, dazed and confused and trying to pick up the pieces.

Now here she was in Spain, about to see him again, and she was filled with trepidation. And there was something else. Some emotion harder to identify. Excitement? Relief? Curiosity?

*Love?*

Her stomach flipped again and Maggie took a gulp of coffee, determined to block out that thought. Each time her resolve wavered, she tried to bolster it with caffeine. It was natural to have misgivings. To be worried that she was doing the right thing. After everything that had happened, who wouldn't be? In her texts she'd played along, letting him think she was falling for his lies. But she was the one who was lying now, pretending to trust him. But there was no point panicking and getting cold feet now. Better still to focus on Flick's reaction afterwards, when she would be able to tell her that he'd agreed to the interview she so desperately wanted. She'd be so pleased, she wouldn't care about the deception.

Because that was now a big part of agreeing to meet him. It wasn't just about being able to confront him and ask him: *why? Why her?* All the deception, the lies, he faked everything, was any of it ever real? The way he'd looked at her, the things he'd said, she thought she'd found love, that they had something special. Losing all the money was terrible, but the emotional impact was in many ways so much worse than the financial loss. Something which she couldn't get the police officer to understand.

It was also about persuading him to agree to talk to Flick. Convince him somehow. Maggie was determined. Before, when she'd turned up at her caravan, she'd just been this random young reporter. A local hack trying to get a story. And Maggie hadn't come on this trip because of her; she'd come on this trip because she'd got nothing to lose.

But Flick *did* have something to lose. She'd staked a lot on this, both personally and professionally. This could be the big break she was looking for. And now, having grown close, Maggie wanted to give it to her. She cared about Flick and despite her conviction that everyone wanted to tell their side of the story, Maggie wasn't so sure. Better that she spoke to him first.

'More coffee?'

'Um, yes, please.'

As the waiter topped up her coffee Maggie took a bite of her pastry.

'*Bueno*, huh?'

Seeing him gesturing towards the pile on her plate, she reddened.

'Mmm, yes,' she mumbled through a mouthful of delicious puff pastry crumbs. '*Muy bueno.*'

He smiled then and she smiled back. A moment of mutual pastry gratification, and something about that brief encounter cheered Maggie up. She'd been so fixated on her meeting at five, she hadn't given much thought to anything else, but now it dawned on her that it meant she was freed up to do whatever she wanted to that day. She could sit by the pool. Head to the beach. Even go shopping, though their winnings were rapidly dwindling and she'd never been much of a shopper.

Sitting back in her seat, Maggie turned to gaze out of the large windows, at the sunshine and blue skies and palm trees beyond, and thought about the whole day stretching ahead. Or better still, she could do her favourite thing in the whole world.

Go look at some art.

# Sunshine and Selfies

Meanwhile, on the other side of the island, Flick was hanging on for dear life.

'Slow down!'

'I can't hear you!'

She was whizzing along on the back seat of a rented scooter, arms tightly wrapped around Rory's waist, trying not to fall off or throw up as they headed high up into the Serra de Tramuntana mountains.

'I said, slow down!' she yelled, trying to make herself heard above the screaming buzz of the Vespa engine. 'You're going to get us both killed!'

'I know, isn't it amazing?' yelled back Rory, as he navigated a series of hairpin turns. 'I knew you'd be thrilled!'

They'd woken late after a boozy night out on the town. She'd wanted to go to bed earlier but Rory had told her not to be boring and ordered another round of Sambucas and she didn't want to be the one to spoil the fun. So they'd stayed up late partying, a word which always made Flick roll her eyes whenever she saw it in the tabloids to describe photos of celebrities. She wouldn't mind if they were *actually partying* but most of the time they seemed to be doing normal, everyday things like having a quiet meal in a restaurant, grabbing a takeout coffee or going shopping.

In which case, she must have been partying with a supermarket trolley in Tesco's last week and never even known it.

But last night they really did party. Starting with dinner in a great little tapas bar – washing down delicious plates of gambas al ajillo, patatas bravas and tortilla Española with carafes of dry white wine – where Flick felt herself slowly starting to relax. Despite her initial reservations, the awkward atmosphere between them both melted away and the good humour returned. Rory was his funny old self. Cracking jokes and making her laugh. Reminding her of why she'd fallen for him all those years ago, age sixteen on the back of the school bus, and making her forget about their differences.

Dinner was followed by several bars and a cheesy nightclub; it was gone 3 a.m. by the time they'd rolled back to the hotel, where Rory had immediately fallen asleep and she'd lain next to him in bed, alarmed by a sudden and unexpected relief that they weren't going to have sex. What was wrong with her? She'd stared at the familiar contours of his back, the broad shoulders with his teenage dolphin tattoo, the soft fuzz on the nape of his neck, and felt both comforted and confused.

Before telling herself she was overthinking things and reaching for her phone to see if Theo Stratin or any of his alias accounts had posted or been tagged in anything. Checking was now a habit. But no, there'd been nothing new for days now.

She must have fallen asleep with the phone still in her hand, because the next thing she knew she was being woken by the light streaming in through a gap in the curtains and Rory's hard-on pressed against her thigh. That was another difference between them. Rory liked to do it in the morning, whereas she was the opposite. She preferred nighttime, preferably after she'd cleaned her teeth and had a shower. When she was feeling relaxed and in the mood, not first thing in the morning with a to-do list running through her head and morning breath.

But they weren't at home with jobs to get to, they were in Mallorca, in a fancy hotel room, and they hadn't seen each other all week. Plus, Rory was being so sweet and attentive and she did love him. Of course she did. She was just going through some stuff. Since her mum died, she'd been all over the place, confused about everything; but, Rory, he was always there for her. 'What would you do without me?' he would say, wrapping his arms around her.

So they had sex and afterwards, lying with her head on his chest, she firmly brushed away any doubts. *It's not you, it's me*, she told herself, over and over. *It's not you, it's me.*

They entered a pretty hilltop village and Flick felt a wave of relief as Rory pulled over and cut the engine in the tiny square. Being completely off the beaten track, it appeared to be devoid of tourists. In the middle was a stone fountain and in the corner a tiny bar spilled tables and chairs onto the cobbles, which were filled with local workmen drinking beers.

'I thought we could stop here for lunch.'

'Great.' Clambering off the scooter, she undid her helmet. Her ears were still ringing.

'Do they serve food?'

'Yeah, it's a tiny bar menu, but the food's supposed to be the best on the island.'

'You knew about this place?'

'Well, don't look so surprised.'

Flick felt a stab of guilt and immediately tried to rearrange her features into an expression of *un*surprise.

'Why do you think we came all the way up here?'

'Um, I dunno . . . sightseeing?'

She felt distinctly wary. Something weird was going on.

'Babe, you always underestimate me,' smiled Rory, stroking her hair and tucking a rogue piece behind her ear. He looked ridiculously pleased with himself. 'C'mon, let's go sit down.'

Taking her hand, he led them over to the only empty table.

'It says it's reserved,' hissed Flick, pointing to the reserved sign.

'It is. For us,' beamed Rory, pulling out her chair.

Pulling out her chair? Reserving a table? Flick felt a jolt of surprise. What on earth was going on with him? In all the years she had been with Rory, he'd never made a restaurant reservation, preferring instead to leave everything to the last minute. Loosen up, you need to be more spontaneous, he would tell her.

Which is why they ended up having the most almighty row last year on her birthday when he was supposed to be taking her out for a nice meal and a movie and they ended up at the local chippie as everywhere was busy.

'But they do the best fish and chips, you've said it yourself,' Rory had said, as they sat in his car, vinegar soaking through the chip paper and onto her new jeans. Which was true, they were delicious, but she probably wouldn't have minded so much if she hadn't just spent two hours with a painful cricked neck, as the only seats left available in the cinema were on the front row.

'*Buenos días.*' A smiling waitress arrived with menus and water for the table.

'*Buenos días.*' Rory smiled, settling himself down opposite her. 'I'll have a small beer, please, and what about you, Flick – one of those negronis you like?'

Flick looked at him suspiciously. Something was definitely up.

'No, just water, thanks. I've still got a bit of a hangover from last night.'

'Oh, come on, have a drink. What about a glass of prosecco?'

'Rory, when have you ever seen me drinking prosecco?'

'I dunno, I thought you might like some bubbles.'

'Bubbles?'

'You know, fizzy.'

'Prosecco is Italian, but here in Spain we have cava,' said the waitress helpfully. 'Personally, I think it's much nicer. Would you like a glass?'

Feeling ambushed, Flick shook her head. 'No. Thank you. Just water.' She smiled, apologetically. 'Sparkling,' she added, then turned to Rory. 'Well, that's fizzy.'

He looked temporarily put out, but quickly rallied.

'And could we have a couple of your famous gazpacho to start.'

'Of course.' The waitress smiled. 'I'll be back to take the rest of your order.'

'*Famous gazpacho?*' Flick looked incredulous.

'I've done my research.' Leaning back in his chair, he pulled out his phone.

'You know it's cold soup, right?'

'It is?' He looked momentarily stricken, then shrugged. 'I'm sure it'll be grand. Like you, babe,' he added, reaching for her hand across the table.

'Are you feeling all right?' Flick wondered if he'd had too much sun the day before.

'Can't a man pay a compliment to his girlfriend these days?'

'Yes, of course, it's just . . .' She trailed off. He was right. It was so lovely here and he'd made such an effort, bringing her up here, booking a table, doing all this research; it was so thoughtful. Why not just sit back and enjoy it?

'Shall we take a selfie?'

She snapped back to see Rory leaning towards her, angling

his phone above their heads, a huge grin on his face. *A selfie?* This, from a man who always said he hated having his photo taken. In ten years, the only one of them both smiling was taken at his brother's wedding. And that was only after his brother threatened he'd kill him if he ruined the official photos.

'Are you sure you're feeling all right?'

'Never better!' Putting his arm around her, he pulled her close. 'I just want to remember this moment.'

'Smile!'

*Stop being so suspicious. Rory is just being nice*, she told herself.

Click. And there it was. A selfie. For ever capturing a moment in time when a smiling young couple had a romantic lunch in a gorgeous little village in the Mallorcan countryside.

*Too nice.*

# The Countdown Begins

*12 p.m.*

A bus ride away from the centre of Palma, at the Fundació Miró Mallorca art gallery and museum, Maggie shifted onto the other foot as she gazed at the paintings by Joan Miró, one of the most famous Spanish artists of the twentieth century. She'd been standing here for who knows how long, so transfixed she'd lost track of time, and the small of her back ached. Still, she couldn't tear herself away.

She'd arrived a couple of hours ago and immediately immersed herself. Art galleries were her happy place. Not just because of how they made her feel, but because they were always where she felt closest to her brother, Charlie. She'd been thinking about him a lot recently. She wondered what he'd say if he could see her now. His little sister, her life fallen apart. As her big brother, he'd always looked out for her. Would he have protected her, tried to warn her? Or would she have been too stubborn and pig-headed to listen?

Remembering their teenage arguments, Maggie smiled. She knew the answer to that already. One thing was for certain, he would have approved of her coming here. She could see him now. *Go get him, sis.* Always encouraging her to stick up for herself. Always giving her the confidence she lacked. He was her biggest cheerleader.

Leaving the gallery, she walked outside into the gardens.

# SO, I MET THIS GUY . . .

It was midday and the sun was high in the sky, beating down. Even with a sunhat she could feel the intensity and, finding a spot in the shade, she sat down. It was lovely here, away from the buzz of the city and overlooking the bay. There was something so magical about art. It centred her. Lifted her. She drew a strength from it. Just coming here today she felt more energized and finally ready to face up to things.

Digging her phone out of her bag, she replayed the voicemail messages from the council and Ainsley, her friend the farmer. She'd been putting it off, but she couldn't ignore them any longer. The countdown was on. She was nearing the end of her journey. Once she'd met with Theo this evening, and Flick had got her interview, she could go home.

Even in the heat of the midday sun, she felt a twist of anxiety.

Still, there was no point putting it off any longer, she had to face up to things.

First up, Ainsley the farmer. She called, but he didn't answer, so she left him a message apologizing for not replying sooner and telling him she'd be home in a few days.

'Sorry you've had to deal with all this, Ainsley. I know you were doing a favour for Charlie. I can't thank you enough, but I'll be gone by the weekend.'

Where she was going to go, she still had no idea yet, but somehow it didn't feel as scary. Coming here, being on this trip, she'd found inner strengths. If she could do this, she could do anything. She knew she'd be OK. That was the power of worst-case scenarios – if you could survive the worst thing happening, you could survive anything.

Next, she emailed the council back, promising to move the caravan by the due date on the enforcement notice. She didn't bother to explain she'd been made homeless, that she'd had nowhere to go, that you can fall in love with the wrong person or make a bad decision and your life can collapse like a house of cards. She was sure the person in the planning department didn't want to hear all that. Or that by being on this trip she'd discovered that home wasn't about four walls, or a structure, it was about a place within.

Finally, she WhatsApped George.

> **Hey, sorry I haven't been in touch.**
> **A lot's been going on.**
> **I'm still away. It's a long story.**
> **I'll tell you all about it when I see you.**

Immediately the ticks went blue and seconds later he was trying to video-call her. She pressed accept and his face appeared on the screen.

'Don't think you can fob me off with a text like that!' he snorted. 'What's going on? When are you back?'

That's how it was with her and George – no need for the usual pleasantries, they just dived straight in.

'Not sure yet. Probably a couple of days.'

'Stop avoiding it.'

'Avoiding what?' Maggie tried to play dumb. She didn't want to tell George who she was meeting later, but neither did she want to lie to him. 'There's not much to tell. We haven't caught up with Him yet.' OK, not *strictly* a lie.

'I'm not talking about The Wanker; I'm talking about your birthday.'

'Oh. That.' Maggie had been trying to forget about it.

'Where are you going to be?

'Um, I'm not sure. Everything's a bit up in the air. We were supposed to be heading to Ibiza tomorrow and after that, taking the ferry to Valencia—'

'OK, I'm coming to meet you.' George didn't let her finish.
'What? No! That's crazy!'
'Do you think I'm going to let my best friend celebrate her big birthday without my fabulous self being there?'
'George, no, I want to ignore it. Pretend like it's not happening.'
'Bollocks.'
'I'm serious. What have I got to celebrate? I'm turning fifty and my business has gone bust, I'm living in a caravan from which I'm being evicted, and the man I thought I was going to marry turned out to be a con artist and stole all my money. I'm a mess.'
'A hot mess,' he corrected, grinning.
'George, I'm being serious.'
'So am I. Fuck all that shit. You're still standing, aren't you?'
'Well, I'm sitting actually,' smiled Maggie, from underneath the shade of a large tree. 'But yes, you're right. And you were right about telling me to come here, about having nothing to lose. I've learned a lot about myself. Plus I've seen a lot of great art,' she added, gazing across at a sculpture.
'See. Always listen to your best friend George.'
'It's just . . . look, there's a lot going on right now, I'm not sure your coming out is a good idea.'
'I'm always a good idea.'
She laughed then, because if one person could always make her laugh, whatever the circumstances, it was George.
'Send me details of where you're staying and I'll get a standby out on Monday and meet you in Valencia. And, no, I'm not taking no for an answer,' he interrupted, before she could protest. 'You can tell me about everything and we can celebrate. Just promise me one thing.'
'What's that?'

'No swimwear selfies.'

'George, I'm not on social media these days, and even if I was, I would never do a swimwear selfie,' she protested.

'That's what everyone says and then they turn fifty and it's get your bits out for the boys.' He grinned, rolling his eyes. 'I've witnessed it with all my friends. If I'm not careful, I'll be next.'

As he pulled a look of mock horror, Maggie shook her head, grinning.

'I've got to go. Bye, George.'

'Bye, beautiful. See you Monday.'

*2 p.m.*

'Thanks for lunch, Rory, it was delicious.'

'Yeah, shame about the building work, though.'

In the hill village, Flick and Rory were leaving the little bar, after their perfect lunch spot had been somewhat spoiled. There they'd been, having a lovely meal, when a truck had arrived, playing eighties power ballads loudly on the radio, and the several workmen next to them had finished their beers and started erecting scaffolding on the church opposite, with much clanking and banging, shattering the peace and quiet.

'I barely noticed,' lied Flick, trying to cheer Rory up, but Rory couldn't be cheered up. Disappointment clung to him, like a cloud.

'They ruined it,' he grumbled, scowling at the workmen as he put on his helmet.

'They didn't ruin it, it was lovely, especially the gazpacho,' she added, then wished she hadn't. Rory had left his after discovering she wasn't joking; it really was cold soup. Worse still, the waitress had greeted his request to heat it up with a puzzled frown.

'Come on, let's go,' he said, turning the ignition.

'Is that to another stop on the magical mystery tour?' she quipped, climbing on the back of the scooter, but Rory's sense of humour seemed to have deserted him and he didn't laugh. Flick wrapped her hands around his waist. It was going to be a long day.

## 2.45 p.m.

Back at the hotel, Maggie stood underneath an invigorating cold shower, relishing the feeling of the strong jets tingling her skin. There were lots of things she missed from her old flat but chief among them was her power shower. Turning, she tipped back her head, washing out the shampoo and conditioner, then began soaping up her arms and legs. She had tan lines. She hadn't noticed until now but this past week she'd gone from pale and freckly to golden. She stretched out a leg, pointing her toe and turning her foot back and forth, and decided she rather liked this new suntanned Maggie.

Turning off the water, she stepped out of the shower and wrapped herself in white fluffy towels. She'd got back from the gallery hot and sweaty and jumped straight in the shower. Gosh, it felt good. Clearing the steam from the mirror, she looked at herself in the mirror. She still had a couple of hours before she had to leave to meet him. Plenty of time to get ready. She wanted to look her best. Ridiculous really. Why did she care what he thought of her? But she did care. What woman doesn't want to look their best when they see their ex? Especially one that stole her life.

Exiting the bathroom, she flopped down on the bed for a

moment. It felt so nice to be clean and cool. The overhead fan circled above her and watching the blades going around and around, she let herself lose focus. She was tired. She'd been on the go all week and now it was almost over. She was going to close her eyes for a moment. Just a few minutes, then she'd start to get ready.

3.20 p.m.

'Shall we get a coffee?'

'No, I'm fine, thanks.'

'How about an ice cream?'

'No, honestly, I'm fine.'

They were in Deia, a picturesque coastal village on the northwest coast. With views out to the Mediterranean below, it was one of the prettiest on the island and had long been a magnet for famous artists, creatives and writers. Now a popular tourist destination, it was filled with crowds of holidaymakers, who meandered through the cobblestone streets, taking pictures and browsing the many galleries and shops.

Two being Flick and Rory.

'Ah, but didn't you tell me that women always say they're fine when they're actually not fine?' Rory tapped his nose, as if he had some kind of insider info, and looked very pleased with himself.

'No, but really I am this time,' protested Flick as they paused to look at a display of painted Spanish pottery. His earlier bad mood had disappeared and he was being so nice, but now it was actually becoming rather irritating. She caught herself. How could someone being nice be irritating? It didn't make sense. And yet, nothing right now was making sense.

'You seem annoyed,' he observed.

'I'm not annoyed.'

'Hmm. Distracted then.'

Flick chewed the inside of her lip and tried to count to ten. He was driving her potty with all this attention. Where was the Rory who could barely drag his eyes away from his phone when she was trying to talk to him? Apparently this was called phubbing. She'd read an article about it once and researchers said half of relationships were affected by phubbing.

Holding her hand tightly as they continued to walk down the street, he turned to her all doe-eyed and brushed an invisible hair from her face. God, what she'd do for a bit of phubbing right now.

'No, I'm not distracted,' she said, smiling.

What I am, thought Flick, is Frustrated with a capital 'F'. She'd had enough of all this lovey-dovey stuff; she wanted to be down by the port, standing guard by the cruise ships, watching the passengers come and go, on full alert for You Know Who. But instead she was romantically meandering the cobbled streets with Rory, who had inexplicably transformed into The Perfect Man.

She glanced sideways at him now.

Gone were the goofy jokes and comedy T-shirt, instead he was being thoughtful, super-attentive and wearing a freshly ironed linen shirt. Freshly ironed! By his own hand no less this morning in the hotel room. She wouldn't have believed it if she hadn't seen it with her own eyes. For a moment she'd lain in bed and thought she was hallucinating with the hangover, but no, it really was Rory in charge of an iron.

'You've been stressed this past year, what with your mum and work and everything; I just want you to relax,' he was saying now, stopping in the middle of the street to stare into her eyes.

He really was being lovely.

'I just want you to be happy. That's all I care about.'

A bit too lovely. Plus, she was really sweating now and she wanted to stop holding hands. It was romantic at first but it must be about a hundred degrees and her palm was all wet and sticky. She tried to casually disengage her fingers – but, feeling her pulling away, he clung on tighter. Out of nowhere, she felt a sudden wave of claustrophobia.

'I love you, babe.'

'Love you, too.'

And panic. There was no letting go.

*4.35 p.m.*

Maggie woke herself up by snorting.

'Huh? What? Where am I?'

She lay there a moment, discombobulated, wrapped in a cocoon of fluffy white towels; all warm and comfy and drowsy and floaty. It took a few seconds for her brain to click into gear and then –

Oh. My. God.

She bolted upright, causing the towel wrapped around her head to collapse over her face, smothering her with damp hair and towelling. She must have fallen asleep. Drifted off after the shower. Shit.

*What time is it?*

Blindly stumbling around the room, she grabbed her bag, rummaging around inside for her phone to check, whilst cursing handbag manufacturers everywhere for always using black lining so you were forever fumbling around in the dark. Not to mention all the rubbish she kept in there. Seriously, *chopsticks*?

Finally she found it and snatched it up – only to discover

it was dead. Fuck. She'd forgotten to charge it. Where was her charger? Panic-stricken, she turned her hotel room upside down. She couldn't find her charger! And then she remembered. She'd lent it to Flick.

FUCK.

Chucking the useless thing back in her bag with frustration, she dived on the phone on the bedside table and quickly dialled reception. She was meeting him at five o'clock so she needed at least a couple of hours to get ready and get to the bar in time. Finally, after what felt like for ever, a chirpy voice answered.

'*Buenos días.*'

'Hi, can you tell me what time it is, please?' she gasped.

There was a pause. Every second taking for ever. Her mind racing ahead. She had all these best-laid plans about what she was going to wear. How she was going to do her hair. Her make-up. She wanted to make sure she looked her absolute best.

'Four thirty-five, madam.'

She went hot and cold.

'Can I help you with anything else?'

'No. *Gracias.*'

Naked in a hotel room, with wet hair, a bare face, a dead phone and several miles to commute to a bar on the other side of town to meet the man who stole her life, Maggie hung up, threw her face into a pillow and screamed at the top of her lungs.

'Fuuuucccckkkkk!!!!!!'


*5 p.m.*

'We can watch the sunset from here.'

'Since when did you like watching sunsets?'

'What are you talking about? I love sunsets. Can't get enough of them.'

Having left Deia, Flick and Rory were now at the beach, lying side by side on a pair of sun loungers, underneath a tropical-style straw umbrella. Normally Rory would have refused to pay on principle, preferring to lie instead in the full sun without any shade whilst getting covered in sand, but this was the new Rory, and Flick was enjoying the novelty.

'Whenever I want to take a photo of one, you always tell me they're boring. In fact, I think your very words were, "Once you've seen one sunset, you've seen them all."'

Rory coloured. 'A man can change his opinion, can't he?'

'Sure.' Flick tried to keep the doubt out of her voice. She hoped that was true; after all, her job as a journalist involved trying to present the facts and change people's views and opinions. But could he change his entire personality?

'Perfect here, isn't it?'

'Yeah, it's lovely.'

'Would you say perfect, though?'

'Hmm . . . yeah, pretty much.' Lying in a bikini, she gazed through the Polaroid lenses of her sunglasses at the waves lapping against the shoreline and the stretch of spotless blue sky. 'But then is anything really ever perfect?'

'What do you mean?' Rory sounded aggrieved.

'I'm just saying in general. Life's not like Instagram. It all looks so perfect in the photos but it's all a bit bollocks really, isn't it? Life's a lot a messier than that.'

Rory looked put out.

'You don't think this is perfect? Me and you. On this beach. This spot. Together.'

And now Flick felt guilty. She'd hurt his feelings. 'Sorry, ignore me, I didn't mean—'

'Do you think that rooftop restaurant is better?' He gestured to one over in the distance.

'Better, how?'

'Well, more perfect.'

'This is perfect.' she said, mostly to appease him, but also because it was pretty goddam gorgeous; it was just her overthinking things as usual. 'It's lovely, Rory, thanks for bringing me here, for today, it's been really special.'

He looked cheered up.

'Shall we do a selfie?'

'*Another?*'

They'd done dozens all day. Flick didn't know what had got into him, he'd been whipping out his phone at every occasion, snapping pictures, instructing her to smile. She smiled dutifully and leaned in and he took a selfie, but he was looking everywhere but the camera.

'Now you're the one that seems a bit distracted,' she teased.

'No, not at all.' Taking the phone, he turned back to her, like a man that had just been caught doing something he shouldn't. 'I'm just going to go to the loo.'

'What, again?'

Rory was acting very oddly. This was about the fourth time he'd gone to the loo and he had a cast-iron bladder. He could drink half a dozen pints and sleep through the entire night without needing the bathroom. It was quite remarkable.

'I'll be right back.'

'OK.'

'Stay right there.'

'Where do you think I'm going to go?'

And then he was off, dashing up the sand, which was too hot and burned his feet despite his flip-flops. She watched him, jumping side to side, like a crazed grasshopper, then dug out her phone and WhatsApped Maggie. No reply. Just one tick. It looked like she hadn't even received it. Huh. Strange. Leaning back on the sun lounger, she closed her eyes. Oh well. Tomorrow Rory was flying home, things would be soon getting back to normal, whatever that was.

5.25 p.m.

'Move. Please! *Señora!* Out of the way!'

Ringing her bell incessantly, Maggie pedalled furiously on her bicycle. She'd taken one from the hotel; it was electric and she had it on full power, and she was racing across town, dodging pedestrians and traffic like being in a video game. So much easier than her crappy old one at home. With any luck, she wouldn't be too late. Or kill anyone.

A man with a small chihuahua stepped out in front of her.

'Arrggghhh, *señor*!' she yelled, swerving just in the nick of time.

After screaming into a pillow, she'd thrown on some clothes, tied her wet hair into a ponytail, shoved a lip gloss in her handbag and jumped on the bike. Luckily she'd been so panicked and nervous about their meeting, she'd already obsessed over Google Maps, working out the route to the bar, seeing how long it would take, zooming in on street view, so she was able to cycle there without getting lost.

Still, that didn't help her appearance. Already, she could feel her curls pinging out everywhere in the humidity. So not the professional-blow-dry look she'd been aiming for. As for her outfit, she was wearing jeans and an embroidered peasant top, which she could already tell was a mistake. It had looked so pretty and bohemian in the hotel gift shop in Taormina, but she had slightly larger breasts than the mannequin and she now feared it made her look less bohemian, and more like one of those actual, rosy-cheeked buxom peasants you see in nineteenth-century paintings, milking cows.

But it was too late to change now. She was almost there.

White-knuckling the handlebars, she careered around the corner. There it was! Up ahead! With the bar in her sights, she slowed down. It was on the opposite side of the street, with large windows and one side almost open, through which you could see the bar and the tables beyond. Braking, she jumped off her bike, locking it against a lamppost, then turned, her heart racing.

He was inside. She could see him, but he couldn't see her. Couldn't see her standing on the other side of the street. Frozen. All those feelings coming rushing back as she gazed at his familiar profile, at the way he rubbed his thumb and forefinger over the cleft in his chin, glanced at his phone, drained the last drops of red wine from his glass. Merlot, probably. Or was he still raving about Rioja?

A flashback to them at her flat, unboxing the latest delivery from *The Sunday Times* wine club, doing research for the wines they were going to have at their wedding, laughing as he told her some funny story about his friend who was a sommelier at a fancy hotel in Beverly Hills. Was any of it true? Was all of it lies?

Finally, this was her chance to confront him, to ask him why he did it, to find out if anything he said was real. To try to get her money back. *To try to get her life back.* Her breath held tight inside her chest, she stared at him. At the man she thought she was going to share the rest of her life with. And she suddenly realized she couldn't move.

## 5.30 p.m.

'Let's go for walk along the beach.'

'Another five minutes . . . I'm a bit sleepy . . .'

'C'mon, babe.' Rory tugged at her hand and Flick opened her eyes to see him standing over her, doing his best puppy-dog impression.

'Have you secretly entered a Mr Romantic competition?' she smiled.

'Oi! I'm always romantic.'

'Is that why you always refuse to send me a Valentine's Day card?'

'That's different.'

Standing up, they held hands and walked down to the waterfront. It was a bit cooler now and the warm water lapped over their feet as they held their flip-flops and walked along the shoreline, their feet making pairs of footprints in the damp sand.

'We can post one of those photos of us holding hands and walking on the beach,' she laughed. 'The ones you always take the piss out of.'

He mumbled something but she didn't hear.

'Next you'll be drawing a love heart in the sand with our initials—'

She broke off as ahead she noticed a love heart freshly drawn in the sand.

'Oh look, how funny . . . and oh, wow, what a coincidence, they've got the same initials as us!'

Silence.

She turned to Rory, except he was no longer standing beside her; he'd dropped to one knee in the sand and out of the pocket of his shorts was pulling a small black velvet . . .

Oh no . . . *oh no, oh no, oh no.*

# SO, I MET THIS GUY . . .

## 5.31 p.m.

It was like she'd turned into one of those sculptures she'd seen that afternoon at the gallery.

*Move*, Maggie implored herself desperately. *Walk over there now. Before it's too late.*

But she couldn't move a limb. Her courage and confidence deserted her and she couldn't face him. Paralysed, she remained rooted to the spot while the world rushed around her and her chance slipped away.

Then he did something. He looked at his watch. It was the smallest of movements; lifting his wrist, turning its face towards him, the light catching on the brass face. But she'd recognize that watch anywhere. It was her dad's watch. The one He took to fix. The one He never brought back. The watch her dad wore every single day of his life, the one she would play with as she sat on his knee, tracing her small fingers along the leather strap that he used to say was made of crocodile, the one passed down from her grandad that was supposed to be left to Charlie, but was left to her instead when he died.

And, like a lightning bolt, she felt a sudden hot flash of anger. It struck her with such force, bursting through her, white-hot and searing, obliterating all the fears and doubts, replacing them with fury. *You fucking bastard.* It was that watch that was going to give her the courage to walk into that bar.

Snapping back, she took a deep breath. This was it. This was her one chance. She took a step forward. Only, she didn't hear the moped speeding towards her. Her heart was hammering too loudly in her chest. She didn't see the driver reaching out to grab her handbag. Her mind was too focused on the conversation she'd rehearsed a million times in her head.

And when it was pulled from her shoulder, and she was knocked to the ground, her head hit the pavement and she thought, *Oh shit*. And then it all went black.

*5.31 p.m.*

At the exact moment Maggie was knocked unconscious, Flick looked at Rory on bended knee. She felt like one of those heroines in the old silent black-and-white movies, tied to the tracks as a train thundered towards them. The selfies, the search for the perfect location, the freshly drawn love heart . . . so this was why he was being so weird all day.

'Flick.'

And now the train was about to crash right into her and there was nothing she could do about it.

'Will you marry me?'

# Ibiza

*Day Nine*

*Five more days to go*

# Freefalling

'Ouch. That looks pretty painful. You really should put ice on it.'

Twenty-five thousand feet up in the sky, Flick looked over with concern at Maggie, who was nursing a huge black eye.

'It's fine, don't worry, it looks worse than it is.' Raising her voice to make herself heard above the engines of the twin-engine turboprop plane, she attempted a joke. 'You should see the other guy,' she quipped, then winced sharply. 'How are you?'

Flick shrugged, then made her own weak attempt at gallows humour.

'Single.'

It was the morning after the day before and Flick and Maggie were on board a short forty-minute flight from Mallorca to Ibiza. A lot had happened in the last twenty-four hours. A proposal. A mugging. A break-up. A fuck-up. A curveball. A concussion. A ride in an ambulance with the sirens on. A stolen handbag. A diamond ring. An official statement to the Spanish police. An awkward goodbye with a now ex-boyfriend in a hotel lobby. And a romance fraudster who got away again. It was more than happened in many a lifetime, and the two women were feeling both dazed and confused.

*

'I'm sorry.'

Maggie threw her a look of sympathy.

'It's OK, I didn't want to marry Rory. To be honest, I don't think Rory wanted to marry me either. He said he could feel me pulling away, so he wanted to put a ring on it.' She gave a small smile. 'I blame Beyoncé.'

'How was he this morning when he left for the airport?'

'Angry and upset. Apparently the jewellers don't give refunds.'

Flick was trying to make light of it, but she looked like she'd had the stuffing knocked out of her. That's the problem with bruised hearts and battered emotions, thought Maggie. You couldn't put ice on them. Unlike physical cuts and bruises.

Speaking of.

'Actually you're right, I think I might ice this,' she winced.

'Of course I'm right.'

Flick attracted the attention of the cabin crew and a few moments later they returned with some ice in a napkin. Maggie pressed it to her eye, which had started throbbing with the pressure in the cabin.

'I can't believe they knocked you to the floor and stole your handbag.'

'The police said there's been a wave of crime.'

'And you didn't get to see who it was?'

'No, it all happened so fast.'

One minute she'd been about to cross the road, the next she was lying on the ground, surrounded by a crowd of concerned bystanders. One of them had called an ambulance. The other the police. She just remembered her head hurting, looking across the street and seeing the bar stool was empty, and realizing her bag was gone and so was he.

'What I don't understand is why you were even there?'

She snapped back to see Flick looking at her, questioningly.

'Why were you even in that part of town?'

Maggie hadn't told Flick. She'd been planning to, before she screwed it all up. Then by the time she'd got back to the hotel from the hospital, it was late, and Flick was in bed. And this morning, she'd found out about the marriage proposal and break-up, and finding the right time seemed to get harder and harder. Plus, was there even any point now? She'd lost her phone and with it his number, as it had been in her handbag. There was no way of contacting him. So what good would it do? Flick would no doubt be furious with her for keeping it all a secret and think her an idiot. Frankly, she wouldn't be wrong.

Still, despite all this, Maggie felt she had to tell the truth. 'Well, actually, I've got a confession—'

'Oh God, it's not another surprise, is it? I couldn't cope.'

'Um . . . well, the thing is . . .'

'Don't tell me, you were on a date,' joked Flick.

'. . . I was going to meet someone for a drink,' she blurted finally.

They both spoke at the same time.

'Oh my God, you *were* going on a date!'

'Well, I wouldn't call it a date.'

'Maggie, you dark horse! Was it the guy at the front desk in our hotel in Palma? I could tell he fancied you when we checked in by the way he tried to help you with your luggage. Oh, wow, he was gorgeous; he looked like George Clooney, only when he had dark hair.'

Maggie's voice seemed to have got lost in her throat.

'Um . . .'

This was not going how she planned at all. Somehow, things had veered completely off course in a completely different direction. She had to quickly corral the conversation.

'Oh my God, it was him. I knew it!'

But it wasn't so easy. Steamrollered by Flick, she had now somehow found herself going on a date with Juan, the young George Clooney lookalike from the front desk.

'Why didn't you tell me?'

She needed to circle back. To come clean and admit everything.

'Well, the thing is . . .'

'Oh my God, is it because Rory and I broke up?' Flick clutched her chest, her face stricken. 'Oh Maggie, you don't have to be sensitive about that. I want you to be happy; I want you to find someone – you deserve it.'

Maggie pressed the ice against her eye, which had started to pulsate. Somehow, Flick thought it feasible that Juan, the handsome Spanish clerk, who must be at least fifteen years her junior, could be interested in her. Which was completely ridiculous. He was far too young and sexy to even notice her.

And yet the way Flick was looking at her, all excited and delighted for her, made the idea seem less impossible and absurd, and she suddenly saw herself in a different light – as Flick saw her, not as she saw herself. And while she didn't want to go on a date with Juan – though, let's be honest, the fantasy was fun – she rather liked this new feeling of fun and possibility. And the truth, which, now felt depressing and quite pitiful, got stuck in her throat.

'Well, good for you, Maggie. I'm so pleased. You really need to get back out there after what that bastard did.'

She couldn't tell her now. She couldn't disappoint her.

'So, are you going to keep in touch?'

'Um, I don't have his number. They stole my phone, remember.'

'Oh God, yes, of course.'

First thing that morning, Flick had shown her how to

change all her passwords and erase all her contacts and data. She'd been grateful but it also struck her that she had no way of contacting Him now. Maybe it was the universe trying to tell her something.

'Along with my credit cards,' she continued, 'though the thieves aren't going to have much of a spending spree with those. They're all maxed out.' She laughed at the irony. 'Thankfully, I left my passport and what was left of our winnings in the hotel safe.'

'Well, that was lucky, otherwise we'd have to give up our search and go back home –' Flick looked at her phone – 'though where we're staying in Ibiza is a freebie.'

Earlier at the airport, Flick had been on her phone, forensically checking social media for any updates to Stratin's whereabouts, while desperately trying to find them somewhere to stay. She'd lost a day – marriage proposals could be very inconvenient – and was frantically trying to catch up. It was peak season and everywhere was fully booked but just as she was losing hope and doom-scrolling, she'd seen an old friend from university was posting photos from her holiday in Ibiza.

'It was so kind of Flea to invite us to stay when I messaged her. She lives in London so I hardly ever see her, but apparently her family have a farmhouse and they have tons of room.'

'You have a friend called Flea?'

'She's from a really posh family, they have all these weird nicknames.'

'You mean, like Flick?'

Flick laughed as she realized the hypocrisy.

'That's better. It's good to see you smiling.'

'I just feel bad.' She shrugged. 'Rory says I've changed, that I'm not the girl I used to be, and he's right. I'm not. Being with you, on this trip, it's opened my eyes. Even if we never find Theo Stratin, I feel like I've found something else. Do you know what I mean?'

Their eyes met and Maggie nodded.

'You did the right thing. About Rory, I mean.'

'Thanks.' Flick smiled gratefully.

Maggie swallowed and when she spoke her voice was heavy with regret.

'You listened to your gut. I just wish I'd listened to mine . . .'

And it was then she told Flick the rest of her story.

# Maggie

The first inkling I had that something was wrong was when I got a missed call from my bank. I never usually answer those calls. You know – the ones with withheld numbers or numbers you don't recognize. So at first I just ignored it. I assumed it was a cold caller trying to sell me something, but then I got a text saying I'd gone into an unauthorized overdraft and to call my bank immediately.

Ironically, I thought it was a scam at first, but a few minutes later my debit card is declined.

'I'm sorry.' The sales assistant looks apologetic.

I'm out shopping for a few last-minute things for our trip to the Maldives and giddy with pre-wedding nerves. After a lot of discussion, we've decided on a small wedding, just the two of us, and what could be more romantic than barefoot on a beach in the Indian Ocean? It was Theo's idea. At first I wasn't sure. In fact, if I'm honest, I took a bit of persuading. I wanted my friends and family there, but as Theo pointed out, we don't have much family; his mum is in a home and mine lives in Spain and it's not like we're close. Plus, all his friends live in LA, so it's a long way for them to travel. Put like that it made sense to fly off somewhere together. Of course, George isn't happy, but you can't please everyone, and like Theo says – this is about us and what we want.

'That's strange.' I peer at my card, checking to make sure it's not expired, then realize the missed call and text must be genuine and feel a slight panic. 'There must be some mix-up, let me call my bank,' I say, trying to remain calm.

This kind of thing happens all the time. I'm always reading news articles about it. Scammers trying to get you to click on links and move money to fake accounts.

'Would you like me to put your things on one side?'

The sales assistant is smiling cheerfully. I've just been telling her that I'm flying to the Maldives to get married in two weeks. That the sarongs and flip-flops in my basket are for our trip but I still don't know what to wear for the actual ceremony. She's so excited for me, especially as it's the middle of November and any talk of tropical islands and sunshine is greeted with sighs of envy and a much-needed distraction from the countdown to Christmas that's already started. She's suggested I check out a brand on the fourth floor of the department store; evidently they have some lovely beach dresses. I'm going to do that just as soon as I've straightened things out with my bank.

'Yes, please, if you don't mind,' I smile back. Normally I'd pay with one of my credit cards, but I just paid for the trip to the Maldives which was an absolute fortune. Theo's going to pay me back of course. He just said it made more sense this way as his US credit card charges a foreign transaction fee, plus this way I can get the airmiles as mine's with BA. 'I'll just step outside so I can get better mobile reception.'

'Absolutely, no worries,' she beams, in that way people always do when you mention weddings. There's so much goodwill and generosity directed towards you when you're a bride-to-be, like you're a beacon of hope for everyone's happy endings. It's infectious.

Outside on the pavement, I call my bank back. Making sure to google the number and not just click on the missed call.

Exactly like they tell you to do on your banking app. Theo laughs at me for being so suspicious; he says I'm being paranoid, but I always say you can't be too careful.

After going through security, I'm finally put through to someone who confirms they've been trying to get in touch. 'It's about your account, Ms Fletcher. Are you aware you've gone over your pre-authorized overdraft limit?'

I feel a beat of surprise that the text wasn't a mistake. 'I've gone overdrawn?'

'Yes, we just wanted to make you aware, as a valued customer.'

'That's weird, I never go overdrawn.'

'You've had a couple of substantial amounts come out of your account recently.'

'Oh yes, I know.' I feel the panic subside. They must be referring to a large chunk of savings I recently moved into the account that Theo set up for the deposit for our new house, plus my investment into the new business.

Sorry, *our future* – that's what Theo always tells me to call it.

'That will be some transfers I made to my fiancé, plus deposits for things. We're getting married and looking to buy a new house.'

'Congratulations.'

'Thanks.'

Since our engagement almost six months ago, it's been non-stop, what with trying to sort out the wedding, find a new house and organize our finances. There's been so much paperwork involved remortgaging the flat, taking out a business loan and setting up a joint account, plus all the complicated international money transfers for the new business as it's registered abroad. There have been times when I feel like I'm drowning in it.

Luckily Theo is so good with stuff like that. He's the one that reads all the small print, then just asks me to sign it. To be honest, I don't know what I'd do without him. All that legalese sends me dizzy. Probably something to do with me having an artist's brain and using the left side, or is it the right? He's the one with the business brain.

'Only, your account will accrue interest unless you clear the sum overdrawn.'

'OK, can I transfer money from my Rewards savings account?'

'Yes, would you like me to check the balance on that for you?'

'Yes, please.'

'OK, one moment while I look into that for you, if you'd like to hold the line . . .'

Annoying elevator music starts playing. I wish they'd just let you wait in silence. I gaze absently at the passers-by. It's a grey day and the skies are leaden. Everyone's wrapped up in winter coats, scarves and gloves. It's hard to believe I'm going to be in bright sunshine and thirty-two-degree heat in a couple of weeks. I wonder again about a beach wedding. I'm not great in the heat, especially not if it's humid. I'll go red and sweaty. Not exactly the blushing bride, more like beetroot. I feel a pang of doubt and imagine a winter wedding, somewhere local in the countryside, all my friends, something stylish with sleeves, woodburning stoves and whisky . . .

'Hi, Ms Fletcher?' The voice comes back on the line. 'Sorry to keep you waiting.'

'It's OK.'

A part of me wishes I hadn't let Theo persuade me. But he was so adamant. And I didn't want him to go into one of his moods. Anything to avoid that.

'That account's been closed.'

'*Closed?*' I snap back.

'Yes, account ending 3774 was closed several weeks ago and its funds were transferred to an external account.'

I rub my forehead, trying to remember doing that. Like I said, there's been such a lot of financial paperwork recently – moving funds around, setting up new accounts – that I've lost track a bit. I must be getting mixed up with another account. I must have closed this one and not remembered.

'Would you like me to try a different account?'

'Um . . . yes . . . can I give you mine and my fiancé's joint account?'

'Yes, that's fine; if you're both named on the account, you can both withdraw or manage payments. If you want to give me the sort code and account number . . .'

It's started to rain. I try to seek shelter underneath the awning of the department store, while I juggle various screens on my phone, trying to find the details of our new joint account. I can feel my happy mood fast disintegrating as stress begins to take over. I'm looking for a screenshot Theo sent me when he opened it. The one that showed our balance so I could check our money was safely deposited. I think it's in my photos. Or is it my emails? Ah, there is it is. Quickly, I read out the sort code and account number, then wait again as the person on the other phone disappears and the elevator music returns.

OK, so I might not be the one with the financial brain, but I'm not going to take any risks when it comes to my life savings and Dad's inheritance.

'I'm afraid we can't find an account with that number.'

'Excuse me?' The person from the bank is back on the line, only they're making no sense.

'Can you repeat the numbers, please? We're unable to verify it.'

It's really raining now. Coming down hard and fast. I say the numbers again, slower this time. Pinching the screen of my phone with wet fingers as I haven't got my glasses, making sure I haven't got them the wrong way round. I can do that with numbers sometimes. I always need to check and check again.

'No, I'm afraid nothing's coming up.'

'I'm sorry, I must have the wrong details.' I hear myself apologizing. 'I'll have to speak to my fiancé, is that OK?'

'Yes, of course. Would you like me to give you a call back later today?'

'No, it's fine. I'll call you. I'm not sure when I'll get to speak to him, he's working abroad.'

'That's fine, Ms Fletcher. Just be aware that as you've gone over your pre-authorized overdraft agreement, your account will be blocked until we've received funds to clear that amount.'

We both hang up. I think about my sarongs and flip-flops put to one side at the cash register. The sales assistant is keeping them for me. I should really go back inside and explain but somehow I can't face disappointing her. She was so excited for me, so hopeful for herself; after all, if this customer in her forties had finally found love and was flying off to a romantic beach wedding, why shouldn't she get her happy-ever-after? But it's lost its sheen, somehow. The rain is really coming down now and despite the awning, I'm getting wet through. I need to go home, talk to Theo, sort it all out. I'll come back for the sarongs another day.

I text Theo straight away, but don't hear anything for hours. He's away working, scouting locations for a film in northern California. He's eight hours behind, so he'll still be asleep. In the meantime I try to look for any paperwork to do with the bank. No one sends paper statements any more, and I can't remember the login details as Theo set it all up, but I want to check the account numbers; I must be getting mixed up somehow. But Theo keeps everything in his briefcase, and if it's not here, he must have taken it with him.

In fact, I can't find any paperwork at all. Considering there's been so much flying around recently, you'd think there'd be some here. Theo's always on his laptop. He likes to sit at the little antique desk that's tucked away in the corner of the living room. It's one of those with the flip-down lid and little drawers and alcoves. But no, nothing. All the drawers and alcoves are empty.

That's when I get the first inkling that something's a bit odd.

It's not until early evening that the ticks finally turn blue. Theo leaves me a voice message. Telling me not to worry, that there must be a mix-up with the bank and everything's in order, but he's on set right now and will call me later.

I'm in the flat with George the cat, sitting on the sofa, when I get his message. I leave one back, telling him I'm worried, explaining again that I'm overdrawn and incurring a charge, asking him again about the account numbers for our joint account.

'What if I've been targeted by one of those online banking scams?' I tell him, feeling panicked. 'You know how sophisticated they are; I'm worried I might have accidently opened a dodgy email, or clicked on a link and now someone's hacked into our accounts . . .'

Even as I'm voicing my fears, I'm worrying about what Theo will say after listening to this message. What if that really has happened? He'd be so furious. I daren't even think about it.

He sends a voice message back: 'You're being silly now, Mags; no one's hacked into our accounts. Hang on, let me check them now.'

A few minutes later and then he sends me a photo. It's a screengrab of the money in the joint account. Several hundred thousand. I feel a wave of relief. It's all there.

Followed by another photo. This time it's a screenshot of our investments and they're all way up. I'm not good at understanding the stock market, or funds and unit trusts, but even I can see we're up almost 30 per cent.

'Plus, I meant to tell you, I just had another Zoom with some potential investors for the business. They're based out in Silicon Valley, so if they come on board, the sky's the limit!'

He sounds so excited in his voice message, I feel guilty. I'm always doubting him. That's what he gets angry about, whenever we argue. That I don't have faith in him.

'Phew, sorry, I was just worried,' I say, leaving another voice message. 'When they said the account numbers didn't match . . . Can you do another screenshot so I can see them properly? They've been cropped off. Or if you can give me the passwords so I can log in myself, I want to call the bank first thing tomorrow.'

A few moments, then he texts back.

> Sorry, I'm actually on set and they've started shooting so I can't leave a voice message.
> I've already logged out of the app and I can't remember the passwords. It's all face ID now.
> I'll send a better photo later.

**OK, no worries.**

Bye, babe. Love you.

**Love you, too.**

# SO, I MET THIS GUY . . .

My phone beeps up a love heart emoji. I stare at it, feeling a sense of relief and reassurance. And yet, something's niggling me. Women's intuition, gut feeling, call it what you want, but I can't get rid of this strange feeling that something's off. That I'm missing something, somehow, but I don't know what it is.

I get up from the sofa, much to the displeasure of George, who has chosen my lap as his bed for the night, and go into the bedroom. I move over to his side of the bed. His dressing table. I open the drawer. Empty. I stare at it. I don't know why that feels so strange, but it does. Surely he'd leave the odd thing behind – a receipt, a bit of paperwork, something – but both his bedside cabinet and the desk he uses in the living room are completely empty.

I open another drawer, this time it's where he keeps his underwear. I rummage through his socks and boxers, before suddenly catching myself, and slamming it shut. This is crazy! What on earth am I looking for? What am I hoping to find? We're getting married in a few weeks – surely I should trust him by now?

After all, it's not like he's done anything to arouse my suspicion. I've seen pictures of his life in LA before he moved here. The house he recently sold, with its swimming pool and palm trees, and his convertible in the drive. I've even looked at his Instagram and Facebook accounts, and there's nothing on there he hasn't shown me himself. It seems to be mostly old ones of him in his convertible, or recent photos of glamorous filming locations. There aren't any of us together. Which admittedly I felt a bit hurt by at first, as if he was keeping me a secret. Or, as my friend George put it, Keeping His Options Open.

That was one of the reasons George and I had an argument a few months ago and stopped speaking. Theo was right all along: George did have it in for him. So now we're no longer friends. I miss him sometimes, but it's easier this way.

Plus, when I asked Theo, he explained that it's not that I'm a secret; on the contrary, it's because he wants to keep his private life private. That what we have together is just for us, and not for public consumption. Put like that, it makes sense. After that I deleted the photos I'd posted of us together on my accounts too. Theo was right. He's right about a lot of things.

I go back and sit on the sofa and turn on the TV. George the cat is pleased to see me and curls his big fat ginger body in my lap. I'm being silly. It must be wedding nerves. Tomorrow I'll call the bank and straighten everything out, then go back to the store and buy my flip-flops and sarongs. I silence the niggly voice in my head. Tomorrow, everything will be fine.

# An Unexpected Invitation

As the taxi from the airport pulled up at the electronic gates, Maggie turned to Flick.

'I thought you said this was a farmhouse?'

'That's what she told me.' Buzzing the intercom, Flick leaned out of the window. 'Hi, Flea . . . yeah, it's me, Flick . . .'

As the gates silently opened, revealing a sweeping driveway lined with olive trees, bougainvillea and droves of French lavender, they entered the kind of sprawling estate you see when you're flicking through glossy magazines at the hairdresser's with your hair in tinfoil. The ones featuring beautiful women in designer clothes artfully posed on chaise longues, while you slump in your chair underneath a monstrous black cape.

'This doesn't look like any farmhouse I've ever seen.'

Thinking of the farm back in Yorkshire where she'd been living in the caravan, with its muddy fields, leaking barns and piles of cow shit, Maggie gave a low whistle.

'This is amazing.'

As they neared the bottom of the driveway, they heard trance music playing from the outside speakers. A skinny blonde girl in a bikini was waiting to welcome them, arms flung out, waving excitedly, like one of those inflatable advertising air dancers you get outside car dealerships.

'You're here! This is SO awesome, I haven't seen you since graduation! And welcome to your friend!'

Throwing her arms around them both as they climbed out of the taxi, she led them through the enormous house, quickly doing introductions to all the other guests while Flick said hello to some people she knew from uni and Maggie tried to remember all their names.

'This is Jasper and Pelly . . .'

Identical twin brothers with identical beaded necklaces looked up from grazing at the kitchen island to nonchalantly wave hello.

'Fabio . . .'

Over by the diving board. Tiny trunks. Less budgie smuggler, more Avert Your Eyes.

'Hattie, Panda, Toots, Kitty, Tigs, Topsy . . .'

They were lazing around the pool in various poses, looking like they'd just come in from a club, which they probably had. It was like *Saltburn* meets the characters of Beatrix Potter. Though the *Tale of Gen Z on Their Phones Smoking Spliffs* didn't have quite the same ring to it.

'Daddy . . .'

Maggie wondered if she'd misheard. Surely she meant Granddaddy? Snoozing in a hammock, he looked like Father Christmas. That's if Santa wore a batik sarong and drank too much rosé in the sun.

'Cousin Haz.'

Red trousers. Signet ring. Socks and sandals. *Financial Times*.

'I'll introduce you to Mummy later – she's gone sailing to Es Vedrà, but she'll be back this evening for her drumming circle.'

'Wow, you've got so many people staying,' said Flick, who hadn't quite realized just how rich Flea really was and was feeling a little intimidated. Though she would rather die than show it. 'Are you sure you have room?'

'We've got ten bedrooms, but it's a bit of a full house,' laughed Flea, cheerfully. 'But luckily we've got a couple of spare tents.'

Uh-oh. She should've known there had to be a catch.

'Great!' Flick smiled brightly and tried not to look at Maggie as they were led away from the house, past the salt-water swimming pool and into the orchard to be with the goats and chickens. It was like being in a game of social mobility snakes and ladders and they'd just slid down the ladder of the British class system.

'So, you said on your DMs you're out here working on a story? How exciting!'

'Yes, we're just here for the one night.'

'Are you a journalist too?'

Flea turned to Maggie who was trailing behind, looking like she'd done ten rounds with Tyson Fury.

'No, I'm—'

'Oh! Don't tell me! You're undercover!' Goggle-eyed, Flea turned back to Flick. 'Is it a major scoop?'

'Well, I'm not sure I'd call it that—'

'Golly, I do love a scoop, though I'm terrible, I never read the news. TikTok is my tabloid of choice.' She laughed gaily, then caught herself. 'Sorry. I shouldn't be frivolous. I mean, it's all so depressing, isn't it? All this terrible cost of living crisis.'

As Flea gave them a tour of her family's private Ibizan estate, Maggie wasn't sure if she was being ironic.

'How's PR?' asked Flick.

'Dreadfully boring. All those tedious book launches and gallery openings. Journalism sounds so much more thrilling!'

Flick thought about her job at *The Local Echo*, sitting next to Tupperware Tony as he told her about his sandwich fillings, typing up endless copy about charity fundraisers and local council committees. There were many words she could use, but thrilling wasn't one of them.

'Here you are.'

By the time they reached a flat terrace, shaded by pine trees and cooled by a soft breeze, both Flick and Maggie had mentally prepared themselves for a couple of nylon tents and some camping mats *if they were lucky*; instead they were greeted by two huge white canvas bell tents, strung with fairy-lights, and complete with real beds, duvets and pillows, and rugs.

'Oh wow, thank you – they're gorgeous!' gasped Flick.

'They've even got their own loo!' exclaimed Maggie, feeling relieved for her perimenopausal bladder. Well, sorry, but she wasn't twenty-six any more; trips to the loo in the night were now the norm.

'They're fully compostable,' smiled Flea, 'and all the lights and charging points work on solar; there's also a solar shower.'

Which of course made Flick beam from ear to ear. A compostable loo! A solar shower! Solar lights and chargers! She was in heaven.

'OK, well, make yourself at home. If you need anything, I'll be up at the finca.' With a wave she turned and headed back through the orchard.

'That's Spanish for farmhouse,' said Maggie as Flea disappeared.

'I finca've died and gone to heaven,' whooped Flick. Diving inside her tent and stretching her arms wide, she flopped backwards and sank into her pillowtop bed.

Twenty minutes later, they were back in a taxi heading into town.

'Couldn't we have just chilled out for a bit?' grumbled Maggie as they left the stunning surroundings of the finca behind and headed towards Dalt Vila, Ibiza's fortified old town. Tired and hot, she'd had to be dragged out of her bell tent. 'I could really do with a siesta.'

'A siesta?' Flick snorted. 'We don't have time for siestas!'

They'd only been in their tents a few minutes when there'd been a shriek from inside Flick's. He was back online! Posting on one of his accounts, his stories showed photos of himself in Ibiza, in the old town and down by the port. Which had caused Flick to leap off her organic cotton sheets and immediately book a cab. They needed to hurry, time was of the essence.

Which is why they were now racing into town.

'The cruise leaves at 11 p.m. tonight – there's no time to lose.'

Maggie gazed out of the window as the red earth of the Ibizan countryside whizzed by. To be honest, after yesterday's events, she was having serious doubts about the whole thing. She didn't know if it was the bang on the head or the memory of standing frozen on the pavement, but there was a big part of her that didn't want to find him. She'd had her chance and she'd fucked it up. She wasn't sure she was strong enough to go through seeing him again – or, more importantly, if she wanted to. She was tired, and right now, she just wanted to throw in the towel and go home.

'We have to find him this time. We just have to . . . we're running out of time . . .'

But, listening to Flick muttering under her breath, all Maggie could think was: how on earth could she admit her true feelings?

Soon after, they arrived in Dalt Vila, the beautiful fortified old town, accessed by a dramatic stone drawbridge. Inside there was a maze of cobbled backstreets and steps, winding steeply up and down, and a plethora of shops, restaurants, art galleries and bars.

'Do you think they'll have a pharmacy?' asked Maggie, after a few minutes of climbing. Pausing to rest, she caught her reflection in a shop window. 'I think I need something for this bruising.'

Flick looked suddenly guilty. In her haste she'd forgotten about Maggie's accident.

'I know, why don't you find one, then go sit at that nice cafe we passed by the entrance and have a cold drink. I'll go down to the harbour, see if I can see the cruise ship.'

'OK, thanks, if you don't mind.'

'No, of course not. Find a spot in the shade and relax. I'll meet you back here in an hour.'

It was only after Flick left that Maggie remembered she didn't have a phone to find a pharmacy. She'd already cancelled it with her phone provider and ordered a replacement to collect when she got back to the UK. Luckily, she didn't have to look too far, and the pharmacist spoke perfect English. Though to be honest, no words were really necessary, as her huge shiner did all the talking. She left with strong painkillers and something for the bruising and swelling, together with a new pair of sunglasses to hide behind, then found herself a nice spot in the shade at the little cafe, just outside the ramparts.

She was just enjoying an iced coffee when she heard a whistle and turned to see a woman approaching in a figure-hugging sequinned dress and heels.

'You know, we've really got to stop bumping into each other like this, people will talk.'

She engulfed Maggie in a perfumed hug.

'Birdy! What are you doing here?'

'Shopping.'

## SO, I MET THIS GUY . . .

'Are you going to the hippy market?'

'Do I look like the kind of gal who goes to a hippy market?' All decked out in sequins and heels, she pulled a face.

'I wasn't a hippy the first time around. All that patchouli and free love, no thanks. If you want love, you're going to have to pay for it, honey.' As if to prove the point, she lovingly stroked the Louis Vuitton handbag on her shoulder. 'Seriously, no one ever looked good in tie-dye. Not even Cher and she looks amazing in everything.'

Maggie fidgeted in her tie-dye skirt she'd bought from a little market she'd happened to pass in Mallorca and hoped Birdy wouldn't notice it underneath the table.

'Anyway, I hear that was yesterday so we're too late, our cruise only arrived this morning.'

At the mention of the cruise ship, Maggie felt her insides twist up.

'We leave tonight, so I thought I'd better make the most of it and see what this party island is all about—' She broke off as Maggie took off her sunglasses. '*Geez Louise!* What happened to your eye?'

'Oh, it's a long story.'

'Are you OK?'

'Yeah. Sort of. At least I think so.' Out of nowhere she had an urge to tell Birdy everything, to get it all off her chest to someone. 'Actually, if you're not doing anything, why don't you join me for an iced coffee?'

'Sorry, doll, but I can't stay. I'm going clubbing.'

'Clubbing?'

Seriously, could Birdy do nothing that didn't surprise her?

'What? This afternoon?'

A limousine with blacked-out windows pulled up beside them and a driver got out to open the door.

'I've got a private table booked at one of the best daytime

parties in town. You should come. I'll put your name on my guest list.'

She handed her a flyer.

'Oh, I don't know.' Maggie smiled politely, shaking her head. It was the last thing she felt like. 'Clubbing's not really my thing.'

Sliding inside the air-conditioned leather interior, Birdy turned and raised an eyebrow.

'I haven't forgotten our conversation in Sicily. Seriously, Maggie, think about it. You never know who you might bump into.'

Maggie frowned, confused. Wait a minute. Who was she referring to?

But before Maggie could ask any questions, the heavy door closed behind her with a soft click and the limousine glided away.

# Song and Dance

'We have to go.'

After exploring the old fishermen's quarter, which was now transformed into a strip of glitzy super yachts, some even with their own helicopters, and finding out that the cruise ships were docked on the other side of the island, Flick had returned to discover she'd just missed Birdy.

'Where?' Sitting across from her, Maggie fanned herself with the flyer. 'The other port?'

'No.' Flick tutted. 'Clubbing!'

Maggie's heart sank. She wished she'd never mentioned the VIP invite.

'I need to ask Birdy a few questions.'

'What kind of questions?'

'I'm an investigative journalist – I'll think of something.'

'I thought you were a community reporter?'

Flick snatched the flyer from her fingers.

'And I'm going to stay one for ever if I don't get this story, now come on.'

One outfit change and a solar shower later, they were now with what felt like a million other people, packed like sardines into a club. Fortunately it was outside and the dance floor was open air. Unfortunately there was no shade and everyone was melting.

'I need some water,' yelled Maggie, trying to make her voice heard above the dance anthems. Despite telling the bouncers their names were on the VIP guest list, they'd had to queue for ever to get in. 'I feel a bit faint.'

Attempting to make their way across the dance floor to try to find the VIP section, Flick turned to see her friend being jostled on all sides by hordes of enthusiastic clubbers. Crikey, she did look a bit ashen. She felt a beat of alarm. It was only yesterday she'd suffered a concussion and ended up in hospital. Perhaps this wasn't such a good idea after all. They quickly needed to divert.

'Let's go to the bar.'

'How will we find it? This place is enormous.'

'Don't worry, follow me!'

Grabbing Maggie's hand, Flick started pushing through the crowds with the kind of determination that only someone who went to a crappy school and tries to get on in life understands. It was like wading through an ocean of waving arms, skimpy outfits and sweating bodies.

Until finally they made it, panting and breathless, to the bar which was thronging with thirsty clubbers.

'How did you do that?'

'Glastonbury.' Flick looked triumphant. 'Once you've made it to the front of the pyramid stage, you can do anything.'

Maggie smiled weakly and wiped her brow.

Flick's triumph quickly disappeared and she felt a beat of concern. Maggie really did look quite odd. And it wasn't just the black eye and bruising. She'd gone a strange sickly green colour.

'Here, sit down, I'll get you a drink.'

Except there was nowhere to sit. For another fifteen minutes they were pushed and jostled until, finally reaching the front, they were served – and Maggie felt even more faint.

'Fourteen euros for a bottle of water!' she gasped. 'What happened to drinks being free?'

'What?' yelled Flick, trying to make herself heard above the rave.

'Wham. "Club Tropicana". It's a song,' she explained, in reference to the famous lyrics. 'You know they filmed the video here in Ibiza.'

'I've never heard of it.'

'You've never heard of it?' Maggie was incredulous. 'First Duran Duran, now Wham, what's it going to be next? Heaven 17?'

'You really did get a bang on the head, didn't you?'

'You don't know what you're missing!'

'I do and it's not Sounds of the Eighties.' Taking a swig of water she looked around her. 'It's Theo C. Stratin. He's here, I just know it. We've just got to get to the VIP section.'

'Do we need to go back into the crowds?' Maggie's chest tightened. She'd never been good in crowds and this was intense.

'Come on, it won't be so bad,' encouraged Flick, looping her arm through hers. 'Let's go.'

And turning away from the bar, they both plunged back towards the dance floor.

Actually, it wasn't bad. It was much, *much* worse. Strobe lights. A sea of sweaty bodies. Pulsating electronic beats and loud drumming techno. A DJ who whipped the crowd into a frenzy. And poor Maggie caught up in the middle of it.

'This is my worst nightmare, I get claustrophobic.'

'It's going to be fine, just keep your eyes peeled.'

'I feel so old.'

'Rubbish, you're only as old as you feel!'

'But that's just it, I feel about a hundred.'

The painkillers had worn off and her eye was throbbing again and her headache was making a comeback. All she wanted to be doing right now was lying horizontal, in a quiet, darkened room. What she wouldn't give for a pair of earplugs right now.

'There's lots of ravers your age here.'

'I think they're called gravers, not ravers.' Maggie attempted a joke, but Flick was distracted as she'd just bumped into Flea and the rest of the Beatrix Potter gang.

'Hey, look who it is!'

All in their party gear, there was lots of hugging and high-fives.

'We got your message so we thought we'd come down.'

'Did you have to queue?'

'No, Cousin Haz went to school with someone who was a friend of someone who got us on the guest list.'

That was the thing about public school, thought Flick, everyone always knew someone. It wasn't about the private education, it was about the connections. Whereas she permanently felt as if she was in a world of missed connections.

Cousin Haz appeared, minus the red trousers and copy of the *FT*, with the rallying cry of, 'What's everyone drinking? Let's get the vodkas in!'

'Has he seen the prices of the drinks?' Maggie looked concerned.

'Don't worry about Haz, that's what his trust fund's for,' laughed Topsy. Or was it Toots?

'Oh, I love this one!' whooped Flick, as a thumping bassline started playing.

'Me too!' whooped Flea.

'Why don't you stay with your friends, while I nip to the loo?' said Maggie, who could see Flick was dying to be with her friends and dance.

'OK, I'll just be a few minutes, it's just this one song.'

\*

Maggie felt a wave of nostalgia. Oh, to be young. It was all right everyone going on about how fifty was the new forty, but the reality was you were fifty. And it didn't matter how good you looked or how great this stage of life was, or whether it brought you reinvention or a new set of abs, you were still well over halfway. The best might be yet to come, but your youth was gone.

And the truth was that mostly Maggie was fine with it. Youth, in many ways, was seriously overrated. All those insecurities and frustrations had meant her twenties had been an emotional rollercoaster of highs and lows, compounded further by the loss of her brother. Yet, there was something about those years. That intoxicating newness. That intensity of joy. That feeling of going out with your friends and wondering what the evening held, that delicious anticipation of What Might Happen? Whereas now, for the most part, she knew what might happen, and it mostly involved an early night.

She remembered how it felt to be Flick's age, being with your friends, the nights out getting drunk and smoking cigarettes and staying up late. Flick had just broken up with Rory. She needed to let her hair down, enjoy herself with people her own age.

'OK, I won't be long, I'll be right back,' said Maggie.

But Flick, always so serious, was already dancing, arms in the air, her face lit up, body swaying, lost in the music. For the first time she looked like a twenty-something should look, like someone having fun without a care in the world. For a few moments Maggie watched her, then, smiling, she turned away.

Only, Maggie had underestimated the size of the club and how easy it would be to find Flick again, and after navigating her way to the toilets, she found herself lost and disorientated. The loud music and flashing strobe lights made it hard for her to think, let alone see, especially without her glasses. Worse still, her headache had returned with a vengeance. And it was when she was trying to move through the crush of bodies, around the large swimming pool, that she looked up and glimpsed what she assumed must be the VIP section. A balcony with separate seating and tables and – oh look! There was Birdy!

Down below, Maggie waved, trying to attract her attention. Wearing her sequinned dress, hair piled up, Birdy was standing against the railing, looking out across the club, swaying to the beats. Maggie called her name. But it was in vain. The music was so loud, Birdy would never hear her, never notice her in the crowd below.

Then Maggie spotted Him.

As he appeared from behind Birdy, suntanned, in a white shirt, her stomach dropped. In his hands were two drinks and she watched as he passed Birdy one.

Was that really Theo? Maggie squinted myopically, trying to see and cursing that she didn't have her glasses. And now they were laughing and he was leaning in and sliding his arm around her waist and nuzzling her neck.

Wait. Was he *with* Birdy? Were they *together*? Her breath caught in her chest and she felt the ground shift beneath her as two worlds collided. No, that was impossible.

Reeling with shock, Maggie suddenly felt very faint. She couldn't take any more. It was too much. The music pumping. The strobe lights. The crowds. She felt like she was about to have a panic attack. And now everything was blurring. She was sweating. Her head was throbbing. Panic rose up in her chest and she felt as if she was going to collapse. She had no idea where Flick was. She didn't have a phone. She didn't know what to think.

All she knew was one thing.

She had to get out of there.

# The Moment of Truth

Maggie couldn't remember much about how she got home, other than she managed to flag down a taxi and get back to the finca, where she collapsed in her tent and slept for thirteen hours straight. And now she was awake and in the clear, sober light of morning, everything about the events of last night looked different.

She must have got it wrong. It had been chaos in the club and she struggled to see without her glasses. Never mind that she'd still been suffering the effects of a concussion and a black eye. In fact, the more she thought about it, the more she was convinced she'd been mistaken about what she thought she saw on the balcony. Or even *who* she saw.

It was definitely Birdy, but now she couldn't be sure it was Theo. There'd been lots of people. Was her mind playing tricks on her again? Like when he first disappeared and she used to think she saw him walking down the street, or in the supermarket, and she'd rush up, only to discover it was someone else and her cheeks would blaze with shame and embarrassment. Was she so stressed and obsessed she was conjuring him up in crowds, like a ghost? Was she never to be free of him?

And it was then she made her decision. She had to move on from this. For her own health and sanity, she had to let it go.

\*

Maggie had always had a sense of reluctance about chasing across Europe, trying to find the man who blew up her life. It was only supposed to be one night, twenty-four hours in Monte Carlo – blink, and it would all be over. But while their plans had changed and the trip had given her life another new and surprising dimension, her doubts had always remained; and as the days had gone by, she'd felt her misgivings multiplying.

And a nagging question.

Don't you run *away* from explosions, not towards them? They always do in the action films. Whenever there's a massive blast, you don't see anyone running back into the wreckage. They're always desperately trying to get to safety. Away from danger. Relieved to still be alive.

Which begged the question, what the hell was she doing? She should be trying to get as far away as possible from him. The Love-bomber. This man who blew up her life. He'd planted the dynamite into the cracks of her heart, the depths of her trust, the foundations of her very being. Lit the fuse and watched it go *BOOM*.

Next time she had a run-in with him, she might not be so lucky.

Having made up her mind, Maggie got up and packed up all her things. She toyed with the idea of leaving a note for Flick, then decided against it. She couldn't do that. She owed her an explanation at least.

'Flick, are you awake?' Pulling back the canvas flap, Maggie saw Flick was fast asleep, buried underneath a large mound of duvet. It had been almost dawn when she'd heard her come home. She stirred as she entered.

'Maggie . . . what time is it?'

'It's early, but I'm leaving.'

'Leaving? To go where?'

'Home. Not that I'll have it for very much longer,' she added, as she thought of her promise to Ainsley to move the caravan. 'Back to the UK.'

'Why? What's happened?'

Bleary-eyed, Flick struggled onto her elbows and pulled off her sleep mask.

'Is this because of last night? I tried to find you. When you didn't come back from the loos I went looking for you, but there were so many people . . . When I finally got to the VIP section I couldn't see you or Birdy, so I just assumed you'd come back here and I stayed out partying—' She broke off. *Partying.* That word again. Except, this time in Ibiza she really was. 'I'm sorry. I was pretty out of it.'

'No, it's not that.'

'I should've left, should've come back to make sure you were OK.'

'Flick, it's fine, I'm a grown-up. You needed to let your hair down and be with your friends. You've been through a lot recently.'

'So why are you leaving? Is it because of what happened in Mallorca?'

'Well, that's part of it.'

'Because, I've been thinking, you could always call the hotel.'

'S'cuse me?'

'To speak to Juan! He works on the front desk, remember?' encouraged Flick. 'I can't believe I didn't think of that at the time.'

'No, you've got it all wrong, I don't want to speak to Juan.'

'Fair enough, I suppose holiday romances never work in real life, do they?'

'Flick, please –' Maggie felt a beat of frustration – 'if you'd just let me explain. I don't want to do this any more, I've changed my mind, I'm done—' She broke off as there was a sudden stirring movement underneath the duvet. 'Wait. Is someone there?'

Abruptly, a tousled blonde head appeared followed by several naked limbs. 'What's that about holiday romances?'

'*Flea?*'

'Oh, hi, Maggie.' She yawned, and gave a sleepy wave.

It took a moment to realize what was going on.

'Sorry, I didn't know you had company, I should go . . .' Maggie suddenly felt embarrassed.

'I can explain . . .' And now Flick was looking embarrassed.

'You don't need to explain anything, honestly, I'm leaving anyway.'

'Wait, let me put some clothes on.'

But Maggie was already walking away.

'Please don't go home!'

A few moments later she turned to see Flick running after her in her bare feet through the orchard. 'I'm sorry about last night, about what happened in Palma, being mugged and your eye and your phone and everything . . . I'm sorry we haven't found him already, I know it's been a bit of a wild goose chase and it's taken a lot longer than I thought, but please don't give up—'

'I found Him.'

Silence. The impact of her words taking a moment to register. And then.

'What?'

'He texted me, I went to meet Him at a cafe.'

'*You met him?*' Flick stared at Maggie, dumbfounded.

'Well, no, that's the thing, I didn't.'

'I don't understand.'

'That was the night in Palma when I got my bag stolen. That's why I was in that part of town, to meet Him . . . except I never did.'

Finally. The truth was out there. The two women looked at each other.

'What the fuck, Maggie?' Flick finally spoke, her face incredulous. 'Why didn't you tell me?'

'I know, I'm sorry; I don't know why I kept it a secret. I just wanted to see him again by myself, to look him in the eye, to try to get some answers . . .'

She broke off and shook her head, trying to collect her thoughts.

'I was worried he wouldn't speak to a journalist, that your being there would frighten him off. I thought maybe I could persuade him to talk to you, that I could bribe him or threaten him or . . . I don't know. I don't know what I was thinking . . . The irony is when I finally found him, I realized I didn't want to find him. I didn't want to see him again. I hate what he did to me, but I was scared—'

'Scared of what?'

'What he was going to say, how I was going to feel. Scared I wasn't going to be strong enough, that he was going to suck me right back in again. That I still loved him.'

She'd finally said it. Finally admitted her worst fear.

Flick listened, trying to absorb this new information.

'I can't believe you're telling me all this now.'

'After I got my phone stolen there didn't seem any point telling you at all. I didn't have his number any more. I fucked it all up.'

'You didn't fuck anything up; you've been amazing, through all of this—'

'Yes, I did and I'm so sorry. I know how important it is to you that we find him, I know that this story could be your big break – and you deserve that, you really do. You're going to be a brilliant journalist, Flick, I just know it. You're the cleverest, funniest person I know, but I can't do this any more.'

'There's something else. It's got nothing to do with my job.'

'It's over.'

'Please, Maggie, I haven't told you the truth either. That's not the only reason I came looking for Theo Stratin . . .'

Something in Flick's voice made Maggie stop and turn.

And there, in the dappled morning sunlight, barefoot and more vulnerable and confused than she'd ever allowed herself to be in her life, Flick finally said aloud the words she'd been keeping inside, for the very first time.

'He's my dad.'

# Valencia

*Day Ten*

*Four more days to go*

# Flick

I found out six months ago.

It was just after Mum's funeral. Colin, my stepdad, asked if I wanted to keep any of her clothes and I was cleaning out her wardrobe, going through her all her clothes and shoes. Mum was a hoarder. She kept everything. Every birthday card, every childhood drawing of mine, all my old toys . . . there were boxes and boxes of stuff up in the attic and we'd already gone through a lot of it together. Looking at old photos. Ones of Mum when she's a little girl, all knock-knees and gap-toothed smile. Me when I'm a baby. The three of us pulling silly faces on family days out.

Mum and Colin got married when I was eight years old. I've never met my real dad. Never known who he was or where he lived or even if he was still alive. My earliest memory is it just being the two of us, me and Mum. Double Trouble, that's what she used to call us. We were so close, almost like sisters. It was only when I got older I realized something was missing. When I'd go round to friends' houses and meet both their parents, or see Father's Day cards in the shops and feel sad I didn't have one to buy a card for. Or when I was picked on in the playground for not having a dad.

I never told Mum about the bullying. Never let her see the tears or the bruises from when I used to fight back. She was a single mum, working three jobs to support us, she had enough on her plate. I used to push the feelings down inside and retreat into my imagination. I remember she had some argument with her sister, my Auntie Pam, one year when we went camping. A vague recollection of them whispering in the corner of the caravan while I played make-believe with my dolls, her looking over at me and saying I should know the truth.

'Know the truth about what?' I remember demanding, curiously, only to be fobbed off with some excuse.

Adults do that a lot when you're a kid. Telling you to go play, pretending like nothing's going on, but kids always know there's something going on and I knew it was about my dad. But Mum would never talk about him. Whenever I'd asked questions she'd always told me he wasn't ready to be a daddy, but she'd wanted to be my mummy more than anything in the world and that she loved me so much, enough for both of them.

So instead I used to make up fantasies about him. He was Prince Charming on a horse and he was going to come and rescue us, like in the fairytales. Or a spy on a secret mission to save the world and one day, when he was done saving the world from disaster, he was going to turn up at school like all the other dads and I'd jump into his arms and he'd swing me around and around and around until I was dizzy.

But he never came to school to swing me around and he never showed up on a horse. And I grew up and shoved it to the back of my mind. And then Mum met Colin and got married and I got a brand-new dad. One that would take me to the fun fair and ride on the dodgems with me, that helped me with my homework and taught me how to drive, and could make Mum laugh, even after she was diagnosed and they were constantly back and forth to the hospital.

Sometimes I'd catch myself looking in the mirror, at my green eyes, and wonder where they came from. Or my long legs and big feet and thumbs that bend funny. Mum was small and curvy with dark brown eyes and tiny features. She always used to clean up in the sales as she only took a size three shoe and they were always the ones left on the rack as no one else could fit into them. I remember she used to laugh and call herself Cinderella.

I came home after graduation to be close to her. All my friends were moving to London, getting jobs and getting drunk, starting graduate training schemes, renting rooms in shared houses, being carefree and living life, meeting new people, getting boyfriends. It's like they were on this new exciting journey, not looking back, no responsibilities, no worries, no one to think of but themselves. They were living these fun-filled, messy, chaotic lives, but mine was organized and sensible and I worried all the time. Their lives got bigger while mine got smaller.

She was good for a while. We thought she'd beaten it, but then it came back and it was everywhere.

I miss her so much. Sometimes I dream about her: I'm little again and lost in a department store and trying to find her, running down the aisles, between the racks of clothes and mannequins, and I'm crying and panicking, and then suddenly I spot her ahead of me, in that red coat she used to love, and I yell, 'Mum!' so loud it makes everyone turn around. And she turns around and smiles and says, 'There you are,' and I sob and say, 'I thought I'd lost you, that I'd never find you again,' and she just scoops me up and wipes the tears from my face and says, 'I'd never leave without you, silly; you'll never lose me, I'll always be here,' and I feel a rush of relief.

It's OK. I'm safe. Nothing bad can happen to me now.

Then I wake up and she's not here, she's gone, and all that's left of her are some of her old clothes, photos, mementos . . . her hairbrush still with a few strands of her hair, a bottle of her favourite perfume, her recipe book stained with her sticky fingerprints.

And then there's her old diary.

I found it when I was clearing out her wardrobe. Running my fingers through the clothes like the keys on a piano, inhaling their familiar scent, it was almost like I could touch her again. She had shoeboxes, stacks of them, filled up with tiny shoes that would never fit me. Except inside one of them was a bunch of stuff. Old stubs of cinema tickets. A theatre programme from a play. A strip of black-and-white photos from a photo booth. Mum and a man I didn't recognize. She looked so young. And a small leather-bound book, tied with two strings of leather. It was her old diary from before I was born.

In it she wrote about meeting a man called Theodore C. Stratin and falling madly in love. She loved how distinguished his name was. She thought he was posh, having an initial. She called him her soulmate. She was so young, barely twenty, and he totally swept her off her feet. They met in Leeds, at the hotel where she'd been working behind the bar. She'd just broken up with her boyfriend and was feeling pretty lonely. He was a guest at the hotel and one day he'd walked into the bar, ordered a glass of red wine and sat at the counter and started talking to her – and boom, that was it.

In her diary she writes so breathlessly. All the entries are gushing and excitable, filled with lots of exclamations marks and declarations of love. She nicknames him Teddy and calls him her Teddy bear, and there are doodles of love hearts and teddy bears in the margin. She sounds like a giddy schoolgirl with a crush. I barely recognized her from the person I knew; she was always so strict and no-nonsense. Especially when it came to me having boyfriends. She wouldn't let me go on any dates until I was much older than most of my friends.

I think that's probably why I stayed with Rory for so long. Because I knew Mum liked him. She used to say he'd look after me. When I told her I could look after myself, she used to shake her head and say I'd understand when I got older, when I wanted to have children, that I was too young to understand.

So when I read that diary it all made sense. He told her he wanted to marry her and that they were going to spend the rest of their lives together, but when she fell pregnant accidentally a few months later he tried to persuade her to have an abortion. When she refused, he just disappeared.

Afterwards I went to see my Auntie Pam. I told her about the diary, what I'd read, and asked her to tell me everything. So she told me . . . about how Mum had gone to her in tears, hysterical, not knowing what to do. He wouldn't return her calls or answer his phone. Soon after, the number stopped working. Apparently even the address he'd given the hotel wasn't his: it belonged to an old married couple who'd never heard of him. My Auntie Pam wondered if he'd been married, if he might have been having an affair then gone back to his wife. She told my mum to forget about him. She called him all kinds of names. My Auntie Pam always had a temper. Uncle Dave said he'd kill him if he ever saw him again.

Only, they never did.

Mum left the hotel and went to live with my grandparents until after I was born and she could get on her feet. I don't think it was a happy arrangement. Mum never really got on with her parents. I don't think they ever really approved of her choices. They were quite religious. But what Mum never told anyone, but which I read about in her diary, is that the whole time she'd been working at the hotel, she'd been saving up to train to be a midwife. She'd been working extra shifts, keeping her tips, being careful with every penny. It wasn't much but it was everything she had and she kept it in a biscuit tin. That little, battered old biscuit tin held her future. It held her dreams of a better life.

But when he disappeared so did that biscuit tin. He took the savings of a pregnant woman. Left her with nothing. She never told anyone. Never wanted anyone to know just what a despicable person he was, least of all me. She never wanted me to feel as abandoned or hurt as she did; she wanted to protect me.

I didn't tell Colin, my stepdad, about the diary. I didn't want to hurt him. He was grieving Mum; I didn't want to drag up the past. Plus, to be honest, in recent years things have been difficult between us. Maybe it was Mum's illness, or maybe it's because I'd started to wonder about my real dad. Instead, I went to work and used my journalistic skills to try and hunt him down. Of course these days, it's different – we've got Google and the internet and social media. It didn't take long for something to finally come up on our internal newspaper server.

It was a photo from a local newspaper in Bath. It was taken last year, at an exhibition at a local art gallery; a local artist had won an award and was exhibiting their paintings and the proceeds were going to charity. There were a few people in the photo and the caption underneath listed everyone, from left to right, and there was his name: Theo Stratin, and he was standing right next to the owner of the gallery, Maggie Fletcher.

Theodore C. Stratin. *Teddy*. It was the same person.

I remember sitting at work, staring at that photo for hours. He looked different, older, but there was no denying it was the same man kissing Mum in the photobooth strip. The same man who'd abandoned and stolen from her. The father who'd seen me as a mistake and something to be got rid of, who'd deserted me before I was even born.

There he was, at a gallery opening, a glass of champagne in one hand, his other around the waist of the owner, his fiancée, all smiles for the camera. Like butter wouldn't melt in his mouth. I was so angry, I had all this rage inside, all these feelings I'd shoved down inside of me for so many years – now they came bubbling up, but I didn't know what to do with them. So for a while I didn't do anything.

And then one day I was in the pub and I overhead some people talking. Local town gossip. I don't usually pay much attention. I was collecting glasses, helping out; it was a Sunday afternoon and we were short-staffed. At first, I didn't pay much attention. They were talking about some posters they'd seen about a missing cat when they'd been out walking their dogs. The cat belonged to a woman who was living in the top field, up on the Pennines. Apparently she used to be quite successful but she'd had her life savings stolen, the victim of a romance scammer, and was renting a field off the local farmer and living in a caravan.

At which point my ears pricked up. I'm always on the lookout for a story, one that's not about Boy Scout fundraisers or missing cats – no offence – so I did a bit of digging around, asked a few questions, found out a name.

Maggie Fletcher.

It sounded familiar. Like I'd heard it somewhere before, but I couldn't place it.

And then I remembered the photo. The woman he'd had his arm around. It couldn't just be a coincidence, so I called up my friend Tariq at the police station, asked if he could do me a favour and look up something on their database. Of course he told me that information was confidential, police-classified and all that, and so I reminded him who gave him the information that led to the arrest of the gang who broke into the jeweller's on the high street and won him a regional commendation award.

That's when I read your statement.

And that's when I knew for sure.

I'm sorry I wasn't honest when I called you, when I drove out that day and trampled mud into your caravan; I'm sorry I let you think it was about your cat. I was scared if I told you the truth, you'd refuse to speak to me – and you were the only person that could help me. When you told me what happened to you, that's when I knew I had to find him. I had to stop him doing to another woman what he did to you and my mum. And because I need answers to the questions I've been asking myself my whole life.

Because if he's my real dad, *who am I?*

# Making Waves

Flick stopped talking and looked at Maggie, who was standing opposite. She hadn't said a word. Just listened while she spoke. She waited for her to say something.

'I'm sorry he did that to you and your mum,' she said finally.

'I'm worried I'm going to be like him.'

'You're nothing like him.'

They were on a ferry from Ibiza, heading to Valencia. Flick was leaning against the railing, the wind blowing her hair away from her face; Maggie stood beside her, looking out across the churning waves as they made the five-hour journey.

After Flick had dropped her bombshell that morning, Flea had appeared from inside the tent, wondering if everything was OK, and so the subject had swiftly been changed. Instead, the next few hours were spent dealing with the practicalities of packing up, thanking their hosts for their hospitality, making arrangements to get to the port. All the while Maggie was reeling with shock at what she'd just been told and bursting with a million questions.

Only once they got on the ferry and they left dry land did Flick open up.

'I'm not talking about looking like him, I'm talking about inside, my genes, my DNA . . . what if I've inherited his personality?' she was saying now.

'That's ridiculous—'

'I'm not being ridiculous! Have you any idea what it's like to find out your father is a criminal?'

'Sorry, I didn't mean—'

Maggie quickly bit her tongue. She was trying to reassure her – Flick was nothing like the man who'd lied and stolen from her – but it had come out all wrong and dismissive.

'I read about it; some studies say as much as 60 per cent of your personality is inherited. I mean, what if there's a criminal gene?'

'Seriously, you want me to answer this?'

'Yes.'

'Have you ever broken the law?'

'No . . . well, maybe once when I forgot to scan an item in my basket and walked out of the supermarket without paying.'

'What did you forget to scan?'

'Frazzles.'

'*Frazzles?*'

'Yes. You know, they're those bacon-flavoured crisps—'

'I know what Frazzles are.'

'A family-size bag too.'

'OK, well, I think you're safe. I don't think you're a criminal for stealing bacon-flavoured corn snacks. Now, maybe if it was a bottle of wine . . .'

Maggie was trying to joke, to lighten the leaden mood, but Flick had the weight of the world on her shoulders.

'But what if it comes out . . . later in life, you know?'

'Look, I'm not a geneticist, but all I know is you are who are you are. Doesn't matter who your parents are, or if you've got the same colour eyes—' Maggie broke off, arrested by the realization that Flick had the same distinctive green eyes as Him. 'You're you . . . and you're a good person.'

'I don't feel like a good person. I've lied to everyone – to you, my editor, myself . . . I hurt my boyfriend . . . I slept with my girlfriend . . . I don't know who I am or what I want . . . I'm a total mess.'

Bare-faced, her hair pulled into a ponytail, and without her signature eyeliner, Flick looked much younger than her years and Maggie felt a sudden maternal protectiveness.

'I didn't feel like a good person for a long time either,' she told Flick. 'After everything that happened, losing the business, my home, my fiancé, my mind . . . I felt so stupid and so ashamed. I hated myself. I didn't know what to think or who to trust – I was just so lost. And then I met you.'

Maggie's eyes welled as she cast her mind back to the person she was less than two weeks ago.

'And you made me feel like me again . . . Driving the car was like getting back behind the wheel of my life . . . it got me out of my head, gave me some control, a purpose, some fun.' She smiled, remembering all the laughter they'd shared, laughter she hadn't been expecting. 'You brought me back to life, gave me myself back, you listened, let me tell my story.'

'That's my job as a journalist.'

'That's not your job, Flick – it's who you are. People talk to you because they like you. Because you understand, you're empathetic, you're kind.'

'I wasn't very kind to Rory.'

'Yes, you were. You stopped him sleepwalking into a marriage, saved him from spending years with someone that wasn't the right person, from you both being unhappy. You had the courage to speak up, to listen to your gut. It means you're both free to be with the right person. Believe you me, many husbands and wives would wish their partners had been so honest.'

Flick turned to look at the waves crashing against the hull of the boat.

'Trust me, I should know. I got married in my twenties and it was a disaster, both of us knew from the start but we just did it anyway. It was short-lived, thankfully. We didn't waste years of our lives, but we did waste a lot of money on a stupid wedding and a dress that made me look like Princess Leia—'

'Wait. *On purpose?*'

'The groom was a huge fan. I even wore my hair in two buns on the side of my head.'

As she cringed at the memory, Flick started laughing.

'Please tell me you have photos.'

'Nope, all evidence has been destroyed.' Maggie shook her head. 'See. Look what you've avoided.'

Flick gave a small smile, then sighed. 'I'm just so confused about everything.'

'That's OK.' Maggie shrugged. 'Truly, most people are confused about most things most of the time.'

Flick looked at Maggie. 'Why are you being so nice to me? You should be angry.'

'I am, but not with you.'

'But I've lied to you this whole time.'

'You haven't lied, you just haven't been completely truthful and I think we've both been guilty of that.'

They looked at each other, both wondering how they got there, both realizing they didn't want to be anywhere else.

'So what are we going to do when we get to Valencia?'

'Meet George and celebrate my birthday.' Maggie smiled ruefully.

'Oh God, of course – happy birthday! I'm sorry, what with everything, I totally forgot.'

'Lucky you, I'm trying hard to forget. I can't believe I'm fifty.'

'I can't believe I got wasted and slept with one of my girlfriends.'

'I can't believe I slept with your dad.'

It just came out.

'Shit, I didn't mean—' Mortified, Maggie cursed at her crassness. 'Honestly, me and my big mouth.'

'I think we're past the point of worrying about hurt feelings, don't you?' Flick smiled. 'And anyway, you gotta laugh.'

'What? Or we'll both cry?'

They both looked at each other, their shared sense of humour bubbling up underneath the surface, the realization that it wasn't the only thing they had in common. If they were close before, they felt even closer now.

'And then what happens after we've celebrated your half-century?' grinned Flick.

Maggie gave a mock grimace, then her face fell serious and she turned to gaze at the horizon. Her mind was made up.

'And then I'm going to go home.'

# Champagne Supernova

'It's the birthday girl!'

As they walked into the hotel bar, George was there to meet them with a bottle of champagne and an outrageous suntan. Arms flung wide, wearing a shirt with a print louder than his voice and, despite being inside, a classic pair of Ray-Bans, he sprang up from the velvet sofa like an excited Labrador.

'Hello, George.'

'Fuck me, you're old.'

'You'll be next.'

'If I'm lucky.'

He laughed loudly, giving her a big hug and engulfing her in his large frame, while Maggie quickly made the introductions.

'George, this is Flick; Flick, this is George.'

Flick looked at George like she'd never seen anyone quite like him, which was to be expected, as that's how people usually reacted to George the first time they met him. He had a presence. Like an actor you might see at the theatre playing the lead role, only George was only ever playing himself.

The champagne was chilling in an ice bucket awaiting their arrival, and popping it open with a flourish, George quickly filled three flutes and handed them around.

'Happy Birthday!' Raising a toast, he took a thirsty glug. 'So come on, spill the beans, what's been happening?'

Maggie and Flick exchanged looks. Still both reeling from the events of the past twenty-four hours, they sank onto the sofa and took dazed sips. The champagne was ice-cold and fizzed as it weaved down to their empty stomachs. Where on earth do you start?

'Caught the bastard yet?'

'Shh, George.' Mindful of Flick's recent revelation, Maggie tried to silence him. But she should've known: George was not a man to be silenced.

'What? Are we not calling him a bastard now? OK, what did we decide on. Liar? Wanker? Total shithead, The Biggest Mistake of Your Life—'

'I went to meet Him.'

'He's my dad.'

They both spoke at once.

George's mouth was still moving but no sound was coming out, like one of those cartoon characters you see running off a cliff and not realizing the ground has disappeared beneath them.

'I think that's the first time I've ever seen you lost for words,' noted Maggie. 'Oh, yeah, and we won at roulette in Monte Carlo and used our winnings to chase him around Europe.'

'We rented a car and drove to Italy –'

'– and Flick threw up all over the Amalfi Coast.'

'Thank God it wasn't in the honeymoon suite.'

'Crikey, can you imagine, over all those rose petals?'

'Mopping it up with a swan-shaped towel?'

They both looked at each other, imagining – it was all so comically awful – then drank more champagne. It was going down surprisingly well.

'Then I hiked up a volcano in Sicily –'

'– and I made lasagne with The Godmother –'

'– and in Mallorca Mags got her bag stolen along with her phone.'

'So I lost his number.'

'They'd been texting each other. I had no idea.'

'I was going to confront him; he was right there, sitting in the bar where we'd arranged to meet, but then I hit my head and got concussion and had to be taken to hospital in an ambulance –'

'– only I didn't know any of this as my boyfriend had surprised me by flying out to propose, but instead we broke up –'

'She did the right thing.'

'But then in Ibiza we went clubbing.'

'Fourteen euros for a bottle of water, George. It was crazy!'

'And I got totally out of it and ended up in bed with one of my girlfriends.'

'And she told me the man who'd broken my heart was her dad.'

'A romance fraudster who ruins women's lives.'

'And The Biggest Mistake of My Life.'

'So there you have it.'

They both stopped talking and turned to George, who'd been sitting, pinned to the velvet sofa, gripping the armrest. He stared at them in stunned silence.

'Well, say something,' urged Maggie.

There was a pause, then, draining the rest of his glass, he slammed it on the table.

'Fuck me,' he said, shaking his head in disbelief, before breaking into one of his classic wicked grins. 'This is better than *Love Island*!'

# An Unexpected Question

A second bottle of champagne later, Flick and Maggie had finished answering all of George's numerous questions.

'That's all happened in a week?' Letting out a low whistle, he rubbed his temples, sweeping his dark hair off his forehead. 'I've barely had time to do my laundry and go to the gym. You must be exhausted.'

But Maggie shook her head. 'You know the funny thing? I was more tired sitting in my caravan all day, doing nothing.'

'Yeah, me too,' agreed Flick. 'I felt the same sitting at my desk at work.'

'I have to say, you both look pretty fabulous considering. Especially you.' He nodded at Maggie. 'Flying here, I was worried it was going to be less of a birthday celebration and more of a rescue mission to bring you back home. I mean, seriously, the last time we WhatsApped you looked *terrible*.'

'Thanks, George. I'll take that as a compliment.'

'Anytime,' he winked.

'But I am going home tomorrow. I've decided. This is my last night.'

There were a few looks around the table, but Maggie's mind was made up.

'Well, in that case, it's even more reason to go out and celebrate.'

'I thought we were celebrating with the champagne?' said Flick.

'No, darling, that was just to get you lubricated,' quipped George.

'And I could have you arrested for sexual harassment,' she fired back, and they both laughed, 'and that's not a double entendre.'

Flick and George had already decided they liked each other and were happily riffing off each other.

'Look, I don't need to do anything for my birthday . . .'

But George was on a roll. 'You're fifty! You're fabulous! And we're in Valencia! This demands much more than a boring birthday bikini selfie!'

That second bottle of champagne was beginning to take effect.

Turning to Maggie, he cupped her face in his hands, and spoke with the same intensity as if he was performing Hamlet with Yorick's skull. 'Do you know what this city is famous for?'

Seriously, George really should have been on the stage.

'Two of my favourite things! Paella and street art.'

It turned out to be true and not just the drunken declarations of a man who'd had one too many glasses of champagne on an empty stomach. Valencia was indeed famous for a perfect double whammy of delicious food and free art. It was a kind of culinary artistry. And after the most mouth-watering and flavoursome dinner of *paella de mariscos* – a giant pan of yellow saffron rice, filled with monkfish, king prawns and mussels, which the three of them shared, heaping their plates high and scraping the burned bits off the bottom until their waistbands threatened to burst – they left the rowdy family-run restaurant to walk off their full stomachs and admire the amazing street art.

\*

'Oh wow, these murals are amazing,' said Flick as they wandered through the El Carmen area of the city. 'What do they all mean?'

'Lots of different things. Street art is a living commentary on the world we live in.' Having armed himself with a map and artists' handbook, George was their unofficial tour guide for the evening. 'It's not just colourful graffiti, it's about artists raising awareness of important issues. By capturing our attention with their artwork, they are literally keeping our eyes open to what's happening around us. Which is pretty incredible, considering most of us spend most of our lives glued to our phones . . .'

'Right, yes.'

Flick guiltily shoved her phone in her pocket.

'And it's not just walls or garage doors, there are some massive murals up ahead, on the side of those buildings,' he gestured.

'Oh, I'm going to go look.'

As Flick hurried on up ahead, George and Maggie continued slowly, arm in arm.

'So what time's your flight tomorrow?'

'I haven't booked it yet. I was going to ask if maybe you could get me a cheap ticket?'

'I knew it. You only want me for my staff discount.'

Maggie punched him playfully in the ribs and he let out a theatrical yelp.

'What about Flick?'

'She wants to carry on until she finds him. She wants to stick to the plan.'

'And you don't?'

She shook her head. 'When I saw him in the bar in Mallorca, I froze. All this time I thought I wanted to see him again, to ask him why he did what he did. I had all these questions.

But then, when I had the opportunity, I just thought: why am I doing this? It wasn't going to change things. It wasn't going to make me feel better. To be honest, I'd probably end up feeling worse.' She paused, her mind flicking back. 'The only reason I crossed the road to go meet him is because I saw he was wearing Dad's watch and I got angry.'

'Too fucking right you should be angry. I'd want revenge.'

'But isn't the best revenge to move on and live your best life?' Maggie turned to George, her face lit up. 'And this evening is a pretty good start, thanks to you.'

'Don't you want answers?'

'I don't think I'll get any. Flick's mum never did.'

'So why did he want to meet you?'

'Who knows.' She shrugged. 'Flick wonders if maybe he caught sight of me somewhere and suspected I was looking for him, that it was his way of trying to get ahead of the game somehow . . . I dunno, I don't think I'll ever understand his motives. And I've finally realized I don't need to try and see inside his head.'

'But what about all the money?'

'He's probably spent it, or gambled it away, or God knows. All I want is Dad's watch back. Saying that, the last time I thought that – *boom*, I was knocked unconscious and had my bag stolen, so maybe it's a sign I should go home. Try to forget all about it. Focus on the future and getting a job and finding a place to live.'

'You know, you can always come and stay with me. I've got a sofa bed, or I could clean out my artist's studio in the garden – you could sleep in there.'

'Thanks, George, that's kind of you, but I'll be fine. Don't worry.'

'I feel like it's my fault.'

'Huh?' Maggie frowned.

'Stirring everything up again. Telling you to call the reporter back, to come on this trip, saying you've got nothing to lose.'

'Don't be silly, you were right to stir everything up! I haven't been living these past six months; I've just been existing. This trip hasn't been a waste of time – it brought me back to life, George. I'm not scared any more. I'm done beating myself up, blaming myself for being such an idiot, feeling like my life was over. I thought I'd lost everything. I know I lost myself for a while, and it took coming here to find myself again.'

She stopped walking and turned to him, her eyes flashing.

'You know, there were times when I didn't think I could survive what had happened. It was impossible to imagine getting over it. I thought I was going to be broken for ever. That my life was ruined and I was never going to laugh or feel happy again. But I was wrong. It's true what they say: what doesn't kill you makes you stronger.'

'And now we're talking in fridge magnets.'

She punched him again.

'Ow, I'm like a peach! I'm going to be covered in bruises!'

'You deserve it, I'm pouring my heart out and you're making fun.'

'I'm sorry. You're right, I'm being a dick.' He was immediately contrite. 'You know me – emotional vulnerability makes me deeply uncomfortable, whether it's mine or anyone else's; I have to make a joke or have a drink or deflect it somehow, which is most likely the reason I'm still single.' George broke off, his face unusually serious. 'But I am listening, and I am very proud of you.'

'Thank you.'

Maggie smiled gratefully as she gave his hand a squeeze.

'But I think you're making the wrong decision going home.'

She looked at him, surprised.

'You know I'm adopted, right?' he continued.

'Yes, of course.' Maggie wondered where this was going.

'And I love my parents, they're my mum and dad and always will be, but it didn't stop me wanting to know where I'd come from, to meet my birth parents. It's just part of who you are, it's part of your identity. Luckily Mum and Dad were always really supportive and they helped me track down my birth mum, and we've got a relationship, but I never got to meet my birth father as he'd already died. He was much older and married to someone else, not a good sort by all accounts, but still, you always wonder.'

George paused.

'What I'm saying is, Flick should get to meet her dad. It's important she knows who he is, like finding the missing piece of the puzzle.'

'Is that wise? He's not a good guy.'

'Doesn't mean you're opening a door; often it's so you can close one.'

'Hey, come and a look at this one! It's amazing!'

Flick's voice broke into their conversation and they both turned to see her standing a few feet away, in front of a large mural.

'Coming,' called George, then turned back to Maggie. Her face was filled with concern.

'I'm just worried he'll hurt her, like he hurt her mother, like he hurt me,' she protested.

'Which is why you have to go with her,' he urged. 'She needs you.'

She fell silent. Everyone talks about the desire to be loved, but it's the desire to be needed that's stronger. Did Flick need her?

'Isn't it amazing?'

Her face lit up, Flick was gesturing up at the huge, colourful alien-like figure on the side of a building.

'It's by Akimbo,' said George, reading from his guidebook. 'Apparently it's in homage to Margarida Borràs, a transgender woman in Valencia who was executed in 1460 because of her identity.'

'Wow, that's pretty intense,' said Flick.

'What I love about street art is that it isn't hidden away in some museum – it's right here, in the real world,' enthused George as the three of them stood and stared up at the powerful futuristic painting. 'So you're an art buff too, Flick?'

'I am now.' She grinned. 'I always thought art wasn't relevant, that it didn't mean anything to me. It was Maggie who told me how to look at it differently.'

'You had a good teacher.' George smiled. 'You know Maggie was an amazing painter herself?'

Maggie rolled her eyes at the flattery. 'He's only being nice because it's my birthday.'

'No, I'm serious.'

'You should start painting again, now all this is over,' urged Flick.

'It's not over yet, I'm coming with you.'

It was a split-second decision. But as soon as she said it out loud, she knew she'd made the right decision.

'But I thought you wanted to go home?'

They say home is where the heart is and standing on a random street in Valencia with Flick and George, it suddenly struck Maggie that perhaps she was already home.

'We're in this together, aren't we?' she smiled.

'Well, if you're sure?' Flick tried to hide her obvious delight.

'OK, now that's sorted, I just have one more question.'

They both turned to look at George as he interrupted.

'Why would a man wanted by the police, who'd escaped to Europe, go on a cruise?'

'Maybe he needed a holiday,' quipped Maggie, with more than a hint of sarcasm. 'Stealing someone's life savings must be hard work. And aren't you outside the jurisdiction of the police when you're at sea?'

'Yes, but not when you're docked at port – then it's a matter for the local police – so it's not like you can escape the law indefinitely.'

'How do you know so much about cruises?' asked Flick.

'I have several friends who work on the ships.' George shrugged. 'I've thought about it myself. All your income is tax free.'

'I don't think he's worrying about paying taxes,' muttered Maggie.

'Well, I think the reason why he's on a cruise is pretty obvious,' shrugged Flick. 'It's the perfect place for a romance fraudster—'

'To meet someone?' finished George.

'To scam someone,' corrected Flick. 'I'm sure he's already found his next victim. Some poor rich, elderly widow—'

'Birdy.'

George and Flick both looked at Maggie, who'd gone suddenly pale.

'We met a rich heiress . . . divorced, widowed, single, in her seventies, I'm guessing. She's on the same cruise. I saw them together at the club in Ibiza.'

'*Together* together?' He raised an eyebrow.

'I thought I'd got it wrong, been mistaken, that it wasn't him.' She was shaking her head, reality dawning. 'He had his hand round her waist . . .'

'And you're telling me this now?' gasped Flick.

'Well, I got slightly distracted by other news this morning.' She shot her a look.

'Maybe this is a silly question, but instead of going on some wild goose chase around Europe chasing a cruise ship, why don't you just get on board?'

George's voice broke into their conversation.

'You mean, go on a cruise with the man who stole my life?' Maggie looked horrified.

'You can't.' Flick shook her head firmly. 'No visitors or members of the public are allowed on board. They're really strict with security.'

'There's no exceptions?'

'No, it's impossible. I've done my research,' added Flick.

'Anyway, it's a crazy idea,' said Maggie.

At the mention of crazy, the two women looked at each other. And that was the moment they both knew what they had to do. Well, you know what they say about crazy . . .

# Málaga

*Day Eleven*

*Three more days to go*

# All Aboard

'Wow, it's gigantic!'

'Like a floating city.'

'I don't think I've ever seen anything quite like it.'

The next day, after goodbyes and good-luck hugs with George at the train station in Valencia, Flick and Maggie found themselves at Málaga Cruise Port, at the Eastern dock, presenting their passports, having their pictures taken, and going through all the necessary security checks, before being whisked down the walkway that led on to the cruise ship.

'Can you believe it's nineteen decks high?' Flick cricked her neck to gaze upwards.

'Can you believe we're getting on board?' replied Maggie in disbelief.

Turning sideways, they both looked at each other; it was a look that said there was no turning back now.

'Welcome to the *Galaxy Goddess*.'

They were greeted at the entrance with a wide smile from a uniformed member of staff who extended her hand in an official handshake.

'It's wonderful to meet you, Ms Lomax. As the ship's press officer, I'm honoured to have such a prestigious member of the British press and their guest sailing with us for the next three days.'

'Thank you,' said Flick, putting on her best journalist face. 'We're honoured to be sailing with you. Aren't we, Maggie?'

'Honoured.' Maggie joined in the smiles and handshakes.

'Well, if you'd like to follow me, I'll show you to your state room.'

'Wonderful!' enthused Flick, giving Maggie an excited thumbs-up as soon as the press officer's back was turned.

'*Prestigious member of the British press?*' Maggie elbowed her in the ribs and they exchanged elated glances that their ruse had worked and they were on board.

'I owe my editor big time,' she whispered with a smile.

'Perhaps you could do a talk on being a top journalist? Our fellow passengers would love that.'

The press officer's voice broke into their whispered conversation.

'How about tomorrow afternoon, between the magician and novelty bingo?'

There was a pause as Flick did a good impression of a deer caught in headlights.

'Absolutely! Sounds great!'

A lot had happened since they'd stood on the street the night before in a different Spanish city and made their decision. Including emails flying back and forth late into the night between Flick and Seymour, her editor, who'd managed to swing them a free press trip on the *Galaxy Goddess*, thanks to one of his old Fleet Street contemporaries, who was now something of a big shot in the PR world.

Not that it was much of a decision, more of an inevitability. George's questioning had triggered one thought after another. Because if it was clear that Theo's motive for getting on the ship wasn't to enjoy the all-you-can-eat buffet and swim-up bar but to commit romance fraud, then they were in no doubt of the identity of his next victim. And no sooner had they realized who it was, they knew they had to get on board. Because it was no longer just about Maggie getting justice or Flick finding her dad. It was also about saving Birdy.

'So, this is your state room, it's one of our superior ocean-view balcony rooms.'

After being led through the reception – a huge five-storey atrium, open to floor after floor of bars, restaurants, lounge areas and cafes, and boasting a jaw-dropping centrepiece of an elaborately carved golden goddess that must have been at least twenty-foot high, rising out of a real fountain – they were taken in one of the two elevators up a dizzying number of floors, led down a maze of corridors, and finally, with the soft click of a key card, shown into their cabin.

Only, it was like no cabin Maggie had ever seen.

'Wow.'

She'd never been on a cruise ship before, but she'd been imagining a poky room, tiny bed – possibly bunkbeds – and a porthole, if they were lucky.

She snuck a look at Flick, who seemed to have been imagining a similar scenario.

'There's a balcony?' she was saying now, in the sort of hushed voice you use in expensive shops full of expensive things you can't afford.

'Where you watch sunsets and sunrises, spot dolphins and feel an ocean breeze,' beamed the press officer, as if reading from her own press release. 'All while enjoying a glass of complimentary champagne.'

'Complimentary?' Maggie's ears perked up. With their winnings almost depleted, she was back to being stony broke and very-soon-to-be homeless. The upcoming weekend was the deadline from the council, and she'd agreed to have the caravan towed. But to where, she still didn't know.

'Yes, as our guests on the *Galaxy Goddess* you've been allocated our luxury package, which includes premier beverages, speciality dining, premium desserts, reserved theatre seating, fitness classes and the most important of all when you're out at sea, free WiFi.'

Flick, who was already out on the balcony, pulled out her phone.

'Don't forget to download our app.'

'You have an app?'

'Yes, it works in conjunction with our *Galaxy* key cards, which can also be worn as wristbands or pendants and act as your ID, wallet and room key. Use it to discover our entertainment schedule, book shore excursions, make restaurant reservations; you can even order a drink and move sunbeds and our waiters will know where you are as it has a unique location tracker.'

'There's an app for everything,' teased Maggie as Flick listened open-mouthed.

'We also have a feature that allows you to discover where your friends and family are on the ship. It's easy to lose people on a vessel of this size.'

'And this will help you find them?' Flick's mind turned.

'If they've accepted your request, absolutely.'

Flick and Maggie glanced at each other. Both thinking the same thing.

'Well, I'll leave you to get acquainted with everything; don't forget to watch the virtual muster drill on your television, it's the safety video in case of an emergency,' she added in explanation. 'It'll explain how to put on your life jackets, where to assemble—'

'It's like the *Titanic*.' Abruptly Flick looked worried.

'Don't worry, I don't think we're going to be hitting any icebergs in the Mediterranean,' reassured Maggie.

'Oh, one last thing.'

At the door, the press officer turned and pulled an envelope from her pocket, which she handed to Flick.

Pulling out a gold-edged invitation, Flick read aloud: 'An invitation to the captain's table tonight for dinner?'

'Yes, he's very excited about meeting such an esteemed journalist and her guest. He can't wait to hear all your stories!' She smiled excitedly. 'And by the way, it's formal attire, so make sure to dress up!'

As the door closed behind her with a muffled click, Flick pulled a face.

'Which exciting story should I start with first? The one about the sheep escaping on the moors, the pole-dancing pensioners or the Boy Scout tombola?'

'Definitely the pole-dancing pensioners,' said Maggie and they both burst out laughing.

'God, I could get used to this,' said Flick, twirling around the room. 'I can't believe we have our own balcony!'

'I thought you said cruises were terrible for the environment?' Maggie raised an eyebrow. 'In fact, I'm sure I remember you saying they should be banned.'

'Well, yes, I was of that opinion *originally* –' finishing checking out the marble bathroom complete with its own whirlpool bath, Flick affected a serious expression – 'but I'm planning to do some journalistic investigating while I'm on board and come to my own conclusions.'

'Would that involve sitting on our balcony and enjoying the ocean view while drinking our complimentary bottle of champagne?'

'It's a tough job but someone's got to do it.'

Popping open the bottle, Maggie filled two glasses and they both went outside onto the balcony. Champagne twice in two days. She could get used to this.

'So what are we drinking to this time?' asked Flick, as she raised her glass in a toast.

*How about to confronting the man who broke my heart and stole my life savings and disappeared?* thought Maggie. *To saving Birdy from the same fate, and bringing Him to justice? Or to finally meeting the man you think is your dad and getting some answers?*

The ship's horn blasted and the water beneath churned.

But as they began gliding away from the dock it struck Maggie that their toast shouldn't be about Him, it should be about *them*. And raising her glass, she chose the most important thing of all.

'Friendship.'

# Keeping Watch

'Can I help you with anything?'

'Why, yes, I'm wanting to buy a gift.'

Meanwhile, lower down the ship, on the fifth deck dedicated to designer retail shopping, Dennis, the sales manager of Fine Jewellery and Luxury Watches, was gliding over to the couple who were bent over an illuminated glass case filled with some of their premium timepieces.

Arms around each other, giggling and whispering, they'd been browsing under his watchful eye for the past few minutes. Years of experience had taught Dennis that was the trick to a successful sale. Give the customer some space to fall in love with a piece of jewellery or expensive watch, to fantasize about how they'll style their hair to show off that pair of stunning six-carat, pavé-set diamond earrings to their girlfriends, or to imagine surreptitiously flicking their wrist to reveal their designer timepiece at their next business meeting.

As a sales manager, you needed to know when to pounce. Ask too early and you could frighten them off. Leave it too late and you risked them being distracted or, worse, snapping out of Cruise Mode, a hypnotic state where real life and money no longer mattered.

Like most things in life, it was all about timing.

He swooped in. 'Is it for someone special?'

'I'd say he's kinda special. What do you think, Louis, are you special?' cooed the glamorous older woman.

'Not as special as you, Birdy,' flirted her middle-aged toyboy.

Dennis didn't blink. Working on cruises for the past twenty years, he'd seen couples in so many different shapes and sizes. There was the man whose wife had died enroute to the Caribbean and the woman who comforted him. He'd bought her a diamond bracelet. The divorcée who'd found love at the singles party and treated him to a luxury watch. The ninety-something widow who chose to live on a cruise ship instead of a retirement home and changed her suitor as often as her sparkly evening gown. She always bought cufflinks.

The high seas did something to people. Show them an open stretch of water and as soon as dry land disappeared so did their inhibitions. People came on board looking for love. It was almost like a dating app. He'd seen so many relationships blossom – some led to marriages, others only lasted as long as the cruise. But he wasn't here to judge; he was here to sell them precious jewellery and luxury watches.

Dennis cleared his throat.

'Would madam like to see anything in particular?'

'Please, call me Birdy,' she said in her distinctive Southern drawl. 'Madam makes me sound like the owner of a brothel.'

She let out a loud cackle of laughter and beamed at Dennis, who felt himself blush.

'Birdy, what are you like?' Her toyboy pretended to reprimand her with a kiss. 'You're embarrassing him.'

'Oh, sir, I'm sorry, don't mind me, I'm only teasing.'

Dennis smiled graciously. He liked this loud American woman, with her flamboyant clothes and mischievous grin. He'd served plenty of Americans in his time. They were often loud but always friendly and polite, not to mention extremely generous tippers. They understood the value of good service.

'See what I've got to put up with?' quipped The Toyboy and winked at him.

Dennis smiled tightly. The boyfriend, however, he didn't like. Handsome, charming, *and a total player*. He knew his type. He'd encountered so many of these shady characters. Con artists, swindlers, heartbreakers. They came on board looking to take advantage of an older woman, or sometimes an older man. Someone vulnerable or lonely or looking for affection. Pretending to be in love with them when all they were in love with was their money.

He might be able to fool her, but he couldn't fool him. Dennis had been married thirty years and raised two sons and a daughter. His family lived in the Philippines where he sent his wage each month. He'd made a good living but he was ready to retire soon. He loved his wife and was looking forward to being with her, though he worried about leaving the ship. He'd lived his whole life on the seas, going to sleep each night in one place and waking up in another every day. It was in his blood now. What if he couldn't settle? What if he lost a part of himself? Without the cruise ship and its passengers, who was he?

'We're interested in one of your watches,' continued Birdy, tapping a long red fingernail on the glass counter. 'A Rolex.'

'Of course.' Dennis went to open the case.

'Sweetheart, please, it's too much,' protested The Toyboy. 'I couldn't possibly accept such a gift.'

It was all Dennis could do not to roll his eyes. If he had a duty-free dollar for every time he'd heard that, he'd be a millionaire and buying his own designer watches, not selling them.

'Nonsense.' Birdy swatted him away playfully. 'Nothing is ever too much. It's my treat.'

'Oh, Birdy, I'm so lucky to have met you.'

'Oh, Louis, the luck is all mine.'

'Is there a particular model you're interested in?' Wearing his white dust gloves, Dennis turned to them both, his eyebrows raised.

'Well, if you insist, I rather like the Submariner,' said The Toyboy.

*Of course you do*, thought Dennis. *Only one of the most expensive.*

'Me too!' Birdy clapped her hands together gleefully. 'Great minds think alike!'

Carefully removing the timepiece from the cabinet, Dennis went to place it on The Toyboy's wrist, but he was already wearing a watch. 'If you'd like to remove your current watch, sir.'

'Oh yes, of course.' He began unfastening the leather strap.

'Here, give it to me, honey,' beamed Birdy, slipping it into her handbag.

Dennis slipped the watch onto his wrist and carefully fastened the clasp. It made a satisfying click. The Toyboy raised his sleeve, turning his wrist back and forth, a smug, self-satisfied smile on his face.

'So what do you think?'

Turning to Birdy and Dennis, he affected the expression of a man unsure and in need of approval.

'It's stunning!' she enthused.

'It's one of our most prized timepieces and a true classic.' Dennis nodded reverently.

'Oh, I don't know. It's so much money.' He shook his head. 'Perhaps we should wait, go shopping tomorrow when the ship stops in Tangier—'

But Dennis quickly interrupted. 'Please, sir, I must warn you. Be very careful of fakes.'

'Fakes?' Birdy looked shocked and clutched her Louis Vuitton handbag to her surgically enhanced chest.

'Absolutely, madam. They have some excellent forgeries. Only an official dealer would be able to tell the difference. Many of our passengers have been tricked by what they thought was a genuine luxury watch only to be left severely out of pocket and very disappointed.'

'Well, that's decided.' Birdy shook her head firmly. 'We must buy you a watch here.'

'We must?' The Toyboy tried not to look too elated.

'It's perfect for all those important meetings you have to attend with your AI technology business you've been telling me about.'

'It's a wonderful choice, sir.'

'And it totally gives the right impression for any new and potential investors,' continued Birdy, looking at him with a glow of pure pride. 'Of which I am now one.'

'*You are?*' The Toyboy swung around, his face lit up. 'You said you were thinking about it, but I had no idea!'

'Well, I've thought about it and the question I keep asking myself is, what's the point of being an heiress if you don't do something with your fortune? Of course there are worthy charities to donate to and godchildren to indulge, but surely an heiress is allowed a little happiness of her own . . .' She broke off, her eyes downcast, and gave a flutter of her new lash extensions. 'So yes, in answer to your question, I'm ready to invest . . .'

'. . . and not just in my business, but in our future,' finished The Toyboy pointedly.

And then, seemingly both overcome with emotion, they clasped each other's hands and stared at each other, like Love's Young Dream, for what felt like an age, while Dennis shifted on his soft-soled shoes and tried not to think about how many years' salary it would take to afford the Rolex on the other man's wrist. Or how many months this affair was going to last before The Toyboy and his new Rolex moved on to pastures new.

Or how much longer before he could take his lunch downstairs in the crew's Mess. He was watching his weight, so perhaps something from the salad buffet.

'So, have you come to any decisions?' asked Dennis, diplomatically. His salary was commission-based so he was eager to make the sale, but he didn't want to appear pushy. Pushy was the kiss of death for retail. 'Just so you are aware, there is usually a waiting list for this particular model, but today you are in luck.'

Gentle persuasion and a little FOMO worked so much better.

With one arm still around The Rich American Heiress, The Toyboy admired his reflection in the mirror, sweeping the hair from his temples and holding his wrist to his face as if he was in a watch commercial, while she gazed on adoringly.

'I love it. *And you*,' he whispered.

'We'll take it!' she declared.

'Wonderful,' smiled Dennis.

Forget the salad buffet. Today he would have the fillet steak.

# The Captain's Table

'You know that scene from *Gentlemen Prefer Blondes*, where Marilyn Monroe and Jane Russell are on a cruise ship and they walk into the dining room?'

A few hours later, Maggie and Flick were all dressed up and in the elevator on the way down to have dinner with the captain. The invitation had said formal attire but they hadn't exactly packed for a cruise. Besides, after nearly two weeks dashing across Europe their suitcases were full of dirty laundry, not cocktail dresses and evening gowns. Luckily, however, they still had the two now-squashed and crumpled dresses they'd bought in Monte Carlo to attend the casino. Luckier still, they also had an iron.

Yet they were both feeling pretty nervous. Being invited to sit at the captain's table was a big deal and neither was quite sure what to expect.

'Is this another one of those old films you're going to tell me I have to watch?' asked Flick, fiddling distractedly with her fringe. She'd trimmed it with her nail scissors and done a terrible job.

'It's not *old*, it's iconic!' protested Maggie, tugging self-consciously at her neckline. She hadn't remembered it being this plunging.

'In that case so are you,' teased Flick.

'Oi!'

Maggie pretended to be offended, but was secretly flattered.

She glanced at her reflection and for a moment she barely recognized herself as the same woman in the caravan Flick had met less than two weeks ago. She'd put on a bit of make-up and done one of those hair colour kits to cover her greys and was really pleased with the results. She admired all those women who embraced going grey, but she wasn't ready to be a silver vixen just yet. If ever.

Plus, if she was going to come face to face on the cruise ship with the man who broke her heart and left her for dead, she was going to do it with really good hair.

But this was about more than a bit of a make-up, a good hair day and a sequinned dress. Gone was the grey pallor and dark shadows under her eyes, the worry etched on her face and the weight of the world on her slumped shoulders. Instead, her eyes were bright and sparkling, her skin glowed with a light golden tan, and her head was held high. The broken woman overwhelmed by weariness and defeat was now filled with vibrancy, confidence and determination.

Maggie didn't look like the same woman, because she *wasn't* the same woman.

The elevator stopped to let more people in and for a moment Maggie and Flick held their breath. They'd done this on every floor, hearts in their mouths, wondering if it was going to be Him on the other side of the sliding doors . . . But no, it was just more well-dressed diners on their way to dinner. Maggie and Flick shuffled to the side to make room. A couple entered wearing a ballgown and tuxedo. Later the husband would get a bollocking from his wife for smiling at the knockout in the sequinned dress.

'So what happens in the film when they walk into the dining room?' asked Flick a few moments later as they exited the elevator on the correct deck and made their way towards the dining room.

'Everyone stops and stares. Trust me, they really know how to make an entrance.'

They both paused by the doorway and looked at each other for a moment. Both a little daunted.

Flick in her satin floor-length dress. Maggie in her sequinned plunging one. But while in Monte Carlo it might have been wearing her, now she was definitely wearing it.

'Well, in that case, seeing as you're a blonde you can be Marilyn Monroe,' said Flick.

'And you can be Jane Russell,' finished Maggie.

Then they both grinned.

'OK, let's go.'

They were greeted by a hostess and led down a two-tier winding staircase to the captain's table, along with the other invited guests. Think *Titanic*, only without Rose and Jack or the iceberg. Everyone was wearing their finest, with the women in cocktail dresses and evening gowns and the men in tuxedos with satin cummerbunds. Immediately Maggie stopped worrying about her outfit – she'd never seen so many sequins and feathers outside of Vegas.

As they walked through the busy restaurant, all eyes were upon them as they made their way towards the designated table in the centre of the vast dining room. Being invited as a guest to dine with the captain at his table was quite the honour and there were more than a few envious stares. Flick thought this is what it must be like to be famous. Everyone staring and gawping. She decided she wouldn't like it. Why did everyone want to be famous when anonymity was so much better?

The hostess quickly seated them. It was an interesting mix of guests, including the ship's officers; and, as was the usual practice, couples were split up. Flick found herself sitting next to a sweet old man called Valentine who proudly informed her this was his first cruise and he'd come away to celebrate his eightieth birthday with his family, while Maggie was next to his daughter-in-law, Liv, who showed her pictures of her recent honeymoon in Mexico and her cute stepson, Stanley, who was asleep in their cabin with her husband Ben.

'The only one missing is Harry,' she laughed, before explaining their beloved family pet was at home with dogsitters.

Finally, and only once everyone was seated, the captain came down in his formal navy uniform and they all had to rise.

'Good evening, lovely to meet you all, welcome to the *Galaxy Goddess*.'

As the Captain greeted everyone, with smiles and handshakes, there began a flurry of introductions around the table, and waiters, who appeared like magic, began pouring champagne and handing out the special menu created for the captain's preference.

'So, I hear we have an esteemed journalist in our midst.'

The captain beamed at Flick across the table as she was handed a flute of amber bubbles. In the last twenty-four hours, she'd had more champagne than in an entire lifetime.

'Um, well, I wouldn't exactly—' She caught Maggie's eye and did a swift U-turn. She needed to play the part. 'Yes, thank you for inviting me tonight; it's wonderful to be here.'

'We're honoured to have you on board.'

'The honour is all mine,' she smiled, crossing her fingers under the table that she wouldn't be called upon to recount her latest leading story and its headline. **WARNING TO HIKERS – EWE BE CAREFUL!** 'I'm sure our readers will be fascinated to read about life on the ocean waves and what really goes on on a cruise ship.'

'Well, we've certainly got some stories.'

## SO, I MET THIS GUY . . .

There were a few titters around the table.

'But nothing we'd want to see in print,' quipped one of the officers.

'What happens at sea, stays at sea,' chimed in another guest and there was a round of laughter around the table.

'How many passengers do you have on board?' asked Maggie.

'Four thousand guests and one thousand, six hundred and fifty-seven crew.'

'So that's almost six thousand people,' said Flick, quickly doing the arithmetic.

Flick and Maggie glanced at each other across the table. They'd both been assuming finding their man was a done deal now they were on board, but unexpectedly doubt flickered.

'Oh, yes, you can be on board and not see the same people twice,' nodded a woman with blonde hair swirled on top of her head, like soft-serve vanilla ice cream. 'I'm forever losing my husband.'

'Are you sure that's not on purpose?' joked the husband.

There was more laughter.

'We have the app so we can track each other,' said Liv brightly. 'It's really useful if we're doing different activities.'

'That's how I got caught gambling away their inheritance in the casino,' chuckled Valentine.

'You have a casino?' Flick's interest was suddenly caught.

'Oh, yes, we have everything here,' nodded one of the officers. 'A casino, spa, gymnasium, cinema, a dozen restaurants and bars . . .'

'. . . a chapel, a morgue,' finished another.

'You have a morgue!' exclaimed the woman with the soft-serve hair, clasping her hands to her chest.

'Over my dead body,' quipped her husband. He was quite the comedian.

There was a brief pause in conversation as the waiters served the starter, a delicious take on the traditional prawn cocktail, with plump ripe prawns drizzled in a delicate sauce. Not that either Flick or Maggie had much of an appetite – they were too busy trying to scan the other tables in the restaurant, both thinking the same thing. He was on the ship, *but where?*

'We also have a jail on board,' said the captain between mouthfuls. 'It's what we call the brig.'

'A prison?' Maggie shot a look at Flick.

'Of sorts, yes. It's more of a holding cell until we get into a port.'

'It's a shortened version of the nautical term "brigantine",' explained the first officer, jovially. 'Which is a two-masted sailing vessel that was often later used to imprison criminals.'

But for once Flick wasn't interested in etymology.

'So you've arrested people?'

'Well, I haven't personally,' said the captain, looking amused by the line of questioning. 'I have a whole security team to do that. Many of which are trained ex-service men.'

'Better not break the law then,' chortled Mr Comedian.

'What if someone was wanted by the police in the UK for a previous crime?' asked Maggie.

'Like a murderer on the run?' gasped Liv.

'Crikey, it's like being in an episode of *Midsomer Murders*, but at sea,' said Valentine, buttering a roll.

'Please, can we change the subject, all this talk is making me quite nervous!' Mrs Soft-Serve began fanning herself.

'Don't worry, you're in safe hands on the *Galaxy Goddess*,' assured the captain. 'I run a tight ship. Anyone breaking the law would be swiftly dealt with.'

He shot a look at her husband, which made it clear he didn't find him as funny as the husband found himself, before turning to Flick.

'Rest assured, the only headlines we'll be making will be for being the best cruise ship in the world.'

And it was right at that moment that Maggie heard a distinctive laugh from across the other side of the restaurant and felt the hairs go up on the back of her neck.

She'd know that laugh anywhere.

Glancing over, she caught a glimpse of Birdy. He must be at the same table, but her view was blocked by the back of a large passenger in a velvet tuxedo. . . and then suddenly the broad shoulders moved and she saw him.

The Man Who Stole Her Life.

Flick heard the laughter too. Saw the reaction on Maggie's face and knew immediately.

*Oh My God. It's him. He's here.*

They both stared at each other across the table. Their minds racing. Shocked and yet not shocked. What did they do now? Protocol said they couldn't leave the table before the captain, but the main course was being served and he'd just launched into an anecdote about the time he steered them into safety during a storm.

'. . . the wind was picking up to fifty-two knots, so I said batten the hatches, we're in for a long night . . .'

And a long anecdote, thought Flick, looking desperately at Maggie, who returned an anguished grimace.

For a few minutes they sat tight as the captain droned on.

And on.

And on.

Right through the entire main course and second helpings of vegetables.

'. . . and I said to my first officer, this is going to make some helluva story!'

Finally, after their plates were cleared away, Flick could take it no more and broke into applause.

'Bravo! What a story!'

'Oh, I'm only getting started.' He gave a flattered laugh. 'Wait until you hear what happened next—'

But Maggie couldn't wait. After all this time, after everything they'd both gone through, they'd caught up with him at last. They had to do something.

'Please excuse me, the powder room calls,' she interrupted, putting down her glass and pushing back her chair. It was now or never.

'Me too!' Flick jumped up.

'Goodness, was it something I said?' The captain looked taken aback.

'I think it might have been the prawn cocktail starter,' apologized Flick.

'Oh no, are you allergic to shellfish?' gasped Mrs Soft-Scoop. 'So is my friend and she blew up like a balloon.'

But Flick and Maggie were already hurrying away from the table. Only the sweet course was now being served and as they tried to make their way across the restaurant a swarm of desert trolleys appeared.

'Sorry . . .'

'Excuse me . . .'

Their way was blocked by a waiter with a huge cart piled high with glazed pastries.

'Quickly, this way.' Flick stepped sideways, only to be blocked by another.

'No, this way.' Maggie gestured towards the far side and a clear route.

It was like being in the old-fashioned video games Maggie used to play as a child with her brother Charlie. Every direction they took, they were obstructed. If not by a dessert trolley, by a wine steward wheeling in an ice bucket or a member of the waiting staff carrying a tray of plates.

And now suddenly guests were getting up and leaving as the theatre was about to start. And Maggie and Flick found themselves in a swarm of people trying to make sure they didn't miss the beginning of the musical production of *Mamma Mia*.

'*I love it in the film when she sings "Honey Honey"* . . .'

'Hurry up!'

'*Ooh, yes, but my favourite scene's got to be "Lay All Your Love on Me"* . . .'

'We're going to lose him!'

And when they finally reached the table, ready for their big confrontation scene, they were greeted by nothing but dirty napkins and empty glasses, one of which bore Birdy's bright fuchsia lipstick. And the sinking realization that in a floating city of nearly six thousand people, he could be absolutely anywhere.

# Tangier

*Day Twelve*

*Two more days to go*

# The Grand Tour

The joy of being on a cruise is going to bed at night and waking up to find yourself in a different port every day. Often a different country entirely. And with it the prospect of being able to get off the ship and explore a new locale with total freedom. Which meant there were four thousand excited passengers who woke the next morning to discover the *Galaxy Goddess* had docked in Tangier, a city famous for being the gateway to Africa.

Correction: four thousand passengers minus two.

'Shit,' cursed Flick, as they sat at the all-you-can-eat buffet having breakfast. 'I thought once we were on the ship there'd be no escape. That it was a done deal.'

'He might not get off the ship,' countered Maggie, stirring sugar into her flat white, but even she sounded unconvinced. After last night, she was feeling frustrated and doubtful. They'd been so close.

'But what if he does?'

'Well, he'll have to get back on again.'

'What if he doesn't? What if he saw you last night at the captain's table and thinks you're going to blow his cover?'

'He didn't see me. Neither did Birdy. They both had their backs to us and must have arrived later, otherwise I would have spotted them when we walked in,' she reassured.

Maggie took in Flick's worried expression and the way she was shredding her croissant into pieces, none of which were going in her mouth. She'd never seen her look this anxious and her heart went out to her.

'Trust me, he has no idea we're on this cruise ship,' she said firmly, silencing her own fears. Flick had been through such a lot. Losing her mother, discovering the true identity of her father, breaking up with her boyfriend. She needed to be strong for her.

Flick looked at her gratefully, then tutted.

'Can you believe it? I had to agree to meet the press officer at ten. She wants to give me a tour of the ship,' Flick was saying now. 'So I'm tied up all day. It was either that or do that talk for the passengers. This seemed like the lesser of two evils.'

'But that's perfect,' encouraged Maggie. 'You can scope out the ship and I'll check out Tangier.'

'OK.' Flick nodded, then paused. 'Maggie?'

'Yes?'

'I'm sorry, for dragging you into all this. For turning your life upside down.'

'You didn't turn my life upside down, you saved my life.'

As their eyes met, they shared a quiet feeling of gratitude and Flick seemed to finally relax. 'Do you think I'm crazy?' she asked, after a moment.

Maggie smiled. 'Depends how you define crazy.'

Tangier. The gateway to Africa. It was like nowhere Maggie had ever been before. As soon as she stepped foot on the shore, into a bustling hive of activity, it felt a world away from Europe. Even the air, filled with fragrant spices and exotic perfumes, smelled faraway and exotic.

The old city was twenty minutes' walk from the port. She'd waited to disembark until after the large queues of passengers going on excursions had dispersed. There was no sign of Him or Birdy, but there were so many people, it would have been easy to miss them in the crowds. Plus, it was so incredibly hot, she wouldn't be surprised if they'd decided to stay on board and enjoy the air conditioning. Perhaps Flick would see them when she did her tour of the ship.

Still, if she did, there would be no way of her knowing until she returned. She was still without a phone, which was a major inconvenience. And yet, rather unexpectedly, one that Maggie was finding completely liberating. She felt completely untethered from her life, but it was a life that no longer fit her. No longer did she feel the dread of an email waiting for her in her inbox, someone's text appearing, a bad news alert or a social media post to remind her that her life was nothing like it apparently should be. The pressure to be constantly checking. The habit of constantly reaching for it, when she was nervous or bored or lonely. She was completely uncontactable.

And in a world where everyone wanted to be connected, Maggie had discovered that actually, what she wanted was to be *dis*connected.

After exiting the ship and having her key card scanned by a crew member, who gave her strict instructions on what time to be back on board, she headed into the old town. It was like stepping into a different world. Encircled by a medieval wall were twisting, hilly streets of cobbles that led eventually to the top of the Kasbah, with its incredible views across the water towards Europe.

With no phone to take a photo or look at a map, Maggie allowed herself and her mind to wander. Meandering through the backstreets, she thought about her future, wondering what was next. Soon she would be back in the UK, but where before she'd felt only dread and trepidation, now she felt a new sense of optimism.

She was fifty. *Fifty!* It was insane and ridiculous and unexpectedly liberating. How strange that she'd always viewed it as some big dead-end when in fact, it felt like a beginning. A much-needed reset. The past was gone and the future was now a blank page.

She'd decided she was going to take up George's offer of his sofa bed until she found a job, saved up some money, and got back on her feet. In her more hopeful moments she even vowed she was going to start painting again. She'd loved having the gallery and exhibiting other artists' work, but in many respects it had been a way for her to hide. When her brother had died, so had that creative part of her. How could she ever feel inspired, when Charlie's life had been so cruelly snuffed out?

And for years she thought it was gone for ever. That desire to create, to breathe life into something. But being on this trip, seeing art again and not just through her own eyes, but through Flick's, had reignited something inside of her. Was it creativity? A passion?

Or was it courage?

The courage to look deep inside herself and realize that part of her had never gone. That little girl who refused the colouring-in books and was forever sketching outside of the lines; the teenager who saved all their money to buy canvases and oils and holed themselves up in their bedroom, her parents' old Roxy Music records on an ancient record player, volume turned up high, trying to make sense of her confused, hormonal world with streaks of vermillion and burnt sienna and cerulean blue.

She was still here.

Her mind flicked back to that night on the Amalfi Coast, when she'd told a complete stranger that she had come to Europe to study art history. Sander, the handsome Dutchman.

Maggie remembered how he'd assumed she was on a sabbatical and taken a photo of her that he'd never sent. Not that it mattered. She smiled fondly at the memory. It seemed so long ago now, even though it was only a week or so ago, but so much had happened since.

Because he was right. She had been on a sabbatical, but it wasn't from work, it was from herself. And it had just taken something extraordinary to find that part of herself again and bring her back to the world. Maybe you have to lose everything to find the stuff that's important. It's like being in the dark, you always look for that chink of light. And that something extraordinary and that chink of light was meeting Flick, and this trip, and their friendship. And realizing she was braver and stronger than she ever thought.

After stopping for a refreshment at one of the local cafes, she ventured further into the ancient medina. Steeped in history, its narrow alleyways were filled with shops and stalls stuffed with an array of goods: kaftans, pottery, traditional leather slippers in an array of vivid colours, bejewelled lamps and perfumed oils. Plunged into the bustling souks, it was easy to get lost without a guide. Tradesmen inviting you to drink mint tea, shopkeepers and street-hawkers wanting you to look at their wares.

Everywhere she looked was a feast for her senses. She passed jewellers and watchmakers, leather craftsmen and basket-weavers. Stalls selling pyramids of brightly coloured spices, reminding her of pigment from paints. It was dizzying. At every corner, she weaved herself further and further into the labyrinthian maze.

Until quite unexpectedly, there he was ahead of her.

He was standing at a stall, haggling over something. He looked hot. Annoyed. The tradesman was holding up a leather bag. They were both shaking their heads. Then, feeling eyes upon him, he turned and saw her.

And suddenly there they both were. In the middle of a souk, in Morocco. Thousands of miles away from her flat where she'd last been together with him.

'Theo.'

Afterwards she was sure she had said his name out loud, but in reality it got caught in her throat and barely came out as a whisper.

A few seconds. The time it takes for the second hand on a watch to move a few clicks around the dial. Then, before she knew what was happening, he ducked around the corner and vanished out of sight.

WTF?

And now her surprise had turned into anger and disbelief. That was it? After all that had happened, he was running away? And for a second time. What a pathetic excuse for a man. And now she was trying to follow him, but it was a maze, a labyrinth. Hagglers and tradesmen waved their wares in front of her, a shopkeeper beckoned her inside – no, please, I need to find someone.

She couldn't have lost him. Not again. Not again.

And then she saw a familiar figure.

'Birdy!'

She was in jewellery shop, being shown something in a glass case, and when she heard her name being called, she looked up and twirled around.

'Maggie! Am I pleased to see you!'

'Thank God I've found you—' She broke off, trying to catch her breath. Inside the medina it was airless. She tried to suck the humid air into her lungs. 'I need to warn you—'

'Warn me about what, honey? Why didn't you come to the club in Ibiza?'

'I did. I saw you with him. With Theo. He's the romance fraudster I was telling you about. The man who broke my heart and stole my life savings.'

It all came tumbling out.

'I know.'

Maggie blinked and took a step backwards.

'*You know?*'

'Of course I do,' said Birdy, as if it was perfectly obvious, and then just when Maggie thought nothing more could surprise her, she laughed mischievously. 'Why do you think I'm dating him?'

# A Little Birdy Told Me

There were so many questions. But they had to wait. They had to get back to the ship. Because the thing about the questions is, the more answers you get, the more the questions multiply. And standing in the middle of a souk in Tangier when their cruise ship was soon to set sail probably wasn't the best time to start asking them.

Much better to wait until they were safely back on board and sitting across from each other on two velvet sofas in Birdy's palatial Galaxy suite. Only, the person firing the first question wasn't Maggie, it was Birdy.

'What took you so long?'

'Excuse me?'

'You told me you were following the cruise ship when we were in Sicily, but when you didn't show up at the club in Ibiza, I got a little worried I wasn't going to see you again.'

Taking off her golf-ball-size diamond earrings, Birdy tossed them into an open jewellery box on the side table next to her, which appeared to be brimming with dazzling bracelets and necklaces.

'And this little plan of mine would all be for nothing.'

'What plan?' demanded a voice and Flick suddenly appeared striding into the room. 'I came as soon as I got your note.'

'What note?' Maggie was even more confused.

'I had Philip, my butler, send a note asking Flick to come to my suite,' explained Birdy. 'You mentioned your room number when we were in the elevator.'

'You have a butler?' Maggie looked to Birdy in amazement.

'The service comes with the suite and it's such a luxury. Philip caters to my every need. If he's not restocking the bar, booking spa treatments or making dinner reservations, he's discreetly sending notes—' She broke off, smiling, as a dark-haired man in a uniform made his entrance carrying an arrangement of fresh flowers. 'Oh, howdy, Philip, I was just telling my friends how totally wonderful you are.'

'All part of the service, ma'am,' he nodded politely, pausing to plump a cushion.

'Everyone should have a Philip; he thinks of everything – it's like having a wife,' she confided as Maggie and Flick both tried not to stare.

'It was getting late and I was worried,' continued Flick.

'We just got back. Sorry, I would've texted earlier but I don't have a phone.'

'It's OK, mine would have been turned off anyway. I was in the spa having a massage after two hours' playing crazy golf. Who knew I'd be such a convert to cruising.' Flick pulled a face. 'So c'mon, what did I miss?'

'I saw Theo in one of the souks . . .'

'Oh my God! Did he see you?'

'Yes, but then he scarpered and I lost him and bumped into Birdy in the medina—'

'Is it true? Are you dating my dad?'

'*Your dad?*'

For the first time Birdy's composure appeared ruffled.

'It's a long story,' placated Maggie.

'And an interesting twist,' reflected Birdy, kicking off her heels and studying them both thoughtfully.

'Look, will someone tell me what's going on?' Flick was fast losing patience.

'My question exactly,' agreed Maggie.

'OK, ladies —' Birdy fixed them both with a steely gaze born from years of coming up against powerful men and never losing her nerve — 'let me rewind.'

Taking a moment to smooth down her skirt and make herself comfortable — by draping herself across the sofa like a reclining nude in a Renaissance painting, only one clad in Chanel — she began speaking slowly and carefully.

'I first met him on the Amalfi Coast. He sat next to me on a boat as we travelled back to the same cruise ship. He introduced himself as Louis, but I knew instinctively that wasn't his real name. Most likely he called himself after my Louis Vuitton handbag that he noticed I was carrying. Of course, I noticed him noticing. It's all in the details and I'm all about attention to detail.'

Unclipping her hair piece, she placed it on the armrest, where it sat like a small fluffy blonde guinea pig.

'He was very flirtatious, but I knew his game. He wasn't interested in me; he was interested in my money. He told me some sob story about being a widower and asked me to dinner, but I told him I was busy washing my hair. Then, a couple of days later in Sicily, I bumped into you again, Maggie, at the cooking class, and you told me your story; about the man who stole your life savings along with your heart. That's when we discovered I was on the same cruise as him.'

Birdy paused for effect. She appeared to be relishing her story.

'Afterwards I put two and two together and realized this was very likely to be the same con man. I don't believe in coincidences, so it was quite obvious really. Con man, romance fraudster, call them what you like, they're quite easy to spot . . . when you know what you're looking for,' she added pointedly.

Glancing at Maggie, she gave her a supportive smile.

'So many people haven't a clue about their tactics – why should they? Most people are trusting, naive . . . gullible, perhaps.' She dabbed at the lipstick at the corners of her mouth with a perfectly manicured finger, then removed the rocks on her fingers and tossed them in the jewellery box as well. 'But Birdy Carmichael is not.'

There was a pause as the ship suddenly listed sharply to one side, then dropped back again. There'd been reports of a bad weather front coming in as they'd left the port to set sail for Lisbon, and outside the skies had darkened.

'It was quite apparent to me that he was on a cruise in order to go big game hunting. And while I say it myself, as a rich older woman, I am a trophy worth having.' She raised a perfectly arched eyebrow. 'Mr Louis, or shall we call him by his real name, Mr Theo C. Stratin, spotted me immediately, and without any need for binoculars.'

Breaking off, she gave a throaty laugh.

'So I let him think he was stalking me, when in fact, I was the one doing the stalking. I was hoping you'd show up at some point, but I couldn't be sure. When I bumped into you in Ibiza, I was delighted. My private table at the club seemed the perfect opportunity for you to nail the bastard. I thought it would be a nice surprise for you. It was kind of a shame when you didn't show. I had to buy him a Rolex.'

Unfastening her own watch, she added it to the jewellery box which was now overflowing.

'So you can imagine what a pleasant surprise it was to finally see you in the souk—' She broke off, distracted by Philip the Butler.

'I've been informed that we're heading into some crosswinds and the sailing is going to get a little choppy. Is there anything I can get for you?'

'Would you be a doll and look after these ladies while I put the diamonds in the safe?' Flashing him a smile, she scooped up her jewellery box and stood up from the sofa. 'And then would you be so kind to make us a round of negronis? All this talking has made me thirsty. What do you say, ladies?'

The ladies didn't say anything. In fact, Flick and Maggie sat open-mouthed, trying to take it all in. This whole time they'd been thinking Birdy needed saving, when in fact, not only was she was quite capable of saving herself, she was orchestrating a sting.

'And don't go easy with the liquor, make those cocktails strong,' she instructed, as Philip began carefully measuring alcohol into the cocktail shaker. 'We all like a stiff one, don't we?'

Seriously. Why were they ever in any doubt that Birdy could take care of herself?

A few minutes later, she reappeared and resumed her place on the sofa.

'Of course the question now is, have we let him get away?' Birdy sighed, as if such minor details were a nuisance.

They each looked at other. Flick was actually starting to feel scared of the way the ship was rolling, and also a little seasick, but she didn't want to lose face.

'Well, he definitely saw me,' said Maggie, 'that's when he legged it.'

'Why would he run away from you when he texted you, wanting to meet you in Mallorca?' asked Flick.

'Who knows,' shrugged Maggie. 'I've given up trying to explain his behaviour. He's a fantasist—'

'And a narcissist. I should know, I was married to a few,' interjected Birdy helpfully. 'This type has no boundaries.'

'Plus, a lot's happened since Mallorca.' Maggie gestured towards Birdy. 'Maybe he was worried I was going to blow his cover in front of Birdy.'

'Have you checked his cabin?'

Birdy shook her head. 'I wouldn't know which one it was. I don't do cabins, sweetie. Only suites.'

'And the crew wouldn't give out that information,' interjected Flick, answering her own question. She was now in full investigative reporter mode.

'Can't we tell if he's got back on the ship with the app?' asked Maggie.

'Only if you're part of the same booking or have accepted a friend request,' explained Flick. After spending the day with the press officer, she was now an expert in cruising and quite the fan.

The ship suddenly lifted, then dropped, as if they were on a big dipper and she swallowed the bile that rose in her throat. Well, she was a fan until now.

'That sounds like a terrible idea. I don't like anyone knowing where I am or what I'm up to,' said Birdy, 'as my ex-husbands will testify.'

'That's why I don't have a Boots Advantage card,' agreed Maggie.

'It's hardly the same, knowing what shampoo and conditioner you use,' Flick snapped, then sighed in frustration. 'Sorry, I'm just . . .'

'I know, I know.' Maggie leaned across and gave her shoulder a squeeze.

'We were so close. If he jumped ship in Morocco, we'll never see him again . . .' Flick trailed off, her voice despondent, as Philip handed around three perfectly executed negronis. She took one gratefully.

'And if he hasn't?' asked Maggie, taking a sip. Crikey, that was strong.

'We're going to need a fucking good plan,' said Birdy, and knocked her drink straight back in one.

# All at Sea

*Day Thirteen*

*One more day to go*

# Maggie

It's like picking a thread. Once you've started, things quickly begin to unravel and fall apart . . .

A few days after the incident with the bank, Theo flew back from the States. Filming had wrapped ahead of schedule, so he was able to come home early. Whenever he went away on trips, he would always come home with gifts of perfume or beauty products. This time it was a gorgeous silk scarf from a famous designer brand, all boxed up with a ribbon and wrapped in tissue paper.

'You didn't have to buy me this! It's far too extravagant!' I protest, as the luxurious silk fabric slips from the box and through my fingers, a gorgeous swathe of lilacs and forest greens.

'Nonsense, you deserve it,' he smiles, shushing me with a kiss.

'I feel like a Parisian,' I laugh, draping it around my neck and pretending to pout, hands on hips.

'*Oh la la,*' he grins, raising his eyebrows and pulling me towards him. 'And now I'm home I'm going to sort everything out with the bank, don't worry, just leave it to me. You've got far more important things to worry about, like what are you going to pack for a beach wedding and honeymoon on a tropical island?'

Feeling his arms around my waist and the silk against my skin, I feel like I'm in a cocoon and I let myself lean into him. The past few days I've felt a bit anxious. After I spoke to Theo on the phone, he tried calling the bank a few times from the States, but never got through. He assured me it was fine, that it was OK to wait until he got back; he even told me he'd hidden some cash in a biscuit tin for emergencies, and to use that if I needed anything until his return.

But still, I did worry, so it's wonderful to have him home.

'You don't seem very excited about marrying me,' he says, sounding hurt.

'Oh darling, I'm sorry, I've just been so distracted,' I reassure quickly, feeling guilty for making such a fuss about the bank when our wedding is just weeks away. 'Don't be silly, of course I am!'

I feel him relax. 'Good. And I'm going to take care of everything,' he smiles, giving me a kiss, as George the cat miaows around his ankles, before suddenly yelping. 'Ow, the little bugger just bit me!'

'What?'

As we break apart, I catch a flash of George's ginger fur flying into the bedroom.

'He bit me!' Theo is saying again, pulling up his trouser leg, to show me the marks on his ankle. I stare at it, aghast.

'George did that? Are you sure? But he's just the softest thing—'

'Absolutely, I'm fucking sure.' Theo is pissed off now, his good mood turned to a scowl. 'I'm probably going to need a tetanus shot.'

'I'm sure it will be fine, he's had all his shots. Let me get some antiseptic cream.'

I quickly hurry into the bathroom, opening the cabinet, rifling through the different bits of medical kit I keep for emergencies. I still can't believe it. George bit Theo? It's so out of character, it's almost laughable, but of course I mustn't do that, he's furious enough as it is. And then I spot a twenty-pound note on the floor. It must have fallen out of his pocket when Theo went to the loo. It's neatly folded up with a couple of receipts. I pick it up. I'm already formulating my joke about him throwing money away when I hand it back, so I don't know what makes me unfold it.

I just have a feeling. Before I even spot it's a bill from a fancy restaurant in London and it's dated four days ago, when Theo was in LA, I can feel myself pulling a thread. Cocktails, a bottle of expensive red wine, two main courses and a dessert to share. Along with the receipt from his credit card. And now it all starts unravelling.

I'm not sure how I make it through that evening without saying anything about the restaurant bill. I keep thinking about bringing it up, but after George bit him, Theo was in a foul mood and I didn't want to make things worse. I could just imagine him, twisting it all round, accusing me of snooping, asking me what I was insinuating. Making me feel guilty for nagging or criticizing him, like I'm the one in the wrong. Tangling me all up in knots with his explanations and reasoning, then stonewalling me until I'm the one apologizing and trying to make things right between us. Because that's what's always happens.

I learned pretty quickly it's better not to say anything at all.

Except the next day I find myself at work in the art gallery, unable to think of anything else. All day, while customers drift in and out, I sell a painting, eat lunch, and talk to a customer who's interested in a small bronze, I turn it around and around in my head, trying to think of a perfectly reasonable explanation, but being unable to. By the time I turn the sign to closed on the door I'm tired and confused and feel like I'm going mad. I really need to talk to someone. By someone, what I really mean is, I need to talk to my friend George.

Only problem is, we're no longer friends after we had that stupid argument. Though to be honest, it wasn't just that; things haven't been the same between us since the engagement party. Theo made it clear he didn't want me talking to George and afterwards I didn't want to make things worse or cause an argument, so whenever George tried to call me or leave messages about us getting together I'd say I was busy and could I call him back later? Only, I'd never call him back, just send a quick text with yet another random excuse. In the end he stopped calling.

I feel terrible about it. I miss him. But I don't know what to do about it. I feel so torn. My wedding to Theo is just weeks away, he's going to be my husband, and yet George is my oldest friend. I would always turn to him first in an emergency. Sitting in the back office, I think about the events of the past few days, compounded with my feelings from the last few months. If this isn't an emergency, I don't know what is.

I pick up my phone, pluck up the courage, and video-call him. And when he immediately answers, his familiar face filling the screen, and says, 'Hello, gorgeous,' and gives me one of his smiles, I promptly burst into tears.

Ten minutes later it's all come blurting out. About the call from the bank. The receipt from the restaurant. The moods. The doubts. The feeling in the pit of my stomach that won't go away. The fact that in just a few weeks I'm supposed to be marrying this man.

'You tried to warn me at our engagement party, you thought something wasn't right, but I wouldn't listen, I was an idiot.'

'You weren't an idiot, you were in love,' says George kindly. He's been nothing but sympathetic and supporting, listening to me as I tell him all about everything that's been going on. 'I just wish you'd told me about all this sooner.'

'I know, I'm sorry,' I say for about the hundredth time, but he shushes me.

'OK, so let me get this straight, you've remortgaged the flat, taken out a business loan and put all your life savings – and inheritance – into a joint account with a man who says he was in America last week working, but was actually having dinner for two in a restaurant in Mayfair?'

Put like that it brings me up short.

'It could've been a business dinner. He's trying to woo lots of investors.'

'So why didn't he tell you he was in London?'

'Do you think he's cheating on me?' My stomach lurches. Suspecting it is one thing, saying it out loud is quite another.

'I don't know what he's been doing—' George breaks off, and for the first time ever I see he looks worried. 'And you've never actually met any of his friends or his family?'

'He's an only child. His dad died years ago and he's had to put his mum into a care home. That's why he sold his house in LA, to move closer to her.'

'But you've never visited her.'

'She's got dementia. He says she wouldn't like me to see her like that.'

'That's handy.'

'What do you mean?'

'Can you remember the name of the care home?'

'Um . . . it's the one not far from me . . . Greenacres . . .'

'OK, let me call you right back.'

'George?'

But he's already hung up.

I sit at my desk, a cold dread creeping over me. I'm trying to keep the feeling of panic at bay. *Don't jump to conclusions.*

*There's always a logical explanation. You're getting married in two weeks.* I fiddle with my engagement ring. At this point I'd be an idiot if I wasn't seriously questioning that decision. Is Theo even the kind of man I should be marrying? I try to imagine breaking it off, being on my own again, and I feel such a sense of loss. *Theo's a lot of things, but he's not a cheater,* I tell myself firmly. *He's not a liar. He'd never do anything to hurt me. He loves me. We're investing in our future.*

My phone starts ringing. It's George video-calling me. I pick up.

'They have no record of any resident called Mrs Stratin.'

'She could have a different last name,' I counter.

'No one called Theo Stratin has ever visited see his mum.'

'Maybe you spoke to a new member of staff,' I suggest, but even I feel I'm reaching.

'Visitors have to sign in and out. There's no record.'

'Maybe I'm getting mixed up, maybe the home is called a different name.'

'Or maybe he's lying, Maggie.' George's face is deadly serious. 'And if he's lying about that, what else is he lying about?'

Dominoes. It's like a line of dominoes. If just one thing I thought was true is a lie, then everything starts toppling. My chest tightens. I feel suddenly faint. George is still talking to me, but my mind is miles away, racing back to Theo.

'I need to speak to Theo,' I blurt. 'I need to find out what's going on.'

I'm suddenly desperate to see him. To hear his explanations. To make all this go away.

'I can drive up from London, it'll just take a couple of hours. I'll jump in the car, wait for me.'

'No, it's OK.'

'I'm serious, Maggie, it could be dangerous.'

I snap back to see George, his face sombre. I've never seen him look so worried.

'I won't say anything until you get here,' I say, but I know I'm only saying it to appease him. 'I'll meet you at my flat.'

'OK, I'm jumping in my car now. My phone says I'll be there in just over two hours.' He pauses, his eyes meeting mine. 'I don't want you confront him until I'm there, promise?'

'I promise,' I fib.

Twenty minutes later I let myself into my flat. I walk up the stairs. Heart racing, but determined to remain calm. All the way over I've rehearsed what I'm going to say when I walk in. In my head are a list of questions. I need to stick to the script, to not be thrown off course by Theo, who is a master in twisting around a conversation so I'm always in the wrong.

*I'm right, I know I'm right*, I whisper to myself as I climb the stairs. Scrunching up my hands into fists by my sides. Feeling my nails digging into the palms of my hands.

The flat is silent. I walk into the living room. He should be home by now. Earlier he'd texted to say he was at the supermarket getting ingredients. He was cooking dinner tonight. A new pasta recipe he'd seen in a magazine. I hadn't wanted to alert him, so I'd acted all normal. Or so I thought. Because as I walk through the living room and kitchen I notice his trainers are gone from the rack in the hallway.

Somewhere in my body a pulse starts beating.

George appears mewing for attention, winding his way around my feet. I pick him up, squeezing him tight, but he doesn't want to be squeezed tonight; he's not looking for affection, he wants feeding. I'm hungry, Mama, he says in cat meows.

In a minute, I tell him, in a minute.

No music playing. No sound of the TV. No overheard conversation on the phone as he talks to another investor about the business. Or the estate agent. Or a work colleague in some faraway destination. Or the carers at the nursing home asking them to take the phone to his mum so he can tell her goodnight.

Thoughts begin tumbling.

Were they real? Was any of it real? Was it just all for my benefit?

My chest constricts, squeezing the air out of my lungs. I can't breathe. I must breathe. I continue through into the bedroom. It's in shadow, the blinds are down, but in the dim light I see the doors to his side of the wardrobe are thrown open and his clothes are gone. Nothing but empty hangers. Never has anything so mundane been so powerful. He's gone. Left. Cleared out. Vanished.

Thump. Thump. Thump. My heart in my chest beats loudly in my ears.

I race around the flat, frantic now. Drawers have been emptied. Some of my jewellery's gone: a pair of diamond earrings I'd got for my twenty-first, a pearl necklace I've never worn that isn't real. What else has he taken? *My dad's watch.* Suddenly I remember he took it to be fixed but never gave it back. I feel myself choke up, then a flash of disbelief. He's even taken the silk scarf he bought me, together with its box.

I start to sob as everything implodes. Thoughts galloping away from me. All my money's gone. There's no joint account. Most likely there's no business venture, or mum in a care home either, or house he sold in LA. It's all gone. Or it never even existed. It was all just a fabrication. My knees buckle and I grab on to the kitchen counter. I feel like I'm going to throw up. He told me he loved me. He told me he wanted to spend the rest of his life with me and I believed him. Bile rises in my throat and I sink to my knees as George the cat circles around me, meowing and meowing and meowing and meowing.

# Nowhere to Run

The storm had hit later that evening. The Strait of Gibraltar was notorious for rough seas, and as they left behind the Mediterranean and entered the Atlantic Ocean to continue up the Portuguese coast towards Lisbon, freak bad weather caused strong winds and big waves. Glasses and dishware jumped off tables. People were warned to be careful walking around the ship. No one was allowed outside. Even with the ship's stabilizers on, it was listing. Worse still, poor Flick discovered that not only did she suffer from carsickness, she suffered from seasickness too.

Was the storm a bad omen? wondered Maggie, as she lay in bed listening to the sounds of retching coming from the bathroom and thinking about what they'd decided. Later, Flick would tell her off for being superstitious.

'But what if something bad happens tomorrow?' she worried.

'Worse than having your head stuck down the toilet all night chucking up your guts?' Flick replied.

She had a point. It had made them both laugh. They needed it.

As daybreak dawned the storm passed and they awoke to clear blue skies. Which was a relief for the passengers as it was the last full day of their cruise and it was going to be spent entirely at sea. It was also a massive relief for the crew who were organizing a huge party that evening to celebrate the end of the voyage. The ship was due to dock in Lisbon the next day, when everyone would disembark, and it was traditional on the last night to give the guests a grand send-off. The Dancing Under the Stars extravaganza was going to be a fun farewell on the top deck, complete with live band, a DJ, dancing, competitions, all-you-can-drink themed cocktails and a speciality menu.

For Flick and Maggie, it also had a bigger significance.

Just after 9 a.m. Birdy called to inform them he was indeed on board. He'd visited her suite after breakfast and left a message with Philip the Butler apologizing for disappearing yesterday. Apparently he'd been so engrossed in choosing her a gift, he'd lost track of time, only making it back to the ship in the nick of time.

'What was the gift?' asked Flick.

'Another necklace I don't need,' deadpanned Birdy. 'And the look on his face when he sees you guys later.'

And so it was decided.

So while the crew spent the day busily stringing lights and balloons, arranging tables, folding napkins, laying tableware, doing soundchecks, decorating the pool deck and unpacking thousands of tiny rainbow-coloured cocktail umbrellas, Flick and Maggie spent the whole day avoiding Him. As the saying goes, there's a first for everything.

As it turned out, it was quite easy. The crew weren't the only ones busy getting ready for the big night and they spent most of the day in their cabin sending emails and making phone calls, alerting various people about various things. Everything had to be timed perfectly. They needed to be ready. Only when everything had been ticked off their list could they finally change into their outfits. Nerves fluttered. This was their last chance. They couldn't mess it up.

*

As arranged, at 9 p.m. they exited the elevator and walked down the corridor towards Birdy's *Galaxy* suite. Dressed in their satin and sequins, Flick and Maggie looked to everyone like a couple of passengers on their way to the party on the top deck. No doubt anyone passing them would mistake their adrenaline and nerves for excitement at the extravaganza ahead. Two women off to have the time of their lives and celebrate the last night of their cruise.

That'll be a lesson to never assume what's going on in someone's life.

Philip the Butler let them in with a warm smile and polite greeting. It was all so easy. So civil. So *undramatic*. As they walked into Birdy's suite, there he was, sitting on the sofa in an expensively cut Italian linen suit, legs crossed, sipping a cocktail, like a man without a care in the world.

He looked up, surprised when they entered. He wasn't expecting anyone. Least of all Maggie and a younger woman he didn't recognize.

'Hello, Theo.'

Disbelief flashed across his features. But it was like lightning, vanishing before you've had the chance to really see it, and he quickly composed himself. Adjusting his features to appear neutral, as if a couple of casual acquaintances just walked in.

'Mags, what are you doing here?'

'I could ask you the same thing.'

'Birdy, darling, you've got a couple of unexpected visitors.'

Birdy was in the bathroom, under the guise of supposedly getting ready. When in fact she'd been ready for ages and had been sitting on the toilet in her evening gown, filing her nails and waiting for Flick and Maggie to arrive and for the show to begin.

She entered the living room wearing Valentino and a steady expression.

'They're actually your visitors; they're here to see you, honey.'

Looks flashed around the room. For a moment it appeared like he might pretend not to know who Maggie was, but then he seemed to change his mind and decide to brazen it out.

'So what is this? An ambush?' he mocked.

'It's not an ambush, it's a get-together,' corrected Maggie. 'Think of it sort of like a reunion.'

She'd been worried coming here that she was going to get upset, break down, burst into tears, get all emotional. Isn't that what he used to accuse her of? If ever she dared to disagree with him, or ask too many questions, or express doubts, he would fly into a mood and she would get tearful and upset. *You're too emotional*, he would say. *You're too much*.

Why had she never stopped to realize it was him who wasn't nearly enough?

'Not a big fan of reunions, I'm afraid.' He wrinkled his nose, his self-satisfied smile never wavering. 'Everyone always looks so much older, they're always quite depressing, don't you think?'

He was treating this all like an amusing joke. Trying to play tricks with her mind and manipulate her. Maggie stared at him, her gaze unwavering.

Two could play at that game.

'I owe you an apology.'

'You do?'

This wasn't what he was expecting at all. He looked caught off balance.

'For standing you up at the bar in Palma,' she continued.

'So I thought I'd better make it up to you. I don't like to stand people up. To just disappear out of their lives. It's kind of rude—'

'Totally,' interjected Birdy, perching on the arm of the chair opposite. She was holding a dirty martini, made by Philip, who'd somehow magicked himself out of the room.

'Look, I can explain everything.'

'Oh really? How you stole everything from me? Lied to me? Left me with nothing? Or are you going to make up another cock and bull story about how you were being blackmailed and the big bad men were going to kill you?'

He'd never witnessed Maggie's scorn before and for a brief moment he was taken aback.

'I don't know what you're talking about.' He looked towards Birdy. 'I'm sorry you've been dragged into all of this, darling. We were engaged and I broke it off . . . I don't know what she's doing here or what she's told you . . . a woman scorned and all that.'

He looked over at Maggie. 'This is embarrassing. *You're embarrassing*. I think you should leave.'

Before she would have crumpled, but now things were different. She was different.

'I'm not going anywhere.' Her voice was calm and determined. 'You're the one that runs away, remember?'

Maggie felt a strange detachment as she looked at Him. Theo C. Stratin. The man who walked into her gallery all those moons ago with his sharp suit and charming smile. Who whisked her off her feet and told her he loved her and proposed in her kitchen on a rainy Wednesday night. The man who made her feel safe and loved. Who she'd invested all her hopes and dreams in. And as it turned out, all her life savings.

The man who spun a web of lies so tangled she nearly

suffocated in them. Who made her feel like she was in the wrong when she dared to ask too many questions, or punished her by not speaking if she disagreed, or cast doubts. The man who alienated her friends and isolated her, who flew into moods and gaslit her, then brought her fresh juice and eggs for breakfast the next morning like it had never happened.

The man who, one day, cleared out his closets, changed his number and vanished. Who left her, heartbroken and devastated, to deal with the bailiffs knocking on the door, the bank calling in the loan and the flat nearly being repossessed and having to sell it. The man who couldn't give a flying fuck when she was forced to live in a damp, mouldy caravan because she had nowhere else to go. Who wasn't there to see her exist on nothing but Pot Noodles and shame and self-loathing, because he was too busy dodging the police, absconding to Europe, and living it up on the French Riviera trying to scam his next victim.

The man who she thought had broken her. Who had caused her to lie in bed, unable to sleep, a heaviness in her chest and fear in her belly so acute that sometimes she feared she would never wake up – worse still, often in those darkest moments she *wanted* never to wake up. And who had no idea that one day his daughter would come knocking on the caravan door looking for him and bring her back to life.

Reminded of Flick, Maggie caught herself. She didn't want to say anything that might hurt her. Whatever her feelings, he was her father and she'd gone through enough.

For so long she'd had all these questions. All this rage. How could you do it? How could you pretend to love someone and take all their money and tell all those lies? How could you be so cruel and heartless? What did she want? Revenge? To hurt him as much as he'd hurt her? To look him in the eye and demand answers to her questions. To tell him what she thought of him. That he hadn't broken her. That she'd loved him. That she'd hated him. But now she only pitied him.

He'd lost a daughter. He'd missed out on a lifetime of knowing the warm, funny, spirited, brave and beautiful human that was Flick. Compared to that, she hadn't lost anything.

She looked at Him and thought all of those things but all she said is, 'You're the loser, not me.'

'OK, I think I've been patient enough.'

Putting down his drink, he heaved a sigh and glanced at his watch, as if this whole scenario was completely tedious.

'We didn't work out, we made a few bad investments – but really, Maggie?' He threw her such a look of contempt it was hard to imagine he'd ever looked at her in any other way. 'I think you should let this go; you're acting crazy.'

'Depends how you define crazy.'

Having been standing there, not saying a word, Flick's voice now broke into the conversation.

'You know that's such an overused sexist trope. Men always call women crazy when they can't handle the truth.'

Everyone turned to look at Flick. With her dark hair pinned up, trademark black eyeliner and figure-hugging satin dress, Maggie thought she'd never looked more striking or more confident. But then Maggie wasn't the only one who had changed since that day they met at the caravan.

'But then you've done it before, haven't you? Lied to someone. Broken someone's heart. Done a runner with someone's life savings.'

'I'm sorry. And who are you?'

It was the way he sneered. The little shrug of his shoulders that intimated to her that she was of no consequence.

'Sally Lomax was only twenty years old when she met you.

She was working behind a bar at a hotel, saving up for college – she had her whole life ahead of her. You were a guest at the hotel. You told her you loved her, that you were going to get married, build a life together, and she believed you.'

In her mind Flick could see her mum's old leather diary, the swirly almost-childish handwriting; could feel the hope in the love heart doodles in the margin.

'When she told you she was having a baby, you did a runner and took all her money. She kept it in a little tin with a sticker that said My Future. You stole her future. You left her pregnant and broke.'

It was more than a quarter of a century ago. In a small, grey, northern, working-class town. Far away from a fancy penthouse suite on a luxury cruise ship in the middle of the Mediterranean. In the years that had passed had he ever thought about her mother or the baby? Wondered how they were? Or had he simply moved on and buried it in the past?

But that's the thing about the past, you never know when it's going to come back and haunt you.

'Sally Lomax was my mum.'

For a moment there was silence as he absorbed what she was saying.

'The barmaid at the hotel? But that was years ago. What? You're telling me you're my daughter? That I'm your father?'

His tone was dismissive. As if he didn't even want to remember or acknowledge her. And in that moment, something within Flick finally broke. Or actually, she realized later, it finally healed.

'No, you don't have a daughter.' She shook her head. 'You're not my real dad, his name is Colin. He's the man who married my mum and raised me. You're just the pathetic excuse for a man who got my mum pregnant and dumped her.'

'OK, well, I think the show's over.'

He was never one to sit and be insulted. Even when it was the truth.

'Birdy, darling, let's call security.' Uncrossing his legs, he put down his drink and made to stand up but Birdy beat him to it.

'Not so fast, Louis,' she said, rising from the seat where she'd been witnessing this whole thing unfold. 'Oh, I'm sorry, sweetie. Shouldn't that be Theo?'

And there it was. The game was finally up. Time to hold up your hands. Admit to your crimes and misdeeds. Accept your punishment.

Only, he was never going to do that. Doing that meant you had to accept you were wrong and express remorse. Doing that would mean getting caught. And fraudsters don't like getting caught.

'Watch out!'

Re-entering the room, Philip the Butler called out a warning but it was too late.

It all happened so quickly. A flurry of movement as he leapt up from the sofa. A scream from Birdy as he pushed past her, knocking the drink from her hand, the glass smashing against the coffee table, her face not far behind. Blood splattering on the carpet. Call a doctor. Call security. Oh my God. Are you OK? Everyone rushing to help her. No one looking at him as the door was flung open and he made a break for it. Go after him. Don't let him escape. Stay still, let me get some ice. You've cut your face. It's just a small gash. Where's my jewellery box? Ma'am, please don't worry. My diamonds! He's stolen my diamonds! Flick and Maggie running after him down the corridor. Quick, hurry. Don't let him get away.

\*

Up on the top deck the party is in full swing. It's the last night on the cruise ship and all the passengers have gathered for the Dancing Under the Stars extravaganza. The live band is excellent and everyone is dancing, having a good time, making the most of their drinks package to consume as many cocktails as they can before they reach dry land. They're going to have hangovers tomorrow, but who cares? The night is young! Tonight's about having fun!

Oh look, people are jumping fully clothed into the pool already! Wow, tonight really got crazy. Wait, what are those two women in evening gowns doing? Running across the deck, they're shouting something but no one can hear them above the sound of the music. It looks like they're chasing someone. And is that security? Hang on, is that a man up by the railing? What's he doing? Oh my God, is he going to jump?

A blink and he's there, the next he's gone. A loud scream goes up from the crowd.

'*Man overboard!*'

# The Morning After

They finally sail into Lisbon, much later than expected. They were delayed as the cruise ship went back to search after Theo jumped, but despite frantic search parties, he's still missing.

'I wonder what's happening.'

'We haven't heard anything yet, we just have to wait.'

'Do you think they'll find him?' asks Flick, worried.

'There's a chance he could have been picked up,' replies Maggie. 'I overheard someone saying it once happened before when a man spent twenty-two hours in the water but survived and was picked up by another cruise ship.'

Maggie and Flick are sitting out on deck on a couple of sun loungers, watching as the cruise ship slowly makes its way into port, where the local police are waiting to interview everyone. It's been a long night and they've barely had any sleep. After the call of man overboard, it had been chaos. Everyone had sprung into action, but it takes a while for a cruise ship that size to stop and turn around to go back to look for someone in the water, so the captain had sent out calls to other vessels in the vicinity. But still, nothing.

Still in shock, they've been up early giving statements to the ship's security team, plus the UK International Crime Bureau. A liaison officer had contacted them after receiving information that a man wanted for questioning in connection with fraud was a passenger on the *Galaxy Goddess*. That information was thanks to Flick and Maggie, who had spent the day before making calls to Tariq, Flick's contact at the local constabulary back in Lancashire, and emailing the detective Maggie had spoken to when she'd first reported Theo. They'd also informed the ship's captain that a man under investigation for an alleged criminal offence was on board, who in turn had informed his security team.

It had taken some organization, but they'd needed to ensure they had everything in place, that they'd ticked every box, prepared for every eventuality, before they confronted him. What neither Maggie nor Flick had factored in was that Theo would do anything to avoid being caught and arrested. Even jump into the ocean.

'According to these statistics, only 22 per cent get rescued,' says Flick, reading from her phone.

'Let's not jump to conclusions, no pun intended,' says a voice behind them.

A shadow is cast over them and they both turn to see Birdy, in a huge sunhat and dark glasses, a bandage on her cheek.

'According to my butler, rumour has it below decks that he was rescued by a trawler and made it back to shore, where he's now on the run.'

'Birdy, how are you? How's your face?'

'Oh, I'll live. A small gash and a few bruises. Nothing I haven't experienced before in the name of beauty. The rather handsome doctor on board said I didn't need stitches. I said are you sure? I think I could do with a little tightening.' She breaks off and laughs. 'Still, I don't want to scar, so it's a good excuse to pay a visit to my cosmetic surgeon in New York. I fly home tomorrow.'

'So do you think he's been found and is still alive?' Flick looks at Birdy hopefully. Despite everything that's happened, no one wants him dead. Not even Maggie, though there were times when she sure as hell did.

'Put it this way, I don't think a man like Theo C. Stratin will be swimming with the fishes just yet.'

Flick's phone starts ringing. 'I've got to take this.' She waves her phone; Colin's name is flashing up on the screen. 'It's my dad.'

That she called Colin her dad isn't lost on anyone.

'Go ahead,' says Maggie, smiling.

As Flick steps away, Maggie turns to Birdy. 'I hope she's going to be OK. You know she only lost her mum six months ago and now this . . .'

'She's got you.'

'Oh, I'm not much use, what can I give her? I don't have anything.'

'You've got plenty to give her. I see the way she looks at you. The friendship you have. The bond you have. She's lucky. You both are.'

Maggie smiles gratefully.

'By the way, I've got something for you.' Reaching into her handbag, she pulls out a watch and gives it to Maggie.

'My dad's watch . . . but how . . . ?' she gasps, astonished.

'I took him Rolex shopping,' she shrugs simply. 'He had to take it off to try on his new watch, so I offered to put it in my purse for safekeeping. He must have forgotten.'

Birdy gave a knowing smile while Maggie shook her head slowly, turning the watch over her in hands, feeling the smooth golden case, the familiar texture of the leather strap; it brought back so many memories.

'You remembered me telling you about my dad's watch.'

'Attention to detail. I've always had a thing for details. So many people don't notice them, but it's amazing what you might miss.'

'And what about your jewellery? Have they found it?'

'Sadly, no. I'd taken it out of the safe earlier, but I couldn't decide what to wear to the party so it was in the living room, on the side table. The police think he must have grabbed it as he ran and it probably fell out of his pockets when he jumped. My diamonds are no doubt on the seabed as I speak. Luckily, I have it all insured.'

'Didn't you once say your jewellery was all fake?'

'Excuse me?'

Birdy frowns, but Maggie's mind is already flicking back. 'Yes, when we first met in Rome. You said your diamonds were all fake and you kept the real stuff in the safe back home in America.'

'Did I? Gee whiz, I can't remember. I must be getting muddled in my old age.' She gives a throaty laugh but she isn't convincing anyone, least of all Maggie, who hasn't seen anyone less muddled and doddery than Birdy Carmichael. The woman is a powerhouse.

'Just imagine that! I'd get to keep my diamonds and the insurance payment, wouldn't that be something? Diamonds really would be a girl's best friend.'

And then she gives Maggie a mischievous smile that suddenly makes her wonder.

'OK, well, I must go,' she says, checking her watch. 'I have to finish packing, it's been so lovely meeting you.'

'Did you buy yourself a new watch too?' asks Maggie, noticing Birdy's Rolex.

Birdy laughs, seemingly amused by the very thought. 'This is the one I bought Louis, I mean Theo.' She shook her head, tutting. 'Honestly, all these names.'

'But I saw he was wearing it last night, in your suite.' Maggie is puzzled.

'Oh no, that a was a fake, sweetie,' she smiles. 'I switched out the real one when he was in the shower earlier. Amazing what you can buy in Tangier. The fakes are incredible. You'd never tell the difference.' Looking very pleased with herself, she gives a little shrug. 'Anyway, I think it suits me much better, don't you?'

'Absolutely,' nods Maggie.

'Anyway, I really must dash. See you around, kiddo.'

Maggie looks at Birdy. There's so much more to her than meets the eye, and for a moment she thinks about asking her a million questions, but for now she's just grateful to have met her.

'See you around, Birdy.'

'So what did I miss?' asks Flick, when she returns a few minutes later.

'I'm not quite sure.' Maggie shakes her head and stands up. 'How's your dad?'

'He's good.'

The two women meet each other's eyes and smile.

'Come on, let's grab our bags. It's time to go home.'

# Declaração da Polícia de Segurança Pública

(using Google Translate)

# STATEMENT FROM THE PUBLIC SECURITY POLICE

Portuguese police have confirmed reports that a man was picked up by a trawler boat after he fell in the water from the *Galaxy Goddess* during the farewell party to celebrate the end of a two-week cruise from Monte Carlo to Lisbon. Theo C. Stratin is a British national wanted for questioning in relation to crimes committed in the UK together with a recent diamond theft on board the cruise ship. It's believed he drifted close to the coast where he was spotted by the crew of an illegal bottom trawler unaware of the search and rescue mission. Since they are undeclared and operating without a licence, they are not tracked by port detection or satellite-based surveillance systems, thus the suspect was able to leave the port without being detained.

Detective Inspector Afonso Henriques commented, 'It's a miracle he survived; and while it's disappointing he was not apprehended at the port and taken into custody, I am confident it is only a matter of time before he is found and brought in for questioning.'

Anyone with information relating to this matter, please contact their local police station.

# Back On Dry Land

# Only A Matter of Time

*One week later*

*London*

Early morning and the city is already bustling as Maggie walks purposefully down the street. Double-decker buses, street-cleaners, traffic, pedestrians and so much noise. It's a world away from what used to greet her when she stepped out of the caravan into open fields and birdsong . . . and quite often a fresh cowpat. It's strange. She only packed up and left a few days ago, but already it feels like a lifetime ago, receding in her memory like something that had happened to someone else. But then that's probably because she had been someone else when she lived there, someone else entirely.

Better still, it turns out she isn't the only one to find her way back. When she returned to the caravan, there was a surprise waiting for her. George the cat. Curled up on the step, snoozing in the sun, like he'd never gone away. He even brought her a gift, a dead mouse, so that was nice. That said, she isn't going to take any chances this time, and is firmly keeping him inside from now on.

So now everything is sorted. She's straightened things out with the council. Thanked the farmer. Towed her caravan to the scrap yard. Even stuck two fingers up at the cyclist in

Lycra when she went back to the farm shop to get supplies for her journey to London. Admittedly it was behind his back and she wasn't 100 per cent sure if it was the same cyclist in Lycra who'd insulted her a few weeks ago, but frankly all those middle-aged men in Lycra hogging the roads and nearly knocking everyone down deserved to have two fingers stuck up at them.

And while she isn't going to miss the caravan with its mould or condensation or leaking windows stuffed with paper towels, she feels grateful to the refuge it gave her to feel shitty and sad, because it's how she got to be the person she is now: a woman walking confidently down a London street on a busy Friday morning. On her way to do what she's been meant to do for ever – to finally get her dad's watch fixed. She took it off when she was packing – she didn't want to damage it – and it's stopped working again. Maybe it needs a new battery.

She checks the address again on her new phone. It must be here somewhere . . . ah yes, there it is. Tucked away down a side street is a shop selling watches and offering repairs. As she pushes open the door, the bell rings.

### *The Algarve*

He steps inside, his eyes taking a moment to adjust after the bright sunshine outside. As the door closes behind him, a man appears from behind the plastic ribbon curtain at the back of the shop.

'Olá, como posso ajudá-lo?'

'I'm sorry, I don't speak Portuguese.'

'How can I help you?'

The man eyes him warily. Not surprising, considering he

## SO, I MET THIS GUY . . .

hasn't showered for a week and he needs a good shave. He knows the police are after him and he's been trying to keep a low profile. If it hadn't been for the shoplifting skills he learned as a kid, he would have gone hungry. That and all the stupid tourists on the beach who think they're hiding their valuables if they put them under their towels when they go for a swim. Amazing, really, how many people still carry cash.

'I've got a Rolex I'd like you to look at.'

The owner of the pawn shop pushes his spectacles up his nose in ready anticipation. He takes it off his wrist and hands it over. It's his getaway money. His way out. He needs a new phone, a new passport. He met a man in a bar last night that says for the right price, he can get him some fake ID, no problem. No way is he going back to the UK to face the music. You don't jump nineteen decks off a cruise ship and survive to meekly hand yourself in to the Old Bill. Admittedly it all got a little out of hand, but them's the breaks.

The owner examines his watch with a magnifying loupe, then places it on the counter.

'One moment, I just need to check something.'

Watching him disappear behind the plastic ribbon curtain, he does some quick mental arithmetic. Fifty per cent of the original value? Seventy-five per cent? He wasn't sure of the going rate for pawning a watch, but regardless, it would still be a pretty penny. What a shame about the American heiress. There would've been plenty more where that came from. Silly old dear, she was so easy to con.

'Hello, *senhor*, is there a problem?'

He was taking ages. What was he doing back there?

A few moments and then the owner reappears, his expression grim.

'Your watch is counterfeit.'

'*Excuse me?*'

He stares at him, dumbfounded, as the owner picks up the watch and hands it back to him, as if it's contaminated.

'It's a worthless fake.'

Is it then Theo realizes he's been had and the game is up? Or is it seconds later, when he turns to leave and hears sirens outside, and he realizes the shopkeeper has called the police?

*London*

'It's valuable?'

Maggie is looking at the watchmaker in astonishment.

'Extremely,' he nods, rubbing his bearded chin and appearing visibly excited.

'But that's impossible. There must be a mix-up. Dad would've told me if it was worth anything.'

'No, I'm quite sure,' he's saying now, 'that's why I went to check it with a colleague of mine, who's a specialist in Second World War watches. It's exceptionally rare.'

Maggie presses her hand to her forehead and looks down at her dad's watch. Sitting between them on the black velvet cloth, with its worn leather strap, slightly scratched gold case and flat, rather unremarkable face, she's trying to process what he's telling her.

'May I ask how you came by this watch?' The specialist now appears, his face flushed by the discovery of what's just landed on their desk.

'It was my dad's,' explains Maggie. 'Well, my granddad's, actually. It was a gift from a Swiss soldier he helped during the war.'

The specialist looks elated. 'It's got everything, even the fascinating provenance.' He whispers something to his colleague.

'Have you ever had this watch valued for insurance purposes, Ms . . . ?'

'*Insurance purposes?*' She's beginning to feel a bit dazed. 'It's Fletcher, Maggie Fletcher, and no, no I haven't . . . I only came in for a new battery as it's stopped working.'

'That's because it works on perpetual motion, the automatic winding occurs when you're actively wearing it. Simply put, if you're not wearing it, the power reserve will run out,' explains the watchmaker.

'So it doesn't need a new battery?'

The specialist looks almost amused. 'No, there is no battery.'

'Oh.'

'Ms Fletcher, this watch is quite some find, from a limited edition of only twenty-four known to the market. It could be potentially worth quite a sum.'

Maggie blinks, still in disbelief. 'How much is quite a sum?'

The specialist clears his throat.

'I believe when one last came up for auction, it fetched close to half a million . . .'

## The Algarve

The doors of the pawnbroker's burst open and several armed police charge in, yelling something in Portuguese as the shopkeeper dives for cover. There's nowhere to run and he throws his hands up in surrender as they push him roughly up against the wall, forcing his hands behind his back. He feels the handcuffs around his wrists, hears the click of the metal. This time there's no need for a translation. Theo C. Stratin is under arrest.

Like the detective inspector said, it was only a matter of time.

# Epilogue

*Three months later*

In a large, open-plan loft apartment, Maggie is unpacking a vase. The shutters are thrown open and light is flooding in, along with a warm breeze, even though it's the end of October. She's surrounded by boxes, scrunched-up newspaper and packaging. George the cat is wrapping around her ankles, paws padding softly on the polished wooden floors, his fat ginger tail stroking her bare skin. She hears her phone ringing and puts down the vase to go to hunt for it. She finds it propped on her easel in the corner of the room. It's Flick trying to video-call her. She must have finished work. She picks up.

'So how's the new apartment?'

Flick's face pops up on the screen, her office in the background.

'The light's fabulous, perfect for painting.'

Sitting down in an armchair, the only piece of furniture she currently has apart from her bed, Maggie hugs her knees to her chest. She's wearing shorts and a T-shirt and still has the remnants of her summer tan.

'And what about Lisbon? Are you liking it?'

'I haven't explored properly yet. The shipping company only delivered my boxes a few days ago, so I've been too busy moving in . . .'

\*

## SO, I MET THIS GUY . . .

A lot has happened since she walked into the watchmaker's in London a few months ago. When just an ordinary day became an extraordinary one, with the astonishing discovery that she was in possession of a rare and valuable watch. One that she could never hope to wear as she could never afford to insure it, she soon realized. Her excitement turned quickly to disappointment and then fear as the experts warned her about the rise in luxury watch theft and threat of violent muggings. Meaning her dad's watch would have to be kept in a safe deposit box in a darkened bank vault.

And frankly, what was the point of that?

Which is why, after days spent talking things over with George, who had known her dad and met her brother, she made the difficult decision to put it up for auction. But while it was difficult, she also knew it was for the best. The watch had huge sentimental value. It was her dad's and his dad's before him, and as she sat with the expert at Sotheby's and wore it on her wrist for the last time, she thought about her dad and all the times she'd seen him wearing it – sleeves rolled up, dancing at parties; in a polo shirt playing golf; pushing his narrowboat through the locks; squashed in his lap as a child with her brother; holding his hand in the hospice.

But, as George gently reminded her, the watch wasn't her dad. He also, less gently, reminded her of the times they'd watched *Antiques Roadshow* together, and how whenever anyone discovered their family heirloom was worth a fortune, her dad would bellow at the TV, 'Sod the sentimental value, take the money!' Which made her laugh and the decision much easier.

It was sold to the highest bidder for a sum she couldn't quite believe: enough for a large deposit to buy a new flat somewhere, give her some savings, and set up a memorial scholarship in her brother's name, to an undergraduate of medicine at his old university undergoing financial need. Charlie never got to be a doctor but this way his legacy would live on. And yet, after a few weeks living with George in London, looking at Rightmove, Maggie realized she wanted a change. A bigger change. The trip around Europe had opened her eyes and broadened her horizons.

Why not try somewhere new? So, after a few weeks researching visas and logistics, she made the crazy decision to move to Lisbon. But like Flick always said, it depends how you define crazy. They'd spent a few hours there after the cruise ship had docked and she liked what she saw so she took a leap. What's that saying, take a leap and the net will appear? And it had appeared in the shape of a year-long lease on a lovely light-filled apartment with a view across the rooftops towards the ocean.

'How about you?' she asks Flick, throwing the question back. 'Is London and the new job everything you ever dreamed of?'

'Yeah, and more.'

Sitting at her desk in the busy newsroom, Flick grins broadly. At last she feels like a real journalist. All around there is activity and chatter. A buzzing workplace, where news is breaking and important stories are being investigated, it's a far cry from the sleepy offices of *The Local Echo* and Tupperware Tony with his controversial sandwich fillings, and she couldn't be happier.

'I've got some news.'

'Don't tell me, you've made the front page again?'

After her exclusive article about the romance fraudster made headlines and got picked up by the national press, Flick was offered a job working for a major newspaper in London. It was the big break she'd always dreamed of and Seymour, her editor, gave her a glowing reference to take with her. Despite his initial reservations, her feature had put *The Local Echo* on the map; he was going to miss her enthusiasm and tenacity.

Not that he told her, of course. He was a Yorkshireman and didn't do emotions. It was just a bit of grit in his eye, that's all.

Colin was over the moon; he'd miss her, but he knew how much she wanted this. Even Rory was happy for her. When he heard the news, he came to the pub to offer his congratulations. He'd seemingly bounced back from having his marriage proposal turned down, and was now dating Kate, who he'd met in Accounts. 'She's nothing like you,' he told her cheerfully, 'she doesn't want to be something she's not.' Which was actually the nicest back-handed compliment Rory could pay, thought Flick, as it confirmed she too didn't want to be something she wasn't either, and that was Rory's wife.

'Ha ha, no, not yet,' laughs Flick, turning off her desktop and reaching for her jacket on the back of her chair. 'But I have been asked to go on BBC's *Woman's Hour* to talk about romance fraudsters, ahead of his court appearance next month.'

It was finally happening. After being arrested in Portugal and extradited back to the UK, Stratin was now in custody, awaiting trial. A substantial prison sentence seemed likely, and there was even a chance Maggie might get some of her savings back. Police raided a lock-up being rented by him and found luxury vehicles and designer goods worth close to a quarter of a million pounds. A police spokesperson, who described Stratin as 'a complete fantasist who constructed a web of lies and showed no remorse', says money doesn't appear to have been the only motivating factor and his crimes were committed over decades. Since news of his arrest, and Flick's subsequent article, several other women had come forward and given evidence against him. Flick was right all along. Maggie wasn't his only victim.

But she was certainly going to be his last.

'Wow, that's wonderful, well done,' she says now in admiration.

Maggie is so proud of Flick. She's handled everything with a maturity beyond her years. Not only has she bravely exposed her biological father to be a serial fraudster, but when he granted her an interview in prison, she used it solely to gain information that would help protect others.

'The captain was right, you're a prestigious journalist now. I'll be seeing you on *Newsnight* next.'

Flick smiles, seemingly embarrassed by her friend's praise. 'You know I owe it all to you. If you hadn't come with me . . .'

'Rubbish. You did this.'

Maggie breaks off to scoop up George, who is meowing by her feet, and places him in her lap. 'By the way, I meant to ask, are you OK for money?'

'Yes, thanks to you and Dad. Plus, I get my first paycheck at the end of the month.'

Looping her crossbody bag over her shoulder, she starts to make her way out of the office.

'Well, if you need anything, you must let me know.'

'I'm fine, stop worrying.'

'I'm not worrying!'

Which of course is a total lie. Despite never particularly wanting to be a mother, Maggie was now in the strange position of finding herself frequently worrying about twenty-six-year-old Flick as if she was her adult child.

## SO, I MET THIS GUY . . .

'Hang on, I'm switching you to audio, two secs.'

Exiting the newsroom, Flick quickly walks down the stairs, through the foyer and out of the news building. The Shard rises in front of her, while London Bridge is behind her, and she glances up at the skyline like she still can't quite believe it. A young twenty-something professional, just moved to London to start her career, her future stretching out ahead of her. There's no feeling more exhilarating.

'Are you heading home now?'

In her earbuds Maggie's voice brings her back.

'No, I'm meeting Flea.'

'Ooh, tell me!'

'There's nothing to tell, we're just friends, it's cool.'

Flick shakes her head and smiles. What is it with the older generation, always wanting to pigeonhole? She starts walking towards the Underground.

'Are you going for a drink?'

'No, we're off to see the new Expressionists exhibition at the Tate Modern. There's a special late-night opening . . .'

Over fifteen hundred kilometres away in an apartment in Lisbon, Maggie gives the air a little punch of triumph.

'Wow, I really did make an impression,' she laughs.

'You changed my life,' quips Flick, but she really means it.

'Mine too,' smiles Maggie, stroking George, who's purring loudly. 'I'll never be able to use disposable face wipes again.'

There's sarcastic laughter on the end of the phone.

'Oh, by the way, I forgot to mention – I did a deep dive into Birdy and I think I found something.'

'You did?'

In recent weeks, Maggie had tried contacting Birdy to say a huge thank you for returning her dad's watch. If it wasn't for her, she might have never got it back, and who knows what would have happened to it. But despite googling, she can't find any mention of her. Usually something will pop up – everyone has some kind of online footprint – but it's almost like she doesn't exist.'

'Yeah, but it's really weird,' continues Flick. 'I couldn't find any mention of Birdy Carmichael, but I did find a newspaper article about someone called Birdie Randolph, with the different spelling, from about ten years ago.'

'How's that weird?'

'They had a photo of her from CCTV and she was her double.'

'Maybe she's a doppelganger – apparently we all have one, can you imagine? There are people walking around looking like me and you.' Maggie pauses. 'Why is there a picture of her on CCTV?'

'She was a con woman who ran up a huge bill at a five-star hotel in Paris by pretending to be a rich American heiress to date men and then disappeared.'

They both fall silent on the phone, thoughts unravelling.

*The husbands. The diamonds. The designer clothes and handbags and Park Avenue apartment. Was any of her story true? Was any of it real?*

'You don't think . . . ?'

'Who knows? Do we ever really know anyone? We're just a collection of stories we tell ourselves. Do we ever really know if those stories are true?'

*That's the thing about getting older*, thinks Maggie. *The older you get, the more you realize you don't know.*

There's a beat, then she smiles, suddenly amused.

'What happens when a romance fraudster meets another romance fraudster?'

'Now *that* would make a good story,' says Flick and they both laugh again. That same shared wicked sense of humour again.

'OK, on that note, I gotta go.' On a busy London street, Flick pauses by a line of rental bikes. 'I'm going to cycle instead of getting the tube. It's a nice evening.'

'You're making me feel guilty, I need to do some exercise, get outside.'

Maggie glances out of her window in Lisbon. It's that gorgeous time of day that artists call the golden hour, when everything glows and the light feels magical.

'You should rent a bike, go explore.'

'Good idea.'

'Bye, love you.'

'Love you too.'

They both hang up.

Twenty minutes later, Maggie leaves her apartment and walks down the hill, along the wide boulevard leading towards the seafront, with its polished mosaic tiles and shop windows filled with pastéis de nata, the delicious Portuguese custard tarts. Despite summer being over, there are still a few random tourists, and she zigzags through them, with only a vague idea of where she's heading. And then she sees what she's looking for. The covered arches. A yellow sign with a windmill. She smiles. Sander really wasn't kidding.

The door is wide open and she walks into the shop and up to the counter.

'Hi, I've heard this is a good place to rent a bicycle.'

His back is turned to her, but when he turns he recognizes her and they both smile. He has a really great smile. Just as she remembers.

'Sure, I just need a credit card and a contact number.'

He passes her a form and she fills it in, then passes it back. He frowns. Then checks his phone and gives a little amused shrug.

'No wonder the photo would never send. I must have written down the wrong number.'

'Well, now you've got the right number.'

They both look at each other. If a picture can say a thousand words, a look between two people who weren't looking for anything, least of all each other, but who just so happened to be at the same pizza restaurant in Rome, meet briefly again on a staircase on the Amalfi Coast, and are now smiling at each other in a bike rental shop in Lisbon, with no idea of what, or if, anything is going to happen between them, can say a lot more.

Her bike is yellow and he helps adjust the saddle then, saying bye, she sets off cycling.

A few moments later, she hears a text ping on her phone. She wonders if it's from Sander and what it will say, but she doesn't stop to read it. Not just yet. She wants to catch the sunset. Ahead, the sea is glistening and the sky is the colour of pomegranates. Exhilarated, Maggie pushes down on the pedals. Without a map she's not sure where she's heading, or what she will find there, but as she cycles away from her past and into her future, she sure as hell can't wait to find out.

# Postscript

*Meanwhile, somewhere in Africa, on a safari*

A group of American tourists are enjoying gin and tonics at the luxury tented camp on the banks of the Okavango Delta in Botswana. It's early evening, the perfect time to watch the Big Five coming to drink at the watering hole. Only, while others are trying to spot elephants and rhino, Birdy has already spotted the prize; his name is Hank and he's a tech billionaire from Silicon Valley. Eighty-five and recently widowed, he's travelling alone.

'Would you know if there's an extra blanket? It's a little chilly.'

Sitting down next to him on the rattan sofa, she gives a little shiver.

'Please, share mine!'

Thrilled by the company of a good-looking woman, Hank lays it over her legs chivalrously. Up close, she notices Hank has ears the size of an elephant, which seems quite fitting, considering she's big-game trophy hunting. She smiles widely and holds out her hand.

'Hi, my name's Birdy.'

# Acknowledgements

When I sat down to write these acknowledgements, I realized it's been twenty-five years since my first novel was published. Twenty-five years! A quarter of a century. Where did the time go?

Well, a lot of it was spent writing novels! *So, I Met This Guy . . .* is my fifteenth, and it's been one of the most fun and challenging to write. I really saw this book as a two-hander. It was Maggie's story, but it was also Flick's. To tell this story properly I needed to move back and forth in time and tense and to switch characters' perspectives. I also wanted to set it across multiple destinations across Europe. To throw in some other cracking characters, like Birdy, who came to me fully formed. And I got to write a villain for the first time. All to a ticking clock!

While the process of writing a novel is just me, my imagination and my laptop (and my famous cork board on which I plot out every scene), I am indebted to so many people for helping, supporting and encouraging me along the way, and this is the bit where I finally get to thank them.

Firstly, my editor, Trisha Jackson. Trisha is everything you can possibly want in an editor: supportive, enthusiastic, intuitive and absolutely passionate about getting the best book. From the moment, some years ago, when I walked into her office at Pan Macmillan to talk about a book I was writing called *Confessions of a Forty-Something F\*\*K Up*, I knew my life was about to change. Thank you, Trisha. So much of my success as an author is down to your brilliant instincts, experience and skill, great sense of humour and sheer hard work, and I am for ever grateful.

I am very lucky to be published by Pan Macmillan and want to say a massive thank you to the talented team for all their enthusiasm, hard work, skill and support: Joanna Prior, Lucy Hale, Poppy North, Josie Turner, Stuart Dwyer, Maddie Thornham, Rebecca Lloyd, Kate Tolley, Andy Joannou, Jon Mitchell, Mairead Loftus, Anna Shora, Hannah Geranio, Chloe Davies, Becky Lushey and Rachel Vale. It's a long list, but so much goes on behind the scenes and every single person plays a huge part. I do hope I haven't forgotten anyone, but rest assured if I haven't mentioned you by name, I thank you from the heart.

Thanks also to all my publishers around the word. It's such a thrill to see my books translated into so many different languages and to know that they are being enjoyed by readers far and wide. And huge thanks as always to all the incredible booksellers. There is no greater joy for an author than to walk into a bookshop and see your book on the shelf.

A big thank you as always to my agent, Stephanie Cabot, who has been with me since the very beginning of my career. I am for ever grateful for her wise counsel, unflinching support, clever instincts and top-notch agenting skills. Not to mention the ability to be completely unflappable in the face of a panicking author with a fast-approaching deadline! Thanks also to the rest of the talented team at Susanna Lea Associates.

A huge thank you to all my friends for all their support over the years, whether it's attending my book launches or understanding when I'm absent for months as I'm trying to meet my deadline. In particular, I'd like to give a special mention to two author friends: Chris Manby and Freya North.

Like I said, this book was both a joy and a challenge to write, and there came a point in the middle when I wondered if I had set myself a bit *too much* of a challenge. Thank you both for all your brilliant authorly advice and encouragement.

If you've got this far, you will know that a part of the novel is set on a luxury cruise ship, and while writing fiction requires lots of 'making things up', sometimes it's good to ask the experts. I want to give a special thank you to David Sanders, an expert in all things cruises, and Charlotte Humphrey of Princess Cruises for answering all my questions and showing me around the *Sky Princess* in Southampton – I couldn't believe how gorgeous it was! I can't wait to go on a real cruise one day.

That said, I want to make clear that the ship in this novel, the *Galaxy Goddess*, is completely fictional and bears no resemblance to any real-life cruise ship or company. And while I had a lot of fun inventing its fourteen-day Mediterranean itinerary, and even more fun having Maggie and Flick chase after it across Europe, sometimes timelines and logistics needed to be tweaked to fit the story. And it goes to say that any errors about what might actually take place on a cruise ship are entirely my own, and purely for plot purposes.

To my family – well, I couldn't do this without you. Thank you as always to my mum, Anita, for your tireless love, support and encouragement – I'm so lucky to have you. To my sister, Kelly, thanks for meeting me in Monte Carlo and joining me at the roulette wheel – all in the name of research! To my dad, Ray, who left this party way too early, but always believed in me as a writer and is for ever in my thoughts. And, of course, to AC, for putting up with a wife who is always drifting off into her imagination, walking Elton when I put my back out in the middle of my edits, and coming up with this fabulous title! I love you all so much.

I also want to take this opportunity to remember Billy Hardaker: thank you for all the years of laughter, friendship, kindness and advice, and for walking me down the aisle when dad couldn't be there. How lucky we were to have had you in our lives.

And finally, but most importantly, to my readers all over the world. Your support over these last twenty-five years has been the greatest gift. Thank you for reading my books and for all your lovely messages and photos. All I ever wanted was to be a writer, and it makes me so happy to hear that you enjoy my books, but also that you find them relatable and that they've meant something to you. I hope you love this one, too.

Alexandra Potter is the bestselling author of numerous romantic comedy fiction novels in the UK, including *One Good Thing*, *Confessions of a Forty-Something F##k Up* – one of the bestselling books of recent years and the basis of a major TV series – and *More Confessions of a Forty-Something F##k Up*. These titles have sold in twenty-three territories and achieved worldwide sales approaching 2 million copies, making the bestseller charts across the world.

Yorkshire born and raised, Alexandra lived for several years in LA before settling in London with her Californian husband and their Bosnian rescue dog. When she's not writing or travelling, she's getting out into nature, trying not to look at her phone and navigating this thing called mid-life.

# HAVE YOU READ THE FUNNIEST 'WTF AM I DOING' NOVEL OF THE YEAR?

'The new Bridget Jones for our times'
*The Telegraph*

'Feistily funny . . . and so relatable'
*Fabulous*

'Say hello to a book that will have you laughing with every page, whether you're twenty, forty or eighty'
*Heat*

A novel for any woman who wonders how the hell she got here, and why life isn't quite how she imagined it was going to be. And who is desperately trying to figure it all out while everyone around her is making gluten-free brownies.

Meet Nell. Her life is a mess. In a world of perfect Instagram lives she feels like a f**k up. Even worse, a forty-something f**k up.

But when she starts a secret podcast and forms an unlikely friendship with Cricket, an eighty-something widow, things begin to change. Because Nell is determined: this time next year things will be very different.

But first she has a confession . . .

'Funny but layered, light-hearted and surprisingly deep, this is a perfect and inspiring read'
*Red*

'A funny, feisty story about the highs and the oh-so-lows of having to start over in your forties'
Mike Gayle